THE SUBTERRANEAN EXPEDITION

THE SUBTERRANEAN EXPEDITION

THE SECOND EXPEDITION

DAVID A. HORNUNG

iUniverse

THE SUBTERRANEAN EXPEDITION
THE SECOND EXPEDITION

iUniverse books may be ordered through booksellers or by contacting:

iUniverse
1663 Liberty Drive
Bloomington, IN 47403
www.iuniverse.com
1-800-Authors (1-800-288-4677)

ISBN: 978-1-5320-1533-5 (sc)
ISBN: 978-1-5320-1532-8 (e)

Library of Congress Control Number: 2017905247

Print information available on the last page.

iUniverse rev. date: 04/22/2017

A NOTE TO MY READERS

On a personal note, I am, as I assume you are, a voracious reader and enjoy Steam Punk. I hate it when Steam Punk authors do not give the back story to the world they have created so that you can follow along and fit their story into the world you are reading about and you wind up spending more time trying to figure out the world you have entered then following the story. So presented here is a highly condensed bit of the back story.

This book takes place about a year and a half after the end of my first book, *The Ratten Expedition,* ends. If you did not read that book, which I strongly recommend you do (let us be honest here, I can use the sales), a brief word of explanation is in order. I have changed history during the American Civil War so that it lasted ten years instead of five (see below), resulting in several significant advances in technology such as steam-powered airships and land attack vehicles. England had declared war on the United States but had been unable to truly follow through on it because of problems in India. Currently the United Kingdom and the United States are in a state of fragile truce, neither side trusting the other. France, under Napoleon III, still holds Mexico. Finally, the south is slowly reintegrating itself back into the Union but hot spots of rebellion are still present.

The Ratten Expedition starts about nine years after the war ends. John Morton, a former officer turned scientist, along with Father Peter Harrigan, a former NCO in Morton's command, were recruited into a secret government agency to deal with two renegade scientists. That is where John met Julia Verolli who was a government spy and top assassin. By the end of the adventure, John and Julia had fallen in love.

From *The Ratten Expedition* where history was changed:

The Trent Incident. On November 8, 1861, the USS *San Jacinto*, commanded by U.S. Navy Captain Charles Wilkes, intercepted the British mail packet the RMS *Trent* after she left Cuba and forced her to heave to. He sent over a boarding party to take off two Confederate agents, Mason and Slidell. No one was hurt, but in the British Parliament, there were cries for war with the United States and that Wilkes be hunted down as a pirate. In my version of history, the Trent was fired on, and several men were killed, including an officer. There is little doubt that England would have come into the war had this happened.

CONTENTS

Dramatic Persona

John Morton, Professor of Natural History at the New York Museum, former NYS militia major in the Civil War

Father Peter Harrigan, parish priest at St Brigit's in the Five Points, former Army 1st sergeant in Morton's Civil War unit

Colonel William Anderson, head of an unnamed Federal agency

Julia Morton, nee Verolli, Morton's wife and former special agent who worked for Colonel Anderson

Dr. Arthur Chesterfield, John Morton's boss and the New York Museum's curator

Simon Thompkins, Dr. Chesterfield's assistant

Isaiah Liman, tinker, corporal, later sergeant, former B Co 2nd U.S. Colored Troops (USCT)

Sarah Liman, young Negro girl rescued by Morton, adopted by Isaiah Liman

Samuel Tinsman, corporal, former member Berdan's Sharpshooters, currently working for Anderson

Sam Kincaid, former member Berdan's Sharpshooters and part of Tinsman's unit

Jason Quinn and Adam Ross, rookie agents under Corporal Tinsman

Clement Hook, Welsh Nationalist and bank robber; his new identity is Carl James Jordan

Spotted Wolf, a young Nez Perce warrior

Strong Bear, Nez Perce Chief

Paul Dasson, first lieutenant, cavalry officer F Troop, Eighth Cavalry, assigned to Fort Freemont

Frank W. Washburn, colonel, commander of Fort Freemont

PROLOGUE

Spotted Wolf worked his way along the trail up to the ridgeline. His pony was very sure-footed as were all the mounts of the Nez Perce. Likewise, Spotted Wolf, in the tradition of the tribe, was an excellent horseman having learned to ride almost before he could walk. Thus he was making good time. Spotted Wolf was looking for some of the tribe's ponies that had been scattered in a violent storm that broke over their village two nights earlier. The task would have been easier in their traditional lands that he was more familiar with; however, after the blue coated soldiers had forced Chief Joseph to surrender two years prior, the remnants of the tribe had been confined to this reservation.

It was not so much that it was bad land, but the problem was that the tribe had not learned the secrets that Father Earth had hidden in this part of the world. It was not home. Spotted Wolf yearned for the ancestral land that he had grown up on. He had been too young to fight in the war but in the two summers just past he had come of manhood. The fact that he was sent out by Strong Bear to look for the ponies was proof of this. He did not intend to fail on this the first task that his chief had given him to perform by himself.

The air was fresh after the rain and the weather fair, and with the exception of spending time with Yellow Bird, the young maiden who had caught his eye, he could not imagine anything that would be better than riding his pony on such a day.

The trail led through a flat area on the side of the mountain. Spotted Wolf thought it would make a good campsite. There was a stream nearby, and a slight overhang made for shelter. Beyond that it was quite defensible with an open vista in most directions except up the mountain. There were trees so that the old growth gave plenty of firewood. Even if Chief Joseph had said, "From this day I will fight no more", that did not mean that the blue-coat soldiers would not attack them again as they did at the start of the war, or that the other tribes would not try to take advantage of the Nez Perce's weakened state.

He stopped, taking in the vista afforded him and letting his horse rest. As he sat there he felt the pony become nervous. Spotted Wolf looked around to see if he could find the source of the pony's agitation. He could not see a wolf along the ridgeline or a rattlesnake coiled up nearby. He could see nothing and yet the pony was becoming harder to control every moment. Soon Spotted Wolf was hanging on to the pony as tight as he could for it was in a great fright. A sudden buck and Spotted Wolf lay hard on the ground. The pony had taken off in total fear. It was not something he wanted to explain to Brave Hawk, his tribal elder, let alone Yellow Bird. It was then he felt it; it was as if Father Earth himself were screaming. It was a very high pitched wail that he could feel travel through his whole body now that he was in direct contact with the earth! What could be happening?

As he worked to get his breath back and figure out what was going on, Spotted Wolf saw, with fear in his eyes, the side of the mountain begin to shake as if something was preparing to burst forth from Father Earth, the way a rat chews through a dead animal to escape. The sound was unbearable now. It felt as if his teeth were being shaken out of his head, his vision blurring. Spotted Wolf managed to get to his feet and run for the tree line, doing his best to put some distance between himself and whatever was trying to break out of the earth. He fell, no longer able to keep his balance from the vibration coursing throughout his entire body. As he lay at the wood's edge, he watched as the very ground began to dance and fall away from the hillside, as a cave opened up to let loose a screaming monster breathing smoke, and with a roar that shook the heavens above. Spotted Wolf could not stand the noise as it seemed to invade his very mind, and then the world went dark as he lost consciousness.

By the time he was found, he was bleeding from his ears, edges of his eyes, and his nose. Additionally he was confused and delusional. It took four days of Yellow Bird's attention to restore him to some degree of sanity.

That is when the trouble began!

CHAPTER 1

WEDDED BLISS, JULIA STYLE

h, spring on the Island of Manhattan in the year of our Lord 1879. It was a beautiful Sunday morning that found John Morton walking home from the Evangelical Church he attended. He wished Julia would come with him but, as she pointed out, she wanted him to come to Catholic Mass with her, so they had agreed to not talk about it. Julia for some reason had decided to go to an early Mass saying she had some things to work on at home, so John was cheerfully anticipating his bride being home when he got there.

Professor John Morton was a very happy man. First, he had a position that he loved as a senior research professor at the Museum of Natural History, with a substantial amount of freedom for his studies. Secondly, he had a wife he loved. Julia was a pint-sized vision. John often wondered how one could pack that much feminine beauty into such a tiny package. Julia stood five foot nothing in her stocking feet and was so well proportioned that she took most men's breath away, including her husband's. Her long, dark hair glistened when it caught the sun like the shine of a raven's wing. She had dusky Mediterranean looks that were to John's mind perfection itself. John was still amazed she would fall in love and marry a dull museum professor, especially after he had soundly spanked her during the Ratten business that had brought them together.

Finally, since their marriage just a little over a year and a half ago, she had managed not to blow anything up or kill anyone. This was some kind of a record for the extremely dangerous former Julia Verolli. Julia had been a special agent for the U.S. Government when John met her. John was never exactly too clear on which agency she worked for. All that John knew was that her former boss, William Anderson, had enough power to make things happen and pull not just strings, but a ship's towing hawsers.

Granted, thought John, there had been several incidents. The first, when a mugger had been hospitalized with a multitude of injuries and broken bones. Julia had stood there shaking, looking like she was on the verge of a complete breakdown when she told the police for their report, in a trembling and tearful voice, that the vile monster just tripped and fallen down some stairs after trying to grab her purse. According to Julia it was John's fault where was he when she needed him to protect her, his innocent little bride. After the police saw Julia's little five-foot, teary eyed body, John felt it was lucky, given the looks they gave him, that the police did not arrest him for failing to protect this poor, tiny, little innocent waif of a female. Then there was the time with a lecherous drunken patron at a museum fund raiser, who had fallen into a fountain, completely accidentally according to Julia who claimed total innocence about the affair, even if she had been the object of the drunk's attentions. At least, other than being soaking wet, he had been unharmed for which John was grateful. Overall she seemed to be settling down to a life of domestic bliss, almost.

Just as he turned up the walk to the door of their house, these thoughts were literally shattered by a small blast which blew out several of the basement windows. John, to put it mildly, went crazy with fear thinking that someone was trying to settle up old scores with Julia. He raced ahead and went in as fast as he could.

By the time he got to the basement he could hear Julia coughing. "Julia where are you, wife?" Morton cried out.

"I am here, sweetheart, (cough, cough)," John heard Julia respond from what was, or more likely what had been, his workshop where he indulged in his woodworking hobby.

John found his wife in the remains of his workshop, looking somewhat disheveled and covered with dust and smoke, with a few more than one or two stray curls loose over her face. "Julia, what happened? Are you all right? Was someone trying to kill you?" All this came out in a rush as John grabbed her into his arms, trying to ensure she was indeed unharmed.

Julia looked up at him and snuggled in closer. The former special agent and assassin loved her husband, and thought that for a dull museum professor, he was truly a man of action. She added the thought to herself that he was also very sexy. "I am all right, dearest, just a little accident. Nothing to worry about," she replied, reassuring John.

John looked down at her with somewhat more than a slight suspicion forming in his mind and, of course as husbands in similar circumstances are wont to do, he immediately started to worry. "Julia what kind of an accident, dear?" he inquired.

John noted that Julia picked up on the change in tone in her husband's voice, and he heard her swallow. "Well, John, do you remember that bomb Ulrich used to help free Chen back in Los Angeles? Well, Isaiah," referring to the black tinker who had been an integral part of their team, "has been working on a small case with a built-in clockwork time detonator so it is without a lit fuse. Well, he sent me some samples, and, well, I was trying to get the formula correct for the explosive part. I think I will call it a thunder-and-lightning-explosive-distraction device. What do you think, dearest?", trying her best to look up at her big, strong, sexy husband for advice in a totally innocent and harmless little-girl way.

John looked around the room again, surveying the scene, including the remains of the windows, most of which were outside in small, very small, pieces. "Sweetheart, did we not agree that that portion of your life was behind you? I thought you were happy working at the museum." He was getting the same feeling that he had the first time he had seen Julia in action down in the Five Points district of the city, which to put it mildly, involved large parts of both fear and amazement. This was not to be confused with the first time he met her; that involved her holding her favorite small Colt revolver on him in a very uncute way, actually, a very deadly way.

Julia, realizing that she was in trouble with her spouse, tried cuddling closer and wiggling so as to take his mind off the basement. "Well yes, John, my beloved, I am happy. It is just, well, sometimes I do miss it. Remember what I told you the instructors at the finishing school always taught us, that a young lady should be prepared for any eventuality," referring to the schooling she had received courtesy of William Anderson when she was an orphan waif who had been picked up for the petty theft of an apple. Instead of jail or the workhouse, which was the usual fate of such children, she was sent to a private school that trained young women in deportment, dance, and literature; however, the curriculum also included other subjects such as seduction, armed and unarmed combat and additional activities involving various dangerous and lethal pursuits. They were all young ladies whom no one would miss.

By this time John was becoming quite aware of his wife's wiggles and was trying to keep his mind on the fact he was supposed to be annoyed at her. "Julia, stop that! What were you doing? My workshop is in pieces!" John demanded.

Julia knowing her husband just kept wiggling. "Well, dearest, the device seemed to work all right; I think the formula needs some adjustment. I think I had a bit too much thunder and not enough lightning. You do remember how I so love explosives." At this last utterance she looked up at John's face with what she hoped was a totally innocent expression. The look included a serious amount of eye batting. The instructors at the school always seemed to recommend excessive eye batting when dealing with men, although, given the circumstances, she wondered if upset, angry husbands, whose workshops were badly damaged, fell into that particular general category.

John was still surveying the remains of his workshop when his eyes lit upon a target board that had been hidden behind the bench. It looked as if the board had been jarred loose from its previous hidden position by the explosion. "What, wife, is that?" John demanded. By now John's body was starting to react to his wife's wiggles.

Julia, still trying her very best to look innocent, said, "Oh that is where it got off to, sweetheart. That is only my old target board for my knife throwing practice, dear. I have been wondering where I left it; very hard to keep track of, my love." She tried adding a smile but by this time she knew she was in serious trouble with her spouse. John most certainly did not seem to appreciate the finer aspects of her former occupation and certainly not the fact that a young lady needed to keep in practice for whatever might come along.

"Julia, some of those cuts look rather fresh for something you misplaced a while ago. Dear, might I ask you how long ago you misplaced it?" By now, John, whether he thought he should or not, was definitely reacting to his wife's wiggling.

"I really could not say, my darling spouse," replied the lovely Mrs. Morton as she added her hands to the wiggling. "Perhaps we should go up for lunch and I will fix us something. Remember it is the servants' day off."

John decided that he was not going to get a straight answer out of his wife knowing her as he did. "Very well, but we have to have a serious talk about this later, my love. No more explosives! Do you understand, Julia?" John was trying to keep his mind on yelling at his wife all the while she was making it very hard to concentrate on anything except what she was doing to a particular part of his male anatomy, the result of which there tended to be substantially less blood going to his brain.

"Yes dear, now come along," as she took his hand, and led him up the stairs using the same walk she had when they were undercover in Los Angeles and on their honeymoon.

John fondly noted the aforesaid walk and was glad he lived in Manhattan where earth tremors were not common as he was quite sure his wife's special walk could trigger one.

Once they reached the first floor Julia started to prepare lunch. "Oh dear, I am all covered with dirt and soot; I should not want to take the chance of getting any in your food, husband," deciding to not mention the burnt powder; no need to remind John, about that. "Well, no problem, I can fix that." She began to hum a bit of a tune, and swaying her hips in time to it began to slowly take off her garments leaving her in just her chemise, shoes and stockings. "John you really do not want to take a chance on getting a food spill on one of your best shirts and puff ties, do you? I mean there is already some dirt on it where you held me in your arms, my big, strong, protective husband, and any food spills could set the stain." Having said this she started to remove her husband's clothes. Needless to say, Julia also mentioned something to the effect that he should also take no chance in messing up his pants, and John was quite shocked later when he realized what had happened. Without realizing it at the time, he not only wound up having dessert before lunch, of all things, but right on the dining room table. Thank God it was the servants' day off. And he thought later how Julia had managed to weasel, or more accurately wiggle, out of a stern lecture on resuming her former trade.

John Morton was indeed a happy man, even if his workshop was somewhat more than a little messed up. He knew he really had to be firm with Julia about that. No more explosives in the house! He had to admit, though, life would be easier if he had not fallen in love with Julia, but it would be nowhere as wonderful as it was with her in his life.

CHAPTER 2

A LETTER FROM SARAH

arly Monday morning found John and Julia walking up the steps to the museum entrance where they were let in by a guard, their arrival being well before the museum opened to the general public. They walked down the hall toward the stairs that took them into the basement where John's office and adjoining laboratory were located. He shared the space with Julia who continued to hold the position as his secretary and field archivist. This had been Julia's assigned cover when they first met to track down two renegade scientists. After marriage John thought that it would be a grand idea if she kept the position. He had explained to her that she was very good at the work, which aided him immensely. He explained to himself, not that the first was not true for indeed Julia excelled at the work, but also allowed that he could keep an eye on his bride and curb her more violent inclinations. He secretly shuddered to think what might happen if Julia had too much free time on her hands!

As they walked down the hall they were hailed by Simon Tompkins, Dr. Chesterfield's assistant and head clerk, Dr. Chesterfield being the museum's head curator. "Good morning, Professor, and to you, Mrs. Morton. I have some mail for you."

Julia reached out to take the mail. "Please, Simon, call me Julia. I have been working here for well over a year; I think we can be on a first-name basis." Julia smiled at the young man.

As with most young men and many older ones, he was quite tongue-tied by Julia's smile. He glanced at the professor who smiled and nodded as if to say it was all right. "Thank you, Julia that is most kind of you." Then he passed the mail over and scurried away so as not to make a fool of himself.

Julia smiled at him and put her arm in her husband's. "Shall we continue my love?" John did not mind as he loved his wife very much even if he took some good natured ribbing from his colleagues. *Imagine having an affair with your secretary. That is all right old boy, done all the time, but when it is your wife, it is simply not done! Gadzooks man! I mean having an affair with your own wife, Morton, what next?* John would just smile at this and chalk it up to the fact that the others were jealous of his luck in marrying a woman like Julia, even if the other members of the staff were not aware of her more lethal abilities and proclivities.

Before long they were in the office and John finished hanging up his coat and Julia's cape. Julia went to her desk and started going through the morning's post. A beaming smile on her face, she looked up at John, waved an envelope and said, "John, a letter from Sarah!" Sarah was the little girl John had rescued in Buffalo's notorious Canal District and who later was adopted by Isaiah, their team's tinker. She had become involved in the Ratten affair even though all concerned had tried to keep her out of it. Julia had been an orphan herself; she had no known family at all. Probably because of this, she had bonded to Sarah almost from the time they first met who was in a similar orphaned situation. This was when Julia was caring for her after an attack by a gang of toughs intent on raping her. Julia loved Sarah and thought of her as her little sister and it made no difference to Julia that Sarah was black. Sarah was her little sister and woe to anyone who would say otherwise.

John returned his wife's smile, as he too liked Sarah; she was full of joy and a very bright little girl albeit a bit of a chatterbox. Although not so little, John thought to himself, as her latest growth spurt left her several inches taller than Julia, even at twelve years old. Granted, that was not saying much given Julia's height. Chuckling, he asked, "So what does your *little* sister have to say, dear?"

Julia snorted in response to her husband's attempt at humor at her expense by emphasizing the 'little'. Julia was a tad sensitive about her height. "Humorous, my dear," Julia replied to her husband, looking at him, her eyes narrowing like she was estimating the range to her target board. However, she was busy opening the letter and reading it. "Let us see," mused Julia. "She has returned from the Hawaiian Islands where she was with the museum's expedition to study the new indigenous non-human tribe that was discovered there." They both smiled at this as it was a way out of a particularly touchy situation devised by John's old Civil War army comrade now turned Catholic priest, Peter Harrigan, that concluded the Ratten problem. "She says to thank you very much for talking Professor Sandusky into taking her along as the assistant archivist. She thought he was very nice and the work was quite interesting although she had to work very hard to keep up, there were so many new discoveries to record and catalog. There were all kinds of flora and fauna to learn about, as well as the new species of non-human indigenous natives."

John smiled. "Donald told me he was very pleased with her. He thought I was ready for the asylum to ask him to take an eleven-year-old girl, especially a Negro girl, on a field expedition a good part of the way around the world, but he told me flat out that she carried her own weight. He was quite impressed with her, especially the way she had managed to win the confidence of the new species, but also the fact that she started a dictionary of their native language on her own initiative. He thinks that she might be an asset on any future expeditions."

Julia smiled at this. She herself remembered that Sarah had surprised everyone with her amazing gift for languages and was quite a hard worker. She laughed a little when one day Julia wound up watching Isaiah's temporary tinker's shop in Los Angeles that had become the team's defacto headquarters. Sarah told Julia she had done quite well. Julia was surprised at the comment but Sarah told her she had to keep good records because her father was terrible at it.

"Well she also says she made a friend among the native children, a female named Cee Cee; how amazing." Julia laughed because this was the friend that Sarah could not have met. A very odd ending to the Ratten affair, indeed. "Now where was I? Oh yes. She goes on to say that she had a wonderful experience, but is glad to be home back in Buffalo, and she is working till late in the evening after school trying to straighten out her father's records for his shop. She says Poppa may be a great tinker but a terrible archivist. She also thinks that Hawaii is much nicer then Buffalo in the winter."

John looked thoughtful for a moment. "I doubt that it will ever catch on; too far to go and too un-America; all that South Pacific-Asiatic influence."

"Let me see what else she says. Oh, here is a part for you, dear. She said to tell the professor that he would like the way the Hawaiian girls dress in very small tops and grass skirts that show their legs quite high up as they dance a hula, whatever that is. She says it is positively quite shocking."

John looked somewhat taken aback and then thoughtfully said, "I might be wrong about it never catching on as a vacation destination."

Julia, her eyes narrowing in that range-finding mode again, said, "Dear, you are not going on any expeditions to Hawaii. I do not care what they find there!"

Morton smiled at his wife, "This from the woman who seduced a man in her own dining room."

Julia turned her nose up in the air. "I was trying to make sure no dirt got into my husband's food when the man in question ravaged me. Oh the shame!" Julia continued after a theatrical swoon, "although I was in shock at the experience. Maybe we should do it again to check to see how terrible it was, I mean just to be certain."

John looked at her, "Not in the office, wife! I get enough comments from my colleagues about having an affair with my own wife now." John kept looking at his wife and smiling went on, "Methinks the lady doth protest too much." He shook his head and motioned back to the letter.

Julia smiled at her husband and thought she was the luckiest woman in the world, well, except for John's silly rules about females being not too dangerous and going around unarmed. Luckily she was able to ignore these without John catching on. Looking back at the letter she continued, "Oh yes, here we go. She is keeping up with her Latin lessons and we should pass along her thanks to Father Peter for making the arrangements. She met some folks from Germany when they came into the shop and is starting to learn the language. She thinks that may help her with the indigenous dictionary project. She says they are getting an even larger German minority in Buffalo along with some Polish. She said Poppa says to tell you that the beer situation in Buffalo is definitely improving with the new immigrants. That is about it, the rest is just some sister stuff. Oh dear, she still thinks boys are impossible but there is one young lad her father hired to help around his shop that she thinks is somewhat cute."

John looked up. "Maybe you should invite her up for the summer holidays so you can have a little older-sister younger-sister talk with her, about boys at least. Isaiah may be a fine father but he is most definitely not a mother."

"Indeed, that would be nice and perhaps necessary. I do miss her so. Buffalo really is not that far, only a two-day train ride or so", said Julia looking at John with a smile. "It is amazing, John, I never had a family except for Uncle William," as Julia referred to her former boss, "and now I have Sarah and you, not to mention your sister Susan and her husband. It really is the most wonderful thing, especially at the holidays. I so enjoyed Christmas last year. I never really had a family Christmas before. It truly was magical, John. I do not know if I told you but we will have to buy extra presents next year. Susan sent me a letter. She told me you are going to be an uncle."

John smiled warmly, seeing how happy Julia was. "Why did you not tell me sooner?"

Julia turned slightly red. "Well, I was working on a project and it slipped my mind. I mean, it only arrived in Saturday's post, my love." Julia decided that not reminding her husband about the project she had been working on was indeed the wiser course of action.

Returning to the matter at hand John said, "I shall have to send a letter to them. What shall we get for a christening present? As for your little sister, Father Peter was right, Sarah does have an absolutely amazing flair for languages. I cannot believe how fast she learns them. I hope Anderson does not find out; he will want to recruit her! And might I inquire, what project, dear?"

Julia looked shocked at this! The last thing she wanted was for Sarah to be involved in the life she previously had even if she had met John as part of it. "Oh dear! Indeed we should do everything to make sure William does not find out about it. It would not do at all. Sarah should lead a normal life and meet a proper young man."

John looked at his wife. "You mean more normal then knowing several languages, being involved with a terror plot and traveling already more than most people do in a lifetime? What project Julia?"

Julia looked annoyed with her spouse. "That was not her fault, John Morton, and you know it; well, the traveling part maybe. However, that was because Isaiah would not leave her at a convent when you found her, and then for a chance to see Cee Cee again." Julia was referring to Sarah's friend, whom she had not met in California, and now lived where she had always not lived, off Hawaii. Continuing, "I do not want her mixed up with William; it is not a proper life for a young girl." John simply stood there without blinking and looked at her. "Well, I was trying to get the formulation right for the new explosive device if you must know."

John smiled blandly, "Oh, you mean you do not approve of proper young ladies keeping explosives around the house, like the kind of thing that would mess up one's spouse's workshop or blow out windows?"

Julia snorted again in that unladylike way. "John Morton, that was only enough for research purposes, hardly enough to do any serious damage. I will clean up your workshop, dear, and do not change the subject! I do not want my sister getting mixed up with William. It is far too dangerous!"

John looked at his wife. "Well, at least I can completely agree with you on that, Sarah is far too nice for the likes of William Anderson and his agency."

CHAPTER 3

ANOTHER EXPEDITION

It was midmorning when Simon showed up at their basement office. He knocked politely on the door. "Simon, seeing you twice in one day, how unusual. So what brings you down to the depths of the lower dungeon, as it were?" Julia said this with a twinkle in her eye as she jokingly referred to the location of John's office and laboratory.

Simon smiled at Julia again and said, "Dr. Chesterfield sends his compliments and wonders if Professor Morton could join him in his office right away."

Julia got up and replied, "Let me check with him, Simon; he is in his laboratory." She crossed the room and opened the door to the adjoining room which served as John's lab. "Dearest, Simon is here and he says the curator would like to see you upstairs in his office. What should I tell him?"

John looked up with a bit of a surprise. First, he had been deep into studying a fossil from the last field trip to Upstate New York near the Erie Canal, in much the same area where he had started his studies as a young man. Second, it was rather unusual to have Dr. Chesterfield summon him to his office. "Please tell Simon I will be up as soon as I put this specimen back in storage and clean up a bit. Thank you, dear."

Julia turned around and started to speak but Simon cut her off, "I could not help overhearing, Mrs. Morton". Julia looked at him and wagged her finger. "I mean, Julia," Simon finished.

"See, now that was not too hard now was it Simon?" Julia said, with a light laugh.

Poor Simon seemed to be getting tongue-tied again and retreated with, "I will let Dr. Chesterfield know to expect the professor."

A few minutes later John came out of his laboratory straightening his tie and pulling on his jacket. Julia smiled and went over and brushed off some imaginary dust and gave his tie a final tug. John looked at her and said, "I wonder what the curator wants? It is rather rare I am called to his office. In fact, the last time was after that fund raiser. Julia, you have not put another patron in the fountain have you?"

Julia straightened up. "John Morton, I had nothing to do with that. The man was drunk and tripped! Second, I do not have knowledge of any other patrons being injured or falling into fountains."

John looked down at his wife. "All right my love, I will take your word for it. Still, I wonder what Dr. Chesterfield could want."

"Most probably a promotion, after all, you are brilliant, my dear." Having said that she stood up on her toes and kissed him.

John started to respond to the kiss in spite of the teasing of his colleagues and his earlier admonishment to Julia. Julia pushed him away. "Dear, museum curators first, wives second, and only when you have the proper amount of time for it."

"I really hate it when work gets in the way of husbandly duties. However, as usual you are right, my love. Let us see what the curator wants. For the record, I doubt that it is a promotion. I am just one of several brilliant people around here." John then let Julia wipe a bit of her lip rouge off his mouth before he went out the door.

A few short minutes and several flights of stairs later John found himself outside the hall door to the curator's office. Knocking, he went in to be met by Simon at his desk. Simon looked up and smiled, "I will let the curator know you are here, sir."

"Thank you, Simon," replied Morton as he waited. Morton stood there as Simon walked over to the curator's door, knocked and went in. Several seconds later he returned and told Morton to please go in. John walked calmly over to the door, knocked, went in and then came to a complete stop! The curator was not alone. In the office with him was William Anderson, Julia's ex-boss. John stood there for a second and tried to mentally regroup. Swallowing, he said, "Good morning Curator and Colonel Anderson. How nice to see you again, sir."

Anderson smiled at John and replied, "John, I do not believe we have seen each other since your wedding. How is my niece? Well I hope?" This was the story that Julia had given everyone at their wedding since that is how she seemed to think of Anderson, that he was her uncle. It would hardly have done to try and explain to everyone that she was a secret agent and assassin for Anderson's agency.

John swallowed and replied, "Julia is fine, Colonel Anderson. She is very happy in her new life. Perhaps you can come over for dinner if you will be in town long enough. I know Julia would love to see you, sir." John fervently hoped Anderson would not have the time for he sincerely wanted nothing at all to do with the man, and especially did not want Julia to have any doings with him.

The curator smiled, delighted to see that an excellent patron of the museum was happy. "John, please come in and sit down would you. Mr. Anderson, or should I say Colonel? John, Colonel Anderson has some wonderful news!"

"Dr. Chesterfield, Arthur, Mister will do fine, in fact, please call me William. The war is long over although I still try to help out the government on occasion with the odd bits of business; the occasional odd problem, you know. I am retired from the army."

Dr. Chesterfield looked happy, "Oh very well, William it is. Anyhow John, the Anderson Foundation is interested in funding another expedition to the western territories and they have asked me if you could be spared here to head it up. Is that not the most wonderful news!"

John stood there frozen and just as he was going to sit down, a series of bugle calls and drum rolls were going off in his head as if he were back in the army and his unit was under attack. They were the calls for all troops to man the defenses. "Another expedition, sir? Well I am still sorting and cataloging the finds from the last major research dig near

Clinton's Ditch, sir. I do not want to get too far ahead of myself," he stammered in response as he managed to find a chair.

Anderson smiled, "Do not worry, John, the foundation has several young candidates who can cover for you here while you are out in the field along with your team. If fact, they were part of your last western dig. They did excellent work in the badlands on that Dakota Territory dig several years back. They were all eager to have a chance to gain such valuable experience coupled with a chance to work with you. You apparently mesmerized them; quite the bit of hero worship there. Seriously, they all think the world of you. To a man they are excited about an opportunity to do some work here at the museum. Apparently, Arthur, your humble institution has quite the reputation in certain circles." The curator beamed at this last remark as Anderson had said it as a smiling aside to him!

Anderson continued, "In fact, the curator here has been singing the praises of the young black girl who wound up on the team last time as the assistant archivist. He tells me you actually talked a colleague of yours into taking her on an expedition to the Hawaiian Islands no less, and she was quite the asset. According to Arthur she has the most amazing flair for languages, and she is, in addition, an excellent record keeper. I hope you can use her on this trip. I remember Julia spoke highly of her father, a genius tinker if I remember correctly. I do believe I met her and her father at your wedding, did I not? As I remember it she was your flower girl? I recall being somewhat surprised at Julia having a Negro girl in her wedding party. However, Arthur, as John here knows, there is no predicting what my niece will do next."

John was feeling trapped. There was no way he could decline without the curator finding out the real story behind the last expedition funded by Anderson. John responded, trying to play for time. "Well, sir, as you know, Julia was not only an orphan, but also had no known brothers or sisters or any family, eh, that is before she was found by you, sir. Then she met Sarah who was also an orphan with no family at all, so they seemed to bond. Julia sees Sarah as her little sister."

Dr. Chesterfield looked somewhat confused. "I thought that at your wedding Sarah was introduced as Mr. Liman's daughter?"

John responded, "Yes, sir, however, Isaiah had bonded with Sarah also so at the end of the expedition he adopted her. You see, Isaiah had lost his family too. His wife had died in childbirth with their first child, a daughter, who also died. It was several years before he was recruited for the expedition. It seemed that over the course of the expedition they healed each other." John swallowed, and looking back at Anderson resumed, "Another expedition, sir. Quite an honor, sir. Needless to say, I would have to discuss it with Julia." Trying to think of a way out he blurted, "We were hoping to start a family, sir. You understand. I mean we just found out my younger sister Susan and her husband are expecting. I would not want my kid sister to get that far ahead, sir."

Dr. Chesterfield seemed mildly shocked at this since John had not mentioned it before. Also, since Mr. Anderson had funded such a major expedition several years before and seemed to want John to head up this new study, that in and of itself was quite a compliment. "John, perhaps you two could hold off for a while. It would most certainly be a big boost to your stature in the scientific community." And, thought Chesterfield, a big boost to the museum.

Anderson smiled, and spoke, "Think nothing of it, Arthur. I know my niece. She is a very level-headed young woman. John, let us discuss this over dinner at the club. I keep up my membership there for the rare times I am in town. As a matter of fact, Arthur here was good enough to sponsor me for it; indeed it was very kind of you, Arthur," this last was said with a brief nod to the curator. The curator smiled and nodded back, as if to say 'my pleasure'. Anderson went on, "Of course, I do not get to make much use of it. Washington business, the government, always seem to have some minor problem or another that needs attention; so hard to get away. You can understand. Shall we say eight o'clock tonight and, of course, Julia must come. I believe they have relaxed the rules somewhat since I first joined. They now allow ladies in as the guest of a member, somewhat different from the first time we met there."

John realized there was no way out of this meeting, so as a gentleman the only option he could see was to give in gracefully. "Eight o'clock, sir, at the club. I know Julia will be excited to see you again. You were virtually her only family."

The curator looked somewhat relieved, after all, John's last trip had resulted in not only a great number of scientific discoveries, but a wealth of very favorable publicity for the museum. This last was due in no small part because Julia had prepared and filed so many stories and illustrations, which she had one of John's interns do, for publication by the newspapers. How did she put it? Oh yes, as if the whole city would be along with them on this expedition of discovery. He actually had been thinking of having that writer fellow, oh, what was his name? Buntline, that was it, have Ned Buntline do a book on some of John's exploits; they were quite exciting in themselves besides the scientific discoveries. That book should really put the museum on the lips of everyone. Maybe '*Morton Among The Savages*' or '*Morton And The Lost World*' or some such. Capital idea, could sell it right here at the museum, raise some revenue. Maybe they could put in a small stand for mementos. Dr. Chesterfield was jarred out of his musings when Mr. Anderson got up to take his leave.

"Till this evening then, John", he spoke as he shook John's hand.

"Indeed, sir. I know Julia will be happy to hear you are in town and want to see her." John was actually wondering what Julia's reaction was going to be. Julia said she was happy but to be honest, a museum professor's life was not exactly the exciting stuff of dime novels by writers such as Ned Buntline! He was somewhat dull, he feared, after her life working for Anderson.

John was in quite a state by the time he returned to his office a short time later. As he arrived he could hear Julia typing away, which took him back to the first time he had found her in his office. How would

Julia react? Filing and typewriting or a life of adventure as a secret agent? Squaring his shoulders, John opened the door and went in.

Julia stopped her typing, and looked up at him smiling. The smile left her face, however, as she noted the look of worry on his face. "John, what is it? Your position has not been cut has it? I know the economy has taken a downturn, but you are secure in your position here, are you not?" John looked so worried, she was scared for her husband.

John smiled at her and plunged in, "No, Julia, nothing like that, actually somewhat worse. Your uncle is here and wants to fund another expedition!" John used neutral language in case someone should overhear.

Julia looked torn. She knew that John did not approve of her past association with Anderson or her past life. However, she did miss it to some extent, she was after all a young woman of twenty-one. She was not exactly a spinster's age yet and still had some high spirits and more than a bit of a swash-buckling adventurer in her hot Mediterranean blood. "Did he say what he wanted, John? Did he give a hint as to what the research was to be about or where the research was to be conducted?" Like John, she tried to watch her language as did her husband for she had found that museum staff was just as prone to gossip as any gaggle of church parish old maids.

John shook his head and answered, "No, but he promised to tell us about it later. We are to dine with your uncle tonight at his club. What may be a bit more sticky," trying to find a word that did not express the worry he felt, "he knows about Sarah. Apparently Dr. Chesterfield let the cat out of the bag by praising her, and telling him about all the help she was to Donald on his Hawaiian research. Anderson seems to think that both Isaiah and Sarah can be of use on this expedition he has planned."

Julia looked stricken. It was just earlier that morning when she told John that she did not want Sarah involved with William's agency, that it would be too dangerous for her little sister. Now she realized that her past life was catching up with her and drawing others that she loved into it! Julia Morton was at that moment beginning to truly appreciate her husband's point of view about her past life. Danger to herself, that she had no problem accepting, she had lived with that prospect for several years of intrigue and spying for William Anderson. Now it was Sarah, John and Isaiah. It was virtually her whole family that was being brought into the arena! Julia wet her lips, calmed herself and asked, "What did you tell him, John?"

John looked at her and answered, "I tried to get out of it by saying that we were thinking about starting a family." John hid a small smile at the thought. "I am afraid that it did not work too well, we are still invited to dinner. Eight o'clock tonight at his club."

Julia looked a little taken aback. Until then she had not thought about children; she and John had not discussed it. A family of their own, that was most assuredly something to think about. "Well, then we shall see what the night brings, besides dinner that is." Julia looked down for a moment and then looked up at her husband and asked, "John, are children something you want?"

John looked at his wife. "I know we have not talked about it, but I had hoped it was something we might want, together."

Julia got up and went over and hugged her husband. Looking up at him she said, "As I remember, it does take two people. I am sure your father had that talk with you about it, at least you seem to know a lot about it," and with a small teasing smile finished, "for a dull museum professor."

John hugged his wife back. "In truth, I read all about it in the various scientific journals," he said smiling, with an added wink and a small but very delightful neck nibble. He went on, "I suppose we might close up a bit early today so we can get ready to find out what your Uncle William has planned."

CHAPTER 4

DINNER WITH A SIDE OF ANSWERS

Later that night, even though the weather was not too bad, John had elected to pay for a small carriage to take them to dinner as the club was a fair distance away from their home. As always, Julia looked lovely in her favorite dark blue dress with the onyx jewelry. These were a holdover from her time working for Anderson for museum professors were not paid well enough to afford a different dress for every day. John seemed to note this, "Julia, I am sorry I cannot afford a new dress for you." He was worried that her old life would call to her.

Julia looked at him, "I am not complaining, John. We do not get out that often anyway. Besides, if we follow through on our earlier discussion, you, sir, shall have to be able to afford some maternity clothes for me or I shall be forced to work naked!"

John turned several shades of red at this last comment and Julia just smiled. John caught his breath and realized that his wife was pulling his leg. He replied "Well, at least the child would have two aunts, Sarah and Susan, and a cousin, so it would seem. It would make Christmas even more magical."

Julia smiled as the carriage drew up at that moment in front of the club. "I believe dinner awaits, sir."

Just as in their first time together, John helped Julia down from the carriage and it still made him catch his breath as he felt the warmth of her body through her clothing. The club was as elegant as John remembered it from the first time he had dinned there with Anderson at the start of the Ratten business. There was an excellent string quartet playing a Mozart piece softly in the background. After he inquired, the headwaiter showed them to Mr. Anderson's reserved room, this time without John having to bribe the man as he had to do on his first occasion at the club. Anderson was there waiting for them. John was surprised in that there were five places set although so far Anderson himself was the only person at the table.

Anderson stood and came around to hug Julia. Smiling he said, "It would appear that wedded life suits you Julia. You look as lovely as ever, my dear."

Julia smiled, for in spite of all that had happened, she did love Anderson as would a niece with a favorite uncle, much to John's disapproval. "Do not try to flatter me so much, Uncle William. What is it that brings you here, and do not try to tell me that you were just in the neighborhood. I know you far too well, sir!"

Anderson smiled and shrugged his shoulders and in reply said, "Not flattery, but honesty, Julia. However, I will not try to fool you, as you say you do know me too well. You were always one of my best, and dare I say, favorite students."

Julia looked at him "Do you not mean agent, sir?"

Anderson simply shrugged and let it go saying, "Well you did graduate Julia, and with honors, first in the class as I remember. You thereafter took care of some modest projects for me with a noted efficacy. Please sit down," as he pulled out a chair for her at one of the settings. "Would either of you care for a cordial before dinner or a glass of wine while we wait for the rest of our party? The club does have an excellent wine cellar you know. As they say, rank hath its privileges." The waiter took their orders. Julia had a small sherry while John took a neat whiskey.

After the waiter left, closing the door behind him, John asked the obvious question, "William, what is this about? My wife paid her dues for your education, and we are in the scientific world now, not yours!"

Anderson looked at Julia with a raised eyebrow. "Is he this blunt and forceful at home, my dear?"

Julia put her hand on John's arm and smiled at him, "I seem to have a way of soothing his very rare occasions of temper." Then she turned back to Anderson and finished, "They seem to show up only when he is reminded of my former life. My *very* former life, William!"

"Really so former, Julia? A purse snatcher in the hospital, a patron in the fountain? I do keep tabs you know. However, as it turns out, your former and your current life may have intersected with the present problem I am dealing with. I need both your former and current talents along with several other persons, who should be arriving shortly."

It was just then that the drinks were served. They could overhear the waiter, who had stepped out after serving them, asking a man if he would like a drink since several of the other guests had already ordered. The man's voice replied that he would take a brandy, please, and then the door was opened to admit Father Peter Harrigan.

Father Peter just stood there much as John had done when he was shown into the curator's office earlier that day, although the good father made no attempt to hide his displeasure. "Anderson, I should have known when I received a note from the archbishop's private secretary, by special courier no less, that said to meet someone for dinner at such an upscale establishment that it would be you! What is it this time! What great threat to the nation has the government unleashed that you need to have cleaned up?"

Anderson smiled. "Father Harrigan, always a delight to see you too, sir. Please, join us. We are awaiting one more guest, then all your questions will be answered, or at least as much of an answer as I can give at this point. Obviously you know the Mortons."

Peter looked less than happy, scowling at Anderson as he assumed a place at the table; however, his face lit up when he looked at the Mortons. He indeed was pleased to see John and Julia. It had been some time since they rarely got down to the Five Points, which is the closest one could get to hell and still be in Manhattan where his parish, St. Brigit's, was located. It was even rarer when he could get away to their section of Manhattan to visit them. He smiled, "John, Julia, it is good to see you two again, how are you?"

John nodded as Julia replied with some pleasantries while the waiter returned with the priest's brandy. "We are well, Father Peter. Our work at the museum is quite fulfilling and enjoyable. How is life in the parish?"

Peter smiled at her. In spite of Julia's former life, he liked her very much, even more so since she had married John and seemed to be leading a mostly violence-free life. "Like you Julia, I find it rewarding, but at times it is tiring. It is not the easiest place in which to be a shepherd in. However my boss seems to think it is the best place for me."

Julia cocked her head at this. "You mean the archbishop?"

Peter smiled his best Irish smile and pointing upward replies, "No, the Big Boss."

Julia seemed somewhat taken aback at this and then smiled. She reached over and hugged Peter and laughing said, "Well I can see where there is no arguing with the head office then!"

Peter smiled and looking at John, "I take it you are happy with the domestic arrangements then, John." Peter was in truth happy for them as he was the man who married them. He had seen them fall in love even if they had not wanted to, or in Julia's case felt she could not, admit to each other or to themselves, to some extent, over the course of their last journey together.

John looked at his friend and former army comrade, "I could not be happier, Peter, although I still have some windows to repair." Julia looked somewhat guilty at that.

Now it was Peter's turn to cock his head, "I somehow think that is not something I need to go into, at least outside of the confessional, do I, Julia?"

Julia looking somewhat like she had been caught with her hand in the cookie jar replied, "So you were saying about the activities in the parish", trying to change the subject while looking as innocent as a schoolgirl at a convent school facing the mother superior.

As they sat enjoying this simple bit of small talk, they heard a slight commotion in the hall outside the private room. Finally the door opened to admit two men. One was tall and lean, reasonably well dressed, handsome in a rough kind of way, about Morton's height but a bit leaner.

They thought it odd that he still had on his coat worn over his shoulders like a cape and his hands were behind his back. The other man looked like a no-nonsense workman with a bushy mustache and dressed in workman-like clothes such as a tradesman would wear to church on Sunday.

Julia noted a slight bulge under the mustached man's jacket that indicated he had a short-barreled pistol in a holster that was being worn in a cross-draw position. She tensed up somewhat although she did not, as an extremely well-trained agent, let it show, her hand moving oh so slightly toward her bag where, unknown to John, her favorite small derringer nestled. John seemed to think that a proper museum professor's wife should not carry deadly weapons, even though John still carried his little Pepperbox along with his so-fancy and even deadlier cane, with its concealed blade. As she had noted to John on many an occasion, a young lady should be prepared for whatever comes up and should not have to rely on her husband, unless of course it was to distract the police from following up on a tripping and seriously injured purse snatcher. She loved John, but at times he could be so stuffy. Really, it was the modern age, 1879, after all. It would seem old habits even at age twenty-one die hard.

The shorter man with the mustache glanced around the table. "Which one of you is Anderson?" This was said in a somewhat bored voice.

Anderson stood up, "I am, sir. Is this Hook?"

The man nodded and replied, "Yes, this is Hook. You are going to have to sign for him." So saying, he pulled out some paperwork from his inner coat pocket. With that, Julia could see his badge, that of a U.S. Deputy Marshal and the gun she was sure had been there. She relaxed ever so slightly at the sight of the badge. The marshal took a pencil and handed both pencil and paperwork over to Anderson for his signature. While Anderson signed the paperwork the marshal asked, "You want the irons off him, sir?"

Anderson looked at the tall man. "Can I trust you, Hook? This could be your lucky day."

The man looked Anderson square in the eye. There was no flinching, no sign of fear. "Fact is Guv'ner, I can say anything I want, but how will you know whether or not it is the truth? However, I can afford to hear you out. Like you said, it could be my lucky day."

Anderson looked at the smaller man, "If you would, please take them off Marshal and thank you for the delivery."

With this final direction the marshal removed Hook's coat and taking a key out of his pocket removed a set of manacles from Hook's wrists. "Mind your manners, Hooky. I do not fancy hauling you all the way back to Elmira." Then the marshal took the manacles, put the papers back in his inner pocket and turning, left the room.

Anderson smiled and indicated the chair. "Please sit down, Mr. Hook; we have yet to order. Would you like a drink before dinner, sir?"

Hook cocked his head while rubbing his wrists, a bit raw from the manacles. "Scotch, single malt, from the Highlands if they have it." He said this as he removed his coat and hung it up.

Anderson raised his eyebrows a bit. "While the situation with Great Britain is not the best, I believe the club has some. Most probably they will say left over since before the war, Mr. Hook, or much more likely smuggled in through Canada." The waiter was summoned and Hook's order placed.

Hook looked at Anderson and continued once the waiter had left and the door closed. "What is this all about? I was just settling into my new home, as it were, before I was brought here. Not saying it is not a better place, especially without all the bars, but what is this all about? I mean, you do not seem the type to be doing such things out of the goodness of your heart, the Father here and the pretty little bird maybe, but not you, sir. As for the other gentleman, him I do not know."

Morton was a bit shocked at the series of events to say the least. He was more than a little putout any man would talk about Julia that way let alone an obvious prisoner. "I will have you know the pretty little bird, sir, is my wife!"

Hook looked at him in a lazy way. "You certainly have good taste, Guv'ner, I will give you that." Returning his gaze to Anderson he again asked, "Do you plan on answering my question about why I am here?"

Anderson looked at the assembled group. "Of course, Mr. Hook, but first, introductions are in order. May I present Professor John Morton of the Department of Natural History at the New York Museum and his wife Julia. Julia is an ex-associate of my agency, currently on leave."

John looked a little shocked at how Anderson referred to Julia's status. Anderson went on as if he had not noticed the look on John's face, "And Father Peter Harrigan of the Archdiocese of New York, despite the clerical collar, an excellent man in a tight spot. To one and all may I present Mr. Clement Hook formerly of Wales. Mr. Hook believed in the cause of Welsh independence, so much so that Her Majesty's government put a price on his head, one commensurate with the trouble he caused. It was a quite sizable one. That led Clement here to immigrate to the United States, in a bit of a rush, shall we say. Unfortunately for him, he combined his former occupation as a mining engineer with his zeal to rob banks as a way to finance plots against Her Majesty's government. Not that I care about the latter but the former is quite the no-no, would you agree, Mr. Hook?"

Hook nodded his head, "I would say that about sums it up, Guv'ner. I believe in a free Wales and to hell with Good Queen Bess. I will admit that your yank peelers were on the spot, picking me up the way they did. However, that still does not explain who you are, or what this is all about."

The conversation stopped for a moment while Hook's drink arrived. As the door closed behind the waiter, Anderson started up again. "Excuse me, Mr. Hook, my apologies. My name is William Anderson and let us just say I am in charge of an agency that deals with various delicate and unusual problems for the United States Government. I hope that answers your first question, Mr. Hook."

Hook nodded his head and replied, "Met your type before, Guv'ner, different accent and look, but I do indeed recognize the type, the type that does his work in the shadows, I do. All right, that answers who you are, but not why I am here."

Anderson nodded and then continued, "With the exception of Mr. Hook, I assume most of you are familiar with the Nez Perce Indian War several years ago."

Hook shrugged saying, "I read about it. Bunch of your red aborigines beat the tar out of your blue jackets right?"

Julia looked at Anderson, "I believe Mr. Hook's brief summary, while leaving out a great many details such as the United States started

the war, is essentially correct. We only won by wearing them down."
She turned and looking at Hook, "And just so you are aware, sir, we
Americans call them Indians and it is blue coats not jackets."

"My apologies, madam. Would not want to offend the natives and
the local militia," replied Hook, in a manner that clearly seemed to
indicate that he did not care one way or the other who he offended.
He tipped his drink to her as if in some sort of a salute and took a sip.
Looking at the glass he then looked up at Anderson noting, "A very
fine cellar, sir."

John and Father Peter had been nodding in agreement, about the
condition of the club's cellar, at any rate. As to the war, Peter looked
surprised and then quizzically inquired, "What do you mean, the
government started it?"

John spoke, "We were able to see some of the reports that were not
released to the press or were downplayed in the news accounts. The U.S.
Government provoked them, and militia and white settlers attacked
them in order to seize their lands. It was most shameful!"

Anderson looked at Julia. "I shall assume that you came across some
of the reports during the last affair. That and/or you still have some
connections, Julia."

Julia looked at Anderson. "We were near enough to the battle area
at the dig site in the Dakotas so it behooved me to stay informed, Uncle,
and as you said, I still have some connections in the business, sir."

Anderson looked at Julia with a somewhat annoyed expression for
no more than a few seconds mumbling, "Top of her class indeed." He
decided to go on replying to Father Peter's question, "Basically, Father,
as usual the lovely Mrs. Morton and her agent-stealing husband are
correct in their brief outlines."

John smiled at this description of himself, for indeed he had stolen
Julia away from Anderson, even if he had to marry her to do it and he
thought he would do it again in the span of a single heartbeat. John gave
his wife's hand a gentle squeeze.

Anderson went on as if unaware of John's thoughts. "The government
did provoke the Indians and then almost managed to lose the war.

Idiots, as if we did not have enough problems on our hands between the French puppet government in Mexico with their own civil war, Apaches raiding out of Mexico, and the Brits in Canada. That is not to even mention the south is still smoldering. At least that is slowly dying down. It was just lucky that the British had trouble in the Indian subcontinent so that they did not feel that they could afford to stir up trouble over here. As it was, it was a closely run race; hardly the army's most shining hour. It took most of the army units west of the Mississippi to corral the Indians before it was over, a mere forty or fifty miles or so from the Canadian border." Anderson paused and took a sip of his drink before going on. "As I was saying, not the army's finest hour, and Julia is right, they basically won by wearing the Indians down. As it was, they almost made it to the Canadian border but they stopped to let the women and children rest and that gave the army a chance to catch up to them. Chief Joseph was shipped back east while the tribe was settled on a reservation in the Idaho Territory."

At this point John interjected, "It would seem that a better use for Joseph would have been to make him an instructor at West Point, considering he out-maneuvered and out-fought the army at every turn. Speaking as a retired officer, his campaign was nothing short of brilliant."

Anderson nodded to John and resumed, "Indeed Major, that was actually talked about in some circles, but the army's pride probably would not have allowed it. Also, your commission is in reserve so technically you are not retired."

John, Julia and Father Harrigan scowled at the implied threat in this statement. All three had served their country, Julia as an agent for Anderson and both John and Peter, before he became a priest, in the war to hold the Union together, not to mention the Ratten business.

Father Peter said, "It would seem to me, sir, that we have proved that we will do what needs to be done for our country, without the need of such threats."

Anderson looked at him, "You are right, Father, it was uncalled for. I do apologize."

Julia looked actually somewhat shocked, for in all her years of working for Anderson she had never seen him be contrite before. She wondered if he was slipping some and started to worry about him. Even though she knew he used people, including John and herself, she did still feel affection for him for all that he had done for her. He was, after all, as John put it, the only family she had known before she met John, and against all the training supplied by Anderson, fallen in love with him.

Hook spoke, "All this is fascinating, no doubt, but it still begs the question, why am I here, Your Lordship?"

The others nodded in agreement with Hook's somewhat rude utterance.

Anderson looked at the group, and after taking a sip of his drink, resumed, "About three weeks ago a young Nez Perce warrior who had been too young to fight in the wars, was send to find some stray horses that had gotten away from the tribe during a particularly nasty storm. From what the Indian agent said in his confidential report, he was trying to prove himself to impress a specific young lady."

Father Peter noted drily, "Some things seem to cross racial and cultural boundaries, I see."

Anderson nodded in agreement, "Indeed, Father, indeed. As I was saying, the tribal elders gave the lad the assignment to get him out of the camp for a while since he was becoming somewhat of a thorn in their side, as we would say, pestering them to prove he was a warrior. It was a reasonably easy assignment and would keep the lad out of everyone's hair for a while."

John broke in, "I take it things did not go quite as expected?"

Anderson looked at John and responded with a deep breath. "Indeed they did not, Major. When the boy went missing they tracked him. When he was found he was in a bad way. He was bleeding from both his ears and eyes and, additionally, was quite delusional. From what the agent was able to gather from talking to the party that found him, the lad was mumbling something about the side of the mountain exploding and a monster coming out. Later there were reports of more monsters on the reservation. Needless to say the Indians are riled up, and the army is in near hysterics at the thought of another Indian uprising or them bolting off the reservation. As was previously noted, they were barely able to contain them the last time. I will not beat around the bush with you. I need a team with the cover of an expedition to go and find out what is happening, get it under control and put a stop to it. Needless to say, the sooner the better. Any takers?"

Hook was the first one to reply, "I still do not see, Guv'ner, what this has to do with me, or for that matter, what is in it for me?"

Anderson looked at Hook. "Simply put, Clement, we believe, based upon the evidence at the scene, that this might not have been a living monster but some sort of new tunneling machine of incredible power. The information supplied was none too clear, quite muddled actually. As of right now, we just do not know. Either way we need a man with your knowledge to evaluate it for us and to help us to understand what we are up against. As to what is in it for you, once the threat has been contained and the information recovered, Clement Hook dies and you receive a new identity and a new life, a clean slate so to speak, Mr. Hook." Anderson took a sip of his drink. "As I said, this could be your lucky day."

Hook looked thoughtful at this. "What has this to do with the others here; why them? A new life is fine as long as it is not posthumous."

Anderson smiled at the other three then looked at Hook. "Do not worry about the others, they have already proven themselves. The major and the good father, First Sergeant Harrigan back then, were in the war together, both are highly decorated veterans. Furthermore, they were on a previous expedition that was handled most satisfactorily, despite the fact that it had a far different ending then envisioned. As for the lady, as I said, she worked for me for several years handling various, let us just say delicate, assignments, and is extremely proficient at all sorts of things. Finally, she is a veritable genius with explosives. The rest of the team you will meet later. In point of fact, Mr. Hook, since you are the questionable newcomer, it is they who should be questioning you."

Julia, who had been watching the exchange, asked, "Who else is on the team, William?"

Anderson looked at her and replied, "It will be the same as before, Julia, less two of the sharpshooters. Bill's injuries, the ones he received during the Ratten business, did not heal as well as was hoped, so we use him on quieter assignments now, surveillance mostly. He is still a most reliable fellow. John now has a family so he wishes to be based in the Washington area. They will be replaced by some of my best young agents. Of course I am hoping that Mr. Liman and his daughter will join you."

Julia looked somewhat annoyed. "I also have a family, William," as she put her hand on John.

Anderson smiled. "True Julia, but John Kirkland's family does not know about his position; they think he works for the State Department delivering documents. That, as opposed to your spouse who is well aware of your former activities not even to mention his own. And do not be so trite with me, young lady; I find it hard to believe that you are ready to settle down fully to a life of typing and filing. As you remarked about me, I know you too well, Julia."

John was getting somewhat nervous as he could sense something was bothering Julia. Julia tensed up. "Why do we need Isaiah and Sarah, William? Sarah is only twelve years old! She deserves a life as a child; she lost so much already!"

Anderson looked at Julia and replied, "Julia, this mission calls for a man of her father's abilities and from the reports I have received he will not go if Sarah is not with him and vice versa. Also, it appears as if young Sarah is a bit of a genius herself. This matter is serious and I need the best I can find. Am I clear Special Agent!"

Julia looked like she wanted to explode, but then it passed and she just nodded and spoke quietly, "I understand, sir, the needs of the mission." Then she seemed to catch fire again, "But understand this William, if I think Sarah is in any danger I will abort the mission! My or even John's life are one thing, but I will not let my little sister be endangered. Are *we* clear, sir!"

Anderson looked somewhat shocked at Julia's response. "When John mentioned this morning that you saw this young Negro girl as your sister, I thought he was exaggerating, but now I see he was telling the truth, without any hint of exaggeration. All right, Julia, but I expect you to be just as dedicated to the mission as to the child's safety. This is very serious business. The British would like nothing better than to stir up trouble out in the west."

Julia stared back at her mentor and former boss. "Have I ever been other than that, sir?"

Anderson looked at her and smiled again, indeed like an uncle with a favorite niece. "No, Julia, you have not. I can live with your terms."

Julia smiled, but again she was wondering about the new softness and condition of her uncle, as she thought of Anderson. It had been drummed into her at the "finishing school" William ran for young ladies like herself that the mission came first no matter what or who was in the way, and everyone was expendable. She had discovered that there were some things more important than the mission, thanks to Sarah. She found that out in a very forceful way when Sarah put herself in the line of Julia's fire to save her friend, Cee Cee.

Hook looked somewhat confused at the exchange. "Your little sister is a darkie?" he asked in a surprised voice.

Julia turned on him. "I was an orphan, as was Sarah when we met, and you, sir, had best remember that skin color notwithstanding, she *is* my little sister. And *no one*, and I mean that very seriously, no one does anything to hurt her. Are we clear, Mr. Hook?"

Hook looked shocked at the change in Julia's manner. It was then that John stepped in, as he had to do in the past. "Sir, a little while ago you referred to my wife as a pretty little bird. A word of advice, do not threaten or make remarks about Sarah or you will see her undergo a metamorphosis into an extremely angry hawk with talons out. Are we clear?"

Taking a deep breath and going through some obvious mental exercises, Julia seemed to quiet down and become steady. Then she spoke in an even tone, "Understand, Mr. Hook, I never had a family I knew and Sarah had lost all of hers. We shared something and we love each other very much. Perhaps it is some kind of compensation for both of us but she *is* my family. I do not like the idea of her being mixed up in all this as it is." This last was obviously being said for Anderson's benefit. "However I do indeed understand the needs of the mission and that there is a potential danger to the country."

Hook shrugged again, "I must say now I am curious; I can hardly wait to meet this young woman who would raise such emotions in you, madam."

Anderson had watched this play out. Picking up his fork to tap the side of his water glass for attention he said, "I am glad to hear that you want to meet Sarah, Clement, and you shall have your opportunity very soon, unless of course you want to return to Elmira. Of course, since you know so much, it will have to be spent in solitary confinement, you understand."

Hook nodded his head at Anderson. "What can I say Guv'ner. When faced with an offer like that, I am in. But I want that offer of a clean slate in writing, sir."

Anderson looked at Clement Hook, smiled and shook his head. "Like you told me, I can say anything I want, but I am afraid you will have to take my word for it. Nothing in writing. In fact, this whole conversation never actually happened."

Hook appeared to be digesting this last statement when Julia spoke up, "For what it is worth, Mr. Hook, I have never known William to go back on his word. Trust is a valuable and somewhat scarce commodity in our world." John looked annoyed at this inclusion of Julia and Anderson in the same world as one another. Julia slid her hand over John's and squeezed it as if to say, I love you and now I am in your world.

Hook smiled and nodded again. "I may not trust you, sir, and as I said, I have met your type before in the shadows and they are indeed dark places. The lady, however, seems honest enough and the good father has not spoken up against what she said. All right, I am in."

Anderson smiled and said to John and Julia, "Your train is being refurbished and restocked as we speak. I remember from the last expedition the problems you had, Julia. This time you will have your own engine and crew right from the beginning along with the highest level of class, as the railroads put it. That should speed up your trip. At least you should not be slowed down as much as the last time. The train should be ready the day after tomorrow."

Both John and Julia looked up at this last comment. John spoke up giving voice to what they were both thinking, "Wednesday, that is hardly any time at all Colonel! We need to take care of various matters and I need to arrange for coverage at the museum!"

Anderson looked at them. "Wednesday. This matter is extremely volatile and I need you out there as soon as possible. Whatever is not handled will be seen to by someone on my staff. As for the museum, here are the names of some of the candidates we have contacted; give me your recommendations. I will have the young man or men, if you feel that it will take more than one, here by the end of the week." It was clear from Anderson's tone that no excuses would be tolerated.

Father Peter, who up to this point had been a bit of a bystander, cleared his throat and began to speak, "Several questions, sir, if I might."

Anderson along with the others looked somewhat surprised at the idea Father Peter might have some questions. Anderson looked at the priest, and with a nod said, "Yes Father, what are your questions?"

Father Peter replied, "First off, why me? I understand John, Julia and obviously Mr. Hook here, but why me? Although I am somewhat ashamed to admit it, I am pleased to think that you seem to consider me an exciting, dashing secret agent of some sort."

Anderson, smiling, replied, "That is easy enough, Father. You are the odd man out." Peter cocked his head at this remark somewhat quizzically. Anderson seeing the look went on, "By that I mean between Julia's basic desire to solve every problem by applying more than enough explosives to demolish it, and John's strong urge to study it till it dies of old age, you were the intermediary who had the ability to get these two to work together and to restrain Julia long enough not to kill John before she fell in love with him, although in retrospect, I am not sure that was a plus considering I lost her services, at least temporarily." Again John's face showed that he disliked the way Anderson referred to losing Julia's services "only temporarily". Anderson went on ignoring the annoyed look on John's face. "Julia's notes on you were quite illuminating, even if she did not think that they were. I can see the look on your face Padre. Do not worry, she did not violate the seal of the confessional or for that matter say anything derogatory about you. On the contrary, she took great stock and comfort in you and in your counsel. She saw you as a person who gave everyone a chance and did not judge them beforehand. Shocking, I know. Julia also seemed to find the way you reacted to Sarah as most warm and genuine; you have no idea what that meant to her." At this Julia blushed somewhat. Peter looked at her and smiled his best pastoral smile. Anderson went on, "Based upon John's notes and the debriefing we got from the rest of the team, yes, Corporal Tinsman and his men were debriefed and John also seemed to see you as someone to lean on when he was not sure of what course to take or to just catch his breath. It also seems that you prodded him when necessary, in a gentle, mild-mannered, First Sergeant kind of way. You are indeed quite the shepherd, Father, of this little flock. I found that it was most remarkable."

Father Peter looked at Anderson and then the Mortons and sighed. "And here I thought it was the dashing secret agent part. Oh well. All right then, the second question, what about my parish?"

Anderson smiled "The new archbishop was very cooperative. As before, your parish will be well taken care of, the archbishop's solemn oath."

Father Peter seemed to digest all of this and then shrugged and asked his final question, "Do we get Chef again? It did make life so much more pleasant."

Anderson laughed at this last utterance from the priest. "I am afraid that I lost the chef to a very fine restaurant here in New York but I do have someone else in mind. I do not think you will find it too hard of a sentence in purgatory, Father."

It was right after this question-and-answer session that the waiter returned to take everyone's dinner order. Just as it was two years before with a luncheon, the meal was excellent.

CHAPTER 5

SHUFFLE OFF TO BUFFALO

Tuesday had been frantic. At home, Julia worked with both of their servants to have the house secured and find them temporary work. She wanted to make sure it was only temporary as she wanted both of them back, and, oh pack! Yes, packing, that was also important. She was pleased to note that her lucky agency issued knife-proof corset, the red one with the black lace trim that had saved her life during the Ratten business, still fit after a year and a half of marriage. She also thought that John did seem to like the way she looked in it, at least by his usual male reaction. She smiled to herself and had a very female reaction herself; she certainly did enjoy that aspect of married life! Now, back to packing. Where was her favorite pair of throwing knives, John's special cane and spare ammunition for his little Pepperbox? She really had to see about getting John a better gun; it was just that he loved that underpowered tiny gun so much. Men! Exasperating, irrational creatures, but on the whole rather nice to have around, she thought, especially when you were wearing a red corset with black lace trim.

While Julia frantically saw to their domestic arrangements, John was working feverishly at the museum to prepare all his notes for whoever Anderson got to cover for him. John had looked at the list of names Anderson provided over dinner and suggested three of them as the best candidates. As Anderson had noted, all three were on the dig in the badlands several years before. Each had proved their worth and abilities to him.

John looked up as Dr. Chesterfield himself knocked on the door frame since the door was open. It was most unusual that Dr. Chesterfield arrived to talk to John in his basement office/laboratory instead of summoning John to his second floor office. "John, what is going on? When Colonel Anderson said they wanted you for another expedition I was very pleased, but my goodness, what is all the hurry? I mean, well, these bones have been in the ground for thousands or more years, my boy. What is all the great rush?"

John fumbled for a reply. "Well, sir, you see, apparently the bone bed was discovered during some preliminary scouting for possible mining sites. While the Anderson Foundation had enough connections to get the, er, interested parties to hold off on development, they do not feel that they can hold them at bay forever, so hence the need for the expedition to move as fast as possible before all is lost."

Dr. Chesterfield looked somewhat befuddled and replied, "Well I can understand, but John, to put such an undertaking all together so quickly, my God, how will you ever manage? I mean the logistics alone could overwhelm you!"

John smiled at his boss, stalling while he pulled an answer together. Standing, he led the curator to a chair and fetched him a cup of coffee. It was handy to have your laboratory attached to the office which was equipped with a Bunsen burner that could keep the coffee hot when not in use for other pressing scientific inquiry. In a soothing tone of voice John said, "First, sir, you have to understand that the Anderson Foundation has many irons in the fire, as it were, and Colonel Anderson himself has a diversity of business ventures so he is able to put things together very quickly and he seems quite used to it. Apparently he has to do it on a regular basis to keep ahead of his business rivals. For example, the train we had the last time has just finished being restored and restocked after it returned from another research use, in the Texas wilds I believe. Apparently we are not the only museum to see Anderson foundation support and greenbacks. Additionally, Colonel Anderson was able to raid one of his own companies for several key staff that will be needed, very handy bit of business there. Finally, sir, do not forget who my Chief of Logistics and Planning is; there is none finer then she, sir!"

Dr. Chesterfield smiled at this. "Of course, John, there is certainly much more to your wife then a pretty face. She is quite the manager and archivist, is she not?"

John, inwardly breathing a sigh of relief, said, "Indeed, sir, there is none better than my Julia." He also went on in his mind with the thought that there were even far more things, of a much nastier type, that Julia excelled at than the curator knew. "Also, Colonel Anderson was able to borrow Father Harrigan for the trip from the archbishop. He has quite the network of contacts. Luckily Father was one of the men I served with in the war and we are good friends. Even though he was a guest on the last expedition, so to speak if you remember, he was a tremendous help, especially teaching Sarah Latin since it helped her with the cataloging. Do not tell Julia I told you this but Sarah knows far more Latin then my wife. Julia told me she could not have managed without her."

Chesterfield looked at John. "Your secret is safe with me, John. I thought the Father was only along as the archbishop's representative to check on several bits of mission work the diocese was doing."

John smiled, relaxing as he realized he was selling his excuse. "True, sir, but that did not really consume that much of Peter's time. Without asking, he pitched in to help with my research along with teaching Sarah. That and helping with wedding arrangements and performing the ceremony." John truly smiled at this last bit.

Chesterfield smiled himself at this last. "I remember, John. He was the one who married you and Julia. I do not know if I ever told you but my wife and I rode with him on the train back to the city, very nice fellow, for a Catholic priest. Well it seems as if he did a fine job of it, although if I remember, I did warn you about the dangers of taking a young unmarried female out to the untamed west, did I not?" This last was given with a bit of a smirk. John laughed at this last comment appreciating the bit of humor to help relieve the craziness that swirled about him as he was trying to get ready.

Then Chesterfield's expression changed and he looked thoughtful for a moment as if mulling something over. He looked at John with a rather serious expression. "John, will Julia be able to prepare articles for the papers again as she did the last time? It was quite the bit of publicity for the museum and science in general. How did she put it? It would be as if the whole city was along on this trip of discovery, or some such. You do not know how far your spouse's words went, not to mention the drawing she managed to obtain. Why, there were several news services that picked up the stories and it was read about all over the country and even overseas."

John looked a little stunned. "Really, sir, I, I mean we had no idea. We did not get the papers out in the badlands and then there was the honeymoon which had its own things to keep us busy." John became somewhat red in the face as he said this last. Clearing his throat he went on, "And then rearranging my house for a family instead of a bachelor and hiring a maid for Julia. Then there was the sorting of all the fossil discoveries and writing them up. I guess neither one of us knew about the stories being so widely circulated we were so busy." In truth John was surprised they really did not know about the newspaper coverage. He went on, "Well, sir, I would have to ask Julia but I am certain that she will do the best she can; however, we are under a serious time constraint on this trip. Colonel Anderson made that quite clear at dinner last night. However, we shall see, Curator. My wife does seem to have an impressive talent for pulling miracles out of her bonnet. Of course part of it will be if we can use Mr. Liman and his daughter on this expedition. Sarah was such a help to Julia last time, it was like having one and a half or even more Julias along, they worked so well together. All that, and there were several young researchers who learned firsthand that new specimens should be put where Sarah directed them before they were cataloged, crated up and put into storage for the trip back. Apparently Sarah picked up some traits from her big sister."

Dr. Chesterfield laughed at this last comment of John's and then still smiling said, "That is settled then. John, I really do hope that those articles can be written. It was a big boost to the museum. Well, you have much to do and little enough time to do it in so I will leave you to it. One last thing if possible, needless to say, when you return since there is no time now, is there any way I can see the train? I really did want to see it last time."

"Very good, sir, you know you can count on Julia and me to do our best. As for the tour, if it is not needed for any other Anderson Foundation business right away, I will do whatever I can to arrange it." John breathed a sigh of relief as Dr. Chesterfield went down the hall and up the steps toward his office. John thought to himself, we can arrange that tour, that is if we can get all the weapons, Julia's explosives and various other non-scientific expedition materials out in time. He also congratulated himself that, for pulling a story out of thin air to cover the rush, he had done rather well! John gave himself a mental pat on the back.

Neither one of the Mortons got much sleep that night as the arrangements and packing went on into the wee hours of the morning. Both John and Julia looked more than a bit blurry eyed as their carriage and the accompanying small wagon they had hired, pulled up to the station where the special train that was to take them on their latest expedition was waiting on a coach track behind the station. John turned to Julia and spoke quietly to her, "You know, Mrs. Morton, this train does hold certain romantic memories for me."

Julia snuggled up. "Well, Professor Morton, you best act on them because Sarah and I will be sharing a compartment together, that is if Isaiah agrees to join us." Her tone changed and was now concerned. "John, I really do not know what to hope for. We need his services and you know how I care about Sarah, but I am so afraid it will be too dangerous for her." She sighed and put her head on John's shoulder.

John put his arm around his wife and held her. "Life is dangerous, but remember, Sarah survived the mean streets of Buffalo, in the Canal District no less, on her own. She is tough and smart, just like her big sister!" Julia smiled up at her husband at this last comment. John, pulling her in a bit tighter went on, "As to this separate compartment arrangement, I do not suppose you can sneak out and down to mine do you?"

Julia still smiling up at her husband, snuggled into him even closer if it were possible, and adding a serious bit of eye batting, "Well I suppose I might be able to do that, sir. Remember, I am a highly talented secret agent and very well trained in the art of sneaking. Besides I think Sarah will understand now that we are married, as opposed to the last time when she had to protect me and my honor, which by the way was in virtual tatters after being dragged to almost every hotel in Los Angeles by the dastardly actions of a certain lecherous professor." As this last was said she gave John a playful poke in the ribs.

John laughed, "I remember the looks she gave me. She looked like she could give a trained attack dog lessons. I was not quite sure which one of you to be more scared of. However, I did tell you that was my dastardly, evil, lecherous plan, to ruin your reputation so that you would have no choice but to marry me." With this last John leaned forward and kissed his wife soundly.

Their laughter and warmth was broken by a voice calling out to them which caused them to break off their kiss quite suddenly. "Major, Julia, we were wondering when you two would arrive." The voice was that of Corporal Samuel Tinsman, who with his men had been such an integral part of their team last time, the mission where she met John, and had served on several missions before that with Julia. Tinsman was a former Berdan Sharpshooter and still a crack marksman, although now he sported a rather bright red plaid jacket and his favorite brown derby hat instead of his dark green uniform and kepi. He turned, and putting his fingers to his mouth, gave a piercing whistle and several more men appeared.

John dropped down from the carriage and turning helped Julia down. Julia hugged Tinsman and then Sam Kincaid who had also been part of their team. "It is so good to see both of you again," Julia spoke to the men, obviously happy to see them. John also joined in with warm and sincere handshakes.

Two young men stood slightly behind the quartet looking somewhat nervous. Tinsman, seeing them out of the corner of his eye, waved them to come over. "Professor John Morton, Major, or sir to you two, and Mrs. Julia Morton." He continued more to himself than anyone else, "Still did not see that one coming even if I *was* at the wedding." Julia laughed and put her arm in her husband's arm. "If I may present our newest members. This is Jason Quinn." A young man who had sandy hair and seemed wiry as opposed to bulk strength put his hand out and gave John a warm handshake and likewise Julia. Next Tinsman turned to a young man who was a bit on the shorter side with the dark looks of a more southern Gallic Mediterranean heritage. Although short he was almost as wide and looked a bit like granite. "This is Adam Rossi." Again handshakes were given. Tinsman continued, "The colonel seemed to think that they would do, sir. Both fresh out of training, Major." Tinsman looked like he had reservations about them like any noncom would of a pair of green recruits.

Morton gave a warm smile, and looking at the pair but speaking to Tinsman said, "Well, Corporal, what do you think?"

Tinsman looked noncommittal and replied, "Well, sir, they have been trained as well as could be at a school but we will see what happens when they see some real action, sir."

Morton said, "Welcome to the team, Gentlemen. We do not have a lot of time for you to become familiar with us but all I ask is that you try your best. Keep on them, Corporal, and when you have a chance, check them out on our various weapons along with some of Julia's little trinkets."

Tinsman all but saluted. "Yes sir! All right you two, help the lady with her luggage and do it smartly, but be gentle, there is no telling what the lady has packed." The two young agents looked at each other and then at Tinsman and finally at Julia who stood there looking innocent as could be, a veritable masterpiece of a picture of innocence as it were. As would any good NCO, Tinsman barked, "What are you two waiting

for, written orders? Or do you plan to move it just by looking at it!"
Posthaste the two young men scrambled to the small wagon and began
undoing straps and moving bags.

John and Julia watched trying to hide some serious snickering as
their luggage disappeared onto the train. John turned to Tinsman and
Sam. "Have Father Peter and our new member, Mr. Hook, showed yet?"

Tinsman started to speak when Sam Kincaid looking up the street,
smiled, and replied, "I think your answer is just arriving, sir."

Morton looked behind him to see a small buckboard pulling up with
Father Peter, reins in hand. Beside him sat Clement Hook looking a bit
more casual then he had on Monday night. Hook was dressed in more
workman-like garb so that he did not stand out as much. Peter pulled up
and tied off the reins. "Good morning Major, Julia", as the good father
reverted back into first sergeant mode. "Corporal and Sam, it is good to
see you two as well." With that he climbed down as did Hook. Again
there were handshakes and backslapping all around between Peter and
the two sharpshooters. As they finished up, Jason and Adam returned
from unloading the wagon and then loading John and Julia's luggage
and supplies on board the train. John introduced Peter and Clement to
one and all. This introductory camaraderie was broken by the sound and
sight of a high-stepping American-type locomotive, belching smoke
from the stack and steam from her cylinders, backing down the track
with a ringing of its bell. The brakeman made sure of the couplers and
connected the air hose. Finally the signal lines were hooked up. While
the train crew was busy with these vital bits of transportation work John
said, "I see we are wasting no time, Corporal."

Tinsman shrugged as he nodded and replied, "I was told in no
uncertain terms to make best speed, sir."

John nodded and said, "We had better get aboard or we will be left
standing at the station." With that, each of the groups began to climb
up the steps and onto the platform of their respective cars.

Before long the whistle screeched as the engineer threw over the
Johnson bar and the bell started to clang again as steam was fed into
the cylinders and the four tall wheels began to revolve, slipping a bit

then catching as the engineer applied some sand to the rails. The train slowly pulled out of the station under the proceed signals and onto the high iron. Next stop was Buffalo and a meeting with an old friend and Julia's "little sister".

Even with the priorities given their train, it was still at least a day and half into Buffalo. While people were willing to work overtime, the locomotive still demanded rest stops on the way for taking on coal and water. And as with people, what goes in must come out. There were ashes to be raked out and axels to be greased, while they waited for a chance to get over the Hudson River near Albany. Even they had to wait for the railroad's crack passenger trains no matter what their train's class was.

Thus evening found them waiting impatiently on a siding, or as the railroaders put it, "in the hole", while dinner was served. The four principals ate in their car while the corporal and his part of the team took their dinner forward in their bunk and storage car. Actually Sam did. Meanwhile, Tinsman put the two recruits through practice after practice at field stripping and clearing imaginary jams and reassembling the weapons, and finishing by making sure they were loaded; all this being done while blindfolded. Secretly he thought they did quite well, although from his comments to them one would think they were the greenest, most ham-handed recruits that any long-suffering NCO ever had to deal with since a new Greek Hoplite dropped his spear outside the walls at the siege of Troy. However, he did try to encourage them by telling them that with six more months of brutal training they might come up to the major's expectations…possibly.

While this was going on, Father Peter said grace and the four friends started their dinner, Chicken Kiev with a fine white wine. Father Peter decided that indeed Anderson had found a completely acceptable replacement for Chef. As he sat savoring the meal he thought maybe purgatory was not such a bad place after all.

After the dishes were cleared, the gentlemen lit their various pipes and cigars. Julia of course abstained as befit a proper young woman. *Truly a vile habit*, she thought. At least she had gotten John to cut down on his consumption of that noxious weed. Without any visible outward expression, she laughed a bit at herself; she was truly becoming a wife, trying to change and civilize her husband. So much for the tough secret agent persona!

After various forms of tobacco were brought up to proper operating temperature, the gentlemen poured brandies while Julia partook of a fine, much more ladylike, sherry.

CHAPTER 6

CLÉMENT'S TALE

s the various tobaccos and libations were enjoyed, the four began their respective tales. Morton and Peter told how they had met during the Civil War, the campaigns, battles and life in the camps. Further, how they had saved each other's life several times.

Peter went on to tell how he had progressed from tradesman to soldier. How, by the end of the war, he had enough of death and destruction, not to mention the seemingly endless streams of injured and broken soldiers and civilians, especially the women and children, harmed or killed. He talked about the sight of families ripped apart. He told them of his decision to enter the seminary to try and rebuild a world torn apart so brutally and radically.

John told how he had been a small college professor before the war but had gone in the army to help preserve the Union after England had sided with the Confederacy. That had occurred after several seamen and an officer had been killed along with several seamen injured aboard the RMS Trent. This occurred when that ship had been holed by a shot from the USS San Jacinto to get her to heave to so that the navy could take off a pair of confederate envoys named Mason and Slidell. He went on to talk about the battle where Peter and he had met Isaiah, and seen his aptly named blunderbuss in action and how his genius had saved the day and their lives. He told how he had started his studies and how that led to his position at the museum. Finally, he mentioned how a summons from his old army companion had drawn him into a new and far different world where he met a certain Miss Julia Verolli and William Anderson.

Next, Julia talked about her life. She related how as a small orphan she had been caught stealing some fruit from a street stand for food. She related how she had been found by William Anderson and instead of being sent to an orphanage or work house she had been sent to a most unusual school for young ladies, young women no one would miss, all of the girls being in straits similar to Julia's. She described in vague terms the curriculum of the school. However, there was enough detail that Hook could get the idea by using a bit of imagination. Peter and John did not have to guess, already knowing far more about the special finishing school for young ladies run by the shadowy part of the government.

She left out most of her work before the Ratten business since it was on a need-to-know basis, much of which she had not even related to John. That was her old life before John and Sarah. While she was not ashamed of it neither was she proud of it; but it most certainly did not fit into the world she now inhabited. She went on to describe some of the aspects of the affair that brought John into her life. She talked about Sarah and what she meant to her. She finished her tale with a fanciful telling of how a certain unnamed professor had forced her against her will to marry him by dragging her to virtually every hotel in Los Angeles thus ruining her reputation in polite society. John and Peter laughed quietly at this part knowing Julia as they did.

The three having finished their stories looked at Clement and waited. Before he started his story, glasses were refilled, and while John did not start another cigar, much to Julia's approval, both Peter and Clement refilled and stoked up their pipes. Clement began his tale by describing Wales. He talked about the deep valleys and lush green scenery, about the country's people and how the English came to dominate them. He went on to tell how many of the valleys were now filled with spoilage from the various coal mines that covered the landscape as Britain fed its seemingly insatiable appetite for the black diamonds to drive the great empire's industrial expansion. The valleys green no more but brown and dirty. How the mine owners, all English, cared not a whit when a village was wiped out when a mountain of muck let go and came down the valley from side to side, obliterating everything in its path, villages, men, women and children gone. He recounted that he had overheard one of the owners joking that at least they were spared the expense of burying the dead.

He went on to tell how he had lost his older brother to the Royal Navy when he was forced into it by a press gang. His brother never came home, just a letter expressing Her Majesty's condolences at his loss at sea. Finally he talked about one owner who had seemed at least to have some decency toward him. Squire Marsh had lost his own son and seemed to see something in Clement and took a shine to him. He realized his intelligence and sharp eye, hence Clements's training in engineering and mining.

However, when one of mud slides buried his village, it was Squire Marsh who made the obscene joke. It was several nights later when Clement had slit the man's throat and slipped away to join a Welsh resistance group. Several years of raids and running followed. But the tide was against them as more and more Welsh countryside became anglicized. The police were closing in. It was then that the suddenly inspired decision to immigrate to the Americas was made.

After a few more puffs of his pipe to get it going again, he finished his tale by telling how he had made contact with some ex-Welshmen and others who had grievances against Her Majesty's government; they in turn led him to an assortment of various criminal elements. It was through these contacts that he had been recruited to help a gang tunnel under the streets of New York to break into a bank with ties to England. He said he thought it would kill two birds with one stone so to speak; remove money from the pockets of the English and then get it back to Wales to help them use England's own funds to finance the rebellion against the Crown. He finished the story by telling how the police department, or peelers as he referred to them, and the judiciary had taken a very dim view of the aforesaid withdrawal. With a final puff he ended his story. "So that is how I came to be a long-term guest of the State of New York, at least until I wound up here."

John and the others looked thoughtfully at him, digesting the tale. John broke the silence by asking him, "Assuming we contain this, whatever it is, and the small detail of our managing to survive the encounter, what then, Clement, more bank robbing? More Welsh-liberation activities?"

Clement shook his head almost sadly and replied, "No, John, the police apprehended us due to a fellow Welshman who ratted us out. He was in the pay of the Crown, the vile traitor. At the trial he laughed at us thinking we were fools. No, I have had enough of England and Wales. The country is too deep into the fabric of England now and I doubt it will ever see its own flag over Cardiff. I am too good an engineer to work on lost causes. Such activity it would seem only wastes energy." He paused to take a sip from his glass before finishing. "Your Mister Anderson's offer of a new life sounds good to me. Running and hiding is no life for a man. Like you, I think that perhaps I will be finding my own good woman and be settling down; that sounds quite nice. I am getting too old to keep on running and jumping at shadows; that is a life for younger chaps. From what I have heard about America there is plenty of work for a man who knows a thing or two about tunneling and mines."

John smiled and told him, "You are indeed right, Clement, if not in mining, although God knows there is enough of that. The railroads are expanding as fast as can be and it seems every other day a new tunnel is started. A man with your knowledge and talents will be much in demand. You should have no problem making a living. As for the women, well I shall not complain, sir. If nothing else I feel I am the luckiest man in the world." He reached over and took Julia's hand and smiled. Julia returned the smile.

Clement looked at him. "What about Her Majesty's government, they still have a bounty on my head. That most certainly does not make for a quiet life."

It was Julia who answered him. "I should not worry, Mr. Jordan, when Uncle William gives his word it will be as if Clement Hook never was. You are not the first who has been resurrected from the grave, as it were, by him. Besides there are enough problems on this mission that we do not have to add in any British threats, assuming they are not at the bottom of this to begin with. Heaven knows the area in question is near enough to the Canadian border."

Clement looked at her in surprise, "Jordan?"

"Indeed, sir, Mister Carl James Jordan of Pennsylvania, Jordan now being anglicized from Jerdanczyk of Polish heritage as was much of the rest of that part of the country. A man who grew up in Carbon County, Pennsylvania, surrounded by good Pennsylvania anthracite coal mines. That is where you learned your trade, sir." Julia got up and went over to the small cabinet where the built-in bar was and opening a drawer pulled out a stack of documents. Returning to her seat she passed them over to Clement, or Carl as it was now. "Your new life, sir. I would suggest that you memorize it and internalize it. Your life depends on it, Carl."

Clement looked at her and the documents. "This will not be easy to pull off; I know nothing about these people and I most certainly do not know any Polish."

Julia looked at him and replied, "Your grandfather, who was a bit of a tyrant, forbad any Polish being spoken in the family after he came to America. You were to be Americans so you got an American name, although you know some odd words. If Sarah joins us she can start teaching you some Polish. As for other things, a flood wiped out the town where you grew up leaving you as one of the few survivors; luckily you were away visiting a dentist for some painful problems with your teeth. There were no dentists in your home town. The family is real but they all died in that flood so you should not run into anyone who might have been related to them. As with many towns in that area, most of the people stayed in the same town so that most of the folks who knew the family died also. Carl was real but he too died in the flood, but with no body found there was never any death certificate able to be issued." Julia smiled although it did not hold any warmth, "William is very thorough."

Now Clement looked truly shocked. "Your sister knows Polish? How is that? I thought you said she was black." It was obvious Hook was floundering for some sort of understanding of this whole new life he was being given and had seized upon that simple fact in order to give his mind time to process this completely new and alien life.

Morton and Peter smiled quite broadly at this, knowing all too well how Anderson worked and the array of changes he had brought about in their lives. Peter knew perhaps even better then John, having, in the span of a single day, gone from parish priest to having been involved with the Treasury Department, and then being promoted to Lieutenant Colonel of Regulars who worked undercover in counter-intelligence, from a retired first sergeant who had served in the state militia. All this in the seeming blink of an eye during the Ratten business.

Peter picked up the narrative. "Clement, or should I say Carl, it will take some getting used to. However, as to Sarah' abilities, she is like one of the new clockwork recording devices written about in one of John's scientific journals. She has an amazing flair for languages and picks them up as fast as can be. She out-stripped my knowledge of Latin in just the several months we were together, along with picking up some Chinese. You, sir, shall be, I think, most amazed at her abilities. Although I did not know about the Polish myself."

Julia laughed a bit and explained, "Her last letter, Peter. She said she was learning German for her Ratten dictionary project, but if I know her she is already picking up Polish. It seems that the Polish community in Buffalo is growing. She said she met some when they came into her father's shop for some equipment to start a brewery. You know my sister, she collects languages like others collect foreign stamps or coins, or more accurately, like other girls collect dolls. She really loves it."

Peter shook his head at this. "She is truly amazing. When I think of the hours I had to study Latin for seminary I am jealous, so much so that I should be doing penance tonight."

John laughed a bit at this last comment from his friend but then looked at Carl. "What do you think, sir, can you become someone else? I know from experience it is hard."

Hook, or Jordan, looked at the three and with a thoughtful expression said, "As your Mister Anderson said, this could be my lucky day. I can only wonder what it will be like to not have to keep looking over my shoulder and to be able to relax around strangers. To think about seeing an attractive young lady and be able to get to know her, instead of being afraid that someone will torture her just to get information about my whereabouts." Jordan paused a moment and then looked at Julia. "What about Clement Hook, what is to happen to him?"

Julia replied, "It must have slipped my mind. Did I not tell you Clement Hook was buried yesterday in the state prison graveyard at Elmira? It seems he was killed in a fight with a fellow prisoner although no one knows which one. Very sad. There was absolutely no one there to mourn him, just the warden, prison chaplain and a couple of guards to lower the pine box and fill in the grave. The event made barely a notice in the newspapers. Of course the State Department will notify the British authorities since he was, after all, one of their subjects. Not a big rush you understand, a couple of weeks, very routine matter."

"A couple of weeks, why not right away?" Jordan was now somewhat agitated.

Julia smiled that female tiger smile, "Because he was no one of any importance and certainly no one to get excited about. These things take time; first the state prison system has to notify the U.S. Bureau of Prisons. Being a foreign national he was to be transferred there eventually anyway. Then they have to notify the U.S. Marshal's Office and they in turn will notify the State Department who then will notify the British Consulate. None of these will be in any rush; very routine thing this, because if it was someone who was trying to be given a new life and was in a very big hurry to end an old one, the British might want to double check. Are we clear, sir?"

The newly resurrected Carl Jordan sat back and looked at Julia, then spoke to John, "Sir, I, like any normal male with any eyesight at all, can see what caught your eye about your wife, but watching her in action it becomes obvious as to what held your interest in the lady. There is far more to her then meets the eye." Jordan smiled and shook his head, raising his glass to John, "My compliments, sir, on your good taste, again."

John looked at his wife and raised his glass to her. He smiled, "Indeed, sir, she is one of a kind and I consider myself a very lucky man." Having said that Morton drained his glass, while a smiling Father Peter joined the toast along with the other two men. Julia sat there and looked delightfully innocent.

In the railroad's interlocking tower, the switchman used both hands to pull and push some levers, aligning turnouts and setting some signals to proceed. It was a short while later that the passengers could hear the whistle and the wheels squeal as they felt the thud pass through the train and it began to move as the signals changed and the crew acted upon the proceed signal. Next stop...Buffalo.

CHAPTER 7

THE TEAM REUNITES

en o'clock the next morning saw the train pull into the Buffalo Central's passenger terminal on Upper Terrace Street and be settled on a coach storage track. A steam line from the central boiler house was hooked up to keep everything warm and cozy since there was still some ice in Lake Erie and the temperature near the lake could be much cooler then even several blocks inland. The team began to retrieve their various hats, bonnet and coats as they heard the engine uncouple from the rest of the train, pull out and head to the railroad's 4th Street round house to be serviced before starting on the next leg of the journey.

The four principals climbed down while the corporal had Sam send Jason and Adam to secure a carriage for them. Meanwhile, Tinsman was busy arranging for an additional baggage car to be leased from the railroad, anticipating Isaiah's joining the party and needing room for his workshop-on-wheels, as he had referred to it the last time, not even mentioning the steam wagon. Soon Adam and Jason returned from their assignment and climbed down out of the carriage they had obtained. Peter and Carl, as he was now known, climbed in while John helped Julia up and into the carriage. Before he climbed in himself he told the two new agents that until Tinsman returned Sam was in charge and they should keep a sharp eye out. Not stand guard or at least not look like they were standing guard, since museum expeditions did not generally post guards on their trains. The two rookie agents swallowed and said they would do their best.

As the four prepared to pull away, John paused and heard Sam explaining to Jason to go into the station and buy a paper and sit outside on the platform looking relaxed and read it while keeping an eye on that side of the train. And yes, there would be a quiz on what he read so he better be able to do both. Adam meanwhile was to go over to the saloon on the other side of the siding's tracks and get a beer and sip it very slowly while sort of staring out into space in the general direction of the train. John watched smiling as poor Sam passed out of sight shaking his head while climbing back on board the train. The other three passengers were curious as to what was so amusing to John. He waved off their questions with a smile.

They made good time to Isaiah and Sarah's new home and shop since on this trip they already had the address, instead of searching all over town for it as they had to on their last trip. The new store was not far from the old location although a bit more upscale since it was on Niagara Street itself instead of off on a side street. It seemed as if the payment Anderson had made to Isaiah for his time and efforts in the Ratten business had been well invested since the shop looked quite well kept. It also looked as if business was good since there were several wagons parked alongside the building seeming to indicate a brisk patronage. The sign over the front simply read

I. Liman & Daughter
Clockworks & Mechanicals

As they alighted, several customers came out with much chatter about the high quality of the work. John thought, happily for his friend, that it was an excellent and most welcome change from the first time they had entered Isaiah's old store. As he opened the door the little bell rang, not exactly the most modern in steam technology thought John, but it worked. Quick as a wink, in answer to the bell, a nicely dressed Sarah came out to meet and see what the new customers were interested in.

As Sarah came around the corner of the counter she saw Julia, broke into a huge smile and called out to her. Both of the girls ran and embraced, laughing and hugging each other. The gentlemen stood quietly while the girls held a joyous reunion. A moment later Isaiah came out of the back to see what all the female fussy noise was about.

When Isaiah saw who it was he called out to a young, light-coffee-colored lad of about fifteen, "Jonah, I have some special customers. I need you to watch the store for a while." Although he made it sound like a question it was obvious to all concerned that it was not. The young man perked up and taking off the apron he had been wearing and putting the broom he had been using behind the door, he replied, "Yes, sir, Mr. Liman. Will Sarah be here too?"

Isaiah shook his head. "No son, this is your chance to solo." Then he pointed to Julia and said, "This is Sarah's older sister Julia, so she wants to spend some time with her."

Jonah, as that was rather obviously the lad's name, looked very confused seeing a white woman named Julia but gamely responded, "Yes, sir," with a look on his face that obviously said he did not have the slightest idea what his boss was talking about and hoping that he was not becoming addled.

Isaiah exhaled and said, "I will explain later, meanwhile try not to put me out of business, all right?" Isaiah told the group to wait while he went in the back and grabbed his jacket and a cape for Sarah.

As he came out Sarah looked at him and with a nod to Julia said, "Poppa, if it is all right with Julia, perhaps we could have some tea here, just the two of us."

Julia smiled and added, "That would be lovely. John, I think you gentlemen can manage by yourselves. We need a little quality time for some sister talk."

The gentlemen in question seemed to find the arrangement acceptable, so handing Sarah back her cape, Isaiah kissed his daughter and told her in a hushed tone, "I think Jonah can handle things by himself for a while, at least I hope so, but keep an eye out just in case. We will see you after lunch." With that taken care of, Isaiah led the way out of the store and down the street to a small restaurant a few doors down on Niagara Street.

Julia smiled at the young man who was busy trying to look very serious and not at all curious about Sarah's white older sister. Julia followed Sarah behind the counter, through the workshop and into the kitchen of the house which formed the back of the building. The first thing Julia wanted to know as soon as the door closed behind them was, "Why are you and Jonah not in school today, young lady?"

This question was put to Sarah as she hurried about putting a kettle on the stove for tea and adding a few lumps of coal to the firebox. As she finished she looked at Julia and replied, "There is a measles epidemic going around and they closed the schools until it passes. I do not mind; I do not like it anyhow, in fact I hate it!"

Julia looked totally shocked at this. "Sarah Marie Liman, I cannot believe what I just heard come from your mouth young lady! You love to learn. What is this about, Missy?" She looked very sternly at the young girl who in all the ways of the heart was her sister and wondered what was going on.

Sarah looked at the floor, not even looking at Julia, and started to cry a little. Julia went over and took her into her arms, seeking to console her, Although she thought it must have looked somewhat odd since even with her shoes that had a bit of a lady's heel, Sarah was still at least an inch taller than her. Sarah, as she felt Julia take her into her arms, began to sob and put her head on Julia's shoulder taking comfort that she could only get from a mother, or in this case, an older sister. "Sarah, what is it, what is so wrong? Please tell me." Julia said this in the same gentle voice she had used to tend to Sarah as she had when John first brought her to the train years ago. Julia stepped back a little and reaching out tilted Sarah's head up slightly, and grabbing a cloth from the sideboard wiped Sarah's tears away.

Sarah, her face still downcast, sniffed back her tears and said, "The other kids tease me. They say they are not even sure I am a girl, I am so skinny, and I know too much for a girl. The one boy said I have to stand twice in the same place to cast a shadow. One of the girls said I was so flat they could use me for an ironing board." Sarah looked as woeful as could be.

Julia looked at her again with all the love a sister could have. "Oh, is your father not feeding you? I mean if the other girls are so filled out all ready...." She said this in a bit of a teasing tone of voice trying to cheer Sarah up.

"Julia, you know better than that. Poppa is a good provider, besides I do most of the cooking. Poppa is not the greatest in the kitchen, in fact, and do not tell him I said this, he is even worse in the kitchen then he is at keeping records, except for making tea," she replied, trying to smile at least somewhat through the sniffling and tears. After another sniffle she went on, "All the other girls are way older than me and have already started to fill out."

Julia looked shocked, this time in a theatrical kind of way, then she smiled and replied, "I think it is time we had a little talk, young lady, because pretty soon you are going to change from a little girl into a young woman, and as much as I like your father and respect him, he is, after all, a male." Julia rolled her eyes in that same exaggerated theatrical fashion at this which seemed to have the desired effect as Sarah reacted with something between a giggle and a laugh, which, because of the sniffling turned into an embarrassing snort. Julia hugged her sister even more trying to give her the warmth she needed. Then she smiled and they both said "Men," together and laughed some more. Julia went on trying to get to the root of the problem. "Why are the other girls all older then you?"

Sarah still looking woeful replied, "I guess you all taught me too much. They skipped me over two grades and then another one because I already knew the material; in fact I corrected the teacher on some things. Poppa got called into school about that."

Julia asked quietly, "First of all, it should be 'all of you', not 'you all.' Remember, proper English and diction are important for a lady. Second, did you get into more trouble?"

"No, Miss Klaus, the teacher, was fair and double checked and found out I was right, that is when they put me ahead another grade after the original first two. I did not ask to be put forward, Julia, I did not! I do not have any friends!" Sarah was obviously very upset.

As they talked Julia finished up by telling Sarah that when she had been on the streets, before she was sent to the finishing school, she was even less shapely then Sarah and had not developed any figure until she was fourteen. "At least you got taller." This brought a smile to Sarah along with a small giggle. Julia looked annoyed and said, "Thank you for the support, Sarah." Then she went on, "The nurse at the school said it was probably because I had been under-nourished living on the streets, just like you. Believe me at that age John would have never noticed me. As for knowing too much, I know you can fool men, let alone boys. I remember Los Angeles young lady." This last was said very smugly and with a hint of a smile as well as pride in her sister. "I know it will be hard for you to believe, Sarah, but in a couple of years this will not mean much to you, it will be just a bad memory. Girls can be catty at times especially if they are jealous of you because you are smarter than they are. As for boys, do not forget they are just younger versions of men, really very delicate creatures, not to mention silly. Remember, I am married to one. Very fragile egos you know. One has to be very gentle with them and let them think they are in charge."

Sarah stared at her for a brief moment and then started to laugh. "I remember Los Angeles too; it is easy to fool men is it not." With that she got up to get more water for another cup of tea.

As she did this Julia looked over her shoulder toward the front of the building and asked, "I assume Jonah is the boy you were talking about in your last letter?"

There was a distinct change in Sarah's complexion as she blushed and nodded. "Indeed. What do you think, I mean is he not the cutest thing?"

Julia shook her head at Sarah. "Handsome, Sarah, boys are handsome, boys are never cute. Remember what I said about delicate egos." She finished this with a look that said do not forget that.

Sarah laughed and said in reply, "I will try to remember that. Anyway, I have more serious problems. I worry about Poppa so, he needs someone. I mean, I do my best to look after him, Julia, but he needs someone more his own age to be with him." Sarah was doing her best at trying to change the subject of her sister's questions to something less embarrassing.

Julia looked at her seriously. "I think your father can find someone on his own."

Sarah sighed, "He could but he is always too busy in the shop making sure we have enough money or trying to take care of me. Julia, he does not take time to look. I am worried. I love him so and want him to be happy!"

Julia looked at her over her refreshed cup of tea. "So, do you have anyone in mind?" raising an eyebrow. She waited for an answer from Sarah as she was adding a bit of sugar and a slice of lemon to her tea, overjoyed that Sarah had been able to provide some lemon slices.

Sarah looked serious. "I think Miss Wilson, one of my teachers, would like Poppa. She is very pretty and quite smart. I am pretty sure Poppa would like her. I just cannot figure out how to get them together." Sarah shrugged and looked at Julia with an I-need-some-help-here kind of a look.

Julia smiled her female tiger smile and said, "Let us talk about Miss Wilson some more, before we return to the subject of boys or at least one in particular."

Before Julia could say anything more Sarah shook her head in a way that seemed to indicate a what-am-I-doing-here moment. She looked at the woman who in truth was more of a sister to her then many sisters who shared blood. "Julia I am so happy to see you but I must ask, why are you in Buffalo?"

While this was going on, the gentlemen were seated down the street talking in the back corner of a diner that, while it did not have an extensive menu, what was on that that list was well-prepared and quite tasty. John introduced Carl to Isaiah. Meanwhile Isaiah, Father Peter and John renewed their warm camaraderie. Carl looked on wondering about this trio, especially Isaiah. To be honest, he was not sure what to make of him since he had really never known any black men, being a very scarce item in Wales and not really having met any, or at least not getting to know any very well as of yet in his short stay in the Americas.

John somehow sensed Carl's hesitation. He looked at the man. "Not to worry my friend, Isaiah is a steady man when he sees the elephant, and his work bench is like Felix Mendelssohn's composing desk, a place where true art works are created. You are in fine company."

Peter looked at Carl and said, "Indeed, sir, a good man and a steady one, a man I dare say I am proud to call a friend."

Isaiah looked at his two friends and former teammates with wariness visible on his face and inquired, "Let me guess, you two are not just in the neighborhood for a friendly chat or Julia just wanting to see Sarah. Dare I ask what this is about? Do I need to order something a bit stronger then sarsaparilla?"

John looked up to make sure no one could overhear them before he replied, "Although Julia was thinking of inviting Sarah down to stay with us for a while so they could talk about various lady sorts of subjects, there is indeed a reason for the visit. I hate to say this, Isaiah, but perhaps something a bit stronger would be in order."

Isaiah looked at his friends and the newcomer. "I guess I knew the answer to my question from the moment you walked in the door. What is this about, John?"

John looked his friend and comrade square in the eye as he replied, "Isaiah, Anderson has a problem and has arranged financing through the museum so that he could send us on another expedition, and this time we have no idea what we are up against." John and Peter told Isaiah what little they knew, and how worried Anderson and the army were about the Indian situation.

As Isaiah took all this in they could tell he was wary and hesitating. "John, this time it is different. I have a family now and I cannot expose my little girl to that kind of danger. My shop is doing well and we are building a life. It is not that I do not want to help but I really do not think I can."

Peter looked at his friend and nodded. "We understand, Isaiah, but again, we do not know how much danger there is to the country. All we know is that whatever this is it is very powerful and the nation does not need another Indian uprising on its hands. The army is stretched thin as it is trying to watch the Canadian border along with the possibility that the French problem in Mexico may spill across the southern border. With no control of the border it is resulting in some truly horrible raids by the Apaches. There is no telling where that will lead. There are many in the south who still do not accept General Lee's surrender at Chattanooga in 1869 and would be happy to renew the war." Peter took a sip from his own glass and went on, "Besides, where else can we find a man of your abilities? We have no idea whether this monster is made of flesh and bone or of steam and metal. If metal and steam, we will need you to help sort it out. If flesh and bone then we will probably need your talents to control or kill it."

Isaiah looked at his friends, deep in thought. With a nod toward Carl, as he had only been introduced to him but beyond his name had received no other information about him, he said, "How do you fit in, sir? What is your stake in all this?" He obviously was weighing whether or not to join in and wanted to know as much as possible before making a decision.

Carl returned his stare and cleared his throat, "That is a fair question, Mr. Liman." He looked at Morton who gave a look and a shake of his head as if to say you can tell this man anything, he is to be trusted. "Let us just say that Jordan is not the name I was born with. Your Mr. Anderson made me a very persuasive offer to allow me to have a new life. My old one, may I say, was having some problems of a red-coated sort. Anyway, I agreed to help in exchange for a chance to start over. I am getting too old to keep looking over my shoulder all the time; as I told Anderson, that is a game for younger men. As for why he made me the offer, there are those who say I am some kind of or at least a bit of an expert on mining and tunneling. He seemed to feel that, since whatever we are after moves through the earth like a fish through water, I might have some value in resolving the problem. I hope that answers your question." He then took a sip of his drink and continued, "As far as it goes, I hope you make your mind up soon since, new name or not, Buffalo is a bit too close to Canada for my taste, it being Crown territory."

Isaiah mulled all this information over while the men finished their lunch. Isaiah looked at John and Peter. "I wish I could help, but I have Sarah to consider. It is not like I can pick up and leave on a moment's notice. I am a family man now John. I am sorry."

John and Peter both said they understood and the quartet left, walking the short distance back to the store.

As they entered, the girls had already come out of the back. Sarah was talking to a customer about a new clockwork butter churn he wanted while she was suggesting that he might be better off with a steam-powered version since he had the steam available. While Sarah was busy at the counter, Julia was talking to Jonah, obviously checking out the lad who had caught her younger sister's eye. Julia's idea of a polite chat was pretty much the equivalent of an interrogation. It was obvious that Jonah was more than slightly intimidated by Julia but then most males and quite a few females were too, so that basic reaction did not prove anything one way or the other.

Sarah finished up with the customer who then left. She made some notes in a ledger book. As Sarah was writing, Julia told Jonah to go get some lunch. She and Sarah would keep an eye on the store.

As the door closed behind the young man, the store was empty except for those who understood the reason behind the reunion. Sarah smiled at her father. "Poppa, when do we leave?"

Isaiah almost exploded! "What do you mean 'leave' young lady? School will not be out forever, not to mention that I have a business to run, and finally, it is too dangerous for you to be anywhere near this, whatever this is!"

Sarah looked at her father somewhat sternly. "Poppa, Julia said she would talk to Miss Wilson to find out what I should be learning in the last months of classes. You know very well that I will not miss anything between her, Father Peter and the professor, and you too. Jonah can watch the shop and Mr. Anderson will send someone to help, obviously not as good as you but we should not be gone that long and he should be able to handle the simple orders. And finally, I am not letting you run off by yourself; who would take care of you?"

Isaiah looked at Julia with a face like a thunder cloud. "You put these ideas in her head did you not? She is just a little girl! I thought you said you cared about her!"

Julia started to protest when Sarah cut her off. "Poppa, Julia did not put any ideas in my head. You taught me that this country, our country, that freed people like us, was worth fighting for. I know it is not perfect but it is better than anywhere else. That is what you told me. Now it needs our help."

Isaiah looked like he was about to erupt. "Not *our* help, *my* help, and I already helped, remember? I am not leaving you behind in Buffalo by yourself!"

Sarah set her face and put her hands on her hips. "Poppa, are you just going to stand there and do nothing while someone or something is out trying to start a war? I heard you telling Jonah some of your stories about the war. Do you want other young men to go to war? Jonah has been talking about going into the army. I do not want him getting killed because we did nothing!"

Isaiah looked at his daughter. "Where did he get a damn fool idea like that?" He looked like he was ready to blow up with an even larger blast.

Sarah firmly looked at him. "From you! You and your stories of the fight to end slavery for the whole country, to free black people. He was stunned at how you got to see President Lincoln in the parade at the end of the war. He looks up to you, he wants to be like you."

"Well, what of it; I did not ask him to look up to me! What is it to you anyhow?"

Julia looked at Isaiah. "Your daughter thinks he is cute."

"What! She is just a little girl!" Isaiah was yelling even louder now.

Julia shook her head. "Isaiah, she is twelve and she will not be a little girl much longer."

Father Peter sighed and made the Sign of the Cross. "Remember my friend when we got back from St. Paul, I told you that you should enjoy your family now because all too soon some young fellow will want to steal her away?"

Isaiah looked like a man who knew he was losing the fight. "All right, I will talk to the Watkins family and see if you can stay with them," looking at his daughter.

Sarah looked as determined as a mule, a Missouri mule at that. "You are not going all over the west by yourself, Poppa; I am going too. I cannot take a chance on losing you." This last in a tone of voice that sounded like an iron door slamming shut.

Isaiah looked beaten. Looking at John he said, "Definitely spending too much time with your wife, sir!" John shrugged as if to say "tell me about it". "All right, but you are staying out of harm's way; ARE WE CLEAR YOUNG LADY!" By this time the windows were starting to rattle in their frames.

"Yes, Poppa," replied Sarah who now was trying her best to look like the perfect picture of the archetypical dutiful daughter. She continued, "I will start packing and working up a list for whomever Mr. Anderson sends to cover for you as to what has to be done. I just hope he keeps decent records." Sarah looked very innocent as she said all this. Julia was very impressed by her little sister, very impressed indeed.

John patted his friend on the back. "Give me a list of what you need for your shop-on-wheels and we can pick it up in Chicago so you do not have to tear up your shop here. You will both be back before you know it. As for spending too much time with my wife, try to look on the bright side, at least you do not have a bunch of windows to replace." John was trying to cheer his friend up without much success while Julia looked totally innocent and uncomprehending about what John was referring to. She wanted Sarah to be proud of her too.

There was still much to be done starting with telling Jonah, who had returned to the shop after his lunch, that his boss was helping out some friends with their expedition to the untamed west, hunting for new animals or fossil things from long-dead animals, or some such thing, for a short while. Jonah seemed quite amazed and very impressed that his boss was helping out on a fancy scientific research expedition, to the untamed wild west no less. Poor Isaiah hung his head at the hero worship. Although unsaid, it was obvious from the look on Jonah's face he was somewhat worried that not even Sarah would stay behind and he would have a new, albeit temporary, boss.

As far as Isaiah was concerned events seemed to be going in an all-downhill direction and picking up far too much speed with no brakes on the steep downgrade.

CHAPTER 8

ON THE TRAIN TO CHICAGO

everal days later the team was assembled on the platform preparing to board the train. Sarah looked the most excited since at twelve she still had a taste for high adventure, with Julia coming in just a tad behind her at a close second. As noted, Julia did miss the life to some extent; to be honest, it was a considerable extent. Not that she did not love married life with John, that part was quite wonderful, but the museum's basement and filing was not exactly the stuff of high adventure.

Soon the party was boarding. The car for Isaiah's mobile shop was mostly empty, with the exception of the steam wagon which had been loaded on the day before after the car had been modified with a drop-down ramp by the first baggage door. As they settled in they could hear the sound of the air brakes being pumped up and then feel the engine take up the slack in the couplers. Then they could sense the slowly building acceleration and shifts in direction as the wheels began to creak and screech. The train's crew threaded their way across multiple switches set by the strong arms of the man in the signal tower with its bank of huge levers, and began making their way through the yard's throat to the locomotive's nature home on the high iron.

It took several days for them to reach Chicago even with their train's priority. It was the simple fact that there are limits given the amount of traffic between major rail hubs such as Buffalo and Chicago, and the fact that only one train could use that particular track at a time. The time was well spent, however. Over meals and training the team began to form as the newest members got to know one another.

For a large part of the trip Carl was under the tutelage of Julia and Tinsman. The two of them put him through a crash course in weapons. The basics of how to use pistols, rifles, shotguns and knives of all sorts of shapes and sizes were drilled into him until he could at least get shots off in the general direction of a target if not on it and not cut himself with an edged weapon. For their part, Jason and Adam worked under Julia's trained eye on various aspects of edged weapon combat also, since both were reasonably fair shots from their previous academy training; not up to Tinsman's standard, but in fairness to them, few men were, but they were fair shots anyhow.

Sarah was happy, for as Julia knew, she loved to learn. Language lessons in Father Peter's poor Chinese were resumed after a lapse of several years; one never knew when and where that might come in handy again. Morton worked with her on science and mathematics, quite enjoying the time since she was a far more attentive student then some of the college men he had taught, and, he admitted to himself and Julia, somewhat brighter than many. Sarah thought Mr. Jordan was nice too, since Julia had press ganged him into teaching Sarah the basics about geology and civil engineering. Finally just as Julia had predicted, Sarah did know at least a little bit of Polish and she was teaching this to Jordan.

While all this was going on they were happy to call an end to the days' activities and get some sleep. Jordan told Isaiah that he was very impressed with his daughter; she was quite the student. Isaiah was still unsure about the whole Idea of Sarah being there. Having lost his whole family once and thinking, mistakenly as it turned out, that he had lost Sarah again during the Ratten business, he was terrified of possibly losing her again!

Sarah began, in the evenings when they were alone in the compartment they shared, in a very roundabout way to ask Julia questions about what she and John were doing when she snuck down to John's compartment in the evenings. Julia began to fill Sarah in on the idea of intimacy between a man and a woman. Sarah had some knowledge of it from watching various animals procreate since almost everyone who had any land available kept some sort of livestock, mostly smaller ones such as rabbits or pigs, so that much she understood. Larger ones like cows were somewhat rare in the city and most horses were neutered. Julia was well trained in such activities courtesy of Anderson's finishing school. So the lessons continued into the evening. It was during this time that, as Julia told Sarah's father back in Buffalo, Sarah began her transformation into a young woman. She had her first menstrual period and Julia had to show her what to do and how to handle it. And perhaps most importantly, explain to Sarah's father why she wanted to take a day off from her studies and just stay in their compartment and rest for the day. Isaiah was trying to take it all in and deal with the fact that his daughter was growing up.

John noticed a change in Julia during this time but could not figure out what was happening to his wife. She seemed to be both focused and yet hesitant about things. John had never seen her like this and was trying to figure out what was happening and not show Julia he was worried about her.

Father Peter took all this in with a grain of salt. He enjoyed spending time with Sarah for her language lessons even though he was running out of words to teach her. As he had noted on more than one occasion she was like one of the new clockwork-powered recording devices that were the current rage. Once she heard a word she seemed to own it. The rest of the time he rested and caught up on his theological journals, an activity that he seldom had time for at St. Brigit's. The parish, while not too large, had more than its share of problems like any spot in the Five Points, so Peter wore out plenty of shoe leather in his parish attending to all the various troubles and concerns.

Peter and John were reading in the car when John said something about Julia. Peter asked a few questions in such a manner that John did not even realize he was being questioned. Peter seemed to know almost instinctively what was going on. Years of dealing with the families in his parish had given him a wealth of information to fall back on. He smiled and went on with the lessons and listening to everyone, just like a good shepherd to his flock.

Before too many days had passed, the train was pulling into Chicago. The train took a siding in the coach yard and steam lines where connected so they still had heat, it being somewhat cool in the evenings still. Lake Michigan was by no means warmer than Lake Erie at this point in the season. And it allowed Cook to still use the steam trays in his galley kitchen. Meanwhile the engine crew uncoupled the extra baggage car and moved it to the team track which served as a general loading point for odds and ends near the freight station. The team could see that several wagons heaped high with boxes and canvas-covered items and hidden piles were waiting. The railroad crew spotted the regular door of the baggage car to be close to the aforesaid piles. The male members of the team began to unload the wagons as Isaiah and Sarah sorted out the various items. It took the rest of the day and a good part of the next before Isaiah told John that his rolling workshop was open for business, whatever that business might be.

The train crew was notified that all was loaded and secure. The conductor went in to speak with the dispatcher. Chicago was an exceptionally busy rail hub so it was evening before the train was cleared to pull out. As before, they heard the bell and whistle and felt the thump as the couplers pulled taunt and the crew set their Iron Dragon to rolling forward to meet who knew what.

CHAPTER 9

A Quiet Stroll
In Sioux Falls

Once they were out of Chicago and the immediate vicinity, their train began to pick up speed. The tracks were relatively new and the traffic was somewhat lighter. While they did have to stop and wait at times, these were minimal since Anderson had, as he said, arranged for the highest class that their train could have so that they had rare occasion to wait in the hole. Still, crews had to be changed along with coal and water being replenished, plus the engine had to be serviced, so all this took time. Life fell into a routine of practice and training; additionally for Sarah and Carl, learning.

It was on one of these prolonged stops at Sioux Falls in the Dakotas to have the railroad equipment serviced and to take on supplies that Julia and Sarah decided to do some shopping, as young ladies are wont to do, and to just stretch their legs a bit. Sarah and Julia were walking along and were so busy talking about their respective dreams that they had inadvertently gotten themselves turned around and wound up on the wrong side of the tracks, as it were. As they were getting oriented to get back to a better part of town, a gang of four somewhat drunk toughs approached and began making lewd comments to Julia and disparaging ones to Sarah. Julia told Sarah to ignore them and they started to walk away when one of the young men grabbed Sarah. Julia turned quickly, and reacting to someone attacking her sister, needless to say her adrenalin was up. She chopped the man's wrist so hard that the others heard the bone snap. The young man let go of Sarah and howled in pain as he fell to his knees supporting his arm. One of the remaining men snarled, "I am gonna make you regret that you did that to my brother, bitch." He pulled a large knife known as an Arkansas Toothpick from his boot and started toward Julia. There was no mistaking his intentions, his face a picture of pure hate and drunken arrogance.

Julia pushed Sarah well behind her and met the attacker head on. As the attacker moved in he used an underhanded lunge at her with the knife. Quite untrained and sloppy, thought Julia, as if assessing the moves by one of the rookie agents during their training sessions. Julia pivoted back on her left foot so that the knife was going past her. The attacker went forward in an uncontrolled motion, there being no body to stab because the body that he had anticipated would stop his forward attack was missing, courtesy of Julia's well-timed move. As this happened, Julia reached out with her right hand and grabbed the attacker's knife hand by the wrist, her fingers deftly finding the nerve cluster and squeezed so that the knife went flying, barely missing Sarah. Using the knife wielder's own momentum, she shifted her weight to her right foot so that her movement followed through and her left fist caught the man just at the junction of the base of his skull and top of his spine. As a final part of the counterattack, her left foot shot out, and even with her full-length dress, connected with the back of the man's left knee. Granted this was made easier since being out west Julia had relaxed her dress code somewhat and not worn her bustle and had far fewer petticoats on than a proper professor's wife and female museum staff member would be expected to wear back in the city. Still, it was a most impressive feat of unarmed combat. This completed the movement that had the result of sending the obnoxious drunk reeling and down on his knees at first and then his face in the dirt, or to be more accurate, into a pile of horse leavings.

The other two started to spread out for a classic two-person attack when Julia, who by this time had had quite enough of this foolishness, pulled her derringer and with a well-placed shot put one attacker down with a medium-sized, bloody hole in his leg. The last man of the drunken quartet looked at his friends, all of whom were wounded or badly damaged to some extent, and then at Julia who still had a bullet in the derringer's second barrel and a decidedly annoyed look on her face. His face drained of color and he seemed to sober up in a quite amazingly rapid way. He took off, leaving the others on their own to face this female bobcat. The other three helped each other up and began to leave. The one with the least damage, being dazed and bruised with a numb hand and skinned knees, along with missing his knife, was trying to wipe horse shit off his face and snarled out several threats which Julia ignored as befit a proper young lady of good breeding. However, since her parents were unknown, this was a bit of a presumption, and excellent deportment by way of the finishing school.

Sarah stood there stunned, with the knife lying in front of her, afraid to pick it up. She had seen Julia in action once during the Ratten affair when the streetcar conductor grabbed her, however she had been too surprised, too young, too scared and had not realized what was happening at the time. It was all just confusion in her mind. Later she had briefly seen part of the interrogation when her sister tortured a man, but nothing like this. That man had been tied in a chair and not free to fight back. Her eyes were big as saucers, as the saying goes. After Julia was sure the men were leaving for good, she quickly reloaded her small pistol before turning around to see the knife on the ground. She bent over, picked up the toothpick, and turning around threw it so it stuck in a tree next to the head of the man who had been uttering the threats, with a solid thunk.

Sarah stood staring at her sister. It was at this point that Julia looked around after the knife throw to see if Sarah was all right. Seeing her sister's face, she swallowed hard and realized that for the first time, Sarah had seen a much darker and dangerous side of her in real action, the one she had wished Sarah would not see again, or better yet, would never have seen. She tried to make light of it saying to Sarah, "Bunch of ruffians. Well good riddance to them. Now we must really get back to the better part of town, shall we?" Julia kept smiling as she tried to make light of the knife throw by saying, "One should always return other people's property, Sarah."

Sarah closed her mouth still looking surprised. That was a somewhat gentle word, shocked or stunned would be much closer. Being an eloquent young lady she just settled for saying, "How did you do all that; there were four of them? I mean what, how did you know what to do?" Sarah continued to stare at her in amazement.

Julia took a deep breath, "Sarah, I told you during the business with the Ratten that I was afraid you would be scared of me if you knew how dangerous I am. I hope you can still love me, because I love you and I do not take well to people abusing my little sister." Julia, while trying to put on a brave front, was scared again. She had been through this on the previous expedition but that did not make it any easier for her. Julia was still trying to deal with this type of fear, the fear of losing her family. Though she did not realize it, Julia needed Sarah since she was virtually her only family aside from John, having no idea of who she was or who else might be family or where she came from. She was a mystery to herself. Her bond with Sarah formed an elemental anchor in her unknown world.

Sarah smiled and reaching out hugged her. "Of course I still love you. You are my big sister. Sisters' Oath, remember?" Sarah felt odd because now Julia was crying and Sarah was holding her and comforting her just the way Julia had done for her in Buffalo.

Julia sniffed loudly in a quite unladylike fashion; she was busy trying to pull herself together. She thought that professionally trained, tough special agents were not supposed to sniff loudly or otherwise, even if they were on leave, as Uncle William put it. She hugged Sarah back, and finally getting herself under control, smiled and said, "Come along, the men will be worried about us poor helpless females, especially your father."

"Poppa will not worry after I tell him about this," laughed Sarah.

To put it mildly, Julia panicked. "Sarah, you cannot tell anyone, especially your Father or John. They will be alarmed at the thought of us in danger! Dear God, they will never let us go shopping again without an escort. Do you want that? Can you imagine your father or John following us into a dress shop, or worse yet, looking for lady's unmentionables? NO, no, no, not a word of this to anyone! Are we clear young lady?"

Sarah looked surprised. "Are you sure Julia? Do you really think that they would do that, I mean follow us all the time? Julia, I really, I mean, I do not like to keep things from Poppa."

Taking a deep breath and letting it out, Julia steadied herself and then looked at Sarah. "I do not like to keep things from John either but it is not so much not telling them as not wanting to get them upset. I have told you men are sensitive, delicate creatures and have to be treated gently and allowed to think they are in control. Do you understand?"

Sarah looked at her and began to snicker. "I think I do," she replied. "I know sometimes I have to be somewhat less than direct with Poppa. Do you have to treat the professor like that?" looking at her big sister, who in Sarah's mind knew everything.

Julia smiled back at her and putting her arm around her replied, "Not all the time, just most of it."

After Sarah got over her shock, the two of them laughed together as they walked back to the better part of town with their arms entwined.

Several blocks later, and in a much better part of town, they stopped to look in the window of a shop at some new fabric, well new to this part of the west anyhow. Sarah looked at Julia and said in a hesitating way, "Um, Julia, could I ask you something?" Julia looked at Sarah wondering what she was concerned about. It was hard enough talking about what she and John did at night; what was it now? "Now what, young lady?"

Sarah got somewhat flushed and started out, "Well, I was thinking, I mean, you know what you did back there, to those men, I mean."

"Sarah, what are you talking about?" Now Julia was scared again worrying that Sarah was having second thoughts and would be afraid of her and not want her in her life.

Sarah looked around to see that no one could overhear her. "Do you think you could teach me some of that, I mean, you know, just in case?" Sarah flashed a small grin at Julia, not knowing how she would react.

Julia stood there stunned which was not at all like Julia. "What?" she sputtered, actually almost shouted!

Sarah looked around thankful that no one seemed to notice Julia's outburst. "Well, I mean, I was thinking that, what I mean is, we are heading into the untamed west and it might be good if I knew something about defending myself." This was said as she seemed to look down and around and bite her lip at the same time. It was a rather interesting look to say the least.

Now it was Julia's turn to be shocked and stunned, to say the least. To be somewhat more colloquial, she looked as if someone had hit her between the eyes with a thick piece of cordwood. "I do not know what your father will think of it. I mean it does not seem to be the most ladylike thing to learn, you know."

Sarah smiled and started to grin. "Well, we do not have to tell him or the professor. After all, it is not so much not telling them as not wanting to get them upset. Someone told me men are sensitive, delicate creatures and have to be treated gently and allowed to think they are in control."

Julia laughed, a totally un-secret agent, un-proper wife-of-a-museum-professor-and-staff-member, out loud, laugh where one's eyes start to water, and hugged Sarah. Smiling at her little sister she whispered, "Lessons start tomorrow."

Once Julia regained her composure, the ladies continued back to the station and their temporary home on wheels, although there were a few stops along the way. They assured themselves these purchases were merely so the men did not suspect them of going shopping and not buying anything. It was purely for appearances and not having anything to do with a new bonnet, ribbon for one's hair, gloves and a few other modest purchases.

CHAPTER 10

TOWARD AN UNTAMED
WESTERN POST

The next weeks' travels reverted back to the routine that had been established, with the small exception of Julia and Sarah sneaking up to the modified car that served as a bunk car that held Tinsman and the other agents. The car was what is referred to as a combine. Normally this means that part of the car is a coach which holds seats for passengers and part is a baggage car. However in this case, the passenger part had been remodeled into a series of compartments and a small common area for meals and card playing for the four agents who were along. The two ladies were aided in this endeavor thanks to the long standing relationship Julia had with Tinsman and Sam which predated her relationship with John. It meant that the gentlemen did not look into the baggage part of the car when the ladies were using it.

The baggage end of the car was partially filled as it was storing a rather large amount of weapons and equipment for whatever the mission might require. These various items aside, the two young ladies had more than enough space for Julia to begin to teach Sarah the basics of self-defense.

This was going along well enough until Isaiah and John began to compare notes as to what their respective ladies were up to. This comparison seemed to show a notable amount of time unaccounted for. At dinner the night before the train was to arrive at Fort Freemont, the post closest to the reservation, the gentlemen inquired about the unaccounted-for time right after dessert was over. After finishing some cake and while all were still seated, Isaiah asked Sarah, "Sweetheart, how did you get that bruise on your arm?"

Sarah smiled at her father. "When the engineer took up the slack in the couplers it caught me unaware and I just fell down, Poppa." She was trying her best to look innocent.

John looking at his wife said, "What have you been doing all day, my love?"

By this time the girls were looking a bit trapped, but bravely trying her best Julia replied, "Just reviewing various reports, my love. How did you spend your day?"

John and Isaiah looked at each other with raised eyebrows. John broke the silence. "Julia, Sarah, there seems to be several hours a day that we cannot account for you two and your activities. What, wife, is going on?" Morton had a rather determined look on his face as he continued to stare at Julia.

Sarah, trying to look cheerful and as dutiful as a daughter should be spoke up, "I should go back to our compartment and study." She made as if to get up from the table.

Isaiah without raising his voice said, "Sit down young lady, this discussion is not over." Sara promptly sat back down.

Morton looked at his wife again. "You were saying, beloved spouse of mine, about your days' activities?"

Julia and Sarah looked at each other and both swallowed as if it was a practiced move. "Well, John, Sarah and I were just working on some ideas for when we are in the field, nothing significant you understand. You really do not have to worry about it." Julia started batting her eyes at John and doing her best to look helpless.

Isaiah, looking at his daughter, did not say a word, just kept looking without seeming to blink. Although she loved her father very much, she thought he was looking like a snake ready to strike. By this time Father Peter was curious himself, whether or not he thought he should be, and cocked his head to hear the conversation.

John was making a face that seemed to indicate more than a slight degree of disbelief. He continued to probe, "What kind of ideas that would involve Sarah being bruised and you wearing your older field clothes, dear?"

Julia had hoped that John would not have noticed that she had been wearing her field rig, minus all her weapons of course. "I was training Adam and Jason, dear, you know, to bring them up to your standards," hoping to shift blame onto John.

John looked at his wife. "Wife, that was this morning and you changed for lunch. What prompted you to change back again, darling spouse"?

Julia realized she was trapped, so she tried to mitigate the trouble. Knowing there was no way out, she decided that they best fess up; it would be easier in the long run. "Well, if you must know, I was teaching Sarah some self-defense moves. I mean, well, I did not want to agitate you or Isaiah, but she was having some trouble in school from some of the other children who are quite a bit older than she." Julia looked mildly guilty at this point. She thought it was exactly the right amount of guilt for the small fabrication she had just told.

Isaiah looked shocked at this revelation. "Sarah why did you not tell me?"

Sarah quickly decided to go along with Julia, remembering her dire warning about going shopping with her father along. "Well, Poppa, I did not want you to worry or make a fuss. I thought it would only make things worse at school. Julia has been teaching me to take care of myself. You know she is quite good at it."

John however was more then used to Julia's ideas of telling the whole truth about something, that idea being that it was something she would hardly ever do. "What prompted the idea of such training now, dear? I mean, we have been en route for several weeks already."

Julia looked at her husband harmlessly while thinking he was getting to be a pain. Not so much a pain that she did not want him, you understand, just enough to rise to an annoyed-wife level. "Well. it sort of came to us as we were talking one night in our compartment, my love, you know, just some girl talk." Julia hoped that that would be the end of it.

John looked as if he was not satisfied but simply said, "All right Julia. I always wondered what it was you two gossiped about."

Julia and Sarah both let out a sigh of relief, at least internally.

Isaiah still seemed put out but thoughtful at the same time. "Well, I guess that it is all right but you be careful young lady. It would not do for you to get hurt. Understand?"

Sarah jumped up and hugged her father and said, "Yes, Poppa, I will be careful."

After listening to all this, Father Peter silently made the Sigh of the Cross, for he too was familiar with Julia's ideas on telling the whole truth. He settled in and dug out his pipe and began preparations for an after-dinner smoke.

Sarah and Isaiah excused themselves shortly thereafter and went forward to the shop-on-wheels to work on the steam wagon. Isaiah had some new ideas for improvements. Sarah was happy to go along and just relieved not to be in any deeper trouble.

Then John got up and most gallantly helped Julia up as befit a proper gentleman not to mention loving husband. He took her arm and without a word steered her toward his compartment. As the door slid shut behind them, John Morton took his wife in his arms in a fierce embrace and whispered in her ear, "What are you not telling me, wife?" As he was waiting for an answer John began some serious neck nuzzling.

Julia gulped and started to respond to her husband's question with her mouth, while the rest of her responded to being held tightly in her husband's arms while he nibbled on her neck in a whole different way. "Why, only what I told you my, love."

John stopped his nuzzling just long enough to respond, "Julia, not that I mind it, but you are wiggling and that tells me you are trying to take my mind off of what we are discussing. So, what prompted the training?" As he was saying this, his right hand had started roaming over Julia's backside with an occasional pinch thrown in. This activity was made much easier by the afore-noted lack of a bustle and extra petticoats. Simultaneously, his other hand was starting to undo buttons on the back of her dress. He breathed in her scent and felt her warmth. It was an aphrodisiac that he never tired of. That and the obviously guilty wiggling which was indeed most delightful!

Julia continued to feel her body respond to John's manliness and felt his rising excitement, her own starting to match it. "All right, but you cannot tell Isaiah, dearest, he would be too upset about it." By this time she was also breathing deeply and starting to have trouble forming words; her nostrils starting to flair doing their best to catch her man's scent as she tried to get even deeper into John's embrace.

John murmured his agreement as he slid her dress down pulling the petticoats with it and found her in her knife-proof corset and stockings which he did not mind at all. He renewed his explorations with his lips working down her front to the top of the lace of her corset and then working under the lace trim to the swelling below. Meanwhile as his one hand continued exploring from the bottom up, a rather moist bottom he noted, the other worked in between lips and the bottom exploring hand, although the hands worked together for a bit to add Julia's pantaloons to the pile of clothing on the floor. While John was thus occupied, Julia briefly described the incident with the toughs and how Sarah had suggested that perhaps it would be good if she knew some self-defense moves, all the while trying to catch her breath. All John's kissing, stroking and nibbling was driving her into a frenzy and making it, as she had noted on previous occasions, very hard to concentrate.

Now it was John's turn to mutter a reply, which basically was that he agreed that it indeed was probably not a bad thing to teach Sarah. This was said as Julia managed to get her husband's pants unbuttoned and slide them down his legs along with his drawers and then went to work on his shirt, trying with what was left of her self-control not to rip the buttons off, as it seemed to take forever to get it open and expose John's chest to her. Like her husband, Julia never tired of exploring her husband's body with every tool at her disposal. She continued this sensual inventory right down to his groin, her hands busy running themselves over John's manhood while her lips and tongue worked their way down his chest to join her hands down below. She thought it was only fair that since John had done all the nibbling, she should strike a blow for women's equality and get in some serious nibbling of her own which started at his neck and worked its way down his neck over his chest, taking a brief pause to work on his nipples awhile. From there it was due south to where her hands were busy with a special part of John's anatomy.

At this point all coherent verbal communication ceased and a far more primitive type of communication took over completely, although there was a noticeable, not to say substantial, amount of incoherent noise. Neither party seemed adverse to this change in communication techniques. It was sometime later, it taking more than a little while, to finish what they were telling each other in John's bunk. In the end they seemed to agree that such conversation as took place was indeed just wonderful. John Morton was a happy man although exhausted. In a similar vein, like her husband, Julia was an extremely contented lady. It was during this quiet time that John fell asleep with a mostly naked sleeping wife on top of him.

Sometime later, Julia woke up due to something or someone tickling her nose. When she was finally conscious enough to realize she had fallen into a light sleep on top of John who was still deeply and soundly asleep, her nose was being tickled by John's chest hair. She smiled again; *I seem to have worn him out. I really must keep in mind that he is older than me; I cannot tax him too much. I very much like the idea of having him around.* Then she was thinking that this man was her man and no one else's, in a very possessive and contented way, in spite of the fact that John was one of the few people who seemed to know when she was adjusting the truth, as it were. She knew she would not want anyone else to fall asleep on.

However, all such wonderful things had to come to an end so she moved with as much delicacy as possible, after all she was laying on top of her sleeping husband and there was an important area of his anatomy that it would not do to damage. No, it would not do at all! She managed to get her feet on the floor without waking John or tripping over her stockings which were down around her ankles. The only reason she still had them on at all was that she still had her shoes on. The red corset with its black lace trim and black ribbon stocking tabs was now part of the pile of clothing on the floor of the compartment so there was nothing to hold them up. She thought to herself that she had to see about getting some garters if this sort of thing kept up. At home they were just as enthusiastic most of the time but generally they took time to fully undress before such activities and hang up their clothes so they did not get wrinkled. Neatness does count, as she had told John, although at times she wore the silk Chinese print robe she had gotten for their honeymoon. John still seemed to like that. Once he muttered something about men enjoying unwrapping special presents just as boys did even when they knew what they were getting.

Quietly as she could, she picked up her things from the floor. As she stood up she caught a view of herself in the wall mirror with a bit of a shock. As she saw her reflection she thought she was the picture of a woman who had been caught out in a hurricane or worse. Part of her hair was loose and going every which way down her shoulders and over her back and chest, she was naked and her makeup smudged. *That would be a wonderful invention for women, makeup that did not smudge. All this steam technology and Babbage's engines are nice, but how about something useful. Men never think about what a woman needs!*

Holding her clothing in her arms and with a final smiling look at John still blissfully sleeping, she quietly slide the door open just enough to see if the coast, or more accurately corridor, was clear before she ducked out and as quietly and quickly as possible trotted down to the compartment she shared with Sarah. A mouse trying to sneak around a cat would have been loud in comparison as she opened the door and ducked in quickly sliding the door shut behind her naked behind. She finally relaxed and began hanging up her clothes and putting things away. She removed her shoes and it did not take much to finish up getting her stockings off. She decided that the hair and makeup could wait until morning.

Just as she was ready to climb into her bunk, Sarah said, "I take it you and John were having some of that man-woman relationship you were telling me about?"

Julia froze. Now what? She turned to face Sarah and replied, "Let us just say that my husband was not altogether convinced about the story I told at dinner regarding your training and he decided to interrogate me some more. Before you ask, young lady, yes, it was a truly lengthy, wonderful and enthusiastic interrogation. Now good night, Sarah. Your big sister needs some rest after the rigors of the questioning that horrible wicked man put me through." At this she arched her eyebrows and with her hand on her outthrust hip, smiled a sultry smile. Julia then climbed into her bunk and was soon fast asleep.

Sarah, becoming used to the idea of what went on between a man and a woman, smirked just a little and went back to sleep dreaming about finding a proper woman for her father and wondering if it would be like that for her some day.

Morning found the entire team rested and relaxed. John especially thought that it was good he found out what was really going on right after dinner so he had plenty enough time to recover. Getting the truth out of Julia could be taxing to say the least, very enjoyable, but taxing. He had to be firm with Julia in more ways than one. As he helped her to sit down, he kissed her very properly on the cheek and whispered in her ear how much he loved her. Julia looked up at him and smiled; *yes, a truly lucky woman*, she thought.

CHAPTER 11

THE FORT

It was about eleven o'clock in the morning when the train pulled into a siding at the station that served the post. As with many such installations, much of it was empty space, with just two high towers that served as mooring points for the great airships. No airships were in residence currently which tended to make the field look even larger and more desolate. Nearby were multiple buildings with a log wall running between them and several additional sections to complete the enclosing stockade. Block houses occupied the two open corners that did not have any buildings occupying them. Two double wooden gates, one facing the train station and one facing the landing field completed the facility. The post's name, Fort Freemont, was over both gates. Nearby, a small town of about fifty to sixty buildings had sprung up with various shops and multiple saloons, mixed in with houses typical to this part of the country and a single church along with a one-room school house.

The post was somewhat larger than the typical army post because of the recent Indian war. A battalion of infantry was stationed there, four companies, along with a section or two of field artillery and two troops of cavalry. Additionally, there was some support personnel for the airships—Corp of Engineers and Signal Corp troops. All told, the Fort had some six hundred and fifty men plus dependents, this being lower than would be expected for the number of units stationed there, but as with most units in the army, none were up to anywhere near full strength. Even at this large number, however, most of the troops were off on patrol or providing escort for various wagon trains, survey parties and telegraph repair details. The upshot of this was that significantly somewhat less than two hundred men were currently in the fort. As John knew, this would be about the right number from his days in the army.

The team climbed down from the train just as the gate nearest the railroad station opened and a detail of five troopers and a small buckboard with extra seats in what would normally be the open cargo space came out heading in their direction. As the soldiers approached, a young first lieutenant spurred his horse ahead and then came to a stop. He dismounted with the easy grace of a man used to a life in the saddle.

Morton stepped forward and smiled. As he offered his hand he said, "Professor John Morton of the New York Museum of Natural History, Lieutenant."

The young officer returned the smile in a somewhat forced manner. "Lieutenant Paul Dasson, sir, E Troop Eighth Cavalry, at your service." It was obvious that the young officer was looking over the team trying to figure out what was going on. "We were informed about you and your expedition, sir. I do not know how to tell you this, sir, but this is probably not the best time to come. There are some problems, Professor Morton did you say? Things are in a bit of unrest to say the least."

Morton smiled and looking confident said to the young officer, "If I may present my team, sir, perhaps you will be somewhat more relaxed. First, my wife and team archivist, Julia."

Julia curtseyed to the young officer and smiled saying, "My pleasure, Lieutenant."

The Lieutenant bowed and kissed her hand and murmured, "Mrs. Morton."

Next, John motioned to Father Peter. "Lieutenant, may I present Father Peter Harrigan of the Arch-diocese of New York, formerly First Sergeant Harrigan of the One Hundred and Sixty-First New York Infantry Regiment." At this the officer's eyes widened a bit.

Father Peter smiled and said, "You remind me of a young officer I knew from back then, Lieutenant, only he was a captain." John smiled at this. Julia raised an eyebrow at this comment, but said nothing. Again the young officer replied with a hesitant greeting.

Next John stepped up to Isaiah and Sarah. "Lieutenant, if I may present our team's tinker, Isaiah Liman, the gentleman who invented the blunderbuss which I believe the army still uses, formerly Sergeant, C Co, 2nd United States Colored Troops."

At this the Lieutenant looked completely shocked. Grabbing Isaiah's hand he broke into a big smile. "A true honor, sir! Your invention got my troop out of a tight spot a while ago. A real honor, sir!"

Isaiah smiled. "I am glad it helped you Lieutenant, but for now I try to stick to less lethal tinkering. May I present my daughter, Sarah, sir." John quickly added, "Our assistant archivist and my wife's fearless organizer. I warn you, sir, never let her catch you putting a specimen in the wrong spot, a court martial would be more preferable and definitely more comfortable."

"Your servant, Miss Liman," this said as the officer bowed to Sarah.

Sarah blushed some and like Julia offered the man her hand, although she thought he was sort of old, he had to be at least twenty-seven, while executing a proper curtsey just like her sister.

John brought forth Corporal Sam Tinsman and Private Sam Kincaid of B Company, Berdan's Sharpshooters. Next he introduced Carl Jordan as the team's excavation expert. Finally he presented the new members of the field team, Jason and Adam.

The young officer seemed speechless after the introductions. It was obvious that he was wondering why a scientific party needed such highly experienced military talent. Regaining his powers of speech he looked at Morton, "You, sir?"

"Major John Morton, army reserve, formerly Commanding Officer of the One Hundred and Sixty-First New York Infantry Regiment, for now trying to be an inactive military officer and an active museum professor."

Now the Lieutenant looked completely surprised. "The John Morton of Sharpsburg, that Morton, sir?," the color draining out of his face.

Morton smiled and holding out his hand again, "I seem to remember I was involved in it along with some other battles, Lieutenant."

Dasson grabbed Morton's proffered hand. "Truly an honor, sir. I read about the battle at the Point, sir. I mean, sir, welcome to Fort Freemont, sir."

Julia smiled at her husband and looking at the young officer who seemed to be starting to go into hero worship mode said, "Lieutenant, please no more. If you swell my husband's head too much I will have to get him all new hats and then how could I afford any new bonnets for myself?"

John laughed and put his arm around Julia. "Besides being my wife and invaluable assistant, Julia also serves the highly important role of keeping my feet quite firmly on the ground, Lieutenant. A truly wonderful woman." At this last Julia turned her cheek to John and he gave her a quick peck on it.

With this bit of introductions over with, the six principals boarded the buckboard while Tinsman and his crew began to check weapons and stand guard over the train. The young officer noted the seemingly non-guard guard detail. It was only a short ride to the fort.

The buckboard went through the gate and drew up in front of a building marked with a sign that read "Post Commander" and the various parties climbed down. John of course turned to help his wife and Sarah down. The lieutenant stepped forward, and knocked on the door and without waiting, opened it and stepped in. He said something to someone inside and motioned for them to come in. The two women were, as was the custom, allowed to enter first and the four gentlemen followed.

The office was typical of a frontier fort. Not overly large but adequate for a staff meeting. A desk and a larger table with maps on it dominated the room while chairs, ashtrays, a couple of spittoons and a pot-bellied stove with a wood-box seemed to take up the rest of the space. Sitting behind the desk was a balding man with a generous set of sideburns wearing the uniform of a full Colonel of Infantry. The nameplate on the desk read 'Col. F. W. Washburn'. Lieutenant Dasson stood to attention and introduced the team's leader to the post commander, as the man obviously was.

Colonel Washburn stood up and as he came around his desk said, "At ease, Paul." The young lieutenant relaxed. He began introductions of the rest of the party members to his commanding officer. After the introductions were completed, the colonel waved them to various chairs. John helped Julia to be seated while the young officer helped Sarah. "Please, Professor, call me Frank; we are somewhat informal out here on the frontier."

John liked the look of the man. Older, probably near retirement, and somewhat overweight but obviously still in good enough shape to lead troops in the field. "In that case, please call me John," Morton smiled. "Like you, sir, we work pretty much on a first-name basis, with the exception of Father Peter," waving at the clergyman. "There is not too much room for formality when you are sleeping in a tent and digging in the dirt all day."

The Colonel looked at the assembled group and turning to Lieutenant Dasson said, "Paul, I believe you have your duties to attend to, no need for you to be held up any longer. Thank you for meeting and escorting our guests." The lieutenant stood up and saluted his commander, which the older officer returned, and excusing himself to the members of the team, smartly exited the office. As soon as the door closed behind Dasson, Washburn looked at John and lost his smile. "What in hades is this about, Morton? I got a telegram from the War Department in Washington, directly from the Assistant Secretary no less, to give you and your team every assistance for your field expedition and to do it quietly. I have the Indians ready to jump the reservation because they are scared out of their minds. I do not know how much you know about the Nez Perce but having dealt with them for over a decade, I can tell you for a fact they do not scare! What, sir, is going on and what is so important about your research on prehistoric fauna?"

Morton took a deep breath. "Frank, I cannot tell you the full details, but my team has been sent out here to find out what it is that is riling up the Indians and put a stop to it. Like you, we have been given our orders from superiors that are as high up, if indeed not higher. We are not here to undermine your authority or cause you more trouble. If anything, just the opposite." Morton then turned to the team. "You are aware of some of the team's background, however, let me add that Carl is an expert on mining and tunneling; how or where he got his knowledge is unimportant and it is on a need-to-know basis. My wife, and, yes, sir, she is indeed my spouse, is a highly trained intelligence expert and exceptionally deadly. Do not let the gentle smile and the innocent look fool you, Colonel, she is a genius with explosives." At this point Morton put his hand over Julia's with a gentle squeeze and went on, "The rest of the team, with the exception of Sarah and Carl, are all well-trained and very steady men, sir. Carl was picked for his specialized knowledge and Sarah is only twelve so you will have to give her some time. However, she has a very useful set of skills that we found invaluable in resolving a previous problem." Sarah beamed at this bit of praise.

Washburn sat back in his chair. "I rather suppose I have to take your word for it, sir." Picking up a telegram off his desk and waving it at them, "You come highly recommended. And as you are no doubt aware, orders are orders. Welcome to the northwest and Fort Freemont." With that Washburn put out his hand.

John smiled and visibly relaxed. He took the offered hand and they shook. Julia took the opportunity to speak up. "Colonel if you would be so kind, can you tell us what you know, and if you have someone available who can show us on a map where the event occurred?"

Washburn replied, "Indeed, madam, but now it is incidents, plural! There have been several sightings over on the reservation, and most recently some of the surrounding settlers have been screaming for army help. My forces are spread very thin. It is over one hundred miles to the nearest fort for support and I have not seen an airship in five months. On top of all that we have no idea what we are up against."

Washburn got up and went over to the conference table and rolled out a map. The rest of the team followed him and stood around the table as the colonel anchored the map with an ashtray, ruler and other items. The map firmly secured, Washburn took a cigar out of his uniform coat pocket and began using it as a pointer. "The first incident that we know of happened roughly here. Spotted Wolf, the young Nez Perce buck, told a tall tale; at least at the time we thought he was delusional from falling off his horse or some such. Although I should have known there was more to it; Nez Perce do not fall off their horses. You would think they were descended from some kind of Grecian centaur stock the way they ride. You would swear some of them were born on a horse."

It was Father Peter who broke in. "Spotted Wolf was the young boy who said the mountain exploded and a monster came out?"

Washburn looked at the priest. "Indeed, Chaplain. I know the lad. Has a chip on his shoulder because of the war but for all that not really a bad lad, bright and normally very steady. From what the agent said the lad was delirious for at least three to four days and in pretty bad physical condition. That alone should have told me there was more to it, the Nez Perce do not get spooked either. Next, there were several reports of huge animals around here and in several cases quite dangerous." Washburn pointed to a different area of the map. "As it was I did not have enough men to send in a decent force to reconnoiter the area. I am sure Major Morton can tell you there are never enough troops for all the various missions."

John nodded his head in agreement. Washburn went on, "At the beginning we thought it was some tribal malcontents looking to stir up trouble as an excuse for jumping the reservation, or perhaps an injured grizzly bear. A grizzly would definitely fit the definition of a large and dangerous animal. I would have liked to do a flyover to take a look-see and show the flag and power of the U.S. Government, but none of the airships are available. I was told that they are needed elsewhere, especially on the Canadian border. Damn Brits, excuse me ladies. Anyway, in the last week we have had three reports from ranchers that something is taking their livestock. They were positive it was not a grizzly."

Carl looked up. "From the way you say that, sir, I assume that it was not the local aborigines?"

Washburn looked at him. "Who?"

Sarah smiled and said, "I think he means the Indians, Colonel."

Carl seemed to realize he misspoke. "Indeed, sir, the Indians. I am given to understand that they raid cattle, sir."

Washburn shook his head. "I thought so too until Lieutenant Dasson's detail returned. Unless Indian ponies have gotten very large and changed their hoof prints, it was defiantly not the Nez Perce or a bear. I have not the slightest idea what it is, but it is definitely not the Indians or any animal we are familiar with."

Morton asked simply, "Are all the reports the same?"

Washburn looked at him. "No, indeed not. There were two similar: Spotted Wolf's story and another about a new cave appearing. Others were about strange sounds and some missing cattle and sheep. There were also the same strange tracks. Those occurred here, here and several around here," the Colonel using the cigar as a pointer noting locations on the map that was spread out.

Isaiah looked at the map. "What kind of country is that, sir?"

The colonel looked up as if seeing Isaiah for the first time. He seemed shocked to some extent at being questioned by a black man. He hesitated in answering, then laughed, "I am sorry, Sergeant, it has been a while since we have had any men of your kind around here, but I previously had several companies of the Twenty-Fifth Infantry under my command. Some of the best troops I ever commanded, bar none. In answer to your question, it is pretty rugged. A lot of hills, stream-cut valleys and woods. Bobby Lee could have hidden a whole army up there and we would have had trouble finding them."

Isaiah looked at John. "Does not sound much like steam wagon country, Major."

Morton looked at the map and pointing, responded to his friend, "Indeed, Isaiah, but it looks like we can use the wagon to stage in some of the equipment so we can set up a base camp for our activities if needed." John was pointing to the map with a pencil he had picked up as a pointer of his own. "I would think that this might be a good location. What do you know about it, Colonel?"

Washburn looked at where John was pointing and grunted. He said at last, "Not a bad location; fresh water and good grazing, but it is on the reservation. You may have trouble. The Nez Perce are really riled up right now. White men camping on their land may not go down too well. I really cannot spare the manpower to protect you and your team, John. We are spread too thin as it is." Washburn got a puzzled look on his face and then added, "What is a steam wagon?"

Morton looked up at him from the map. "In answer to your question, Frank, it would be better to show you, but for a quick answer, it is a horseless wagon powered by a steam engine; a sort of a much-smaller utility version of Ericson's Land Monitors, one of Isaiah's inventions, a handy gadget indeed. As for our approach I think it is best to talk to the tribal elders. Do you have anyone who can translate for us, Frank?"

Washburn looked at him. "Translation is not so much of a problem; many of the Indians already speak English as they attended the mission schools. I would suggest that you have Lieutenant Dasson accompany you. He knows many of the elders and is on as good a term as any man around here to introduce you. Additionally, he knows the territory quite well."

John smiled. "I think that would be an excellent idea. That and we will need a guide. Would you be able to spare the lieutenant tomorrow morning? It is best we get started as soon as possible before this whole thing gets even further out of hand."

Washburn smiled. "That should not be a problem; and you are getting a very fine officer. I will have my orderly let him know. Do you want me to tell him that you are a little more than just a museum party?"

John looked thoughtful for a moment before he replied, "No, let us leave that out for now. The fewer people who know the better. If needed I can tell him later."

The meeting broke up but not before the gentlemen enjoyed a drop of Kentucky's finer spirits and some cigars. The two ladies decided to tour the fort, the truth being that Julia did not want Sarah around such behavior. Not that she did not understand, as she had noted she was married to a male, but it would not do for her little sister to be around such smoking and drinking. So while the men socialized, she and Sarah checked out the trading post and managed to meet some of the army wives, some of whom were more than a little shocked at Julia introducing Sarah as her younger sister. Julia seemed to ignore it and by now Sarah was used to it.

CHAPTER 12

A BUSY DAY

It was early morning and a small party consisting of Lieutenant Dasson and three troopers from his unit, Morton, Father Peter and Carl, headed out of the fort. Dasson told them before they headed out that this should be a small party since they were there to parlay and it should not look like an invasion. He also had suggested that the good father join them since the Nez Perce seemed generally well-disposed toward the missionaries.

Shortly thereafter another party headed out going in a different direction to visit some of the ranches that had reported missing stock and other odd goings on. The detachment was led by a sergeant, and was composed of a corporal and an additional ten troopers. It also included Julia, Tinsman and Adam.

Meanwhile the rest of the team stayed behind. Sam Kincaid and Jason used the time to unpack various items of equipment. The two men meticulously began the process of laying out ready-packs of extra items and equipment they might need. Sam knew that having what you needed at hand and ready for action can save lives, generally, and most importantly your own. The last things to check were the team's weapons to make certain they were in peak condition after the trip. After checking them in the combine which served as the team's armory and equipment car, they took them to the post's range and double checked that they were sighted-in properly. While they were at the range, Jason was curious and asked Kincaid about the gun he was sighting-in. "Why are you taking an old single-shot rifle, sir, and what is the arrangement with the two triggers? Would not the repeaters be better?"

Sam sighed and shook his head. "First of all, kid, I was a private, not a ruddy officer, so it is Sam not sir. Second, this particular rifle is a Sharps falling block, chambered for the forty-five one-ten with double set triggers and I am sighting it in for three hundred yards. At that range it has at least three times or better than the knock down power of the forty-five Long Colts the repeaters are chambered for, and even more than the forty-five seventies the army uses, not to mention way more accuracy. They use ordinance like this to shoot the Creedmoor matches and hunt buffalo. The second trigger when pulled sets up the regular trigger so that it is a hair trigger; only takes about five ounces of pressure to touch this beast off. The major said the reports were that something big was taking down livestock. Now sheep are one thing, a wolf or cougar could do that and the repeaters will handle those. Might take a second shot but they will get the job done. However, a range steer is a totally different animal. We are talking grizzle bear or some such. If we have to face a mad grizzle or something else that could take one of those down by itself, I surely would like it to be at as long a range as possible. I have no burning desire to be up close and personal. I do not need it in my face, whatever it is; nothing to prove, as it were. I want to kill it, not just make it mad, so I plan to be shooting something that hits like a great big cobblestone or some other piece of Irish Confetti through a plate glass window. Understand?"

Jason smiled and replied, "I guess that makes pretty good sense, sir, eh, I mean, Sam." Sam rolled his eyes and waved for Jason to check the spotting scope to see where his latest round hit on the target before adjusting the telescopic sights some more. This bit of target practice took most of the rest of the afternoon, since it had been a while since Sam had a chance to do some serious shooting and was quite enjoying himself, even more so because he had Jason to clean the guns after shooting off a whole bunch of Black Power; a truly messy, smelly and dirty job that was. Ah, it was truly wonderful to have a newbie along for such chores!

Sarah wanted to go with Julia and the party going out to the ranches, but Isaiah had said no quite firmly. He went on to explain that she really knew nothing about riding horses and he needed some help with the steam wagon and other gear and his daughter was the best person around for that. Sarah sulked a little bit but decided her father was right. In thinking about it, she realized that what she knew about horses consisted mainly of trying not to get run over by them when she was on the streets by herself back in Buffalo, before she had been adopted. She knew also that her father was right, in spite of having to hide it upon occasion. She was a help around the shop besides keeping Isaiah's records and cooking. She realized that she knew somewhat instinctively that she had been hiding it from Jonah so she did not intimidate him. She remembered what Julia had told her "men are sensitive, delicate creatures and have to be treated gently, and allowed to think they are in control", and giggled a bit to herself. Her father looked at her out of the corner of his eye, but sagely said nothing.

They worked together all morning to improve the engine power. By the afternoon she had decided to take a break from working with her father, and told him she was going to go over to the trading post in the fort and get some pieces of penny candy. Isaiah gave her a nickel and told her to bring him back a piece or two as well. Sarah smiled, and kissed her father before she headed for the fort. It was not a far walk from the station, only about a quarter of a mile or so. The guard at the gate smiled at her and let her in without comment, not seeing her as much of a threat to the U.S. Army in general or the post in particular.

While she was in the trading post Sarah saw a young girl behind the counter who was perhaps just a little older then herself. She smiled at the girl and said hello. The girl had red hair that was as red as Sarah's was black. She also had pale skin and freckles. The girl's name was Molly

Sullivan and the two began chatting. It turned out that Molly was one of the few children on the post, although at fourteen she was not quite a child anymore. Her father was a sergeant in one of the cavalry units stationed at the fort. Like Sarah she did not have many friends, not that anyone was rude or nasty to her, just that there was no one her age. Sarah thought she was pretty, although she was undecided about that bright red hair. Molly did say that one or two of the younger soldiers had noticed her, but when they found out her father was the post sergeant major, the highest enlisted rank in the army, they generally decided that kind of trouble was not worth it no matter how pretty they thought she was. Perhaps it was the lack of companionship that the two felt but it became obvious rather quickly that they would become friends. Sarah was pleased that Molly did not see her as inferior because she was black. Unknown to Sarah, Molly felt the same because she was of Irish descent. She remembered as a young child the "No Irish Need Apply" signs she saw when her father was stationed back east for a while at Fort Niagara. She found out that they had something else in common; Molly worked at the trading post, so Sarah told her how she helped her father in his tinker's shop back in Buffalo. As they continued their conversation Sarah found out that Molly's father had been with Colonel Washburn for quite a while. Molly told her how she had met some of the Buffalo Soldiers; she told Sarah so she knew she was used to blacks. Sarah looked oddly at her new friend. "What is a Buffalo Soldier? Is the army recruiting buffalos or do they come from Buffalo like I do?" She was really confused.

Molly laughed at her new friend. "No silly, Buffalo Soldiers are the units that have enlisted troops of black soldiers. The Indians called them that since some of them had tight curly hair and it reminded them of the mane on the buffalos that they hunted."

Sarah thought about it for a minute. "Did they not mind it, being called after some animal?"

Molly looked at her "You do not know much about soldiers do you? Maybe at first but then they seemed to like it and made it their own. They seemed proud of it," she finished with a shrug.

Sarah smiled, "I do too know about soldiers, my father was one in the war, although he does not like to talk about it much, at least not to me."

Molly shook her head in agreement with Sarah. "I know what you mean. Mostly I overhear him talking about it to the younger troopers. I guess it is too much for us poor delicate females," this last with a wide-eyed look which Sarah knew well since she shared it often enough with Julia, and she laughed. Molly asked what was so funny and Sarah told her about her big sister, Julia.

The girls were interrupted by a customer who was ready to purchase some supplies. Instead of using the new cash register that was sitting by itself on the counter, Molly pulled out a pad and pencil and began to add up a column of numbers. Sarah just stood by and used the time to look over the selection of candy. When the woman had left, Sarah asked Molly why she had not used the register. Molly looked scared. "Sarah, I think I broke it; it does not work right. I am so afraid that Mr. Wilkins will dismiss me."

Sarah looked at her friend, as she now considered Molly. "What do you mean you broke it?"

Molly told Sarah that she was not too familiar with it and earlier that day when she tried to ring something up the machine would not total the items or open the drawer, so she had reverted to the old fashioned pencil and paper.

Sarah looked at her friend who by now was almost crying. "Maybe I can fix it, Molly."

Molly looked stunned, "But you are a girl, how could you fix it!"

Sarah replied with a smile, "Did you not pay any attention to what I told you? I help my father in his shop and do a whole lot more than just keeping his books. Do you have any tools I could use?"

Molly shook her head in a negative way. Sarah patted her hand. "I will be back shortly. I will have to go back to the workshop in our train and get a few supplies. I will be back quickly."

Sarah dashed from the shop and ran down to the railroad station and her father's shop-on-wheels. As she ran into the shop from the end door, Isaiah looked up. "What is all the hurry and where is my candy?"

Sarah smiled at Isaiah and replied, "Poppa, I made a friend and she needs some help. This should not take too long and I will not forget your candy."

Isaiah grunted and said, "This friend is human, right?" Sarah remembers her friend Cee Cee, now where she "always" lived on one of the Hawaiian islands after the Ratten business and smiled.

Sarah laughed. "Yes, Poppa, although she does have this really bright red hair. But not to worry, she is quite human."

Isaiah laughed to himself and asked what kind of problem it was. Sarah told him about the cash register not working. Isaiah nodded and said, "All right but get a small bag and take some of the various sized springs, pins and screws so you do not have to keep running back and forth from here to the post." With that he went back to work on the steam wagon.

Sarah grabbed up the small parts like her father suggested, along with her tools, and headed back to the post. Before long Sarah had the cash register apart. Molly was beside herself. "Sarah, if Mr. Wilkins sees this apart like this he is going to dismiss me for sure!"

Sarah just kept looking at the machine's innards while Molly was busy looking out the door for her boss. A few minutes later she squealed, "He is coming, Sarah. I am done for!"

Just then Mr. Wilkins came in the door. Molly was trying to figure out how to tell him about the register when there was a small noise from behind her and Sarah said, "Excuse me, Miss, could you ring me up please."

Molly turned around and Sarah was standing there by the now reassembled register smiling, looking innocent and holding out some candy. Mr. Wilkins seemed confused and asked Molly what the matter was. Molly looked a little stunned, but could see Sarah out of the corner of her eye mouthing the words *you forgot how to use the resister.*

Molly swallowed and looked at her boss. "Sir, I have to admit I have been using a pencil all day; I forgot the lesson you gave me on the new cash register."

Mr. Wilkins shook his head and said, "All right, let me show you again and this time pay closer attention, Molly." Quickly, explaining as he went, he tallied up Sarah's candy and pushed the handle down to open the drawer and make change. Then he closed the drawer and said he was going in the back.

Molly looked like she was going to collapse but managed to stay upright. Sarah snickered. "It was just a broken spring, not your fault at all."

Molly hugged her. "Sarah how can I ever thank you?"

Sarah looked thoughtful for a moment. "You said your father was in the cavalry, did you not? Do you know anything about riding horses?" Molly smiled a big smile at her new friend.

CHAPTER 13

A Meeting
On The Reservation

I t was after noon by the time the small party reached the main village on the reservation. Along the way Carl had asked Dasson why he had not seen any Indians.

Paul laughed and replied, "That is because they did not want you to see them. They have been watching us since we crossed over the boundary. The Nez Perce are some of the best light infantry in the world. They could give advanced lessons to the Apaches."

Carl swallowed noticeably at this, knowing very little about Indians other then what he had read about in the sensational novels sold in Wales. He started looking all around. "Lieutenant, are you quite sure about them being here?" He was wondering what he would look like without any hair.

Paul smiled and replied, not even bothering to look at the mining engineer, "Quite sure, Mr. Jordan. There have been at least three braves that I saw, which means there are probably nine that I did not see. That answer your question?"

Carl swallowed again and tried to relax, although it did not seem to be working very well.

Only a short time later the party broke into a clearing and before them stood the Nez Perce village. Dasson dismounted and motioned for the rest to follow suit. Before long several men advanced, looking grave. One of them looked at Dasson and spoke, "Greetings Dasson of the long knives. What brings you to our home?" There seemed a wariness in the tone but not exactly hostile.

"Greetings, Strong Bear, it is good to see you again. I bring several persons sent by the Great White Father to find out what is bringing trouble to the land of the Nez Perce."

Strong Bear looked over the rest of the party. The troopers he seemingly dismissed. Shaking his head and going on with a snort, "Paul, what does Washington care about us? You throw us off our land and kill our warriors." This last was said in quite good and colloquial English much to the party's surprise. Strong Bear merely shrugged and said, "Come in and sit down." He then turned and went into a tepee and Dasson and the rest followed him.

Father Peter looked at him and asked, "You seem to know our language quite well; where did you learn it?"

The Indian returned his look, "From your kind, Father, at the mission school. The priests were quite insistent that we learn English to the point where we were beaten if we were caught speaking our own language. A most effective instruction technique I assure you."

Peter looked saddened and ashamed. "I am sorry, Strong Bear. I had heard of such things but I never believed them. It makes me sad that such methods would be used to bring the words of Our Lord to you and your people."

"Father, I would say that the men in black were in good company with the Indian agents who cheated my people of supplies for the winter; they and the others the Great White Father has sent. It has indeed done so much for the lives of our people and enriched our culture," he finished with a strong note of sarcasm.

Morton looked at the man. "I am sorry to hear what you have gone through. We are aware that your people did not start the war, but that it was the greed of my kind that did. I could apologize but I do not suppose it would mean much."

The chief looked at Morton. "Who are you? Your words are true, but as you said it does not mean much to us. Why are you here on our land, what little of it was left to us?"

The lieutenant cleared his throat, "Introductions are in order. Strong Bear of the Nez Perce may I present Professor John Morton of the Museum of Natural History, Father Peter Harrigan, who is working with him and Carl Jordan, also of the museum." While the last was not exactly true, the party decided to let it go since it would be easier than trying to explain Carl's real reason for being there. "They are here to help find out what has been disturbing the Nez Perce and try to stop it, Strong Bear."

The Indian looked thoughtful for a moment. "Three men, that is all Washington could spare? How generous. I see the Great White Father is as generous with help as he is in giving us back some of our land."

Morton shook his head. "No, sir, the rest of my team has split up. My wife, Julia, and several others have gone to check out reports from several of the ranches in the area near the reservation to try and find out more information. The rest of my team is still at the post getting our equipment ready for whatever we will find so we can deal with it. While not huge in number they are the best that there is."

The Indian looked somewhat less then believing. "So, Professor, what do you plan to do? This is not some oversized cougar or wild bison; this thing burst out of the side of a mountain. Can your team handle that?"

John shook his head. "If we cannot, I do not know anyone who can. As I said, my people are the best at what they do."

Strong Bear looked at Morton in all seriousness. "These people of yours include a female and a priest? What is their role, to serve coffee to the beast and convert it to Christianity? Oh, you can call me Kevin; it was the name I was given at the mission school."

Morton looked at Kevin, as he thought of him now, "Father Peter brings a different perspective on what we find, and helps to hold us together. As for my wife, Julia, trust me, sir, you would not want to make her mad. And in answer to the question you were going to ask, I have seen her in action as has the Father and we were just glad she was not mad at *us* at the time."

Father Peter gave a small smile and made the Sign of the Cross. "Amen to that, John. John means what he says Kevin. You are sure about the name?"

The Indian laughed. "Indeed, Father, I grew used to it and it seems to help you whites to relax."

Morton looked serious. "Whatever this is, it is obviously big and we can assume dangerous. We need to get started as soon as possible. Can we meet the lad who first saw this, whatever it is?"

The Indian looked thoughtful. "Spotted Wolf is in the village. How much you get out of him is up to him. He is an angry young man. War does that to people."

Peter looked sad and spoke softly, "I understand all too well, Kevin. John and I served together during the Civil War and I saw men change. For me it was a call to go into the priesthood, for others it was a far darker journey."

Strong Bear, or Kevin, looked at Dasson, "What say you, Paul? Since I have met you, your word seems good and one that can be trusted. I remember how you stood up for one of the other villages against that corrupt Indian agent."

Dasson was trying to take in what he had heard. "Strong Bear, I am not sure what to tell you for I just met these people myself. However, my commander thinks well of them and they seem to be telling the truth."

Strong Bear looked at the young officer, "As usual, Paul, your words are honest. You freely admit what you do not know, and you do not swear to it. All right, we will give you the help you request, for now." Strong Bear said something in his native tongue to a brave outside the tepee and the men waited. Before long the flap opened and a young Indian brave entered. Strong Bear motioned to the lad to sit. It was obvious that it was Spotted Wolf and that he was uncomfortable.

Morton looked at the young man. Although the clothing and skin color were different, Morton could see the fierce pride in the young man's face and especially the eyes. It took him back to the time when their regiment was being formed, that same fighting spirit and will to engage the enemy, although those troops wore butternut or gray. In

Spotted Wolf's case it had not been diluted by time, having recently seen his friends torn apart in battle; it was still fresh. Morton spoke quietly and slowly, "Spotted Wolf, do you speak the white man's tongue?"

The brave looked at him. "I speak your language, white eyes. We do not need your help!"

Strong Bear said something. Although it was in his native dialect, Morton could guess the meaning from the way Strong Bear spoke and the look on the young man's face. The chief was rebuking him in no uncertain terms. He thought to himself that a dressing down by your commanding officer sounded the same in any language.

The lad looked down and said something back, which sounded like some sort of contrition.

Morton smiled at the young man and started over. "Spotted Wolf, whatever this is we will need your help in order to protect your people. I have no doubt about your courage, but something that can tunnel through the earth itself and blow out the side of a mountain, that is a whole new category of trouble. I fear the kind of trouble that will not be impressed by your rifle. My teammates and I wish to help if you will let us."

Spotted Wolf looked at Strong Bear. It was obvious to Morton and his team that the younger Indian respected the chief. Again Strong Bear spoke in the language of the Nez Perce and the younger man nodded. He looked at Morton and spoke, "Perhaps you are right; this Manito is powerful. We will need your power, holy man, to send it back into the earth whence it came," this last spoken to Father Peter.

Father Peter looked at the young man, "I am not sure holy water will be better than a rifle, but if needed, I can handle both." Smiling quietly he finished, "Although I prefer the holy water."

Morton looked a little more confident. He asked, "Can you show us where this creature came out of the ground?"

Spotted Wolf smiled ruefully and nodded. "It is hardly something I will forget. If you wish I will get my pony; there is still enough of the day left."

John's reply was simple, "Get your pony, let us ride and try to seek this beast out."

With that the meeting broke up; Strong Bear looked at Morton when it was just the two of them. "His father was one of my closest friends, like a brother to me. He was killed in the war. I would like him to come back, and so would my daughter, Yellow Bird."

John smiled. "I wondered what power you had over him that he would be so meek. He did not really strike me as that type." Strong Bear laughed and Morton went to get his horse with the rest of the party.

The party headed out following Spotted Wolf. Morton had to say that, indeed, the country was beautiful. The skies were the bluest he had ever seen, especially when compared to the city's coal-smoke-choked atmosphere. Even the scents; Morton could smell the pine and the perfume of the wild flowers. The trail went along till Spotted Wolf held up his hand. Dasson and Morton moved up alongside of him.

The young Indian spoke quietly, "Just up around the next bend is the spot where the Manito broke out of the mountain." Dasson motioned to his men, so they drew their carbines and began to spread out in a skirmish line. Carl and Father Peter also drew weapons but stayed behind the three troopers, John and the lieutenant. Although in Father Peter's case it was the lever-action twelve gauge shotgun Julia had gifted him with. It was not his original trusty old back-in-the-parish double barrel, but Peter had grown rather fond of the new gun. Not that he would tell the bishop but its butt had quieted many a drunk ready to beat his wife. *God does indeed work in strange ways,* thought Peter. *Indeed, the word of the Lord is powerful, although at times you do have to catch the sinner's attention before delivering the homily.*

Slowly the line began to move forward. The horses seemed steady and there were no unusual noises to spook anyone. As they pressed on, John leaned over and asked Spotted Wolf if he was sure this was the location. Before he could answer, Dasson spurred his horse and let out a loud whistle. Hearing that, John spurred his own mount but suddenly came to a halt.

The rest of the party moved up to see. They were all deadly quiet, for what was in front of them was a hole in the side of the mountain that had to be at least twenty feet in diameter. It looked as if one could have moved a small two-story house through it. Carl was the first to move forward, his face showing total wonder. He dropped down off his horse and looked around.

Dasson meanwhile had his three men spread out to watch their flanks. A little while later Carl called out to the rest of the party, "I think you can all relax somewhat. Whatever did this is long gone."

Morton dismounted as did Father Peter and Spotted Wolf and they went up to Carl. Carl spoke, "John, I have never seen anything like this; however, I am willing to bet it was not an animal or some sort of evil spirit." Looking at Spotted Wolf, "Or whatever you called it. This tunnel is too straight and relatively smooth and regular, and further back in where the rain and wind have not gotten to it so much, are tracks, John," as he turned his attention back to Morton. "This was done by some machine of incredible power. It is frankly nothing like I have ever seen, read about or even heard whispered about, but definitely man made."

Spotted Wolf looked at the cave and tracks. "This is what I saw, a machine. I cannot believe it but you are right, I had not come back here since I saw it. Now we can hunt it and destroy it!"

In this case it was Father Peter who put his hand on the young brave. "Son, no one is accusing you of being any kind of coward. I do not know that any of us would have been any better than you, given what happened, especially the way this machine shook you up. We heard about the bleeding from your ears and eyes. We will get them, whoever they are, but just remember, if it can move though mountains, I do not think it will be impressed by your Winchester. We need to do a lot more investigating before we charge in, guns blazing, and probably ineffectively at that."

Spotted Wolf looked at the priest and nodded. Morton spoke, "Besides, I am given to understand that a specific young lady will be quite upset if we do not bring you home in one piece."

Spotted Wolf looked defiant for a second, and then smiled and said, "Yellow Bird".

John replied, "Well, we still have some daylight left so let us see if we can find any further information, and while we do that I will tell you about my wife."

CHAPTER 14

ON THE TRACK OF WHAT?

ulia and the men pulled up at the first ranch where problems had been reported. It was located about eight miles from the fort and just off the reservation. Sergeant Bodkins took one look around and ordered his men to assume a defense parameter with carbines drawn. Tinsman and Adam had their repeaters out after they dismounted. Before they had a chance to knock, the door opened and an older man came out. Bodkins smiled, and by way of greeting said, "Howdy, Curtis, what is going on?"

The man smiled and looked around. "Morning, Sergeant. Looks like you are ready for war. You can relax; whatever it was is long gone."

Bodkins looked over at the corporal and said, "Lew, tell the men to relax but post a picket and have the rest of the men rest and water the horses, roll 'em and smoke' em if they got 'em." The corporal acknowledged by way of an easy going salute, drew in the ten troopers and selecting several began setting up the picket. Meanwhile the others dismounted and loosened the saddle cinches and led the mounts over to a small pond fed by a gentle stream to water them. Several took out paper and tobacco and began rolling cigarettes. Curtis invited the sergeant, Julia and Tinsman in for coffee. Adam, as the rookie, was left to take care of their horses, and following the lead of the experienced cavalrymen saw to the horses and led them to the water.

The interior of the cabin was simple with log walls and bulls-eye glass windows. There was a sleeping area and some roughhewn chairs, but all were comfortable and serviceable. Finally there was a table where Curtis placed a coffee pot that he took off a pot-bellied stove which served for both cooking and heating. He finished by fetching some tin mugs and set them on the table with some canned condensed milk and sugar. Julia did the honors pouring the coffee. She did this with the same grace as if she were back in the city at the home of a socialite for afternoon tea.

When they had all been served, the sergeant started out by introducing Julia and Tinsman as part of a scientific research party to discover what was behind the strange goings on. Curtis looked at her. "I did not know scientists were so pretty; I might have paid more attention in school and stayed a bit longer."

Julia smiled over the rim of her coffee cup and replied, "I am not the scientist, sir, that role is reserved for my husband. I function as his field assistant and archivist."

Curtis looked befuddled for a moment "A who or what did you say, ma'am?"

Julia smiled again. "Archivist. I keep his records and notes. I also help catalog the finds he makes so that we can put all the pieces together later when we get back to the museum. I hope that answers your question, sir."

Curtis laughed. "Indeed it does, Missus Morton, and you don't have to 'sir' me none, Curtis will do just fine. I am just a broke-down old cowboy who had drifted long enough to want to put down some roots and have a place to call home and a peg to hang my hat on."

Julia smiled and looked around. "And it seems to be a fine home indeed, Curtis, quite delightful. Like you would have me do, please call me Julia." Curtis smiled. It was obvious to the other men that Julia had charmed him. Julia turned toward him again. "Curtis, if you could, can you tell us the details of what happened out here?"

Curtis shrugged his shoulders. "Not much to tell, ma'am. I have lost several head of cattle lately and it weren't no wolves or a puma either. Whatever it were was fast and big. Left tracks like nothing I ever seen before."

Julia looked at him earnestly, not giving even a hint of disbelief. "Are you sure about the tracks, Curtis, I mean could it have been something that just messed up the tracks so you did not recognize them?"

Curtis took another sip of his coffee and looked at the men and then straight at Julia. "Ma'am, I been a cowboy and drifter for over forty years and that included a time working as a buffalo hunter with Bill Cody before he got all civilized and fancy with his show. These tracks were fresh as a daisy before they petered out on some rocky ground; I tracked it for a while you see. No, whatever it was ran down a full-growed steer, killed it quick like and then dragged it off by itself."

Julia looked at Bodkins as if to ask what he thought. The sergeant looked at her. "Curtis is one of the best trackers in the area. He done some work for the army here and there and he is telling you straight. He ain't a drunkard, braggart or a liar."

Julia looked thoughtful for a moment glancing at Tinsman who just nodded at her unspoken question. "Very well, Curtis, I seem to have it on good authority that you are a man of your word and quite knowledgeable about such things; what then would be your best guess, Curtis, as to what it was?"

Curtis looked hesitant before he spoke. "Missus Morton, I hope you do not think that I am funnin' you, ma'am." The old man looked deeply serious for a moment and went on, "To be honest, I am not sure, but if I was forced to take a guess I would have to say some kind of a pig, but like nothing I have ever seen before. I have seen some of the razorbacks down toward Arkansas after the war, as I said I was a bit of a drifter, but the tracks were huge compared to them. The tracks were similar, but bigger, and whatever it is it was way faster too."

Julia looked confused, "A razorback you say?"

It was at this point Tinsman spoke up, "A wild pig, descended from domestic swine that got loose. They are large, four to five hundred pounds, sharp tusks and mean as a grizzly that someone just woke up halfway through winter. Bad-medicine brutes."

Julia looked at her friend and fellow team member, then at Curtis. "Are you telling me that whatever these things are they were like that?"

Curtis took a final sip of his coffee and replied, "No, ma'am, I am not telling you that, but whatever it is that took my cattle were a lot bigger, a whole lot bigger and a whole lot stronger if it carried a steer off by itself, although the tempermate sounds about right."

They talked for a bit longer getting more details along with locations of the attack, trail and approximate times from Curtis before the party got up to take their leave and head for the next farmstead. As they rode along Julia asked Bodkins what he thought of the tale Curtis had told them. "Ma'am, I have known Curtis for about six years now, ever since I was stationed out here. Like I said, he is a solid man, the kind of a man you would want behind you in a tough spot, that and he knows how to track. I have never seen him too drunk or afraid, but something has him spooked for sure." Julia was left alone to ponder these comments and the story Curtis told them.

Several hours had elapsed as the horses trotted on at an easy lope that would cover ground but not tire them out. As the party topped a rise they heard a flurry of gunshots. Bodkins told Julia in no uncertain terms, "Ma'am, you and your party keep back." Then in a command voice, "Form a skirmish line to the left, ho!" The troopers spurred their mounts and the column began to change and form a line to the left of the sergeant with the corporal on the far left, and Julia, Tinsman and Adam close behind the line. "Draw carbines, ho!" as the men pulled their weapons out as one. "At the gallop, ho!" and the line surged ahead.

As the distance closed to the farm they were heading for, they heard a final fuselage of shots over the pounding of the horse's hooves, and then the only sound was from the rapidly advancing line of soldiers, civilians and their mounts.

As the line cleared the final ridge they could see something the size of a buffalo disappearing in the distance. Several of them saw something dangling from its mouth. Whatever it was, it was moving too fast and was too far to even begin to contemplate giving chase what with the lead it already had and the distance their horses had already galloped. The homestead was almost completely demolished. The house looked like it had been hit by a tornado; it had been reduced to kindling. The barn or what was left of it still partially stood. The line came to a halt in the yard as the sergeant held up his hand. "Lew, set a picket; keep your carbines ready."

Julia and Tinsman dismounted to look for survivors. Tinsman went to look at the house, or more accurately, what had been the house, most of which was no more than kindling-sized pieces of wood to start a fire with. While he did that Julia went toward the barn. She started to pull some boards out of the way when a shot came through the wood over her head missing her by scant inches. She dropped to the ground and for once was decidedly glad for her diminutive stature, that being she was short. There was an anguished female cry from inside, "Get away you monster from hell, and leave us alone." This cry was punctuated by another shot going through the wood.

By this time, Tinsman, Adam and the sergeant had come over with weapons drawn. Julia cried out, "It is all right, we are here to help; whatever it is is gone."

Bodkins added in his deep baritone, "Jennifer, it is Jim Bodkins from the fort. It is all right, put down the gun and come out."

The voice answered in a totally shaken way, "Jim, is that really you? Oh God please be you!" This exclamation was followed by the sound of crying.

Bodkins replied, "Jennifer it is me. Now relax, I am going to pull some of the boards out of the way so you can get out. No shooting now."

Again the voice came, "Jim, oh thank the Lord above it is you! I will pass the kids out!"

Bodkins said, trying to keep the woman calm, "Give us a minute Jennifer, we need to do this slowly, the barn is pretty shaky. Just hold on. After all this we do not want to bring down what is left of the barn on you." Slowly Adam and Bodkins turned to pulling some of the debris carefully out of the way so whoever was in the remains of the barn could get out without collapsing the rest of the damaged, rickety structure in on them. Before long two young children crawled out and were picked up by Julia and Tinsman, a boy and a girl, young, maybe five to eight years old. Finally a battered woman, cradling a Winchester, crawled through the exit hole the men had made. She looked as if she had just returned from a trip to Hades and was shaking like a leaf. Bodkins picked her up to get her on her feet and held her as she cried and shook. He gently took the rifle away from her and handed it to Tinsman.

Bodkins asked her gently, "Jennifer, where is Paul?"

Jennifer cried, "Gone, Jim. That thing, that monster, must have killed him while he was trying to fight it off and give us time to get into the barn. He's likely dead!" With that the woman collapsed into unconsciousness. The sergeant caught her and picked her up in his arms being as gentle as possible. Moving over to a level spot where several of the men put down some blankets, Bodkins laid her down as he would a sleeping child.

As Julia looked after the woman and children, Bodkins gave orders to picket the horses and start a fire. It was obvious that the woman and the children were in no immediate shape to travel. Before long a coffee pot, along with some rations, was set to heating while Tinsman and Adam looked through the remains of the house. Julia sat with the children who themselves were exhausted, most probably from fright, and Jennifer who was resting under some blankets the men found in the remains of the house. Meanwhile, several of the troopers began to look for tracks while the rest stood guard in case whatever the creature was came back. Julia told them that if they found any tracks to let her know and not to disturb them.

A short while later, Tinsman, Bodkins and Julia were speaking quietly while the three survivors slept, the children having drifted off and covered by more army blankets. Julia looked at Bodkins and asked, "Was Paul her husband?"

Jim Bodkins looked tired and gazed off a bit before responding, "No, her brother. Her husband, another Paul, was killed in the Nez Perce War a couple of years ago. Good steady folks, the kind you need to tame the wilderness. After her husband was killed, Paul came out to live with her and help with the farm. Nice fellow; never married himself. I got the idea he was never much interested in women, if you catch my drift. He was a good man, quiet, not flashy but solid, always ready to help. He must have been trying to drive off whatever it was when it got him."

Julia looked sad. "It will be hard for her; first her husband and now her brother. Kids to raise by herself, home destroyed and no one to help. I do not envy her." Julia was thinking about John and how she would feel if she lost him. These, again, were new emotions to her, very scary ones.

Tinsman spoke up, "We will have to take them back to the fort with us; they sure as hell cannot stay here. If I can use some of your troopers, Sergeant, there is a buckboard behind the barn that seems repairable, even without Isaiah's help, Julia." Tinsman forced a weak smile at this trying to lighten the mood. "Course horses are all gone but someone will have to drive it so that will give us a horse."

Bodkins nodded. "No problem, I will detail a couple of my men. We can camp here tonight. Jennifer will want some time to try and salvage whatever is left of her life." As he said this last, all three of them looked at the remains of the flattened cabin. "So far all the attacks have taken place in the daytime but we will post a picket." He looked at Tinsman. "Can you and Adam help?"

Tinsman smiled, again that same weak smile given the circumstances. "Would not be the first time I stood picket; as for Adam, there has to be a first time for everything."

Julia spoke to Bodkins, "I can help also, Sergeant."

Bodkins looked at her somewhat curiously. "No offense meant, ma'am, but I think it would be best if you just saw to Jennifer and the kids." It was somewhat obvious that he was trying to figure out what a woman, an office secretary from an eastern museum at that, thought she could do on guard duty.

"None taken, Sergeant, and perhaps you are right, it might be better if there was another woman here to talk to." Julia smiled at Bodkins thinking that perhaps it would be best if the good sergeant did not know how lethal she could be. *Remember Julia, just a simple secretary,* she thought to herself. Tinsman said nothing and did not even give a hint of a smile even though he had a very good idea of just how dangerous his boss could be. As Julia finished her thought she looked again at the woman and her two children. Julia estimated that Jennifer was about thirty and taller than her by quite a bit, perhaps five foot six inches, and lean. Plenty to do on a farm so there was not much of a problem keeping extra weight off. Her complexion was tanned and a bit wind-burned and her hair a medium shade of brown. Overall she was pretty but there was an obvious air of sadness about her, even in her sleep.

The sun was just coming over the horizon when Julia was awakened by the sound of the traumatized woman waking up. Jennifer started to have a panic attack so Julia moved over to her to comfort her. As with most frontier folk she recovered quickly; the frontier was unforgiving and tended to weed out the weak fairly quickly and most times fatally. She looked first to make sure the children were safe, then at Julia. "Who are you and where is Paul? Is it gone?" All this came out in a rush as she tried to gather her wits about her.

Julia looked at her. "My name is Julia Morton. I am the person you almost shot yesterday. Thank goodness you were aiming high and I am somewhat short. Whatever it is took off as we rode in and we have not seen anything of it since. As to your brother, we found no trace of him except his rifle which was smashed and bent. I am so sorry." She held out her hand and touched the woman's shoulder with the other.

Jennifer started to shake and cry. She grabbed and held on to Julia as a drowning person holds on to a log to stay afloat. "Paul, Paul, why did you have to die?" Jennifer was crying harder now.

By this time Sergeant Bodkins had come over. "Jennifer, we think from where we found his rifle, Paul must have been trying to draw the creature away from you and the kids. He gave his life to save all of you. There are worse ways for a man to go."

This seemed to help the woman pull herself together and she unwrapped herself from Julia's embrace. "I know Jim, it is, just, what will we do now? I cannot manage the farm by myself and what about Little Paul and Jenny, what do I tell them?"

Julia spoke quietly, "Tell them their uncle died a hero."

Jennifer internalized that, looking at Bodkins and then at Julia. "Thank you. I am sorry I almost shot you. God it was terrible; it smashed everything, killed both of our cows, the horses managed to run off, then it came for us. Paul yelled for us to go to the barn and lock ourselves in and we heard the shooting. It started to attack the barn but then it left. I was so scared I did not even hear you all ride in. When you started to shift the boards I thought it was back!" Jennifer seemed out of breath as this had all tumbled out in what seemed to be a single breath while she started to shake again.

Julia looked at her and put her arms around her, trying to help the woman deal with the horror she had gone through. "It is all right. You thought I was the monster back again. At least from now on I will not let my husband's teasing me about being short bother me so much." She smiled with what she hoped was a gentle and reassuring look to Jennifer. "We are going to repair the buckboard and take you back to the fort with us. Perhaps, while that is being done, it hurts to say this, but hopefully you can find something in the remains of your house to take with you, Mrs...?"

Jennifer looked resolute and took a deep breath while sniffling back a tear. "Yes, thank you Julia, it is Swenson, we were from Minnesota. I am glad you are here; it is good to have another woman around." As she said this she noticed that the two children were awake. "Let me introduce my children." Taking her son's hand, "This is Paul, Jr. or Little Paul", and then putting her arm around the little girl, "this is my daughter Jenny. These are the people who saved us yesterday. You have met Sergeant Bodkins from the fort and this is Missus Morton and you, sir," looking at Tinsman, "I do not know."

Tinsman doffed his hat. "Sam Tinsman, madam, and young sir and little miss," as he nodded to the three people who were now refugees.

Conversation stopped for a moment as Adam showed up and brought over some plates and cups he had found in the remains of the farmhouse. Turning quickly, he brought over a kettle and spooned out some beans, bacon and hardtack. While perhaps not the ultimate in breakfast cuisine, the family had missed several meals during the attack and aftermath so there were no complaints. After they finished their army breakfast, the family started picking through what was left of their home. Jenny, at least, seemed happy when she found a yarn-and-rag doll that was under some boards. To her five-year-old mind, Missus Yarn was part of her family and at least it was another survivor. She still did not quite grasp the fact that Uncle Paul was not coming back. Little Paul at seven understood all too well, having lost his father in the Indian War when he was five. He would cry later but now he felt he had to be the man of the family and stoically went through the remains and began to pile things up to take back to the fort.

Tinsman, Adam and two of the troopers worked on the buckboard and found some tack in the remains of the barn. Meanwhile, one of the troopers on picket duty brought in one of the horses that had escaped the farm during the attack. Thus, by about ten o'clock the party prepared to move out back to the fort, the buckboard was piled up with a small collection of things, the pitiful remains of a life.

While all this was going on, Julia did her best to make sketches and take measurements of the tracks left by whatever had attacked the farmstead that one of the troopers had found and reported to her. She measured the dimensions, shape and depth of the prints and distance between the tracks. She thought that she had at least learned that much from watching her husband in the field during the Ratten affair and on several later digs. She smiled as she thought about watching John on the various digs they had worked on together, especially one last fall in upstate New York. That one ended with a side trip to Buffalo and several wonderful evenings in a lovely hotel room, like a second honeymoon. *Those were some good times,* she thought with a quiet smile, then the smile vanished as again she was thinking what it would be like to lose John.

As the small column moved out, Jennifer and Jenny rode on the seat of the buckboard with Julia handling the reins, her horse tied behind the small wagon. Meanwhile, Little Paul sat quietly among the small pile of goods that was all they had to show for their life thus far. After about half an hour of travel Jenny let out a cry, "Mama, there is Toby," as she pointed to a young horse just coming over the hill. The corporal rode out and put a lasso over the young stallion's head and led him back. At least one more member of the family was safe.

Julia considered all they had seen and heard and knew that the question was quite simple: what were they dealing with this time? But harder, what was the answer?

CHAPTER 15

BACK AT THE FORT

It was late in the day when the members of the column heard the guard at the gate yell out, "Open the gate; patrol returning."

As the party rode through the gate, John and most of the rest of the team appeared from the building where they had been assigned quarters. The men who had visited the reservation had returned much earlier. Sarah, who had been practicing riding under Molly's tutelage, rode over and dismounted. She turned the reins over to Molly. Isaiah who had not been aware of the lessons was somewhat shocked but held his tongue.

The team that saw the pathetic pile of goods behind the seat and the faces of the three refugees instinctively knew something dreadful had happened. The sergeant pulled up his detail as Lieutenant Dasson appeared and he saluted his troop commander. "Detail reporting, sir. All men and research party accounted for."

Dasson returned the salute and looked over the party. "I take it there were some problems, Sergeant. Dismiss your men, see to the civilians and then come into the Duty Officer's office and give me your report."

"Yes, sir. Patrol attention. Prepare to dismount; dismount!" The troopers climbed down and the Sergeant continued, "Attend to your mounts. Lew," speaking to the corporal, "see about temporary quarters for the Swenson family. Dismissed." The dismounted men began to disperse to follow orders. The corporal turned the reins of his mount over to one of the troopers and helped Julia, then Jennifer, down, and finally picked up Jenny and set her by her mother. Little Paul climbed down on his own. Then the corporal told the three members of the family to stay in the shade by the commander's office while he found them temporary quarters. He would come back for them once he found a space. Meanwhile, one of the troopers who had stayed back, took the reins of the wagon horse, along with Julia's mount and Toby; both horses had been tied behind the wagon. He told the family he would see that their things were stored in the post's stockade, since it being in the very unusual circumstance of being empty at the current time. With that he led the wagon away.

John rushed over and grabbed Julia and held her close. "What happened, are you all right?" This came out in a rush as the rest of the team came over.

Julia smiled up at her husband. "John, I am fine, however you are lucky, sir, that your wife is not very tall, so no more smart remarks. John and the rest looked somewhat puzzled by this. Julia gestured at the Swenson family and began introductions. Jenny seemed especially nervous and held Missus Yarn tightly.

Seeing the fear in the little girl's face, Sarah, who to the family's confusion was introduced both as Julia's sister and Isaiah's daughter, came over along with Molly. "Hello, my name is Sarah and this is my friend Molly. She lives here at the fort. What is your name and who is your friend?" gesturing at the rag doll.

Jenny looked at her mother for guidance. Jennifer nodded at her daughter as if to say it was all right. Jenny licked her lips and whispered, "My name is Jenny and this is Missus Yarn, she is my friend."

Sarah and Molly both smiled down at her. Molly spoke, "Would you and your brother like to come over to the trading post and get some lemonade?"

Jenny stood quiet for a minute and again looked at her mother who nodded her approval. "Can I bring Missus Yarn?" It was obvious the little girl was trying desperately to hold on to some sense of normalcy in a world that suddenly was both terrifying and strange.

Both girls nodded with a smile and held out their hands. The four children and yarn doll moved off in the direction of the trading post.

Julia smiled at her sister's retreating back, feeling very proud of her. Jennifer spoke quietly, "Please thank, your sister did you say? for helping the children. They have been through so much." With that she began to quietly cry.

Father Peter came over. "Can I help?" This was said in a quiet, gentle voice. "Sometimes it makes it easier to have someone to talk to."

Jennifer looked at him and responded with, "But we are not Catholic."

Father Peter smiled in his disarming Irish way, "Well if you promise not to let the archbishop know I was ministering to Lutherans, it will be all right. After all no one is perfect."

Jennifer looked at Peter with surprise on her face. "How did you know we were Lutheran?"

Peter looked at Isaiah and replied, "From your name and accent. Mr. Liman and I spent some time in St. Paul several years ago. Nice town, even the jail was clean. So it seemed like a safe guess." Hearing this Isaiah snorted and then laughed remembering the incident all too well.

John looked at his wife. "Julia, we have been assigned quarters. Perhaps you and Mrs. Swenson would like to come in and sit down. We will let the corporal know where everyone is."

Jennifer replied, "Please call me Jennifer. My husband has been dead for a long time, now my brother. Your wife and friends helped to save the children and myself."

The group moved off in the direction of the building John and the others had come from. Jason was sent to find the corporal and let him know the whereabouts of the Swenson family. As the party went into their assigned quarters, Isaiah piped up, "I will put some water on for tea, unless you would prefer coffee, ma'am."

Jennifer looked at him. "Either will be fine, Mr. Liman, please do not trouble yourself. Julia and Jim have done so much already."

Isaiah looked relaxed and replied, "I know of few problems in the world that a good cup of tea cannot help, maybe not fix, but definitely help. Besides, Jennifer, I know Julia well enough to know that after drinking army coffee she is desperate for a good cup of tea."

Julia laughed at this last. "Isaiah, keep that up and I will have to think about leaving John for you." This said she grasped her husband's hand to let him know she would never leave him. John smiled knowing all too well that she had been poking fun at him.

Jennifer looked a bit shocked at this exchange before she realized that Julia had been making a joke at her husband's expense.

He looked at his friend and comrade's back and said, "Just to be safe Isaiah, I think you had better give me some lessons on the art of proper tea brewing."

Isaiah replied over his shoulder, "Sure thing, Major, I have one female to worry about and that is enough."

Julia thought back to her conversation with Sarah in Buffalo and was not sure about that statement.

After the tea was served for Father Peter, Carl, Isaiah and the ladies along with coffee for John and Adam, everyone took a seat and looked at Jennifer. Julia opened the conversation, "Jennifer, would you please recount what happened out on your farm for my husband and the rest of the..." here she hesitated just a second, "research team," she finished.

Jennifer looked tired, but taking a sip of the tea as if indeed there was some kind of life support contained in the old stained china mug, started to tell her tale. "It was a usual day. I was out back hanging up some laundry with Jenny while Little Paul was stacking some firewood when we heard the animals getting riled up. We did not know what was going on, but Paul, my brother, came out of the barn and went in the house and got his rifle. That is when we saw it!" At this point Jennifer started to break down and began to have a panic attack. Julia and Father Peter went to sit on either side of her holding her and speaking softly to her so that after a minute or so she recovered enough to take another sip of the tea and begin again. "I am sorry, it was just so horrible!"

John spoke quietly to her, "It is all right Jennifer, we all have been through some rough, scary times." John thought back to when he had helped to load a badly injured Julia into the landing basket of the dirigible, thinking she was dying. "Just take your time and relax. If you need, we can talk tomorrow, but if at all possible I would like to do it now while it is still as fresh as possible in your mind."

Jennifer took a deep breath and started again. "Thank you, all. As I was saying, Paul came out with his rifle and an extra which he handed to me. I am not much of a shot but I can handle it if needed. That is when we saw it coming over the ridge behind the house. At first I thought it was some kind of a white or pink buffalo, it was that big!" She stopped for a minute to gather herself and then taking another sip of the tea went on. "But it was no buffalo; it ran down one of the cows tearing a huge chunk out of its neck. God, there was blood shooting everywhere." She gasped a lungful of air and then continued, the rest coming out in a rush as if she was almost vomiting the memory like someone does when they have eaten bad food. "It did not stop there. It went for our other cow that was running away. Dear God it was fast! Before the poor thing had gotten fifty feet, that thing was on it, knocking it down and tearing it apart. It was fast, strong and brutal. Paul yelled for me to grab the kids and head for the barn and lock ourselves in." She stopped again. Peter took the tea from her before she spilled it as she started to shake once again. Peter stroked her arm while making gentle, quieting noises to her. It took a while but she managed to get her shaking under control. She resumed her story again, slower this time, her panic beginning to subside. Taking the tea back from Peter she took another sip and went on, "I got the kids into the barn and latched the door shut then braced it with some old fence posts that were in there. I could hear Paul shouting at it and firing his rifle. I heard something being smashed; that must have been when it knocked the house down. That was the house I had built with my husband, now it is gone, just like him!" The woman broke down sobbing.

Julia took a minute to talk quietly to Jennifer, "It is all right, your children are alive and that is something you made with your husband too."

Jennifer looked at Julia and cried a bit more. "You are right, thank you." She closed her eyes took another deep breath and opening her eyes went on, "I heard a number of shots then nothing until something, I can only think it was the creature, slammed into the barn. It must have known we were in there, smelled us or something. Anyhow I thought we were done for and I fired a couple of times. I have no idea if I hit it or not. Then it stopped. The next thing I heard was something pulling at the boards of the barn and I fired. Lucky for your wife I fired too high. That is all I know, until I heard Jim's voice saying it was all right, it was gone and they were going to get us out."

John and the others looked at Julia and Tinsman. Julia replied simply, "The sergeant, Jim Botkins; he knew the family. He talked Jennifer and the children out."

John went over to Julia and knelt before her. "She fired at you; that is what you meant about my teasing you about your height? Julia, I may tease you but you are perfect, just the way you are." Now it was John's turn to envision a life without the woman he loved beside him.

Just then there was a knock on the door and the corporal came in. "Found some quarters for you with one of the ladies in the village, Mrs. Swenson. I can take you there if you are ready, ma'am."

Jennifer looked at the team. "Thank you all for listening to me. I best collect my children and mourn my brother. We will have to figure out how to start all over again. One would think I should be getting good at it, first my husband and now my brother."

Father Peter smiled sadly as he rose to help her stand. "Some things never get any easier, Jennifer, no matter how often we have to repeat them."

She returned the look. "Thank you, Father. For a Catholic you are quite nice. I shall keep your activities from the archbishop," trying her best under the circumstances to return the humor he had started with back on the parade ground.

Carl stood up. "If you do not mind the company, I will walk with you so we know where to find you in case we have any more questions later."

She looked up at Carl. "Thank you, Mr. Jordan. If you do not mind I could use help transporting some of our personnel items to our lodging. I do not know how I will even pay for it."

John spoke up, "It is all right, Jennifer, I have some discretionary funds available from the museum to aid in our research. I think your story should count toward that end."

Jennifer looked relieved and turned to follow the corporal out with Carl close behind she said a weeping thank-you to John.

As the door closed, John looked at his wife. "You were almost shot again, Julia, you have to be more careful. This is getting to be more than my nerves can handle!" This was said as John was still kneeing in front of Julia.

Julia shook her head, "Now dearest, I was not hit, not even close. The bullet missed me by at least four inches so it really does not count. Now behave." With that she kissed him on his nose and touched his forehead with hers. Straightening back up she smiled and said to the rest, "And what did the rest of you come up with?"

Tinsman spoke up and related the visit to Curtis's homestead.

It was Father Peter who spoke next. "Was that all you found?"

Then Julia smiled, "I have sketches and measurements that I took, John. I thought they might be of help." She opened her lady's bag, her one concession to being a female while dressed in pants, work shirt and boots. Pulling out a stack of papers she handed them to John who got up and took the papers over to a table and began to study them.

While John was studying Julia's field notes and sketches, Father Peter told her, Tinsman and Adam about the trip to the Nez Perce village and the strange cave. He emphasized that whatever made it was a machine, a very large and powerful machine, and not an animal.

Julia took all this in and asked the question that had been forming in all their minds, "It would seem that we have two totally different problems, or are they somehow related, and if so, how?" The rest of the team, or such as were there, was asking the same question.

It was some time later that Sarah rejoined the group, after saying goodbye to the children and Molly. Isaiah, seeing his daughter, looked at her and said, "What were you doing on a horse, young lady? I thought I told you no riding!"

Sarah smiled at her father. "No, Poppa, you said I could not go out with Julia and the patrol because I did not know how to ride very well, actually at all. When I thought about it I decided you were right. Now remember, Poppa, you said we should always get paid for our work. Do you remember when I told you I made a new friend? Molly is the person I fixed the cash register for. She did not have any money but her father is in the cavalry and she is an excellent horsewoman, so in exchange she is teaching me how to ride. Payment in barter."

Isaiah snorted; not at all sure it was safe. He did however grudgingly admit that that was what he said. His daughter was growing up much too fast! He was struck by a scary thought that the way she was thinking and arguing she might grow up to study law and become a lawyer; in his mind that would be even worse than an actress, which had been his main concern in Los Angeles.

Julia smiled at her little sister. "Very good, Sarah, soon we shall be able to take rides together."

Both John and Isaiah looked up. "Not with whatever this beast is that we are out here to put a stop to!" thus spoke John while Isaiah shook his head in agreement. Both men looked very firm.

Julia sighed, "Yes, dear, just around the fort, my love."

Again John and Isaiah looked less then sure, as both had a burning question about what the phrase "just around the fort" meant to Julia who tended to take some very liberal definitions about such things. It was Isaiah who replied this time, "We will see about that."

It was somewhat later when Carl finally returned after helping Jennifer and her family to their temporary quarters. He explained to Mrs. Schmidt that the museum would pay for the family's lodging since Jennifer had helped them with their research project. The woman seemed happy at this although she would have taken the family in at no cost to the army, based upon simple Christian charity, however, being a widow she could well use the extra coin.

Carl's arms were a bit tired since he had helped carry a pile of the family's belongings to the house but he did not mind. He felt good; it was nice to be able to help someone without worrying about Redcoats over his shoulder. The family looked like it could use all the help it could get after what it had been through the last several years, especially including an Indian War.

The team again went over everything trying to figure out what they were up against. John told them he would talk to Colonel Washburn and suggest that he should increase the size of his patrols. He knew Washburn would be worried about where to find the additional men, his force was being stretched thin as it was. Besides the increased patrolling, they should alert all the outlying farms and ranches. Father Peter suggested that they inform Strong Bear about what they had found. It might help to keep a lid on the growing trouble with the tribe.

Julia asked John "Did the sketches and measurements I brought back help at all, dear?"

John shook his head, "Yes and no, Julia. They are like nothing I have ever seen before. Thanks to you, my love, I at least have some idea of the speed and weight of this creature. Although the rancher, Curtis you said his name was?, was right about one thing, they are probably from the same family as pigs. The shape and stride pattern are very similar. However, whatever made these prints had to weigh in the nine hundred pound or better range from the depth of the prints you measured. Are you sure the ground was dry, Julia?"

Julia looked at John. "Quite sure. During our conversation over coffee Curtis mentioned that they had not had any significant rain in two weeks, so the ground was definitely dry. Why do you ask, John?"

John ran his hand over his face, "Because if the ground was damp that might have explained the extra depth of the print, but if it was as dry as you say, we are dealing with a very large exceptionally fast creature. Obviously a carnivore at or near the top of the food chain. A very dangerous animal. The questions are now, where did it come from, where did it go and how many more are we dealing with?"

It was apparent that no one had any answers. The team decided that they may as well get some rest and see what tomorrow might bring. Julia whispered to Sarah that she wanted to spend some time with John. Sarah just smiled and nodded.

A little later John was holding Julia close because they both seemed to need the warmth and comfort of the other and the fact that army bunks were none too wide. Julia snuggled into her husband and whispered, "Why, sir, are you holding me so tightly?"

John whispered back, "I do not want you to fall on the floor, I mean for someone your height it could be quite a drop down."

With that comment Julia punched him in the ribs and then tried to snuggle even closer. They were like that as they fell asleep.

CHAPTER 16

A New Day
And New Problems

The day started out with Sarah making breakfast. Isaiah wanted to help, however, Sarah, mindful of her father's skills in the kitchen, or more accurately the lack thereof, managed very gently, keeping in mind Julia's advice about letting men think they were in charge, to have him brew the tea and make coffee, meanwhile she got Jason to help with the grunt work. Before long the team settled down to a delightful breakfast feast.

As they sat around the table, Father Peter was truly enjoying himself and looked at Sarah with a grin, then turned to Isaiah. "Remember what I told you about some young fellow wanting to steal your daughter away? After tasting her cooking you will truly have to mount a substantial guard detail, my friend. Sarah, that was an excellent meal. I dare say, Mrs. Kelly my housekeeper, could not have done better." Sarah blushed and smiled.

The rest of the team agreed. Julia leaned over and whispered to her, "Sarah, the eggs were wonderful. You are going to have to teach me how you fixed them. I am afraid cooking was not a strong subject at the school except for special subjects." Sarah smiled. She was always impressed by her big sister and the thought that she could teach her something just thrilled her. Of course what Sarah did not know was that the "special subjects" were how to disguise the scents and flavors of various poisons and knockout drops. In general, these skills were not considered useful for making husbands happy according to *Mrs. Proctor's Guide for Young Housewives*. That had been a gift, although a bit of a joke from Marie who was just about her only friend from the finishing school. Julia had hoped that Marie could be part of her wedding party but she was on a mission at the time.

The team had pretty much finished and were lingering over a second cup of coffee or extra bit of tea when there was a knock on the door. Jason being the closest immediately went to answer it. When the door opened Lieutenant Dasson was standing there. Stepping into the room he nodded to Morton and said to the assembly, "I hate to interrupt your breakfast, but the colonel asked me to escort Professor Morton to his office at once."

Morton looked up at this. "Please relax for a minute Lieutenant, we were just finishing up and then I will fetch my jacket and we can be off. Did the colonel say what this was about?"

"No, sir, although I got the impression that time is of the essence. The colonel was quite agitated."

John frowned at this. "Julia, I think you might want to join us if you do not mind, my dear," as he pulled on his jacket and then picked up Julia's cape to ward off the early morning chill before the day warmed up.

Julia smiled and standing up turned her back so John could put her cape over her shoulders. She spoke to her husband, "Shall we, my love." With that she put her arm in John's and they turned to follow the young officer out the door. As the door closed behind them the rest of the team looked at each other and wondered what was going on now.

The walk to the colonel's office was brief and the lieutenant held open the door for them. He came to attention and saluted his commander. "Professor and Mrs. Morton, sir."

Washburn returned the salute. "At ease, Paul. I think you better stay for this."

The Mortons looked at each other and then at Washburn. "I assume there is a problem, Colonel?" asked John for the both of them.

Washburn let out a sigh. He started in, "First of all, Paul," addressing the young officer, "there is more to this scientific party then meets the eye. I am sorry I could not let you know sooner, but it was on a need-to-know basis. However, I think things have come to a point where you need to now know. They are part of a special unit that was sent out here to look into what has been going on. Wherever the orders came from it was very high up in the War Department hierarchy, VERY high up!"

Dasson smiled. "I thought there was something going on, sir. The fact that almost all of them had extensive military experience, including a priest, and their tinker, who is a genius. Also from what Sergeant Bodkins told me, Mrs. Morton seems to handle weapons and field conditions far better than would be expected of a shy, eastern, big-city secretary, from a museum no less."

Julia smiled and nudged her husband. "A possible future recruit John. Very observant, Lieutenant." She smiled at the young officer.

The colonel did not look happy. "Please Mrs. Morton; Paul is a fine young officer so I would appreciate you poaching someone else's command."

Julia smiled again at the post commander and replied in her most innocent young girl voice, "Colonel, you certainly cannot blame a girl for trying, sir."

Washburn looked somewhat less than soothed by Julia's reply and continued, "They are indeed a scientific party. I had an old army comrade who is retired and now lives in New York do a little checking. The professor is apparently quite well-known in scientific circles for his research and there is a lot of good-natured gossip at the museum about him having a torrid affair with his beautiful secretary and archivist."

Julia smiled at this last comment and put her arm through John's. While John mumbled something about Kramer and his teasing, Julia asked John, "Indeed, sir, just who is this woman?"

The colonel seemed to think this had filled Paul in enough, so he lost the somewhat lighter air that he was using up till now. "I received word from Strong Bear that there are big problems and he wanted you back out there."

Morton looked serious. "Did he say what or give any hint?"

Washburn shook his head. "No, but it was obvious that whatever it is, it is something big and also very bad news."

As Washburn finished this they could faintly hear a cry from the guard at the gate of a wagon approaching. In mere minutes there was a knock at the door. "Enter," growled the colonel.

A young corporal stood there and saluted. "Sir, Sergeant Bodkins told me to fetch this fellow up to see you, says it might be related to the attack on the Swenson place." They could see a tall and strongly built, grizzled rancher behind the corporal.

The man strong-armed the soldier out of the way. "Let me through, sonny!" The man barged into the room in an obviously highly agitated state.

"What is the meaning of this, sir?" From his tone it was obvious that the colonel was not amused by the rude interruption.

The man did not seem fazed at all by the outburst. "You the ramrod of this here outfit?"

The colonel looked extremely put out. "That is what the sign on the door says," he replied trying to control his temper.

The man took off his hat and for the first time seemed to realize where he was. "Sorry General, my name is Mark Lemat. You gotta take a look at what I kilt this morning; I got it out in the wagon."

Washburn seemed ready to explode. "It is Colonel and you broke into my office in the middle of a meeting because you want me to look at your hunting trophy?"

It was Morton who realized that there may be more to this interruption, remembering what the corporal said about Sergeant Bodkins sending the man over to the fort's commander who was so annoyed at the interruption that he was not putting the pieces together. "What are you going on about, Mr. Lemat?"

The man looked sheepish but firm as he responded to Morton. "Looky here mister, I did not mean to disturb your meetin' here, but this ostrich thing kilt three of my head this morning and tried to get one of my hands to boot afore I was able to bring it down."

Julia looked at the man "An ostrich you say, sir?"

Mark Lemat looked at her. "Yes, ma'am, I seen a picture of one in a big pitchur book in the library back in the city once when my pa took me when I was just a kid. They are a kind of a big bird."

Julia smiled at the man, trying to put him at ease. "I am familiar with them, sir, but I do not believe they are carnivorous, at least not to the point of attacking cattle."

Lemat looked confused. "I do not know about the carnivus part, ma'am, but this one was a killer who surely eats meat."

At this outburst the four persons looked suddenly interested. Morton was the first to respond, "Indeed, Mr. Lemat, if you would be so kind to as to show us your rather interesting trophy." As the party started for the door of the office, Morton turned to Washburn. "Colonel, if you do not mind, I would appreciate it if the corporal here would fetch the rest of my team." The young enlisted man was standing off to the side where Lemat had pushed him.

Washburn nodded to the corporal, "If you would, Samuels, please fetch the rest of Professor Morton's team." The corporal hastily saluted and dashed off in the direction of the quarters John and Julia had recently left.

As they approached the farm wagon they could see the back was filled with something, although there was a tarp covering it so that it was a bit of a mystery, although the tarp had bloody patches on it. They gathered around and Morton could see his team approaching from the temporary quarters. Lemat wasted no more time undoing some ropes that held the tarp in place and pulled the covering off the mound in the back of the wagon. All that could be heard was a sharp intake of breath for there lay an enormous bird approximately ten feet in length. The beak was as big as a farmer's sickle and looked just as dangerous. The eyes were huge and set well toward the front like a predator would have. The feet ended in vicious looking claws that appeared as if they could rip out a man's guts without even trying. Its colors ranged from gray to bright red. Lemat looked at them. "I had to empty all eight rounds from my repeater into that damn thing to bring it down. Thought Jimmy was a goner for sure!" He swallowed and looked at Julia saying, "Ah, sorry, ma'am, for my language."

Julia looked ashen. "No need to apologize, Mr. Lemat, I think confronted with this, I might tend to use a few strong words myself."

The rest of the team arrived and were staring down at the sight of the giant bird. Jason was the first to speak, "If that thing can fly and spread out over the territory, we are in a whole lot of trouble!"

By this time Morton had climbed up into the wagon and was examining the bird. "I doubt that it can fly, Jason, the wings are way too small for the lift needed. They are most probably used for balance and to give it better control of direction while running down prey." Now muttering to himself, "It must be extraordinarily maneuverable." Speaking up he went on, "That beak must be its primary weapon, but needless to say, these claws, given the power by the look of the leg muscles, must look like one of McCormick's reapers in action."

Peter looked at the bird. "Dear God, where did this come from? First a pig from hell itself and now a bird from someone's nightmare. John, what are we dealing with?"

The colonel finally recovered his composure after seeing the bird. It was one thing dealing with Confederate troops charging your position or even trying to flank Indian warriors who were so amorphous as to seemingly have no flank at all, but this had shaken him to his core. "Mr. Lemat, I apologize for my outburst in the office; this indeed was worth interrupting me for." He did not look at the rancher as he said this but continued to stare at the strange and horrible sight in the wagon as if he were mesmerized.

Morton jumped down off the wagon and used a piece of the canvas tarp to try to wipe some of the dirt and blood off his hands. "Mr. Lemat, would it be too much of an imposition to ask you to take your wagon down to the train station? Our train is there on the siding and I would like to do an autopsy on this, whatever it is, so that we have some idea of what we are dealing with."

The farmer looked at him. "Sure, Mister, as long as the government is taking me seriously. Who are you anyhow, and do a what?"

Morton smiled. "I am sorry. I guess with all the excitement we did not make any introductions. I want to open it up and study it." With that

John then introduced his team and how they were a museum scientific party from back east. After this he finally let Washburn and Dasson introduce themselves.

Lemat went forward to climb up onto the wagon, but hesitated. Looking over his shoulder at Morton, "Look-a-here Professor, I am not a greedy man or nothing, but I do not suppose there would be any reward for this here specimen thing, did you call it? I mean it did take down three of my best steers." He looked hopefully at Morton.

John looked at Julia for a second to see her give her head a brief nod of approval. "I think that the museum would most certainly feel that an appropriate finder's fee would be a legitimate cost for such an interesting specimen, sir."

Lemat seemed to breathe a sigh of relief and climbed up onto the seat of the wagon. "Thanks, Professor. Like I said, I am not a greedy man but it is tough making ends meet out here you know."

Morton smiled. "If you do not mind some passengers, Adam, Jason, please accompany Mr. Lemat and unload our feathered nightmare here into the laboratory car." Jason hopped into the back of the wagon while Adam climbed up to sit next to the rancher. With everyone seated, Lemat gave the reins a shake, and with a giddy-up the wagon started for the gate facing toward the station and was soon passing out of sight.

Sarah, who had been standing quietly through the whole exchange, looked at Julia and said, "I hope those things are not too common. I have no idea where I would find an oven big enough to cook it."

The whole team looked shocked for a moment and then broke into laughter. Julia looked over at Sarah, hugged her and said, "Indeed little sister, I think even your consummate skills would be taxed with that as the main course, not to mention I think you would have to put the entire rest of us together to make enough stuffing."

As the group paused to recover from this bit of tension-relieving levity, Washburn cleared his throat, "John, I know you would like to have a look at that bird, but Strong Bear was most insistent that you come out to the reservation as soon as possible. Something has him highly spooked in a serious way. Things are dicey enough as it is."

John looked up. "Indeed Colonel. Julia, would you please start taking some measurements and notes for me. I will take Isaiah, Peter and Carl with me. Carl can show Isaiah the cave; I would like his thoughts on it. Father Peter seems to have reached out to Strong Bear and the rest of the tribe, so I think he would help. And to be honest, we have no idea what we are dealing with, so I think both Isaiah and I would feel much better if you and Sarah were in, or at least near, the fort. If you do plan on any trips, take Tinsman and Sam with you. Otherwise, I would like them to take a patrol and look over the area near the homesteads and see if they can pick up any more information."

Julia looked at her husband and while she smiled at him she was thinking that, like him objecting to her carrying her derringer, John was being silly. "Yes, dear. Sarah and I will hide behind the fort's walls and stay safe."

John, looking like a worried husband, "Julia it is not that I think you cannot manage to handle anything on two feet, but to be honest there are things here that are not making any sense at all. And we still have no idea about what made the original tunnel." Stepping close he looked down at her. "I told you once before, Julia Morton, I need you in my life!"

Julia smiled up at her husband. "I love you too John and be careful. Likewise, I need you in my life you tall, silly man. I saw the look on Jennifer's face at the homestead when she told me about losing her husband. I do not want to lose you." She reached up on tiptoes and whispered in John's ear, "Besides, I like falling asleep on you."

John did not care who was watching, he hugged his wife. "We will be back. Sarah, just for the record, no turkey for dinner." Sarah laughed and nodded.

The meeting broke up and the four men went to the stables to obtain horses and tack while Dasson went to form a small detail to accompany them. Julia and Sarah headed off in the direction of the train to begin the examination of the strange bird that was waiting in the laboratory car for them.

As Julia and Sarah made their way into the laboratory car, they found Jason and Adam waiting there not quite sure what to do. The ladies dismissed the men, although they told them to stay close in case they needed some muscle power. Julia turned up the gas lamps and found aprons and gloves for Sarah and herself. Looking at Sarah, she gently spoke to her, "Are you sure you want to do this? It is not the best way to spend a day." Julia was worried that Sarah would be upset with the blood and handling of the dead bird.

Sarah smiled at her and replied, "I do not see it as any worse than getting a goose ready for Christmas dinner, although, just between the two of us I never thought about doing one this big!"

Julia laughed and decided that little sister Sarah was going to be all right. The ladies set to work. Most of the time Julia took measurements and Sarah, as the expedition's assistant archivist, duly recorded them in a field notebook in a precise hand. There were times, however, when Julia needed help simply because the creature was too big for her to reach the needed measurements. Twice she had to send Sarah to ask Adam and Jason to help reposition the bird. All this took time. During all this, Sarah tried her best, which was really quite good, to make sketches of the various features of the bird.

Several hours later, Sarah stretched to loosen the muscles in her back where she had been tense during all the measurement recording and sketching. Julia looked at her and smiled. "I think you are right, there is not a lot more we can do without opening this creature up and I know John wants to do that. However, it may be a while before the men get back. I suggest we have Adam and Jason go down and get some ice from the ice house on the siding. Thank God for the railroad using ice for shipping produce. It should help to preserve this creature and hold down the smell." With that the ladies removed their aprons and gloves. Standing on the Laboratory Car's end platform, Julia told the two young agents what she wanted and they disappeared while the girls decided that since they were on board anyhow a hot bath in their compartment sounded quite like a bit of heaven.

CHAPTER 17

A STRANGE THEORY

While Sarah and Julia began the work on the strange and deadly bird, the men saddled up and started on their ride to the reservation and Strong Bear's village. The party consisted of the four team members and Lieutenant Dasson and his three troopers. Once again, Dasson wanted to keep the party small so that the natives did not feel it was some sort of invasion. Shortly thereafter Tinsman and Sam left with a detail to sweep the area near Jennifer's homestead.

The ride toward the reservation was quiet, much like the first time the team had gone to meet with the Nez Perce. Carl rode up next to Paul Dasson. "I assume we are being watched again?"

Dasson smiled. "Spotted four so far so I think it is a safe enough bet. Are you nervous again?"

Carl replied, "Not so much but still I do have the sensation of riding into an enemy camp."

Dasson shrugged. "It was not always so; the Nez Perce where a peaceful people till they started getting pushed off their ancestral lands. It did not have to be like this but greed always seems to find a way."

Carl looked thoughtful for a minute "I well understand that Lieutenant; I have seen it all too close up. Let us hope we can resolve this before any more blood is shed."

Dasson seemed curious. "Where did you see it, Carl?" He wondered since he had never thought of Pennsylvania as a hot bed of such problems.

It was Father Peter who answered the young man's question, "Paul, indeed there are those everywhere who do not care about anyone else's problems or suffering, just feeding their own perceived needs."

Carl was indeed happy for the Father's timely interruption since it gave him a chance to think before he started to talk about the Welsh problems. Instead he added, "Poor quality and weak mine timbers for top dollar among other things, Lieutenant." He thought this would satisfy the young officer.

The hours and miles went by. It was late afternoon when the party arrived at the village. Strong Bear came out to meet them. The party dismounted and after the briefest of greeting, Strong Bear ordered them to follow him.

The men looked at each other; they could feel the tension and fear in the village. It was both directed at them but not directed at them as if the villagers were trying to determine if they were behind whatever the problem was. They followed Strong Bear and several other members of the tribe out of the village a short distance and then into another clearing with a single lodge in it.

Stopping, Strong Bear turned and looked at them, "Morton, I need to know if your people did this." It was obvious the Nez Perce chief was shaken to his core. John and the rest remembered what the colonel had told them, *"Nez Perce do not get spooked"*. Finally, Strong Bear seemed to regain his thoughts and went on, "Strong Elk came back to the village yesterday feeling sick and his face had changed. When his wife awoke this morning this is what she found where he had been sleeping." He pulled back the flap and they went in. There was a collective gasp from the men. There on the pallet lay not quite a man. Although the creature was clothed in Indian garments, he looked far more brutish, with heavy eye ridges and a thick nose.

Father Peter, stunned, mumbled, "Dear God in heaven, what is that?"

Strong Bear spoke from behind him, "That is my friend."

Morton sank to one knee and began to examine the creature, or man, or former man. He was unsure in his own mind how to refer to him.

The man on the pallet opened his eyes and tried to speak, but the words spoken in the Nez Perce tongue were garbled as if his mouth could not properly form all the sounds. Strong Bear moved closer and leaned over his friend trying to make out what he was saying.

After a short time the creature closed his eyes and appeared to go back to sleep.

Morton looked at the chief. "Were you able to make out what he was saying, anything at all?"

Strong Bear stood up and motioned for them to step outside. When they were outside he stated, "I made out some of what he was saying; he was confused and his speech was hard to understand, it was as if he could not form the words. I am not sure of it at all. The best I could make out was he had explored a new cave with a yellow haze in it. He saw several strange animals near it that he had never seen before." The old Indian looked up at the sky as if in prayer and then went on, "I was able to make out the general location of this cave but that was about all. His thoughts were rambling. It was as if he were struggling to control himself. His emotions were like one in the grip of a fever."

John stood there with a look on his face were one could see him trying to put all the pieces of this puzzle together. As they walked back toward the village, Morton spoke to Peter in a low voice, "Peter, do you remember how we found Chin and Ulrich using their serum to push up evolution on the Ratten?"

Peter, making the Sign of the Cross, replied in a similar soft voice, "It is hardly something one would forget, John, why?"

John, looking worried, replied, "Because, I think we are seeing the opposite of it here, Peter."

Peter's head jerked up and in a somewhat louder voice he replied, "John, what are you saying?"

Hearing this, the party stopped and all faces turned toward Morton. "Indeed, Professor Morton, what are you saying?" asked Strong Bear. "Do you have an idea about what happened to my friend?"

Morton looked nervous. "There are certain details that I am not at liberty to reveal, but during a previous encounter we saw that it was possible to speed up evolution. In other words, make species smarter and more civilized. The pig from hell and the giant bird that was brought into the fort seem to be earlier versions of the creatures we are familiar with today. Your friend, Strong Bear, has the features of an earlier version of a proto-human. I think we are dealing with something or someone who has found a way to reverse evolution and create earlier versions of various creatures, including man."

Dasson looked stunned and then said, "Are you sure, I mean evolution is just a theory is it not? I mean it is not what the Good Book says."

Peter looked at the young officer. "Paul, it says God made the world in seven days. However, you have to ask yourself, what is a day to God who was and is and evermore will be?"

John looked at the young officer. "It is not universally accepted, Paul, but it is getting there. So far it is the theory that best fits the facts. However, it came to me that I had read an article in one of my scientific journals that when a fellow researcher discovered the bones of a giant pig, he dubbed it a 'Hell Pig'. I think what attacked Jennifer's homestead was just such an animal, an animal that died out thousands of years ago or longer. The bird that Mr. Lemat brought to the fort today looks like some kind of early ostrich, again a creature that has never been seen before. Finally, Strong Bear, your friend is definitely reverting to an earlier form of man. We have found such in the fossil record." Morton stopped and took a deep breath and went on, "Gentlemen, I think the theory fits the facts in an all-too-terrifying manner. We are seeing some sort of devolution at work here; and quite frankly I am scared. So far the creatures we have seen are manageable but some of the species that have been found would be a far different proposition."

"What kind of things are you talking about Professor?" asked Dasson.

John looked at the rest of the small group. "The kind that weigh in the multiple-tons range and have appetites to match. So far the pig and the strange bird, not to mention your friend Strong Bear, are, speaking in geological terms, quite recent, but if this continues there are far more dangerous creatures that we could encounter; the kind of monsters that rifles will not stop. In fact, they would in all probability just make them mad, if they noticed at all. We would need field artillery."

The men looked stricken. Carl managed to ask, "John, please tell me you are just joking."

Morton shook his head. "It is no joke, Carl. We have to stop this, and to do that we have to find the cave with the yellow mist. At least I hope that is what the source of these regressive creatures is so we can seal it up. Because if we do not, mankind may be fighting for its very existence."

The group returned to the village. Strong Bear said they would watch Strong Elk and let Morton know of any changes. Dasson told him they would have the fort physician come out to look at him. The Nez Perce seemed conflicted over the idea but grudgingly gave their assent; then the party mounted up and headed back to the fort. The side trip to the original cave forgotten in the face of these new revelations.

It was becoming apparent to all that time was very much not on their side.

They arrived at the fort just as darkness was falling. They dismounted and left the enlisted men to handle the horses while the team went in with Dasson to brief the colonel. It was not a happy meeting.

After listening to Morton, Washburn exploded. "Morton, have you lost your mind? This is utter poppycock, men turning into some kind of monkeys or apes! This is craziness!" The colonel was erupting as they recounted what they had seen. "Lieutenant, do you expect me to believe any of this?"

Paul Dasson looked as forlorn as a man could be, visualizing the end of his career in the army. "Sir," he stood up, almost at attention, and looking as firm and serious as he could said, "I thought the same thing, but you did not see Strong Elk! He was not human anymore, sir." Almost shaking he took a deep breath, "I know how crazy this sounds but that man or creature, whatever, was not a man anymore. I do not know about this evolution and devolution theory the professor is talking about, but something changed that Indian. Something bad, sir!"

The colonel took a breath, and trying to calm himself, walked over to the sideboard in his office and poured himself a hefty shot of whisky in a tumbler. He motioned to the others to avail themselves. No one took him up on the offer. After taking a gulp he turned and spoke as if to the room rather than the group in front of him, "All right, Morton, I know you come highly recommended but this theory is preposterous; however, Paul is a fine officer and clearly sober, so I have to take his word for the fact that something is changing men and animals out there, and not for the better." He paused and a noticeable amount of whiskey was drained from the glass. "What do we do about it, whatever 'it' is?"

Morton looked at the colonel. "We find whatever it is and destroy it or seal it off. We have to before this nightmare spreads. Right now it is contained in a small area but the longer it goes on the worse it will get. I am also concerned that the longer it goes on the greater will be the change. As I told the others, what we have seen so far is manageable but there are things that could be in quite a different category altogether." The colonel did not look reassured at this last statement, and less so as Morton described some much earlier and much larger creatures from the museum's collection.

Dinner that night brought a planning session. John started by asking what each of the principals had in mind. Carl and Isaiah still wanted to take a look at the tunnel; they had since stopped calling it a cave. The discovery in the Indian village had completely knocked the idea of going on their last foray out of the picture, so they planned on a trip the next day. Julia stated that she wanted to go out to the homestead to see if she could find any more information about the creature that had attacked it and that Jennifer had told her that she wanted to go to check on the property when Julia looked in on her and the children. Sarah said she too would like to go with Julia and Jennifer.

Needless to say Isaiah was less than thrilled at this plan. "I thought I told you that you could not go, Sarah," he stated firmly.

Sarah looked at him. "Poppa, that was because I was not a good enough rider, but Molly has been teaching me. In fact she has been going over jumping with me." Sarah smiled at this.

Isaiah looked like he was trying to decide between exploding or having heart failure at this statement from his daughter. "What do you mean, she was teaching you jumping!"

Sarah smiled at her father as innocently as possible. "Molly said I am already a good rider and excellent horsewoman, and they were just small jumps, nothing too high. I was fine, Poppa."

Julia smiled at Isaiah. "Isaiah, I watched Sarah practice. She is a fine horsewoman, why she looks as if she was born in the saddle. I think it would be all right if she came along. You have no idea how much help she is in the field."

Isaiah looked thunderheads at Julia. "You knew she was jumping and you did not stop her? As for this going out into the field with monsters on the loose, there is no way that is going to happen!"

Julia calmly replied, "I watched her with Molly. Not only is Molly a highly talented rider but she is an outstanding teacher. Isaiah, you do not think for a minute that if my sister was in danger I would have put a quick stop to such activity?"

Meanwhile Carl seemed to be uncomfortable with the idea of the ladies going out there and voiced some concern. Turning to Carl Julia said, "Jennifer wants to check on her homestead, Carl; she is a grown woman. What is your concern?"

Carl looked stunned; maybe it was the fact that he had said anything. He hesitated a moment as if marshaling his thoughts and said, "Julia, it is just that she has been through so much; can you count on her if anything comes up?"

Julia looked thoughtful for a moment and replied, "Carl, the frontier does not tolerate weakness. Jennifer is a strong woman, she can handle it." Julia decided that she needed to talk to Carl after the meeting.

John looked at his friend. "Isaiah, Julia is right, Sarah is a huge help. Tinsman and Sam can go with the ladies and help keep them safe. This

DAVID A. HORNUNG

project is rapidly getting very serious and we will need all the hands we can get. Your daughter is an expert at keeping information straight."

Isaiah looked as dark as a thundercloud, but even he had to acknowledge how talented his daughter is. "All right but you are not going out unarmed. I have something I have been working on that you can use." As he stood he motioned for Sarah to follow him and they left for the train.

Carl also excused himself and said he wanted to check on Jennifer and her children; he got up and went out the door. Julia jumped up and told John she would be right back. She rushed out and called to Carl. He stopped and turned around, waiting for Julia to catch up.

Julia looked at him, and steeling herself, spoke quietly to him, "Carl, one of the things that was drilled into us at the finishing school was that it is bad for teammates to become involved; the mission has to come first."

Carl smiled; it was the same smirky kind of smile he had used when they first met him. "That advice seems odd coming from a married woman, to a teammate no less, unless you are trying to tell me you do not care about John. However, watching you two together I do find that very hard to believe, madam. Secondly, Jennifer and the children are not part of our team."

Julia looked back at him, thinking. After a brief time she simply replied, "Point taken, sir. Please enjoy your evening. However, do keep in mind that missions can put a strain on things and there are most serious events occurring now."

Carl nodded; all traces of the smirk gone. "Thank you, Mrs. Morton. Again, I think John is a very lucky man. I know after seeing Strong Elk, I truly do understand the gravity of the situation and the threat it poses. But I am beginning to care, after far too many years of not being able to nor allowing myself to do so. I have the feeling you did too; at least I believe so after hearing some of Father Peter's stories."

Julia gave a lady-like, "Humph. Father Peter is spending too much time with the churchyard biddies in his parish, picking up bad habits, like gossiping. But I do understand, Carl. Yes, I did begin to care for

John before the mission was over. I did not know how to handle it. That feeling scared me so much knowing that I might have to do something that might harm him or allow him to come to harm in order to see the mission to a successful conclusion. As it was, it was Sarah who taught me how some things can come before a mission. Be careful, sir. Please have a good night."

Carl said good night and turned back in the direction he had been heading and Julia returned to her husband thinking about how the mission had to come first. That *and* what Sarah had taught her.

CHAPTER 18

THE LADIES TAKE A RIDE

he next morning proved to be clear and bright, a most perfect day for a ride. Julia, Jennifer and Sarah set out accompanied by Tinsman, Sam and Adam, in the direction of Jennifer's property. Julia was curious about the strange looking piece of equipment in a rifle scabbard on Sarah's horse.

"Sarah, I have to ask, has your father come up with some new sort of rifle?" Julia was not shy about asking about new weaponry, truly a subject near and dear to her heart. She tried to curb it around John; he never seemed to remind her about those silly male ideas about women not being able to defend themselves but should rely on the men in their life. *Granted*, thought Julia, *some compromises had to be made*. She still favored her thirty-six caliber navy revolver, although it had been modified into a breach loader so that it could handle the new thirty-eight caliber metallic cartridge; much neater and faster on the reload, thank you. She had to admit that although she could use it, the more standard forty-fives that the men favored were a bit much for her both in size and recoil. Her rifle had also been modified. Although a standard Winchester repeating lever-action, Corporal Tinsman had cut down the stock and made some other modifications so she could handle it more easily and accurately. The corporal had disassembled it, then stoned and smoothed the action so it was like skating on an icy pond after he reassembled it. *Very satisfactorily*, thought Julia. Of course she had several varieties of explosives along with her, just in case. One never knew what one might need; a young lady should always be prepared.

Sarah looked over at her. "No, Poppa does not want me to have a gun. If truth be told, I really do not know how to shoot, could you..."

Julia cut Sarah off at this point. "Let us just concentrate on hand-to-hand for now, young lady!"

Sarah looked annoyed but went on, "Well, as I was saying, Poppa did not want me to have a gun so he gave me his new electric stick. He said depending on the setting, it should allow me to fight off any attacker."

Julia looked interested. "An electric stick? What does it do and how does it work? I mean it looks somewhat bulky and cumbersome."

Sarah smiled. "Well, this is supposed to be a test run so to speak, although I really think Poppa does not want me to need it at all; you know Poppa. Anyhow, there are some storage capacitors and batteries in the stock and the mechanism charges it just by the moving of the gun, such as now when we are riding. There is a hand crank that folds into the stock if you are in a hurry to recharge. It delivers an electric shock that can be set by a series of switches in the handle with multiple settings. The stick can be set to sting, stun or kill, as needed. As to the size, this is, as Poppa put it, a prototype. Once he has worked out any possible problems he will make it smaller and easier to carry."

Julia looked intrigued and told Sarah, "Your father is most clever, Sarah. When we take a break can you show it to me?"

Sarah looked delighted at this since showing something new or teaching her big sister something was wonderful, almost magical, as she was convinced that her sister knew just about everything. "You really want me to show it to you, Julia?"

"Indeed, Sarah, you know how I love such things. Although please do not tell John." This last with a look of exasperation on her face.

Sarah smiled and said, "I do not see that as a problem since it is easy to fool men, is it not?" With this reply the two laughed out loud together.

The men ignored the laughter; after all they were womenfolk, even if one of them was the boss, and continued their vigilance. Jennifer spurred her horse and rode closer. "Am I missing something?" she asked with a smile.

Julia was glad to see her smile. It was the first time she had seen that look on Jennifer's face. She thought Jennifer looked quite pretty when she smiled. "No, just some sister stuff. I was asking about the new weaponry that Sarah's father invented."

Jennifer looked at the strange contraption on Sarah's saddle but was more interested in Julia's comment on Sarah. "I hate to be rude, but I am confused, I really do not see much of a family resemblance between you two if you are sisters."

Both Julia and Sarah laughed. Sarah said while trying not to laugh, "It is all right, we get that a lot."

Julia smiled and started to explain, leaving out the classified details. "John and I were on a previous expedition, for the museum, before we were married. Sarah was an orphan living on the streets, as I myself had been. I never even really knew my family; I only had a last name that was found stitched into my clothing, and some vague memories. I was lucky that my uncle found me, took me in, raised me, and saw to my schooling. Anyhow, John insisted that we stop in Buffalo on our way to the research area to find Isaiah. He was attempting to recruit Sarah's father as part of the, eh, research team; they had met during the war. Thankfully, one of Isaiah's inventions saved John's unit during a rebel attack. While we were in Buffalo, one night he rescued Sarah from being used by a group of toughs in Buffalo's Canal District after they beat her senseless. He brought her back to the museum's train and I took care of her. We just bonded, two young orphan girls. Now we are sisters in all but blood."

Jennifer looked even more confused looking at Sarah. "But how are you an orphan, is not Mr. Liman your father?"

Sarah smiled. "I wound up as the assistant archivist on the expedition, thanks to the sponsorship of a certain special lady and a gentleman who said if I was forced to leave he would too." She looked lovingly at Julia who smiled. "Poppa had lost his wife and baby daughter in childbirth several years before all that and as Julia said about us, he and I also bonded over the course of the trip. Julia and the professor were able to help him with the legal stuff and he adopted me when we all got back to Buffalo after the trip. I was very lucky to gain a most wonderful family, as well as a very good, almost too good, an education."

Jennifer looked at her. "Thank you, Sarah. It is nice to know that you can rebuild a life after such losses. If you do not mind me asking, Julia, is that how you met John, at work?"

Julia took a minute to respond, organizing her thoughts trying to make sure nothing classified slipped out. "My uncle's foundation sponsored the original expedition and he most generously recommended me to help keep detailed records of the discoveries. In truth, I think he wanted a spy to make sure his funds were being properly used, that, and he offered to pay my salary. It was, I guess, the adventure of being out in the wild, untamed west with such a handsome and dashing gentleman as John Morton. You could say that he picked me up off my feet, right Sarah?"

Sarah giggled at this and responded with, "I dare say you could describe it like that," trying her best not to laugh out loud, as she recalled that day in her father's store in Los Angeles after they had gone out to warn Cee Cee and her people at the end of the Ratten business.

The miles passed as the small party continued riding toward the destroyed farm. Before long the party arrived at the farmstead. After checking as well as they could and finding nothing immediately dangerous, Tinsman dismounted and began to look for any fresh signs. He had been kneeling, looking at the ground, when he stood up pointing and said, "Looks like the beast went off this way."

Jennifer looked at the remains of her home as she dismounted and saw nothing but the wreckage, all that was left of her home! She heard Tinsman's statement and shaking her head spoke, "Let us see if we can follow it. I want a chance to get even with the thing that destroyed my home, attacked and tried to kill my children and myself, and killed my brother!"

Julia hesitated but a moment before nodding to Tinsman. Tinsman remounted and the small party moved out, each of them trying to see what the surrounding brush and dips in the ground might reveal. None of them was taking this lightly. Tinsman kept a good pace as the track was relatively easy to follow. The area had not seen any rain since the attack so the track was still fairly fresh. The trail seemed to wind around and they found several sites where the creature had attacked something and then fed.

After about two hours, the party pulled up short at the sight that greeted them. The remains of the killer that they had been tracking lay scattered around and a totally new set of even stranger and more numerous tracks took over.

Julia was shocked as were the others. The shock was enough to make her forget herself and revert to special agent mode. "Corporal, what do you make of these tracks?"

Tinsman dismounted again and walked around a bit studying the scene before him. "I can only guess, boss. It looks like a pack of something and I am not sure what. Birds or lizards of some kind, based on these tracks, tore this thing up. But it was not without a fight, you may want to take a look at this," he said while pointing to a nearby dip in the ground.

The ladies all dismounted and carrying their various weapons, went over to look at where Tinsman was pointing. In the depression, actually more like a natural ditch or dry stream bed, lay two lizard-like creatures, each about eight or more feet long head to tail, although from the look of them they most probably would have walked on their two hind feet and been about four-and-a-half to five foot tall. The smell was awful and there was a swarm of flies around each of the creatures that were obviously very dead for each had large fearsome looking wounds. The one had its gut opened up and the intestines laying out. Julia talked to Sarah while still staring at the creatures, "I do not think we will be able to get any specimens for John." Shaking her head she looked at the corporal. "How many do you think were in the pack, I guess we would call it, Sam?"

Tinsman, still looking at the scene and the tracks leading away, rubbed his jaw and replied, "Somewhere between seven to eleven I would guess. Pretty hard to tell, boss. The obvious fight messed up the tracks pretty good."

Julia looked thoughtful as she was calculating the odds in her head. "These things look tough but nothing our weapons should not be able to handle. We will follow, but we need to move very carefully. Looking at them and how they are built, not to mention they brought down the pig, they must be fast. Sarah, you better set your electric stick to kill mode, but be careful. I cannot lose my family."

Sara nodded and went back to her horse. Pulling the electric stick out she checked the setting and looked at several gauges to make sure the new weapon was fully charged.

Julia turned and started back to her horse. Jennifer hurried after her. "Julia, a moment please!" Julia stopped and turned back to her. Jennifer wet her lips. "What is going on? You called Mr. Tinsman corporal and he called you boss. You were giving orders like this was a military operation. What are you really? And please do not treat me like an uneducated farm girl."

Julia looked at her and seemed to be weighing her options. Taking a deep breath she started in. "Jennifer, there is much I cannot tell you, but as you have guessed, we are somewhat more than a museum research team. We are that, but let us just say that the funding for this expedition comes from somewhere other than a philanthropic foundation. In fact, it is a Federal Government agency that as far as most people know, deals with other problems of a far more innocuous nature, such as what we are looking at here. Much of the rest we have told you is the truth. John is my husband and I do see Sarah as my sister. But that is about all I can tell you and you did not even hear that from me. Are we clear?"

Jennifer looked at her in shock; however, she seemed to handle it, as noted the frontier did not tolerate the weak. She nodded and started back toward her horse and Julia turned and started in again for hers. Just as Julia was about to mount, Jennifer spoke again, "Is Carl part of your team? What is his story?"

Julia without turning replied, "Yes he is, but only a recent and temporary addition. As to his story, that is up to him to tell you what he wants you to know." After saying that she finished mounting and as soon as Jennifer mounted the party moved out following the new tracks.

CHAPTER 19

THE GENTLEMEN TAKE A RIDE

ith the ladies and their escorts already in the field, Morton, Carl and Isaiah headed out to look for the cave where Strong Elk was changed into whatever it was he was becoming. Meanwhile Jason was left to keep an eye on the "nightmare bird", as Father Peter had christened it. The good father had volunteered to watch Jennifer's children.

The men were quiet as they rode along, each one trying to figure out what had happened and if they would suffer the same fate. John, Carl and Isaiah also wondered if specific ladies were safe, although for all three it was a different woman or girl, in Isaiah's case.

It took several hours to reach the area where as best as could be made out due to his increasing changes, Strong Elk had said the mysterious cave was. The members of the team were sure they were near the correct area as they began to see several strange-looking animals, although so far they had not seen anything that looked too dangerous. They were on edge and each had double-checked their pistols and rifles, just in case. Suddenly the horses started to buck and refused to go forward. Morton told them all to move back toward the way they had come. Some fifty yards later the party pulled up. Morton told Carl to hold the horses while he and Isaiah dismounted, and taking their rifles, began to move slowly and carefully forward. Both men straining to determine what had frightened the horses.

It was Isaiah who first saw the faint movement in the grasses. "Major, up ahead just to the left of that pile of rocks, low down."

Morton slowly turned his head to see the area in question. "I do not see, wait, got it, whatever it is."

Isaiah pulled something out of the haversack he was wearing and put it in his pocket so that it was ready at hand. As he did this the creature, for it was not obvious at first that it was some sort of animal, began to move forward with an undulating, ground-hugging motion. Suddenly a primordial fear gripped the two men. This was a giant snake some twenty-five feet long and at least two feet in diameter at its largest visible point. Morton raised his rifle and fired at the creature's head and body as fast as possible. The rounds struck home, indeed, it was hard not to miss such a large target at that close range. Angered, the giant reptile hissed and reared up, mouth open, ready to strike, when a small device landed in its open mouth. The jaws snapped shut in response to this and not quite two seconds later a blast scattered the head over the immediate area, including the two men. The body thrashed for a bit but soon the violent movement ended and the snake lay quite dead.

Isaiah, his ears ringing from the blast, looked at the blood, brains and viscera covering a good part of himself and muttered, "Perhaps a bit too much of a blast. I think that a full pound of TNT might have been a tad excessive."

Morton, standing there, also well spattered including a bit of snake blood dripping off his nose, replied, "Isaiah, not that I would complain about not becoming that thing's lunch but is there any way next time to be a bit neater about it?"

Isaiah looking around merely mumbled, "I guess I will have to experiment in making these with different capacity charges for various situations." Then in a somewhat louder voice to John, "Still, it did work quite well. I do not know if Julia told you I sent some empty cases with the timers to her to experiment with."

John, looking up in disgust as he attempted to wipe some snake brain off his shoulder, replied, "Indeed Isaiah, I do believe my darling wife showed me the results of her experiments. I still have to finish putting my workshop back together when this is all over."

Isaiah merely raised an eyebrow at this response, and decided wisely not to ask any more questions about his clockwork-detonated explosives casings that he had sent to Julia. He just went back to trying to remove snake debris from himself.

Shortly after this Carl called out, "I think you will have to come back here, the horses will not come any closer."

John returned the hail, "I want to take a look at what we found first. I doubt that we will be able to get it back to the train." Morton started forward, with Isaiah a few paces behind keeping his eyes wide open, since he had seen how absorbed Morton could be when looking at a new discovery. He well remembered the time spent in the Dakota badlands.

Morton looked at the creature, and then proceeded to pace off its length while trying to estimate the girth. When he had done all he could without any proper field equipment he turned to his friend and said simply, "Let us get going, there is not much more I can learn here and we have to find the source of all this."

Isaiah was happy to comply, for even dead the huge snake gave him the shakes, like it would any sane man. His brain wanted to run around in his head being totally irrational. Turning, he started back still keeping an eye out for any other monsters. "Well, what do you think, John?"

Morton looked perplexed. "I honestly do not know Isaiah. It was definitely a snake. Since the head is mostly gone I have no idea if it was poisonous or not. I have never seen anything in the literature about giant snakes in western North America but that does not mean much; there are far too many blank pages in mankind's knowledge of the various life forms in this part of the country, and this is a very sparsely populated area even by the Indians. However, I would guess it was some kind of primitive species, as opposed to just an overly large snake of a type unknown."

Isaiah, still turning his head to try and watch in every direction at once, replied, "What makes you say that?"

John, lost in thought replied, "It looked as if there might have been some vestigial legs, or maybe it was a deformity. But I would venture a guess it was another case of devolution. Given that snakes, at least the ones we know, seem to be territorial I would say we are near the reason for whatever is causing all this."

Isaiah shook his head, and replied, "Is that not a cheery thought."

After using some water from a nearby stream to finish cleaning themselves as best they could, Morton and Isaiah mounted and the trio resumed their search for the cause of the strange animals.

Unknown to them, but much like their ladies' party, they saw several strange animals but no more that looked too dangerous. The day wore on and still they continued their scouting ride. It was about two in the afternoon when they topped a low rise and spied another opening in the side of a hill, much like the first cave, or tunnel, that seemed to start this whole strange business. This time Morton and Carl dismounted, while Isaiah held the horses. In the bright sunlight neither man noted the yellow haze lying near the bottom of the cave's floor. Both men were armed with their rifles and advanced slowly, while Isaiah backed off with their mounts.

The pair entered the opening and Carl looked around. "John, this one is like the first tunnel, man-made, not natural." The cave, or more accurately tunnel, was fairly smooth and quite large in diameter. The floor had traces of tracks indicating that an incredibly powerful boring machine had been at work although these had been somewhat disturbed by a series of other tracks. These were of several types of animals.

John yelled to Isaiah that he and Carl were going to explore a bit. Isaiah continued to scan the area, fervently hoping to spot nothing at all. He thought the snake was more than enough excitement for one day. Isaiah heard a snarl from over the top of the ridge that sent the horses into a nervous bucking. When he looked up he saw the largest cat he had ever seen with fangs that were well over eight inches long and a body that was at least as tall as a man, and well-muscled.

The cat snarled again and the horses took off with Isaiah hanging on to his as tight as he could trying to stay mounted. John and Carl heard the commotion and came out to look, only to see Isaiah and the horses disappearing. Then they heard the cat's savage snarl and both backed into the tunnel to find a defensible position, guns at the ready. The problem with the tunnel was, being relatively smooth and straight, not to mention fairly wide, that there were no really good positions to take. Both men were charged up, their adrenalin pouring into their blood streams, and both were rapidly breathing deeply.

They heard the cat outside the entrance. The beast had obviously gotten their scent but yet it seemed hesitant to enter. They gripped their weapons, but all the while things seemed to be getting fuzzy.

Julia and the rest of her small party resumed trailing the strange tracks of whatever had attacked the killer pig, each person at the ready. The tracks were starting to change direction when Tinsman yelled out upon seeing three horses running full out with Isaiah holding on for dear life on one of them. It was obvious that they had stampeded and that Isaiah had absolutely no control over his horse. Tinsman yelled to Adam to stay with the women even as he and Sam went after Isaiah and the horses. Sarah, on seeing this took off going after her father. By this time the three horses that had been running full out for a bit were quite winded and the three riders were able to rapidly overtake them, with Sarah being the lightest in the lead. Isaiah looked white as a ghost, or as pale as he could ever be, when he looked up to see his daughter holding the horse's bridle as she had reined both horses in.

Sarah looked at him "Poppa, are you all right? What happened? Where are the professor and Carl?" All this seemed to come out in a single breath.

Isaiah sat there trying to catch his breath and regain his composure, simultaneously hoping his heart rate would slow down as he breathed deeply. While this was happening, Tinsman and Sam rode up with the other two horses. Quickly Julia, Jennifer and Adam also arrived.

Before Julia or anyone else could say a word, Isaiah, trying to talk and gulp air at the same time, said, "We have to go back! The professor and Carl are trapped back at a new tunnel!"

Julia and Jennifer both looked stricken; Julia almost yelling to Isaiah as she was fighting panic, "What happened, why did you leave them?"

Isaiah looked at her. "They dismounted to check out the tunnel. John had me stay back with the horses. There was a cat like a puma, saw one that a customer had shot up in the Adirondacks but bigger, at least three or more times bigger than that, with teeth you would not believe!" He paused for a minute gasping for air, "Spooked the horses, I could not get mine under control, was just barely hanging on." Another gulp of air, and looking at Sarah said, "No more complaints about you riding or taking payment in trade. Those lessons came in very handy Sarah." Still breathing deeply, he looked over his shoulder. "We have to go back for the Major and Carl!"

Julia ordered, "Lead on!"

Tinsman and Sam gave the reins of the two extra mounts to Jennifer and the party took off, heading back the way Isaiah had come, at a trot, that being as fast as Isaiah's horse and the other two could manage after their terrified gallop, the extra tracks completely forgotten about for the time being.

The party crested a rise and saw the tunnel and the huge cat with its giant, almost saber-like teeth, pacing back and forth in front of the opening and snarling while its stumpy tail twitched. Sam dismounted and pulled his falling block out of its special scabbard. He slowly began to move forward and settled into a kneeling position. While this was happening the cat, the size of a tiger or larger, became aware of the party and started to move forward toward them, the quarry in the tunnel forgotten. Sam's breathing steadied and he loaded the gun with what looked like a small artillery shell taken from a bandoleer across his chest. The cat continued its forward movement, almost in a crouch. Sam put the gun up to his shoulder and steadied down, sighting on the giant beast. There was a small click, which seemed loud enough to have an echo since everyone was holding their breath, as he pulled a second trigger to turn the front trigger into a hair trigger. All of a sudden the cat, now close enough to charge its intended prey seemed to leap forward out of its crouch and spring. The day exploded with a thunderclap and a dense cloud of smoke came from the gun's muzzle. In mid leap the animal executed a back flip while there was a spray of grey matter and red blood. The cat landed on its back some fifteen feet in front of them laying dead with a large part of its head missing. This kitty was no longer a danger to anyone.

The party started forward, and perhaps because they were coming in from a different direction, Julia saw the yellow haze near the mouth of the tunnel in a shadowed patch of ground. She pulled up and told everyone to dismount. The men wanted to know why she stopped. Pointing she said, "Look at the shadowed section near the mouth of the tunnel just to the right; you may have to squint a bit." She started to dig in her saddlebags and found what she was looking for. Holding one up she handed it to Sarah. She would have preferred Isaiah but he was still too winded and shaken to be of much use.

Jennifer looked totally confused. "What is that and what does it do?"

Julia showed it to her as she had finally removed another one of the strange objects from the saddlebag. The strange items looked as if they were made of rubber or a tar-impregnated canvas with pieces of glass embedded in them. "These are aetheric-freshening protective coverings for you," as she pointed at the one she had handed to Sarah. "They are worn so," said Julia as she pulled on one of the coverings. "As you can see, the device seals out the gas while the unit removes it as you breath thus allowing you to move in the contaminated aetheric." This last was clear but muffled somewhat. She looked at Sarah, "I do not like to take you into this Sarah, but your father is in no shape and we may need your electric stick."

Sarah looked determined not to let her sister down, and after she was dismounted she pulled the strange face covering on as she had seen Julia do. Then she pulled her untested weapon and started forward.

"What is going on here? You cannot take my daughter into who knows what!" Isaiah was still shaking, but trying to dismount and go after both women.

Julia turned and looked at him, her face unearthly in the protective covering, as if she was some Julia-monster-like creature. Again, muffled but clear, "Isaiah, my husband and your friend is down there along with Carl; we have to go find them and you, sir, are not in any condition to help yet! Sarah is the only one who has had the training for the new electric stick. I do not think there are any more creatures down there since the lion or tiger or whatever it was would not go in. We will be safe. Now wait here." At that the pair started forward again. Just to be safe, Sam ejected the spent round and reloaded another artillery shell into the big Sharps and kept watch. Tinsman turned, his rifle at the ready, and scanned the area behind them and off to the sides to make sure the party was safe from attack on its rear and flanks. The pack they had been tracking was still out there somewhere.

John's head was foggy but the beast was gone and the pair staggered forward into the light. As they cleared the mouth of the tunnel they saw two females coming toward them and instinct took over as they went forward, John coveting the shorter one.

Julia noticed the movement at the mouth of the tunnel and saw John alive along with Carl, but her relief was short-lived. She was shocked to see that they were dragging their rifles like clubs and their faces already beginning to change, their features becoming coarser. "John, stop where you are," as the John-like creature started for her, with the Carl-like creature somewhat behind. She could not shoot; it was John, or at least whatever he was becoming. Then the thing was on her tearing at her clothes. She heard Sarah yell to break free which she easily managed to do. The thing John had become seemed to have no knowledge of close-quarter combat except to grab and hold.

Sarah watched intently. As soon as Julia was no longer in contact she jabbed forward with the electric stick making contact. The John-creature jumped while screaming and had a huge spasm. It fell down and lay there. Furiously, she pulled out and rotated the emergency handle to recharge as the Carl-thing yelled and moved forward. She shouted, "Julia, I need more time to recharge," rotating the crank as fast as she could.

Julia, seeing that John was down, moved forward, not even having time to check on him. She intercepted Carl before he got to Sarah. She danced around the Carl-thing keeping it distracted from Sarah for about two minutes. Finally Sarah yelled for her to keep clear as she moved to strike. As before, the creature that had been Carl screamed and dropped as the stick made contact with him.

As soon as the creature went down and was still Julia ran to John's side his features a strange mask looking like a sculptor's first attempt at a bust. Sarah looked down at the stick and screamed, "Julia, oh my God, I still had it on the kill setting!"

CHAPTER 20

THE REPRIEVE

Julia checked John's pulse and breathing. Despite Sarah's hitting him with a full charge, John was somehow still alive.

By this time they had been joined by the rest of the party. Tinsman grabbed Morton, and Sam and Adam seized Carl, and they carried them back up the ridge as fast as possible to where they felt sure the air was not tainted by the yellow gas.

Sarah was beside herself. "I killed them, I killed them! Julia can you forgive me?" She fell on her knees crying. Julia grabbed Sarah and pulled off her mask while dragging her up the hillside with the others.

Julia removed her own mask and looked at John again to be certain, and held him. "Sarah, he is alive, you did not kill him, but what has happened to him? Maybe it would have been better if you had!" While she was at John's side, in a similar action Jennifer was at Carl's and made the same assessment.

Shaking herself, Julia quickly gave orders, "Hurry, help me tie them up and get them over to the horses so we can get them back to the train." Isaiah, now a bit more recovered, and Adam started to work while Tinsman and Sam kept a sharp eye out for any other problems of the hungry, dangerous variety. Before long the two not-quite-men-anymore creatures were tied over their saddles like some kind of bizarre hunting trophy, as the party was heading back for the fort.

Isaiah looked at Sarah, "You did good Sarah, and you helped capture John and Carl before they could escape or hurt anyone."

Sarah was still crying. "I could have killed them; I should have checked the setting before we started down the hillside, Poppa. I was careless!"

Julia rode up. "Indeed, but I cannot say anything, it was so confusing. Besides, they lived through it. I just hope that whatever it is wears off." Julia was so afraid, remembering the look she had seen on Jennifer's face when she had talked about her late husband.

Isaiah looked at her with an obvious heavy heart. "Julia, I do not want to say this but I do not think it will wear off. It did not for Strong Elk or any of the animals we have seen."

Julia tried to hold back a tear and fervently prayed that Isaiah was wrong. Knowing that she did not get to church too often, she prayed anyway that God would still forgiver her, hear her plea and heal John.

About an hour later, as the party rode along, they heard Morton start moaning. The party stopped, and dismounting, Sam and Adam got John off his saddle and laid him down. Meanwhile Isaiah and Tinsman did the same with Carl.

Julia looked at her husband and was stunned. There lay John, looking quite a bit worse for wear but it was John again! Falling to her knees beside her husband, Julia threw herself on him, crying. John seemed to wake up at this sudden deposit of weeping wife on him, tiny though she was. "Julia," came a small distant voice, "what is going on? God I hurt. My side feels as if it were burned." Trying to move a bit he tried to yell, "Why am I tied up?" This last came out in only a slightly louder voice.

Julia, openly crying now, looked down at him. "John, do you not remember what happened?"

John was still trying to pull himself together. "I remember, but it is fuzzy. Carl and I were at the new tunnel mouth and Isaiah was riding away. Kind of looked like he was just trying to hang on. There was a saber tooth cat blocking the mouth and then there is not much of anything till I just woke up."

Julia looked at him and then started yelling, "You tall, silly, stupid man! If I did not love you so much I would kill you myself! You went into a tunnel with that gas and almost got yourself killed for it!" By this time Julia had sat up and was straddling John's chest while continuing to yell. "Did I not tell you I need you in my life John Morton? Of all the dumb, idiotic, stupid things to do! Why did you not take some of the aetheric-freshening protective coverings if you were looking for a gas-filled tunnel! For that matter, why were you down there? You know nothing about tunnels or machines, you egotistical idiot! You think you have to be in the center of everything!" With that she collapsed on John sobbing while holding him.

John for his part looked stunned at this, obviously trying to put it all together. "What gas? If you could kindly untie me, wife. What about Carl?"

Jennifer answered from a short distance away, "He seems to be recovering but a bit more slowly; he is still out of it."

John tried to nuzzle Julia's neck and whispered, "Ropes, dear. I take it there is somewhat more to this story then I recall?"

Julia sniffed back a tear and sitting up again looked at her man. "I should leave you like this, John Michael Morton, for scaring me like that, you big idiot! That is even without mentioning trying to rape me in public, in front of my sister no less!" Julia stopped yelling only because she ran out of breath.

Morton's thoughts returned to their time in Los Angeles and not for the first time, though maybe he should have, at the very least, studied some groveling in school since he was obviously in the dog house with his spouse for sure. "Rape?" This last came out in a squeak.

By this time Sarah was there and crying. "You did not die!"

Now Morton just added, "Die?" This was no doubt going to be a bad day for sure.

Before long both John and Carl were untied, although Carl was out of it for a while longer then John. Still, much like John, he seemed to have no residual effects except for a burn like John's where Sarah had contacted them with her electric stick, and extreme exhaustion. John and Isaiah thought that perhaps the application of the electric stick somehow reversed the effects of the gas for reasons they could not understand.

Jennifer also looked relieved at Carl's recovery although she controlled herself better then Julia. Sarah noted, however, that it was obvious that she cared about Carl. Soon the party was headed back to the fort.

By the time they got to the fort, both John and Carl headed straight for bed. Meanwhile, Isaiah and Father Peter found Lieutenant Dasson and they headed out to the reservation with the electric stick; however, it was too late. Strong Elk had died, his body unable to handle the continuing changes it was going through.

CHAPTER 21

A Splendid Blast

The next morning Julia sent Isaiah to unload the steam wagon and get it ready to travel. While he was doing that she spoke with Sarah for a while privately and gave her a small device. Then she took Adam and Jason to the train and used them to help her unload assorted tools, supplies, explosives and detonators from the team's supplies.

Sarah was feeding Carl and John back at their quarters in the fort. Father Peter was checking on the two men as best he could. Tinsman and Sam, getting into the spirit of the day, began to unload the Gatling gun and after the training Isaiah had given them on the way out west, they set it up to be steam-powered with a hose from the wagon's boiler so that in a pinch one man could operate it effectively with a very high rate of fire. About an hour later John and Carl, along with Sarah and Father Peter, showed up at the siding behind the railroad station.

Julia spotted the pair and approached them. John spoke, "What is going on Julia? Why is the steam wagon out and some of the supplies?"

Julia looked at her husband and replied quite firmly, "We are going out to seal up the cave or tunnel where the gas is coming from to at least solve that part of the problem, I hope." Turning to Carl she continued, "Tell Jason and Adam what, if any, more materials and tools you will need so that I can set the charges."

Carl nodded and left, heading for the supply part of the bunk car. John looked at Julia. "What should I do, wife?" This said in a conversational tone, knowing he was still on thin ice with his spouse.

Julia looked at him her eyes glaring. "Go to our quarters and go back to bed. You are not needed for this part of the operation, Professor."

John, knowing his wife all too well that when she used his title instead of an endearment such as beloved or husband or even you big idiot, he was still in major trouble with her. Best to tread very gently. "Julia, I am fine, the gas seems to have worn off thanks to Sara's electric shock." Putting his hands up in a placating gesture he added, "Not perfect, I admit. My side is still raw from the burn but I will be all right."

Julia looked, if it were even possible, more put out. "John, I said go rest and I will see to this!"

John started to get his own dander up. "Julia, you are taking Carl but I have to stay back while my wife goes into danger? I do not think so, madam!" John was now standing over Julia looking as mad as she was.

Julia looked even more determined. "I need Carl to tell me where to plant the explosives for the best effect to seal the tunnel. But that, husband, is all. In point of fact, Jason and Adam and I will be doing the work. You, sir, do not have anything to offer to this aspect of the mission, are we clear, Major!" By using his old army rank Morton now truly knew how mad Julia was. He started to say something when Julia nodded just once. Morton felt a sting on his butt and starting to turn around saw Sarah holding something in her hand, then everything went quite foggy and then dark.

Julia caught John as he slumped to the ground so he did not get hurt any more. "Thank you, Sarah, for that timely assistance." Julia looked at John's sleeping form. "I need you in my life John Morton, you tall, silly, stupid man. Now have a nice day's rest. I do love you so." With that she kissed his sleeping form and then called, in an alarmed voice, over to Jason and Adam for help. While the two were coming she took the needle from Sarah and hid it. "Gentlemen, if you would, please help Sarah get my husband back to his bunk on the train. I fear he is not as recovered as he thought he was; he seems to have collapsed again. The bunk on the train is far more comfortable and closer. Oh dear." This last was said with a sound and look of deep concern as would any loving wife express for her sick husband.

As the two men carried John away, Sarah looked at Julia and said, "Can I go with you? I am afraid he is really going to be mad when he wakes up."

Julia looked at her and replied, "Do not worry, even if he wakes up he will be so groggy that I do not think he will be able to do anything more violent then taking up knitting. I will be back before he is awake enough to be really mad. I am sorry I had to ask you to do that Sarah. I honestly did not think he would be strong or quick enough to see you. I cannot take the chance on him getting hurt and in all honesty he does not have any useful skills for this part of the mission."

Sarah looked more than a little worried. "All right, but please do not be late. I do not want to face him alone."

"Not to worry, Sarah, I will be back in plenty of time," then Julia turned on her heel and headed for the steam wagon.

Father Peter, who by this time had joined the rest of the team at the train, saw what had happened. He called out to Julia. Upon hearing him she stopped and turned around. "Yes, Father, what can I do for you?" She said this in as sweet and harmless a voice as possible.

Father Peter looked at her with a worried look on his face. "Julia, I saw what just happened. What is going on?"

Julia looked as if she was trying to decide between the truth, not generally Julia's first choice, and a lie, the latter being the more common Julia route. Peter gave her his best and quite serious *lying to a priest is a mortal sin* look, which stopped Julia dead in her mental tracks. "Father, I know that was somewhat extreme, but John was not going to listen to me no matter what I said. I do not want him hurt. And you, of all people, should know how he is. He would insist on going and protecting me, but in truth just generally getting in the way! To make matters worse, he would want to explore the tunnel completely before we closed it in case there were any specimens in there. I need him in one piece; I cannot take a chance now Peter, especially now!"

Father Peter raised an eyebrow at this last and replied, "I know how you love him, Julia, remember, I was there to watch it happen. But John is still the team leader and it would not be right for you to undermine him like this. What may I ask is so special about now?"

Julia looked hard. "That is why I told everyone that it was just the aftereffects of the gas. Even leaders are entitled to be sick once in a while, especially when exposed to a deadly poison. Right now it is just Sarah, you and I who know, besides John of course. Actually I did not think he would be quick enough to see Sarah behind him. Silly, strong, man!"

Father Peter, still looking at Julia, his face softening and looking much more like a counselor than the rector of a church school asked, "Why now Julia, what is it about *now?*"

Julia looked at him and swallowed, "Because our child will need his or her father, at least if my calculations are correct."

Peter broke out in a radiant smile. "Does John know yet?"

Julia laughed. "Do you think for a single moment I would be allowed to go if he did? That silly man would be fussing over me till I killed him myself." Julia took a breath. "Besides, do you think he could keep it a secret? You cannot tell him, Father; we need to finish this up before he can be allowed to act in a normal male way, that being stupid. No offense, Father."

Peter smiled. "All right, but it will cost you; I get to perform the baby's baptism," this with a tip of his head.

Julia smiled quite warmly and kissed him on the cheek. "There was never any one else in mind, Father. Now, if you would be so kind as to keep an eye on my sleeping husband, I have a tunnel to close." At that, Julia turned and made her way to the steam wagon.

By this time, Jason and Adam had returned from the train car and depositing John into his bed. The team finished up loading the various tools, detonators, lanterns and explosives that they thought they would need. Since Julia wanted to make sure everyone continued to think that it was just the aftereffects of the gas that caused John to black out, she had Carl ride up front with Isaiah. However, as an experienced steam wagon passenger she remembered to bring several cushions to compensate for the lack of springs in the wagon's design. With the team in place and several packhorses tied behind for the last part of the trip, Isaiah opened the valves, worked the various control levers and they were off.

It took several hours because Isaiah could not use the full effect of the steam wagon's speed advantage since, even lightly loaded, the packhorses had to rest periodically unlike the steam wagon. Still, all in all they made good time. They were able to get within about one-and-a-half miles of the tunnel before Isaiah had to pull up. He got down and explored a bit on foot, checking for the best route. Resuming his place at the controls, he worked the wagon forward and did manage to find a spot where it was mostly downhill to the tunnel opening and he had a fairly clear field of fire for the Gatling. Julia did not want to take any chances on being trapped in the tunnel with lit fuses. The team climbed down and began to unload various items from the wagon and the burdens on the two pack horses.

As this activity was going on Carl asked Julia, "Is John all right? I mean I feel quite fine except for the burn from Sarah's electric stick."

Julia looking concerned replied, "I believe he is all right, I just assume that different people react somewhat differently to the gas as with many chemicals. I think that by the time we return all will be well with him," thinking to herself, *at least I hope he will have calmed down.*

When they were ready, Julia told Isaiah and Sam to stay with the wagon and keep an eye out for any creatures that may have been affected by the gas from the tunnel. Isaiah finished the final steam-line connections to the Gatling and completed his preparations by seating a magazine into the breach of the gun from a pile of extra ready-use magazines. He finished his battle-readiness by hand-cranking the gun to load the first round. At the same time, Sam pulled out his falling block and buckled on his cartridge belt. Thereafter each man picked up a pair of binoculars and began to sweep opposite parts of the horizon on the lookout for any threats.

Julia and the rest started down the slope, stopping about seventy-five yards short of the opening. Julia went over to the packhorses and handed out her special face coverings so that they were all protected.

Before putting them on she spoke, "Carl, just so you and everyone else understands, this is not a research mission, we are here to close up this tunnel and seal off the gas that is causing so much damage and danger. Carl, your job is to tell us where to place the explosives, how deep to make the holes. After that, since you have already been exposed once, you will retreat to the steam wagon while the rest of us plant the charges and set them off. Do you understand?"

Carl acknowledged the instructions and replied, "Bring the star drills and hammers. In order to collapse the tunnel we will have to get into the walls, otherwise the blast will just blow out the opening and back up the tunnel without doing much damage."

Tinsman pulled out a picket pin and screwed it into the ground. Finally he tied the horses to it so he had both hands free. Next he pulled his rifle and stayed with the horses while Julia, Carl, Jason and Adam set off with the drills, explosives and detonators. Their field of vision was somewhat limited by the masks but they knew they could count on the others to keep them safe from anything coming up on them were they could not see. At the mouth Julia set up two of her lime light lanterns, although these were not the special exploding ones she was so fond of, so the team had plenty of light with which to work. Carl took a good look at the walls and began to make a series of chalk marks along the sides about every six feet. This went on for some thirty five feet into the tunnel and then back along the other side. He called the others over. "You need to make the hole about five feet deep and three feet off the floor. Then make another set of holes the same depth in between the first ones but up as high as you can. Julia, can you set the charges so there is a few seconds delay between the bottom holes being blown and the top row and if possible go from back to front? That should allow the roof to cave in and seal the tunnel."

Julia thought for a moment. "I can cut the fuses longer so I do not see a problem. How much charge in each hole?"

Having found out the type and power of blasting agent Julia planned to use, he waited till the two rookie agents drilled the first three holes to ascertain the composition of the material forming the tunnel walls before he gave the answer. Julia turned to the two rookies and told them to keep working while she told Carl in no uncertain terms to retreat to the wagon. As the others worked she started to set out the charges, detonators and fuses.

The two young men made excellent time as the walls were quite hard at first, but once the surface was penetrated by seven to eight inches, the underlying material was fairly soft. As they continued down the tunnel, Julia followed behind staying at least two holes behind them so as not to risk any stray sparks from the hammers hitting the drills and catching the fuses on fire.

Some two hours later all was in readiness and the three people retreated out of the tunnel trailing the fuse that all the others connected to out with them. When they were out of the tunnel by some twenty feet, Julia motioned the others on and then lit the fuse and ran. They were well clear when there was a series of thumps they could feel through their boots and then the mouth of the tunnel belched fire and dust. Julia looked back; the tunnel was completely sealed. She smiled and thought to herself, *Carl does indeed know his business.* The smile was replaced with a frown as again she thought that at least part of the problem was resolved. Now where was the machine that made the tunnels and who or what was operating it?

Julia joined the two young agents and Tinsman where he had been holding the packhorses waiting for them to reload the tools. They were about ready to start up the hill toward the others when suddenly the two watchers yelled and started shooting. With a quick look behind them they saw a pack of about eight relatively small creatures coming at them, small compared to what they had dealt with so far. They appeared to be some type of what looked like reptiles, about six feet high and eight to ten feet long to the end of their tails, moving down the other slope and toward them on their hind legs, their front ones in the air like some kind of prize fighter. Julia recognized them as the ones that had killed the hell pig. Worse yet, they moved quite fast, and their jaws and teeth were not small; they looked like something out of a nightmare or one of Mr. Poe's novels of dark horror.

Tinsman levered a round into his repeater, and kneeling, began to fire while Julia told the two young agents to run, the two packhorses bolting on their own, ripping the picket pin out of the ground in adrenalin-fueled fright. Julia pulled her revolver and began waiting for a shot, the current range being too great for accurate fire from the shorter-barreled weapon. Meanwhile, one of the creatures dropped and it flipped over backwards as Sam's big falling block boomed from the top of the hill like an artillery piece. The creatures came on, and suddenly there was a prolonged thunder as the earth around the creatures exploded and the reptiles were torn apart. Isaiah had opened the steam valve on the Gatling and was feeding it as fast as he could. Even over the sustained roar of the rotating barrels, broken only by the amount of time it took for Isaiah to change magazines, the thunder of the forty-five one-ten could still be heard. The last members of the pack died only ten feet from Julia and Tinsman as they both emptied the last of the rounds from their weapons into them. Both were shaken. Tinsman looked at Julia and dryly said, "Cutting it a bit close do you not think, boss lady?"

Julia shook and tried to pull herself together. "I think we just found out for sure what killed the pig. Look at the teeth on those things—like some kind of obscene shredding machine that one would find in a butcher's shop. Indeed, Corporal, please do not tell John. He will be upset enough for not being here today. If he finds out I was in any danger he will be, well, let us just say facing those things would be preferable. I personally do not plan to take any specimens back with us which will only upset him more."

Tinsman laughed and after wiping the sweat off his face started reloading the rifle. Better to be ready; no telling what else was around. Julia looked at her hands and tried to reload her revolver. She had to stop and take a deep breath and force them to stop shaking. Laughing a bit at herself, she thought, *I hope this does not last the whole nine months!*

The rest of the time was spent reloading the wagon. The packhorses were long gone. Julia looked at Carl. "So, sir, what do you think?"

Carl, looking a bit pale at the sight of the chopped and diced creatures with chunks of flesh and guts littering the hillside, replied, "I am not used to dealing with the likes of these."

Julia, having regained her composure, smiled. "No, sir, not the creatures, I mean the tunnel."

Carl shook his head and breathing deeply replied, "A splendid blast, madam, most satisfactory."

The team climbed into the steam wagon and Isaiah took the controls, and slowly at first but steadily gaining speed since there were no horses to worry about, headed back to the fort. The sun was setting as they rolled into the railroad station and their train.

CHAPTER 22

BACK AT THE TRAIN

The steam wagon pulled to a stop near the first car which housed Isaiah's shop-on-wheels and everyone climbed out just as the day was beginning to fade. Julia told them to unload the tools and extra unused supplies, being careful with the unused explosives, while she dutifully checked on John's condition, being concerned about his earlier collapse.

As she headed down the cars she ran into Sarah going the opposite way. She was obviously agitated and in a rush, and looking quite nervous. Seeing Julia, Sarah blurted out, "He is awake and really mad!" Looking over her shoulder as if to make sure John was not standing there, "He is still groggy but I think he wants to do more than take up knitting." This last came out as a bit of a high-pitched and very scared squeak.

Julia smiled to reassure her, and with a pat on the shoulder said, "I will see to John, you just go and help your father with the steam wagon. Remember, John passed out." Then Julia moved past Sarah to the parlor car where their various rooms were, where she could hear Father Peter talking to John, trying to calm him down.

"John, you cannot spank Julia again, it is quite out of the question."

John's voice came back, although slightly slurred, "Yes I can; just you watch me. Running off like that, having Sarah drug me. I should spank both of them!"

It was at this point Julia entered the parlor. "John, darling, I see you are up, how do you feel, dearest? Well rested I hope." Julia was smiling hoping against hope that John would calm down.

John staggered over to her. "Wife, how could you do that, you could have been hurt. I know just what you need." With this John reached out to grab his wife.

Considering Julia's training, background and normal lethal tendencies, that, coupled with the fact that John was still trying to shake off the woozy feeling from the effects of the sedative Sarah had injected him with, this was a *very* bad move. Grabbing John's out-stretched arm and with a quick duck under and her foot in front of his foot, John found himself face down on the floor with his nose buried in the carpet and his arm up in the middle of his back in a most uncomfortable position in what one could actually say was a quite painful predicament. He lay there with his face very seriously pressed into the carpet and his shoulder feeling as if were coming apart and an exasperated Julia sitting on top of him. "Now, dearest, there is no need to act in such a rude and uncouth manner, especially in front of the good father. Besides, this is not Los Angeles and you are not taking me over your knee again. In fact, if the Father were not here, I have it in mind to give *you* a good spanking."

Morton was still groggy, but the pain in his shoulder was causing him to rapidly throw off the last vestiges of the drug that had been so unceremoniously delivered. "Julia, you should not have gone alone. I am your husband!"

Julia shook her head while Father Peter, deciding that Julia had everything under control, went out to check on the rest of the team. "Now, John, dearest spouse, I was hardly alone, I had all the other men, well, except for Father Peter. And remember that I had Isaiah and the steam Gatling if it was needed." She refrained from mentioning that it came in very handy too. She felt it was prudent, given John's worries, and basically decided not to add the fact that a pack of the strange, devolved animals wanted to snack on her and the rest of the team. Reducing the pressure on John's arm she went on, "Now if I let you up, do you promise, dear, to behave yourself like the gentle, loving husband I know you are?"

John grunted. "I will take that as one of your affirmative grunts, dear," and with that she released John's arm and got up off her husband.

John weakly got to his feet and looked at his spouse. "Julia, you know I am in charge of this unit. How can I lead after this, being drugged and knocked out by my own wife and her sister?"

Julia went up to him and hugged him. "I love you, you tall, silly man. First of all, when it comes to explosives or removing an obstacle I am the expert not you, dear. Second, except for myself, Sarah and you, not to mention Father Peter since you told him," no point in wasting a perfect opportunity to make John feel complicit in letting even more people in on the secret, "everyone thinks that you were still having some aftereffects of the gas you inhaled so your mantle of leadership is totally intact. John, you must know I would never do anything like that to you, and there is no reason to be mad at Sarah. She loves you too you know. She did it because and only because I asked her to. You should know I had to insist, since she really did not want to do the deed."

John looked down at his wife, who, as mad as he was, still loved very much. "Why, Julia?"

Julia, knowing her husband as she did, knew that the worst of the storm was over, looked up at him before replying, "Because you really did not have anything to add to what had to be done, John. I had all the firepower I needed and you would have insisted on checking for specimens when time was of the essence. I love you but I do not need you to hold fuses for me. You see, you tall, silly man, I wanted to be sure you were all right when I came back."

John sighed and wrapped his arms around his wife. "Is the tunnel sealed for good?"

Julia wiggled in a bit closer. "Yes, unless whatever, or whoever, digs it back up again. Carl thinks that we collapsed at least forty feet or more. No more gas from there."

John held her. "Julia, I was so mad because I was so worried. I meant it when I told you I need you in my life. Do not take such chances again. Remember, we were discussing starting a family. I want to do that with you."

Julia turned her head down and hugged her husband even tighter. "I want that to, John." She smiled a warm Cheshire cat smile with her head down so John could not see the look, and just enjoyed loving her man. However, the mission was still not complete, so losing the secret smile, she turned her face up to John's again. "John, who has been doing this and is the gas part of it or just an unhappy side effect?"

John, still not completely clear-headed, held Julia and rubbed her back while almost purring. However, all such warmth has to have its own time and place. "I do not know, Julia. We are going to need help to find whoever is doing this."

Julia stepped back and looked up at John. She too would have liked nothing better than to prolong the moment they had, but duty, as the saying goes, is a harsh mistress and they had to complete the mission. "Where do we start to look, John?"

John yawned a bit, looked down at Julia and said, "First we look for some coffee and dinner. It seems that the lingering aftereffects of that gas have left me groggy and hungry after sleeping all day. Then we tackle the mission. Priorities, you know, madam."

Julia looked at him, "Indeed, sir, now what kind of a secretary or wife would I be if I let you pass out from lack of sustenance." The two went to find out what Cook could plan for dinner since the team had been, for the most part, eating in the fort. Julia and John thought that a quiet dinner alone would be nice, however, not all things go as planned as Father Peter, Isaiah and Sarah decided to join them. Carl had chosen to meet with Jennifer to tell her of the day's activates. Julia approved since Jennifer understood the special nature of the team and the need for secrecy. Finally, Tinsman had his part of the team field-stripping and cleaning the weapons, including the Gatling, in case they were needed again, which, by the way things had gone so far, could be any time. Not for the first time, Sam thought having rookies around was a fine idea since the Gatling had burned up what must have been ten or more pounds of black powder at the rate Isaiah had been firing.

The team filled John in on the closing of the tunnel, although at Julia's request before dinner, no one mentioned the attack of the reptile pack. As she had explained, John would have been too upset not to have gotten any specimens, along with other concerns, but she kept that part to herself. Sarah sat as far from John as possible. It would only be after dinner when Julia could talk to her privately that she could give her little sister the all clear.

When the ladies took a brief break after dinner to use the facilities, that was Julia's chance to tell Sarah that it was all right. That young lady was, to put it mildly, extremely relieved since she had been very worried. She had to use the electric stick on the professor and help Julia drug him. Sarah was afraid that she had used up more than her share of forgiveness. She loved him like an uncle and even more so respected him, that and as Julia noted, she loved to learn and he was an outstanding teacher.

Cook was upset that he did not have more notice and felt that it was not up to his standards having to throw a simple five-course meal together. This seemed to amuse the team since they had been subsisting on army rations, and even with Sarah handling most of the kitchen duties, all agreed that army cooks and supplies were nowhere in Cook's league.

Finally with the meal finished and after several cups of strong coffee during the course of a fine dinner, John felt up to turning the conversation to what to do next. Father Peter spoke up, "First, it seems that we would have to make sure there are no more surprises roaming around the territory due to the gas. Also, we do not know if there are any of the other tunnels and if so are they emitting this gas. I would think that patrols of mixed Nez Perce and army troops should be sent out. Also, just to be sure, there should be an observation post set up near the sealed-up tunnel mouth."

Julia looked up in surprise. "Why would you want to send out mixed units, Father, given that there is so much mistrust after the war?"

Father Peter smiled. "Just so, Julia. The enemy of my enemy is my friend. Perhaps by working together to confront these monsters some of the trust that was lost can be rebuilt. At least we can pray it is so."

John looked at his old comrade. "Good idea, Peter; I will talk to the colonel about it if perhaps you and Lieutenant Dasson would talk to Strong Bear. Also, we best find the rest of the tunnels and seal them up. As you noted, that might not be the only one leaking that gas."

Peter smiled. "Assuming that the colonel has no objection, consider it done."

John continued, "Next on the agenda we need to locate what is doing all the tunneling and where. I believe that all concerned have ruled out giant prehistoric gophers or wildly mutated prairie dogs. Any suggestions?"

Julia looked thoughtful for a moment. "John, we need to cover a lot of ground. I do not like to go over the colonel's head but we need to use an airship for this. I will send a wire first thing in the morning."

The rest of the team seemed to mull this over. It was Isaiah who finally spoke up, "Perhaps you should talk to the colonel first so that it might be as if the idea came from him, chain of command and all; no ruffling of feathers."

Julia looked at him. "An excellent idea, Isaiah. I believe John and I shall pay the colonel a visit after dinner. What do you say, John?"

John nodded and replied, "Yes, I most assuredly believe that would be the best approach. Meanwhile, I would like it if you, Isaiah, along with Carl and Tinsman, would check out the tunnels we know about and see if there is anything about them that would give us some clues as to their origin. However, be careful; we have no idea if any more of them have the gas in them. I can vouch for the fact that it is none too pleasant. Then have Adam and Jason close them up under Carl's direction. Meanwhile, Sarah, I would appreciate you putting your archival skills to work and obtaining a map of the area then start noting all the finds the others have made. A visual interpretation may help us to make some sense of all this."

Sarah perked up at this as she felt that, by being put in charge of recording the information, the professor still trusted her. She replied in a happy voice that she would do so. John saw Isaiah out of the corner of his eye looking very relieved that Sarah would be safe in the fort dealing with paperwork.

John finished making assignments and the meeting broke up. John and Julia headed for the colonel's quarters. It was only a short distance to the fort commander's office and before long they confronted the

Corporal of the Guard and inquired if the colonel was in. Quickly they were shown into the colonel's office. It appeared that the colonel had been working late. Several empty plates off to the side indicated that he had already eaten dinner. John smiled and said, "Sorry to bother you so late, Frank, but we have some things to discuss with you."

Washburn shrugged and offered them chairs and replied, "End-of-the-month army paperwork, John. It will be trying but I think I can handle the distraction for a bit."

John helped Julia to be seated and Washburn retrieved several extra cups and poured coffee into them and then refilled his own cup from a large pot on the stove in the corner. Putting out some cream and sugar, he took a sip of black coffee and looked at the two over his cup. "So what is so important that it cannot wait till tomorrow? Not that I will strenuously object to being pulled away from the monthly reports."

John smiled and remembered the reports he had to fill out during his time in uniform. He laughed a bit. "I can well understand your deep and heartfelt sorrow at being pulled off your reports, Frank." The colonel smiled at this bit of military humor. John went on, "Frank, the team managed to seal off the one tunnel we know for sure was emitting the gas that seemed to be the cause of the strange animals. However, we are not sure it is the only one. We need to scout out the area further and check for any more tunnels that we can find. If there are any emitting the gas we will seal them up."

Washburn looked strained. "John, I do not have all that many men for such scouting parties, not even thinking about closing off the tunnels. On top of which, it is a huge area to cover and very rugged terrain."

Julia looked at him and spoke, "Colonel, Father Peter suggested that we ask the Indians for help, after all it is their land, and the Nez Perce are having the most trouble or at least as much trouble as the white settlers. As for scouting the area, do you have any suggestions on how to increase our coverage of the area?"

Washburn looked stunned for a moment. "Use the Nez Perce to hunt for these tunnels? I am having enough trouble keeping track of them. It is out of the question!"

Julia smiled her best alluring smile. "We understand, that is why Peter suggested mixed parties of army and Nez Perce. It would allow more ground to be covered by doubling the number of parties and any further mutated animals to be brought down, and your troopers could keep an eye on the braves."

Washburn looked skeptical. "I do not know; there is a lot of bad blood right now. As for the area to be covered, if we had one of the airships that would really help. Unfortunately I do not have that kind of pull."

John spoke up, "Frank, I know it is a bit dicey, but having the tribe jump the reservation because of all this would be worse. Besides, having to face danger together might restore some of the trust. The idea of using an airship is an absolutely splendid idea. You know that we work for the same government and with your permission I believe that a telegram from my wife might help." Glancing at the very innocent-looking Mrs. Morton, John went on, "She does have the ear of several well-placed people in Washington."

Julia looked at John. "Well, dear, if you think it will help and you do not mind, Colonel."

Washburn, giving Julia a puzzled look, replied, "Mrs. Morton, be my guest if you think it will make any difference."

"Thank you, sir, I shall send a telegram forthwith. What about the mixed patrols?"

Washburn blew out his breath. "I have my reservations but it might just help. You are right, we need all the bodies that we can get; it is too big an area to cover otherwise and I have nowhere near enough manpower. I will have Dasson talk to Strong Bear and see what he thinks."

There were some more pleasantries before John and Julia left. As they walked back to their quarters John looked down at his wife. "As usual, my love, very well played."

Julia smiled. "Uncle William's schooling was very complete, dear." Leaning in close to him she kept smiling and with a bit of a laugh said, "Dear, keep smiling, I believe we have an audience."

John returned the smile and gave a small chuckle. "What are you talking about Julia?" This was said as he bent down almost as if he were kissing her.

Julia smiled again and replied, "I am not sure, John, just a tickle at the back of my neck. However I do think we are being watched."

Still bent down, John replied, "I have not noticed anyone, my dear."

Julia looked up at her husband letting the slightest look of wifely frustration cross her delicate features. "Perhaps if you paid attention, dearest, to what is going on around you…"

John smiled "I am; I am taking a moonlit walk with an angel."

Julia rolled her eyes; it seems she had learned that from Father Peter. "That is very sweet, John, but really do try to pay attention. I do believe we are under surveillance."

John pulled his wife in closer to his side. "Where wife? I have not noticed anyone. Are you sure Julia?"

Julia decided that having a husband to snuggle up to while spotting watchers was a nice idea, a very enjoyable cover indeed; she should tell the other girls in her class. "Over in the corner by the trading post where Molly works, you know, Sarah's friend. You can barely see him. I am certain it is the same man that has been hanging around the fort the last several days. The one with the dog."

John looked thoughtful for a moment. "I have noticed him. Not too many people with dogs beside them wherever they go. You are sure of it?"

Julia poked her husband in the side. "Really, John, if something is not thousands of years old and partially or mostly buried I swear you would never see it. Yes, it is the same man. I only wonder where the dog is."

John knew his wife's abilities so he did not question her suspicions any more but simply accepted them. "What to do, my love?"

Julia, looked up at John like a young woman in love, which she was, but now she was in dangerous agent mode. "I think Corporal Tinsman and his fellows should invite him in for tea and questions." With that the couple continued arm in arm to the quarters they shared with the rest of the team.

It was not long before several members of the team slipped out a back window of the building and blended in with the shadows cast by the fort's walls and other buildings. John and Isaiah went out onto the porch to enjoy a cigar while in the background Julia could be heard yelling that she did not want those truly nasty things indoors and they should stay outside if they were going to indulge in such a vile habit.

The man by the trading post took in all this interplay and was not aware of the three men closing in on his position until he heard a familiar growl at his side. "What is it, King?" he spoke quietly to his four-footed companion.

The question was answered by Corporal Tinsman, "Fine looking dog you have there, sir, be a shame to hurt him, so it would be best if you keep him quiet and at the same time keep your hands where we can see them."

The man looked at the man who appeared in front of him and noted the way he held himself. There was no question in his mind that this man was highly trained. Then he noted the other two men. "Easy, King, it seems that we are surrounded."

Just then a new voice spoke up, "I would say, old fellow, that it is I who have the drop on you."

Tinsman laughed a bit. "We were wondering if you would show up or we would have to look for you, mister. Considering that the odds are four to two, I think it would be smart if you just handed over your gun and be real friendly. No offense to your friend King here, sir, but I do not see him packing any iron."

The new man started to say something but froze as he heard the hammer on a gun being cocked from a short distance behind him and another voice, Bill's, say, "Do as the corporal says, please, sir. We would not want any gunfire to wake up the fort now, would we? The colonel seems a might touchy about such things."

Jason and Adam moved in and removed the guns from the two men. The six men and one dog started walking toward the quarters the team had been assigned. Smiling, John opened the door and said, "Welcome gentlemen, please come in."

CHAPTER 23

TEA AND QUESTIONS

s the men passed into the room, Sarah looked at the dog. "He will not bite or anything, will he, mister?" Sarah was eyeing the dog with some trepidation, not being accustomed to them. In Buffalo they had mostly been used to guard property and were generally not at all friendly, and that was putting it very mildly.

The taller of the two men replied to Sarah's nervousness by saying, "Be nice to the young lady, King," then he looked down at Sarah and said, "You can pet him if you like; he is quite friendly, at least when people are not threatening me with guns." This last was obviously meant for the male members of the team who had escorted his partner and himself to the quarters.

Sarah came forward slowly and began to scratch the dog behind his ears then broke into a smile. Meanwhile, Julia was setting the table. "Tea, gentlemen, or would you prefer coffee?" This was in a quite pleasant tone but neither of the two men made the mistake of thinking this was a friendly meeting.

The somewhat older of the two said, "Tea please, madam," in what was an obviously somewhat harsh and workman-like British accent. He was on the shorter side, a little sallow-faced, a dark-eyed fellow with a bit of a ferret-like look to his face. He watched Julia as the other man responded by asking for coffee. "I assume I have the pleasure of meeting Miss Julia Verolli," said ferret-face. At this utterance the two men took chairs and sat down.

Julia smiled and finished pouring the beverages. "Indeed not, sir, it is Mrs. Julia Morton. I believe you met my husband when he welcomed you in." Julia finished her hostess duties by pouring coffee for John and tea for Father Peter and herself, then sat down. The other men sat down in chairs around the room.

"Really. You look very much like a woman who has a rather extensive dossier back home."

John was getting somewhat nervous at all this but Julia just smiled at him. "Verolli was my maiden name, sir. Now, who would you be and where would home be that it would have such a file on my little harmless, innocent self?" There was a smile on Julia's face but the older man knew that it was not a friendly one or, in spite of the lady's statement, harmless.

"It would seem that the records that were sent over to the Yard from the Foreign Office are somewhat behind the times. My compliments, sir, on your good fortune; she is quite a catch," this last to John. The man looked around and decided that the men in the room where too experienced to be trifled with, even the priest. "Home would be London, madam, and my name is Guiles Lestrade. If I may present my traveling companion, George Preston, and of course you have met King," gesturing toward the dog who at the moment was being scratched and petted by Sarah, who seemed to be ignoring the business being conducted by the adults while being enchanted by the rather large husky.

Julia looked at the man and spoke, "The name Lestrade. Mmm, I am afraid it does not ring a bell, sir. I know of no person in Her Majesty's Secret Service by the name of Guiles Lestrade or," glancing at the other man, "George Preston. Where do you two fit in, gentlemen?"

Lestrade replied, "That is because I am not in the Secret Service, madam. Detective Constable Lestrade of Scotland Yard, Special Branch, at your service."

The younger man looked for guidance at Lestrade who nodded as if to say we are caught. "Constable George Preston of the Northwest Mounted Police, madam, at you service, and as Constable Lestrade noted you have met King. You will forgive him if he seems playful; he is young yet, still a bit of a pup." King looked at him upon hearing his name but the mountie smiled and said, "It is all right boy." The dog returned to being pampered by Sarah. Indeed, he seemed to feel that this was quite an enjoyable doggy way to spend one's time.

Julia smiled at the young policeman. "Welcome, Constable, I hope the coffee meets with your approval." Julia, looking at him, decided he was quite good looking, tall and broad shouldered with dark hair and mustache and gentle features. She thought to herself, *perhaps I should keep this one and pass him along to Marie*, one of her former classmates at the finishing school who was still in agency employ.

The mountie looked at her and replied, "Indeed, madam, very good. If you do not mind me being forward, what do you have planned for us?"

Julia said, "As of right now I have not decided. It quite depends on why you gentlemen have been following and spying on us, although I have been considering keeping you and turning you over to a friend of mine, Constable, a fellow classmate. You are not married are you, George?"

The mountie seemed shocked at this and quite nervous. "No, madam, I am not married; life in the remote parts of the Yukon is not much to build a relationship on. Why do you ask?"

"Not to worry, Constable, it was not for torture, well maybe a little bit but nothing too objectionable. I believe my husband will vouch for that. It is simply that a classmate of mine, Marie, has not found her man yet. Like your agency puts it, we always like to get our man." Julia gave a sly smile at John at this last. "I think she would find you quite charming," returning her gaze to the Preston. The policeman looked quite abashed at this.

John entered the conversation at this point. "Julia, really, do not scare the constable so. I can assure you, sir, my wife was just joking."

Julia gave her spouse a look and an unladylike snort. "Not really, John, he is handsome, much like you, dear, and having a husband around does make life much more enjoyable, indeed a quite wonderful cover for various activities. I do however believe that Uncle William is generally not happy about married agents so it would have to be a special reason, like planting an agent in Canada. Besides, there is nothing wrong with Marie; she is very nice, quite attractive and used to the kind of hardship that I should think a mountie's wife must face."

It was Father Peter who now entered the discussion since he was beginning to sense a tension building between John and Julia. "Julia, not that I am against the Sacrament of Matrimony but perhaps there would be a better time to discuss it, after all, we do have other rather serious business pending."

Julia had an annoyed look on her face for just a second, after all, Marie was one of the few friends she had in the class. The school tended to bring out the competitive nature of its students and discouraged close relationships. "The mission must come first" was the school's motto. She decided the Father was right. "As I was saying, gentlemen, what has brought you to the United States? It is not as if our countries were best friends." Nodding to the mountie, "I will include you in that, Constable, since I do believe you are acting in the Crown's interest. Before you decide to give me some fairly tale, I want you to know I do not enjoy being lied to. I assume, Detective Constable, that my dossier was clear on that point?" looking at the Englishman.

The Englishman looked thoughtful while the mountie looked concerned as he had not seen the documents in question. Both of the men realized that they were quite outnumbered and unarmed. Lestrade looked thoughtful for a moment before speaking, "It would seem, ladies and gentlemen, that it would be best if we were up front with each other. Yes, madam, your folder was quite clear about that last point. However putting that last point aside, I do believe that we are working on the same problem."

Lestrade stopped as Carl walked in on the tea party, as it were, and stopped short trying to figure out what was going on. There were two men who were new to the group seated with cups in front of them and a dog that Sarah was busy scratching the stomach of, and it was obvious that there was tension in the room.

Lestrade and Preston both looked at the man who had walked in. Preston's face was merely curious with no hint of recognition, while

Lestrade's face seemed to be going through some sort of mental pile of wanted posters in his head.

Julia spoke up, "Gentlemen, if I might introduce another member of our team, Carl Jordan from Pennsylvania. Carl, may I introduce to you Detective Guiles Lestrade of the Metropolitan Police, from London's Scotland Yard's Special Branch, no less, and Constable George Preston of the Northwest Mounted Police."

Carl stopped in mid stride and looked at Lestrade. He was obviously shaken, but Julia's training kicked in and he put out his hand and merely said, "Sorry if I seem surprised, but you are a rather long way from home Detective and the United States is not the most hospitable place for an English copper or even a Canadian one, Constable," with a nod to Preston.

Lestrade took the man's outstretched hand and replied, "You remind me of the wanted poster of a Welsh terrorist named Clement Hook. Have you ever been to Wales, sir?"

Carl shook his head. "As the lady said Constable, I am from Pennsylvania. This is really the first time I have traveled outside the state, except for one time I went to Buffalo, which is in New York, looking for work with the railroad."

Lestrade kept up his stare. "Relatives in Wales?"

Carl knew that he was on thin ice but kept smiling. "No, Constable, my family was from Poland; my grandfather, just after he immigrated, changed the family name from Jerdanczyk to Jordan to be more American. He stated that our family was to become American. We were only allowed to speak English in our house. He was a bit of a tyrant about it."

Lestrade looked as if he accepted it, sort of. Turning back to Julia, as he perceived her to be the leader, he went on after the interruption. "As I was saying, Mrs. Morton, I was assigned along with several other police to track down a new cabal seemingly bent on bringing the world under their rule; they call themselves 'The Teamwork'. From what we have been able to piece together, the type of teamwork these fellows believe in is that all the animals be under the same whip, if you catch my drift."

Julia nodded, "Indeed, sir, I have met the type before. However that begs the question, why are you here on American soil?"

Lestrade took a breath and another sip of his tea. Then he went on, "I was coming to that, madam. By the way, the tea is excellent, thank you. It seems these fellows are very well financed and have their fingers in quite a few pies, as it were. It also seemed as if they are quite enchanted with powerful technology. We keep missing the leaders but did pick up some of the underlings and henchmen who spoke under some, shall we say, spirited questioning, although even more of them committed suicide before they could be questioned. Apparently the cabal has some wide-spread operations going on, one of which is some sort of operation in western Canada involving gold mining to help finance their other schemes. The Yard thought these were a bit of long odds but still worth checking out. I had read much about the Dominion; it sounded like quite the place, well, compared to London anyhow. Very curious about it I was, and thus I decided to volunteer for the trip, that and I was the junior detective, which is how I came to be over the pond and across the continent to wind up here. Likewise the constable's involvement; he was my liaison out here when I was sent to check into it."

Julia cocked her eyebrow at this but it was John who spoke, "The last I knew, gold mining was hardly illegal in the Dominion. Why the interest?"

It was Preston who took up the story at that point. "Mr. Morton."

John responded with, "It is Professor Morton, but please, Constable, call me John."

The mountie nodded and his face showed a sign of recognition. Taking another look at Morton he went on, "Professor John Morton of the New York Museum? Even out here we have heard of your discoveries. Most impressive, sir!"

Julia jumped in again, "Please, no more Constable, I need to keep my husband's feet on the ground. His head seems to swell when he receives too much flattery, and we will all wind up listening to stories about long dead animals for the rest of the night."

John smiled at this, reached over and kissed Julia on the cheek. "Am I that bad, my love?" Julia rolled her eyes but reached up and held John's hand to her cheek.

Preston looked a bit surprised but smiled, even under the circumstances, and started in again, "As I was saying, we have had substantially less trouble with the native people then you have had south of the border, and my government would like to keep it that way. The men in question were not only mining Indian land without permission, but their work was poisoning the water supply so it had to be stopped. We tracked them but missed them up north in Yellow Knife. They managed to clear out before we could close in. We kept up our search and then we picked up the trail and followed them down to British Columbia. Again they slipped through our fingers!" The mountie looked highly vexed at this.

Lestrade picked up the tale again. "We were fairly certain that they jumped the border and came down here to the States but had no idea of where. I must admit, to a London Copper, this is quite the large country between you and our Canadian cousins. As I was saying, we did not have any idea where to look when we saw in the papers about the Indian problems around here. I wired London and was authorized to cross the border quietly and to try to stop and apprehend them."

John spoke up again, "I assume without the knowledge of the U. S. Government."

Lestrade looked at him and shrugged. "Indeed, sir. As I said, we were to try to do this quietly. However, as we have been around the post and listening in on various conversations, it was becoming obvious that two men would not be enough to handle this, if indeed it was the men in question. We were at a bit of a loss on how to proceed. Should we return to Canada or should we approach your party since it was obvious you were somewhat more than a mere scientific team, although we are not sure just what you are. That is about where we were when you invited us in for tea."

Julia looked at John who shrugged his shoulders as if to say *your call, wife.* She looked deep in thought for a moment then spoke. "Gentlemen, as you said, we should be upfront with each other. Indeed we are a bit more than a scientific party, at least if there are no fossils around. They tend to distract my husband." John looked annoyed at this statement. She looked at him with an *I-am-only-telling-the-truth* look before she went on, "We are having the same problem with unauthorized mining along with some rather nasty side effects. I do not suppose that you encountered any unusual side effects from the tunneling?"

Preston responded, "Unusual, in what way, madam?"

Julia looked at him thinking, *yes, Marie would like this one, very polite and dreamy eyes.* "Strange animals, Constable."

Preston looked at Lestrade. "No, I cannot say that we did, although at the beginning there was not a lot of wildlife around since it was winter and everything was pretty much in hibernation. We were traveling by dogsled most of the time."

Sarah looked up from scratching and petting King. "What is a dogsled?"

Isaiah tried to quiet his daughter who looked determined to find out what the man was talking about.

Preston smiled, "It is how we travel up north in the winter; teams of dogs pull sleds. King here is a lead dog."

Sarah looked at her father and then back at King as if to confirm such a strange idea. Isaiah replied, "We will talk about it later. Now be quiet while the adults finish their talk." Sarah frowned but went back to fussing over King. King for his part seemed to find this quite acceptable.

Julia smiled at her sister then looked at Preston. "You were saying, Constable."

Preston resumed his tale. "We received no reports of any unusual animals in British Columbia. If there were any we know nothing about it. If we are being open with each other, may I ask why your interest?"

John spoke up, "You are quite sure, gentlemen?"

Both Lestrade and Preston nodded in the affirmative.

John went on, "If that is the case and these events are linked and I think we can at least assume they are, that part of the problem is not manmade or some weird side effect." The other three principals agreed with John's assessment. "Simply put, gentlemen, there was a gas emitted from at least one of the tunnels that seemed to mutate various animals, and men, quite unfortunately, also having been on the receiving end of it." At this Julia looked at John with the eyes of an annoyed spouse.

John swallowed knowing that he was still in the doghouse, so to speak. "We did not know if it was part of the tunneling or a natural substance that had been released. It would seem that it was just an unfortunate natural release, assuming it is the same gang and using the same techniques."

Carl and Isaiah then began to ask questions of the two men about the tunnels to determine if indeed the same machine or techniques were being used. Based upon the descriptions and answers they received, Carl nodded to Isaiah and then said, "It sounds pretty much the same, Major, although based upon what the gentlemen said about the size of the tunnels and depth, those must have been small-scale test bores making sure the idea worked in the field, a proof of concept so to speak. I think we are dealing with the same gang."

During the interchange, Lestrade kept looking at Carl as if going back to that wanted poster. Julia noted the look on his face and filed it away, fearing that she might have to make the English detective disappear before the problem was resolved.

Julia took over, "What do you know about the men who are doing this other than they are possibly working for The Teamwork?"

Lestrade looked at her. "We do not have too much to go on, however, we are fairly certain that they are indeed members of The Teamwork. There are, as far as we know, at least five of them. One is a chemist, a Prussian, two are mechanical engineers, one is an American and the other we think is a Russian. The next is a tinker; we have very little information about him but we believe he might be an ex-Japanese Navy man. Finally, a musician, named DeBilio, French. As to the last one, we have no idea how he fits in but we are fairly sure about him."

Isaiah and Carl looked at each other. Isaiah spoke, "I have an idea. Whatever this thing is, it must be enormously powerful, so that would explain the two engineers and possibly a new fuel source. That accounts for the chemist. The tinker is easy enough, someone has to keep it running and do repairs; it must be a real challenge. I think I may know why the musician; sound is vibration. They are using acoustic energy to literally pulverize the rock in front of the machine."

Carl looked at what was fast becoming his friend. "Of course, Isaiah! That would explain the hard finish on the tunnel walls. The machine must use the material that is just outside the immediate sound projection path that is being pulverized, the energy must ram pack the walls into a thick and dense enough lining to hold up with no support. It is shear genius, evil but brilliant!" Carl thought again and then went on, "They must need to control the pitch and volume depending on what type of soil and rock they are moving through, that is why they need the musician along to make adjustments as they proceed with their tunnel and as the material they are tunneling through changes."

Isaiah took up Carl's thought process. "Yes indeed, Carl, it must be like playing an organ, constantly changing pitch, volume and tone, not to mention the duration of the sound. The control must be based upon some kind of vibration or instrument readings or both. Probably very challenging. It must take a truly outstanding musician to pull it off."

John broke in, "But what is it for? I mean, yes, you can mine gold with it or other precious metals, but the enormous cost of the thing and such a highly talented crew? It does not sound very profitable."

The team plus the two Crown representatives looked at each other. Preston spoke, "What if it has nothing to do with mining, that it is just a cover or a test run?"

Morton's face lit up, "Of course, that is it!"

Father Peter looked at John. "You are right, John! It must be; this device is a weapon of war."

Lestrade, Preston, Julia and the others looked at the pair. It was Julia who asked the question, "John, Peter, what are you two talking about?"

As it was, it was Father Peter who spoke, "Julia, imagine being able to come up behind the enemy's front line with a tunnel to bring your troops in, spilling assault units out before they could react. No army would have a chance. The Union tried it at Petersburg at the Battle of the Crater. It took a full regiment weeks, men who had been recruited from Pennsylvania, coal miners who were used to digging tunnels, and it was truly effective. It only failed because the rest of the army did not think it would work and the general in charge of the assault was drunk most of the time, so the army was not prepared to follow up fast enough. That took an enormous amount of time and manpower, but what if it could be done in a matter of days?"

John spoke than, "Even worse, whole cities could be held with hostage tunnels bored under them packed with explosives. Sneak attacks so devastating war would be changed forever. No area would be safe especially with The Teamwork controlling it. The slaughter would be incalculable."

They all looked sick. The future with The Teamwork controlling such a machine was too horrible to envision.

After a time Julia looked at Preston and Lestrade. "Gentlemen, I believe we can agree that this is a threat that confronts all of the people of the world not just our respective countries. We work together?"

The two lawmen looked at each other. It was Preston who replied, "Indeed, madam, I cannot see bothering Ottawa with such speculation; no telling what the higher-ups might want us to do, even if by some miracle they believed such a story or, on a personnel note, what would happen to my career."

Lestrade was next. "Mrs. Morton, I am not sure if I am authorized to procure trans-Atlantic cable services to report back to the Yard; quite the expense you know. Just left to my own devices so to speak."

Julia looked at John as he smiled and nodded at her. She looked at the two. "Indeed, why upset Washington with such a farfetched theory that would make us look foolish. Better we look into the matter, resolve it and then file a report. I think that is acceptable to all."

As the meeting broke up, the two foreign policemen told the rest where they were staying. Julia followed the men and dog out the door and said, "Constable Lestrade, might I have a word with you, privately?"

Lestrade looked at her, and then took a step closer while Preston moved a distance away. Lestrade simply said, "What is your concern, madam?"

Julia looked at him. "Constable, I fully believe you realize just how enormous this problem is to both our countries as well as the rest of your country's empire, compared to one criminal who I can assure you died in prison a while ago, is relatively insignificant, would you not say?"

Lestrade looked at her. "Indeed, madam, this is quite a serious problem. Anyhow the fellow in question was Welsh and a bit outside my jurisdiction, that being London. Died, you say? Well as long as his ghost does not come back to life in any Crown territory, I do believe that Her Majesty's law enforcement will close the book on the matter. That 'died part' is in writing, is it not?"

Julia smiled. "Of course, sir. I believe by now Her Majesty's government has been properly informed of his death in prison, or will soon be. You understand going through channels and all is rather time-consuming, after all he was no one of any real importance."

Lestrade smiled. "As long as it is official, madam, I believe the case is closed. Good night then."

Julia dipped her head. "In writing, sir. Good night." As she watched the two leave she breathed a deep sigh of relief.

CHAPTER 24

A Plan of Action

arly the next morning while Sarah and the rest of the team started breakfast preparations, Julia went to the fort's telegraph office. Since this was a permanent installation, compounded by the recent Indian war, the fort had its own office instead of relying on the railroad, as most such facilities did. After seeing that the coded message she had prepared in their quarters was sent, she returned for breakfast with the team, along with Preston, Lestrade and King, who had been invited the night before.

Preston seemed the most happy. "Miss Liman, might I say that was an excellent meal." King looked up from the bowl that had contained some leftovers from Sarah's cooking and was now very clean and shiny. King barked quite loudly. "It would seem King agrees with me." The mountie laughed a bit at this.

Sarah smiled and curtsied, "Thank you, sir, and you too, King. Would anyone like anything else?"

All the gentlemen and Julia agreed that they were too full to think about any more food. Isaiah smiled at his daughter, again thinking how proud he was of her.

After the dishes were cleared, John called the meeting to order. "We need a plan of action. Julia has sent a telegram to try to obtain the services of one of the army airships for scouting. We do not know yet if it will be approved, or if approved, how long it will take to get here. Meanwhile, the colonel has approved the good father's idea of mixed patrols. Peter, I would like you to accompany Lieutenant Dasson to the village to talk to Strong Bear and enlist his support for them."

Peter smiled. "I will be happy to, John. How soon will the lieutenant be leaving?" Then he swallowed while looking just the slightest bit green and asked, "Just for the record, I do not have to ride in the airship, do I?"

Isaiah, Julia and John snickered at this since they remembered Father Peter's strong and highly negative feelings on airships and traveling within them from the previous expedition, that being it was the most terrible way to travel yet invented by mankind. John, controlling his laughter replied, "In answer to your questions, Peter, the answers are, as soon as possible and no, there are no plans for you to have to ride in the airship. Is that all right then?"

Father Peter looked very relieved. With a nod to the rest he answered, "If that is the case, then I shall go to see about a mount and tack and find the good lieutenant. So if you will all excuse me." With that the priest rose and quickly exited the quarters.

Both Preston and Lestrade looked somewhat concerned. Preston spoke for the both of them. "Are you sure such an old man should be going, especially a man of the cloth?"

Julia smiled at the mountie. "Former First Sergeant Harrigan is very capable, Constable. He is quite tough underneath his clerical collar but his heart is as warm as it can be, he is truly a Godly man. Beyond that he is also as dependable as can be and because of all that he seems to have forged a friendship or at least a thaw in the relationship with the Nez Perce."

The mountie looked slightly taken aback at this but seemed to come to terms with it.

Julia smiled. "I know it seems strange but he is truly a wonderful man. I know because he helped me when I had to sort out feelings about Sarah, who had become my sister. It was hard when all your training and upbringing was about completing the mission and that nothing else should matter."

Sarah overhearing this last looked at Julia and smiled, and Julia returned the smile.

Preston, appearing somewhat more confused, looked between the two women. Both Sarah and Julia laughed and said together, "We get that a lot." Then they just laughed some more.

Morton took pity on the constable and said, "I will explain later, George. Now if you two can stop being humorous for a bit." The two ladies in question smirked but then got serious. With this bit of female silliness over Morton got back to business. "Sarah, as I said last night, I would like you to secure a map or perhaps maps of the area and begin to log in the information we already have. When Father gets back with Lieutenant Dasson have the lieutenant show you the recommended search patrols. He knows the area better than any of us. That should get you started, then show the known tunnels and direction they went on your map. Are we clear?"

Sarah perked up. "Yes, Professor. You want me to fill in the data we have and the planned search pattern so that every area is covered at least once; just like on the dig site?"

John smiled at her. "Exactly, Sarah. I knew I could count on you."

Lestrade looked somewhat surprised at this exchange. Julia caught his eye and said, "Do not worry Guiles, Sarah is our assistant archivist and performs her duties exceptionally well. Trust me, if there is anything to find by visualization, she will spot it." Sarah looked proud and lowered her head.

John looked at his wife and sighed saying, "Dear, could you, and I truly shudder to ask this, prepare some of your thunder-and-lightning devices? We will want to take this gang alive if possible. I know our two Crown representatives, myself included, would like to ask them some questions."

Julia looked at him in a totally innocent way. "Dearest, did you just indicate that you might need some of the devices that I was working on around the house that you got so upset about?" She added a serious amount of eye batting to her question.

Morton looked less than amused. "Indeed, my love, but do not push the issue. We still have my workshop to set to rights when we get home after all this is over."

Julia, feeling that the ice was thinning under her feet, smiled and replied, "Point taken, husband. You shall have my devices, that is if Isaiah can be spared to prepare some more of his cases."

John smiled at his wife and then looked at Isaiah. "You heard the lady, my friend, any problem with her request?"

Isaiah shook his head. "Already ahead of you, Major. I have made some up, although I will have to empty them and remove the TNT. It should be simple enough to do and then refill them with Julia's special formula."

Morton smiled. "Good. Please, as soon as possible. We have no idea when we will catch up with them. Jason and Adam, I want you two to accompany the patrols and take notes on what they find, if anything. Corporal, Sam, same detail. I would prefer that the new men work with you but we will be spread thin. There seems to be no help for it." Next, John looked at the mountie. "George, would you ride with Jason or Adam? Your experience at tracking could be useful."

The constable replied, "And it would keep me under the eye of one of your operatives." Transferring his gaze to Julia, he asked, "If I might, thunder-and-lightning devices, madam?"

Julia replied before John could. "Indeed, Constable, a low power-explosive, but a bright flash with quite a loud bang to stun or shock rather than kill. It should help us to capture one of the gang at least."

John nodded in agreement with his wife and then went on, "To answer your question to me, George, I will not lie to you, sir. I trust you but only to a certain point. However I do feel that your experience would be of great use. I am not sure if you should take King. No offense but we are not sure all the mutated animals have been accounted for."

Preston looked at King. "He is a good part of my tracking ability; he will be safe." King merely looked up and barked as if to say, *Indeed, sir, it hurts that you should question my abilities, I am, after all, a member of Her Majesty's Northwest Mounted Police.*

John smiled at Preston and his four-legged partner. Then shifting his head slightly, looked at the other Crown officer and continued on, "Constable Lestrade, I am somewhat at loose ends with what to do with you. You do not seem to have the skills for field scouting. Any suggestions?"

Lestrade looked quizzical for a moment and then replied, "I suggest, Professor, that I go back to doing what I had been doing, that being hanging around and listening to the folks around the village and fort. These men must need some supplies or perhaps a bit of relaxation, so someone may know something about our quarry without even being aware of it."

Morton nodded. "That sounds good. I suggest that you take Father Peter with you when he returns from his trip. He is not only a good listener but he knows the idiom better than you do. He could be a big help. Going to the Indian village is one thing, but spending day after day in the saddle is another and he is not that young."

Lestrade returned Morton's nod and noted, "And like the constable, keeps me under the eye of one of your people."

Morton smiled, "Just so Guiles. As with the constable, I do trust you, but I will still keep both eyes open." Morton looked around the table. "I believe we all have our assignments. Julia, after you have finished working with Isaiah, perhaps you would assist the constable and Father Peter. You could blend in with some of the shadier ladies in the area in case our evildoers are looking for that sort of relaxation."

The mountie and Scotland Yard man looked a bit shocked at this last. Julia smiled at them. "Not to worry, gentlemen, it would not be the first time I have played that role; after all, it is good for catching the eye of shy, quiet, dull museum professors." At this last as she smiled at John.

The two men looked at each other. Finally Lestrade laughed and nodding to Morton remarked, "As I noted previously sir, quite the catch."

Morton smiled and reached over to Julia just to stroke her cheek again. "Indeed, Constable, indeed."

At this the meeting broke up.

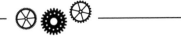

There was little for most of the team to do for the next several days since it would take that long for Lieutenant Dasson and Father Peter to talk to Strong Bear and organize the search parties. So the two sharpshooters and the two rookies practiced their skills; in this they were joined by Preston along with King.

Sarah was busy however. She obtained the maps that the professor requested and began the painstaking task of filling in the data they already had. This included the tunnels they had found so far. She also noted the various attacks and animal sightings, as well as possible sightings or other activities such as strange tracks. A large part of it was interrogating the men who brought in their team's information to make sure the positions and details were as accurate as possible. It was after being put through one of Sarah's post-scouting reports, as she referred to them, that Lieutenant Dasson remembered back to his first meeting with Morton and his team and how Morton warned him about a court martial being preferable to misplacing a specimen in Sarah's charge. He most assuredly, after intense questioning from Sarah about another tunnel, began to truly understand the profound depth of that comment. As usual, Sarah's work was meticulous.

Julia was also doing her duty although looking far different then she had up to that point since she had donned her working clothes, as she called them. These consisted of her bottle-green dress which showed her cleavage and rather shapely legs up to her knees. Black fishnet stockings and high-heeled, black ankle boots with white pearl buttons completed the ensemble, along with far more makeup then she normally wore, and long, flashy earrings. She remembered that John liked the look which he had seen during the Ratten affair, which he affirmed several times when she returned to their compartment after working the saloons. John was very rigid on his still liking the look, much to her satisfaction.

Julia began to hang around the saloons in the bar area and music houses while Lestrade worked the crowd. This allowed them to keep an eye on each other. Julia on Lestrade because there was still a question of whether or not he was working with them or using them, while Lestrade served as a backup to Julia in case a man got out of hand. He also steered her toward some promising leads. In truth, none of them turned up much relating to their problem, but some of the leads and information were forwarded to the local sheriff or U.S. Marshal since they would be interested in information related to smuggling, claim jumping and theft, along with other assorted crimes.

It was six days later that things finally started to move forward. Led by Strong Bear, some thirty Nez Perce braves arrived at the fort for the scouting details. Although the air was tense, there was at least no violence. Part of this was due to the civility that Washburn and Strong Bear showed toward each other. The former enemies respected each other's skill, bravery and integrity. Additionally, Sergeant Bodkins and his troopers had talked to the rest of the command over beers about what they had seen, along with the members of the museum's scientific research team, the result being that the fort's troops had enough knowledge that this was a serious danger and that all hands, even Indian ones, were needed. The braves that Strong Bear brought with him had either seen the strange animals or understood what happened to Strong Elk. They also grasped clearly the seriousness of the situation. They knew well that their families were in danger and understood that the whites were needed. Whether it was Father Peter's suggestion about "the enemy of my enemy is my friend" or all the men involved on both sides were experienced solders or braves and understood the value of following orders. The details were set. Based upon Tinsman's suggestion, at least one man in each patrol was issued a Sharps fifty-caliber Buffalo Rifle in case they needed something with more power than their standard-issue trapdoor 45-70s or the Indian's forty-five Long Colt repeaters.

A week after Julia had sent her telegram, the fort received a reply stating that an army airship would be on station soon. Colonel Washburn on hearing this wondered exactly who Julia Morton knew. Her husband's statement that it was high in the United States Government's hierarchy, indeed seemed a bit of an understatement, however he wisely decided that it was perhaps better if he did not inquire too deeply into the matter.

As the days and weeks progressed Sarah began to fill in her map. Lieutenant Dasson, along with one of the Nez Perce braves, reviewed Sarah's map and set up the patrols such that slowly they covered section-by-section areas around the original sightings of tunnels and animals. There were numerous encounters with more strange animals, some of them deadly. Three army troopers and four Nez Perce braves were injured or killed in the first week. As Father Peter had predicted, there was less tension between the two groups as the days passed. When you need to depend on the man next to you for your life, the color of his skin tends to take a far distant second place in importance to whether or not you can count on him when it seems as if you are in the middle of the road where the devil was moving hell and a new load was passing by.

Tinsman's suggestion about the Buffalo Rifles was also proven sound as time progressed. The animals they found tended to be more primitive and larger, not to mention hungrier. Even those who were not meat eaters were dangerous. The size and defensive weaponry, such as horns or tails with spikes, could kill not just a man but gut a horse with little or no problem. Also, there had to be constant vigilance as even the smaller ones were quite nasty; these tended to spout a wicked set of razor sharp teeth or had a poisonous bite. It became apparent that the more time elapsed the greater the regression became. John theorized that the changes brought about by the gas had something to do with their ravenous appetites as the creatures were rapidly changing form and gaining size.

It was now obvious that the one tunnel that had been closed could not account for all the strange animals being seen and dealt with. Isaiah, Carl and Tinsman were kept quite busy sealing up newly found tunnels, so much so that Julia found it necessary to send for more of her preferred explosive. They also found that, while not all of them did, several of the tunnels were emitting the gas that caused the strange mutations.

Days and evenings passed without any new leads. The team, which now included the Scotland Yard man and the mountie, was wondering if they would ever catch a break in this mystery. Everyone kept working as hard as they could, but, as with most things in life, a lead came from a totally chance encounter.

For a change from the frantic pace and since there were no new tunnels to check out and then close, Carl asked Jennifer if she would like to go into the small town for dinner, to which she agreed. He had arranged for Sarah and Molly to watch the children. It was obvious to all that the two adults were attracted to each other. Jennifer had been trying to find a way to ask Carl about his involvement with the museum's expedition and was still sorting out her feelings in her own head. Carl found that Jennifer was sensitive, and, he thought, very pretty. He had also noted that even though she received an emotional battering over the last several years she was still holding together. He remembered Julia's comment that the frontier did not tolerate the weak.

The small eatery, hardly an elegant restaurant, actually more like a rundown cafe, had an old and somewhat battered piano in the corner that no one was playing. The two lonely people sat there over a plain but tasty dinner talking about inconsequential things, each looking for the right way to go into deeper subjects. It was at this point that a man who had been eating alone said something to the waiter. The waiter replied and pointed to the piano in the corner with a shrug. The man got up and went over to the musical instrument and pulling up a chair from a nearby vacant table sat down. With no music in front of him he began to play. Even though the poor battered piano was out of tune the man managed to pull some beautiful melodies from it.

At first Carl really did not notice the music but then something caught his attention and he began to listen very carefully to the music, much to Jenifer's annoyance. Finally Jennifer made to get up and leave. Carl began to panic, for he was really beginning to feel affection for Jennifer and the children.

"Jennifer, please, I cannot explain right now, but this is important," Carl spoke quietly to her while he reached over the table and held her hand.

Jennifer, her eyes flashing with annoyance replied, "I can hear that the man plays well, but what is so important?"

Carl looked at her. "I really cannot explain now, but I need you to go and fetch John or Julia as quickly as you can." Jennifer looked as if she was ready to issue a harsh retort. Carl went on, "I am not being flippant when I say that man playing the piano may be involved in the death of your brother. Please do it!"

Jennifer looked torn between wanting to leave Carl or do as he said. "Are you sure?" she hissed.

Carl looked at her and replied, "I am not positive, but I honestly believe that it is a strong possibility."

She looked for a moment as if she were fighting some internal battle but then looked at Carl who she was beginning to see a future with. "If you say so, I will be on my way."

As she got up and left, Carl sat there and ordered some more coffee. It was in the third saloon in the town that she found Julia. Her world was shaken by the cowboys and farmers who leered at her, even in the plain dress that she had worn to go out with Carl; actually it was about the only dress that she had salvaged from the remains of her home. In truth, it was Julia who saw her first. Carl had told her that Julia and another man were working undercover in the saloons. She had no idea what undercover meant but she bravely went in to look for the pair. Julia saw Jennifer enter the saloon and began to make her way over to her. When she got up to her she noted that Jennifer was scared as some of the drunks where giving her the eye. She jumped when Julia whispered in her ear, "Jennifer, what are you doing here? I thought you were going out with Carl."

Jennifer wheeled about and her eyes went wide looking at Julia, seeing her in her working clothes. Shocked seemed to be a very mild word to describe the look on her face. Sputtering, she said simply, "Julia, why are you dressed like that?" Her whole face flushed with shock.

Julia took her arm and led her out the door to a shadowy patch of ground at the front of the saloon. "I am working, trying to find a lead on the men who are creating all this chaos. Why are you here?"

Jennifer was still trying to process this entirely new world, never having been in a saloon before except for the first two where she had been trying to find Julia before Julia found her. She most certainly had not seen one of her friends, as she now thought of Julia, dressed in such a lascivious fashion. "Does John know what you are doing and how you are dressed?"

Julia looked annoyed but before she could say anything, Lestrade showed up. "Julia, is everything all right?" He was concerned since he was to act as her backup and up to this point had not met Jennifer.

Julia replied, "I think it is, Guiles. Yes, Jennifer, John knows what I am doing and how I am dressed. I cannot take the time to explain now but it is part of my job. Now why are *you* here?"

Jennifer seemed to pull herself together. "Can we talk in front of this man?"

Julia smiled, responding, "Indeed Jennifer. May I present Detective Constable Guiles Lestrade of Scotland Yard from London, England. Guiles, may I present Jennifer Swenson. Her brother was killed and their farm was destroyed earlier by some of the strange animals."

Lestrade said hello and that he was sorry for her loss. Julia cut him off. "Jennifer, why are you here?"

Jennifer shook her head as if trying to assimilate all this new information. ""Carl and I were having dinner at the cafe when a man began to play the piano. Carl started listening intently to it, I do not know why, I mean it was good and all..." Before she could ramble on Julia grasped her shoulders to bring her back. Jennifer mentally regrouped and went on, "Anyhow, he said I should find you or John and to tell you that the man might have something to do with Paul's death. What could a piano player have to do with his death?" This last was almost a shout as Jennifer was on the edge of hysteria.

Julia assessed the situation quickly. "Guiles, I need you to go to the cafe and give Carl some back up while I return to the fort and change into something a bit less flashy. Jennifer, will you take Guiles to the cafe?"

Jennifer looked at the two of them, trying to sort things out in her mind. She realized that something might indeed be up as both Julia and the new man seemed to find Carl's interest in the musician worth following up. She wet her lips, and straightening up she replied, "Yes, I can do that. Please come along Guiles." With that she started out for the cafe.

Julia said after the pair, "I will be there as quickly as I can."

CHAPTER 25

More Tea With Questions That Julia Did Not Want Asked

arl was so intent on watching the man playing the piano that he did not see Jennifer and Lestrade come into the cafe, thus he was somewhat surprised and nervous when Lestrade pulled out a chair and sat down next to him, although he was pleased when Jennifer also appeared and sat down. He smiled at Jennifer and then looked at Lestrade, and speaking very quietly, he asked him, "Are we working together, Constable?"

Lestrade held the man's eyes steady on his own and replied, "Carl, Mrs. Morton asked me a similar question and I will give you the same answer. Wales is outside my jurisdiction so I was only mildly curious. Furthermore, the lady assured me that the man in question died in prison, so as far as I am concerned, as long as his ghost does not show up in Crown territory the case is closed."

Jennifer wondered what it all meant and was determined to find out, but before she could ask, Carl spoke again, "I think I can assure you that there is almost no chance of that ghost turning up in British territory. We work together then." Carl put out his hand and the London copper took it and they shook on it.

Carl then nodded toward the man playing the piano, "DeBilio?"

Lestrade nodded. "I have never seen the man but the general description fits and the fellow is obviously a talented musician."

Carl rubbed his jaw in thought. "Well, this is more your area of expertise then mine, Constable. What is our next move?"

Lestrade thought for a moment. "I would like to have him in for questioning, but it is not as if we can pinch him here in the cafe. I suppose we will just have to wait for him to leave."

Jennifer looked at the two men. She licked her lips as if to build up her courage. "Do both of you think that this man may have had something to do with Paul's death?"

Lestrade looked at her. "Indeed, madam, it is highly possible. I am not sure but it seems to fit."

Jennifer appeared to be looking inside herself as if weighing some serious matter, and squaring up her shoulders, reached a decision. "If I can lure him outside, would that work?"

Carl looked ashen but it was Lestrade who responded, "Indeed, madam that would be most excellent."

Jennifer smiled at Carl and undid several of the top buttons on the front of her dress. Running her fingers through her hair and with a bit of a forced smile, murmuring more to herself then her two companions, said, "If Julia can do this so can I." She got up and walked over to the man playing the piano. She leaned against the piano and looked down at the man.

The man looked at her from the corner of his eye and said, "Do you like it?" He had a trace of an accent but Jennifer had no real experience with foreign accents except some Norwegian ones from back home before she moved out west.

She smiled and replied, "It is very pretty. Do you know any romantic songs that might warm up a lonely widow lady?" She gave her hips a bit of a sway in time with the tune he was playing.

"I believe I do, madam. My name is Mikhail, what is yours?" He changed the tune into a slow waltz tempo that certainly would do the trick for what the lady wanted.

As the two men watched from the table they saw Jennifer smiling at the man but could not make out the conversation over the sounds of the piano. Guiles tapped Carl on the shoulder and they paid their bill, and then moved easily out the door and into the shadows. Lestrade pulled a small bottle out of his pocket and a piece of cloth along with a pair of manacles. He handed the irons to Carl and the pair stood ready.

Inside, Jennifer kept smiling at the man Mikhail. "You have been playing a long time. Would you like to take a break and get some night air?" As she said this she was running her hand along the V of her neckline where she had opened the extra buttons.

Mikhail smiled and finished the tune he was playing with a bit of a flourish and stood up. Smoothly he took Jennifer's arm, and stopping by the front counter, paid his bill. As they exited, Jennifer ran her hand up the man's arm and turned so that they were headed into a bit of shadow, so they were hid from prying eyes. Jennifer turned and smiled up at the man. *Too bad,* she thought, *he is rather handsome.* It was at this point that a very quiet Lestrade put the piece of cloth over the man's face. His eyes opened in surprise and he started to turn but he suddenly slumped and Carl, who had moved as soon as Lestrade accosted the man, helped to catch him.

Jennifer, who was shaking like a leaf in a strong breeze, tried to smile. Lestrade took the irons from Carl and applied them, looking at Jennifer and said, "Well done, madam, you did very well indeed."

"What did you use on him? He went down so fast," asked Jennifer hoping that the man was not hurt, even if he had something to do with her brother's death and her home being destroyed.

Lestrade smiled and seemed almost cheerful. "Not to worry, Miss Jennifer, just a touch of chloroform. He will be sleeping like a baby for a while, at least till we get him someplace where we can have a nice friendly chat." To finish off securing the man, Lestrade reached into an interior coat pocket and pulled out a bag and slipped it over the man's head. Then he seemed effortlessly to pick the man up and put him over his shoulder. Both Carl and Jennifer were surprised; it seemed that the good constable was quite a bit stronger than his small frame would suggest. He looked at the pair and seeing the looks on their faces, shrugged, even with the burden he was carrying, and said, "Special Branch lightweight boxing champ back home." With this simple statement he started off in the direction of the train since he explained to the pair in his wake that he thought it would be a bit of a bowl of sticky pudding to explain why he was carting a chap over his shoulder in irons, with a sack over his head no less, to the sentry at the fort's gate.

With those words of explanation from Lestrade, Jennifer separated from the men and went to find Julia at the fort and tell her to meet them at the train. Before long Lestrade, with some help from Carl, had the man secured in a chair in the parlor of the train's main car.

Shortly thereafter Jennifer led a more modestly dressed Julia, along with John, Constable Preston, with King of course, and Father Peter into the parlor. The rest of the team was busy at other things. The group took positions just as some noises and movement indicated the man was coming around. The group stood in front of him as Lestrade pulled the sack off his head. Julia had a sharp intake of breath and the color drained from her face. "Mikhail!" gasped a stunned Julia.

Mikhail looked around blinking and letting his eyes adjust to the light again. He looked at Julia, smiled and replied, "Ah, my beautiful dark-haired American czarina, just as lovely as when I last saw you after our work in Anchorage. I believe that you are still working for your uncle's agency?"

John Morton looked furious; Julia looked somewhat sick. Finally she pulled herself together enough to say, "Please untie this man. If I may present to you all, Mikhail Cznerka of the Russian czar's secret police." Julia swallowed and started introductions, somewhat forcefully, with John, "Mikhail, may I introduce my husband, Professor John Morton."

Before she could continue, Mikhail, looking sad, spoke up, "You mean to tell me, my czarina, that you are, as you Americans say, off the market? How sad. I had given up hope of ever seeing you again and when I do meet you, you are with another man. Ahhh, such tragedy!" This last delivered in a totally dramatic way.

John looked thunderstruck and Father Peter looked like a cross between embarrassed and curious, since he was aware of some of Julia's life before John Morton came into it. The others were wearing looks of just plain confusion.

Julia tried to make light of the whole incident. "Mikhail and I met on a previous assignment in Alaska during the purchase of the territory from his government. We worked together as a team. Even if we were working for our own governments, the ends we were working for were the same. Mikhail, how have you been?" Under her breath she murmured, "Married I hope."

By this time Carl and Lestrade had the ropes and irons off the man. He stood up and grabbing Julia's hand and with a low bow kissed it with a typically Russian flourish. "I will always treasure the time we spent in San Francisco after we finished up that assignment, but you were introducing me to you companions, da?"

Putting on a brave front, Julia continued with the introductions. John looked as if he was ready to explode. Father Peter looked as if he thought he might have to tackle John. Just then Sarah came in having finished as much as she could on her maps. She looked friendly enough since she had missed the previous conversation.

Mikhail looked at her and Julia with a raised eyebrow. Julia said, "Mikhail Cznerka of the Russian czar's intelligence service, may I present my all-but-blood sister, Sarah Liman."

The Russian looked confused for a moment, then smiled, and clicking his heels together bowed and said, "Miss Liman, your humble servant."

Sarah curtsied just as Julia taught her and replied, "Thank you, sir. I am pleased to meet you."

Mikhail went on, "Mistress Liman, I must hear the story of how you and Julia became sisters; I can only assume it is a fascinating tale, young miss."

Julia jumped in, "Later Mikhail, right now the question is, what are you doing here? I assume you are not on vacation."

Mikhail, looking around, spoke, "Let me see. A beautiful American assassin with her professor husband, an English policeman along with a Canadian gentleman of the same persuasion and several others whom I am not sure of their part yet. I believe we are all working on the same problem, The Teamwork."

This time it was John who spoke up, and the irritation in his voice was evident. "What are you talking, about, sir?"

Mikhail looked at him and then back to Julia. "Please let us not waste time. I am on the trail of a Russian subject. He is an engineer named Glinka. We believe he has tendered his services to an international crime syndicate that is known as The Teamwork."

Julia was still trying to figure out how she was going to explain all of this to John, however, she realized that she must put that concern on the back burner and deal with the immediate problem. "Mikhail, first of all, it is Agent," her eyes darting down towards Sarah, "and for the record, we have decided that whatever problems exist between our governments, it is not relevant to the immediate problem of stopping The Teamwork and their monster war machine. Do you wish to join with us on that basis?"

Mikhail looked at the assembled group and with a note of surprise replied, "War machine?"

John took up at this point, "Indeed, sir, an immense subterranean tunneling machine that we feel is being tested as an instrument of war."

The Russian looked somewhat stunned at this idea. "We were aware of the fact that this syndicate was up to no good, but an immensely powerful engine of war, are you sure?"

John looked at the man. "It seems to be the only logical conclusion for their activities. While it would aid mining operations, the construction and operating costs would be prohibitive, but as an engine of war it quite unfortunately makes much better sense. Yes, we firmly believe they are testing such a weapon."

Mikhail looked at the faces surrounding him and came to a conclusion. "There were some whispers that The Teamwork was preparing to come out of the shadows, but for open warfare? That is far beyond anything we had heard. However, knowing what we do about this group, I believe it is something they would do. They are truly diabolic."

Seeing the looks going across John's face, as well as noting the paling of Julia's complexion after seeing who they captured, Father Peter spoke up, "Before we tell you what we have so far, what can you add to the pool of information, sir?"

Mikhail looked at the priest with a bit of surprise on his face since in his experience found it rare to meet actively involved clergy in his work. "Father, it is nice to meet you. Glinka is a brilliant engineer well known to my government. He worked on several of the designs for the czar's newest ironclads and is perhaps one of the foremost experts on steam engines in the world. When he suddenly disappeared we thought he had been kidnapped. Sadly, our investigations showed us that he had left voluntarily to join a shadowy organization called The Teamwork. I was assigned to bring him home. My government did not feel comfortable with his working for others knowing he had valuable information about our navy."

By this time Morton had calmed down if only because the analytic portion of his brain kicked in trying to fit these new pieces of the puzzle into place. He brought Mikhail up to date on what they found and on the strange gas that had almost killed him and Carl, not to mention the strange mutations of the various animals.

The entire group seemed to be mulling over the new information the Russian supplied, but, as before, there were serious gaps in their knowledge starting with where The Teamwork agents were camped out. They filled the Russian in on what they knew so far.

The group decided to reconvene in the morning so they could sleep on the new events and knowledge.

John and Julia returned to John's compartment, which Julia was dreading. John started, "Just how well do you know this man?"

Julia looked at her husband. "John, it was before I met you and I fell in love with you. I was younger then, about seventeen, and it was one of my first field assignments, actually it was my second, but the first was just a minor affair. Secretary Seward had started the land purchase, but with England in the war things had become much more complicated with England trying to ruin the deal. Our government wanted to finish up the transaction since it was taking far too long. Uncle William sent me to help move things along; that is where I met Mikhail. Mikhail was older and a dashing, well-established undercover agent. I suppose you could say I was a bit smitten, with a touch of hero worship, since I was new in the active field business, but for what it is worth, I was not in love with him, more like a bit of lust. It was truly the first time I realized I might die during an assignment and I guess a good part of it was myself just showing me I was indeed still quite alive."

John looked at his wife, trying to sort through his own emotions. "How many more are there, Julia?"

Julia looked at John somewhat sadly and replied, "And you John, how many women before we married? You seemed to know quite a bit on our wedding night for someone who got all his information out of his scientific journals. I never presented myself as something that I was not. I was a spy and an assassin; you knew that going into our marriage. Especially after you saw me working in Los Angeles, did you have the idea that using my body to gain information was out of bounds?"

John Morton continued to look at his wife, a woman who had captured his heart and his very soul. "Julia, I guess knowing it and being able to not think about it, is much easier than having it thrown up in my face. They are two different things. I am trying to get used to the idea of another man knowing you."

Julia reached out to John and stroked his face. "John, know this then, you are my love and the man I want to have a family with, not just to prove I am alive but to build a future with. Last week at the cave when I thought you had been changed forever and I had lost you, I felt like I died inside. I could not get over the look on Jennifer's face when she told me how she lost her husband. There is no one, nor has there ever been anyone who can take your place, my love."

The two embraced. John whispered, "Are you over him?"

Julia snuggled into her man. "Over you, never sir. That other fellow, I was never in love with him. Like I said it was more to prove to myself I was really still alive. That, my beloved, is the truth."

The rest of the evening passed passionately but deep and tenderly as it can only be between two people who love each other and want so much to assure themselves of that love and bond.

CHAPTER 26

SARAH BEGINS TO SEE A PICTURE EMERGE

By the time the team started to trickle in, Cook already had breakfast started and had allowed Sarah to assist. Sarah thought this grand since he shared some of his deep, dark, culinary secrets with her. She thought it was a mark of what he thought of her abilities, which in truth, indeed it was.

Next in was Julia who made for the tea storage and hot water so that a cup of that most delightful beverage could start its timely process of transforming water into the elixir of life, which tea was as far as she was concerned. While the transformative process was started, Sarah finished up her immediate task and looked at Julia. Wetting her lips a bit nervously she asked, "Julia was there something going on between the professor and Mr. Cznerka?"

Julia looked a bit shocked at this question believing that Sarah had not noticed. "Oh dear, Sarah, how do I explain this. John was a bit jealous when he found out I knew Mikhail from the time before I met him. Thanks be to God I was able to calm him down. I convinced him of the truth, that John Morton was the only man in my life who I really care about. The one I truly love. It is sometimes difficult when your past catches up to you." Julia stopped to remove the tea ball and add just a bit of sugar and lemon, then taking a sip, "So you see, little sister, why you should be careful of what you do now."

Sarah looked at Julia. "Did you care about him, Mr. Cznerka I mean?"

Julia smiled, "No, not really that way Sarah, only as a friend, it was just a young girl's relief at being alive after almost being killed on my first major assignment as a field agent, and Mikhail was handsome and very dashing. You remember last night how he made you feel when he was bowing to you." Sarah smiled at this for indeed he had. Julia went on, "But in love, no, I was never in love with him. He was a fantasy not a husband. The John Mortons of the world are the ones you fall in love with. Honest, stable and dependable, the ones who come home at night after work. The ones you want to have a family with, the ones you want for a father for your children." Sarah looked thoughtful at this advice from her big sister. Julia hugged her and with a lighthearted laugh, "With just the right amount of adventure in their blood and very handsome and sexy too."

Sarah giggled at this "Like Jonah?"

Julia smiled. "Who knows, give it time, Sarah. You have time, enjoy and savor it, little sister."

John had overheard the conversation as he stood just outside the entry into the kitchen. He smiled and felt much less worried. He thought to himself, and not for the first time, how much he wanted and needed Julia in his life; damaged workshops notwithstanding.

John did his best to look as if he had overheard nothing and opened the door and entered. After extending a good morning to Cook and the ladies, he prepared a cup of coffee. Mumbling something about too many cooks spoiling the broth, he retreated to the parlor and seated himself.

The rest of the team finally arrived with Corporal Tinsman joining them since the other three men of his unit were out on scouting patrols while he rotated back for a bit of rest.

John opened the meeting as the breakfast dishes were cleared. "While I was sitting here waiting for the rest of you, the colonel sent a note saying that the USAS Franklin would be on station today and did we have any specific areas we want her to scout. I am open to suggestions—anyone?"

The rest of the team looked at one another and of all people it was Sarah who raised her hand. Morton acknowledged her with a nod of his head and spoke quite formally, "The chair recognizes Miss Liman."

Sarah spoke quietly, obviously somewhat nervous, "Professor, if I may get my map, I will be right back."

John looked at her. "Very good, Sarah. Personally I could stand to have another cup of coffee, so off you go."

Sarah disappeared from the table in the direction of the compartment she nominally shared with Julia although she was getting used to the idea of it being just hers since Julia spent most evenings with John. Morton, retrieving the coffee pot, proceeded to pour another cup of Cook's excellent brew. He had just finished his second sip when Sarah returned. She unrolled her map, which both Julia and Father Peter noted was very well done. Both were quite proud since Julia and Peter had been responsible for Sarah's lessons when she first joined them. Sarah, having anchored the map down with the creamer and sugar bowl and stealing several coffee cups from Father Peter and Tinsman as well began to point out the details on the map.

Sarah had been meticulous with the information she put on the map. "Professor, I think that we should search in this area here." Sarah, using a fork, noted an area on the map that seemed empty.

Carl spoke up, "Why there, Sarah, there has been no activity noted."

Sarah gulped and tried to build up her courage. "I know, but if you look at the pattern, there were several tunnels found in this area which you thought were the oldest, based upon, I think you called it deterioration. Then the next series were here," pointing to another area just east of the first." Continuing on, "Then these were found," again pointing to an area further east. "If your dating of the tunnels is correct, then I would guess that they would start moving to a new area, and based upon the last two moves it should be in this valley area."

John stood up, along with Father Peter and stared intently at the map. Peter smiled, and looking at Sarah said, "I wish we had had you instead of that showman Pinkerton during the war. I dare say our intelligence operation would have been vastly improved, Sarah."

John spoke up, "Even if they change their pattern, Sarah, this is a very nice bit of work. All right, we can shift two of the patrols into the new area along with the Franklin."

Julia looked at John, "Why only two, John?"

John still looking at the map replied, "First, we still have to account for all the tunnels. There may be ones we have not found yet with the gas that could lead to future danger to both the settlers and the Indians. Second, these men may not have gotten Sarah's memo." He looked at Peter, "Just like the rebels did not at Sharpsburg, remember Peter?"

Peter looked up and smiled. "Indeed John, but if I were a betting man I think I would put my money on Sarah's work. Quite the detective would you not say, Constable?" looking at the Scotland Yard officer.

Lestrade laughed a bit then looked serious. "We could use you at the Yard, Miss Liman. Should you ever feel the urge to travel across the pond, I would be happy to put in a good word for you."

Sarah beamed at this praise while Julia just smiled. Isaiah was very proud of his daughter and was busy trying to figure out how he could get a ride in the Franklin.

As the meeting broke up, John sent Tinsman to have Lieutenant Dasson rework the patrols to cover the area suggested by Sarah and still keep looking for tunnels in the previous areas. It was about eleven-thirty in the morning when a giant shadow passed over the fort and the USAS Franklin came to a hover. About an hour later the ship's crew and the ground crew had the airship secured to a mast. The great ship began taking on supplies and the ship's captain and first officer reported to Colonel Washburn's office.

It was there that they met John, Julia and Sarah, with the exception of Father Peter who was taking some time to minister to the fort's soldiers, dependents and townspeople, there being no Catholic priest in the area currently. The rest of the team members were out searching for new tunnels, or in the case of Carl, Adam and Jason, closing up existing ones. Colonel Washburn made the introductions. "Major Ian

Fraser, Captain of the Franklin, and his First Officer, First Lieutenant William Fox, I would like you to meet Professor John Morton of the New York Museum, his wife and assistant Julia Morton, and Miss Sarah Liman, Julia's assistant.

Captain Fraser looked at the three and then spoke with some strain showing, "Frank, please explain to me why I was pulled off my patrol to help a museum scientific team?" It was obvious to all that Captain Fraser was not a happy man.

Colonel Washburn looked at the annoyed major and simply responded, "Ian, Bill, I think you better sit down. The information you are about to receive is above classified and to be honest it is one hell of a tale. Would either of you like a drink before you hear it?"

Both of the new officers looked at him as if he had just sprouted an extra head, then they turned their attention to the three museum staff. It was obvious from the looks they gave them that they thought Sarah was the true wild card. What could a young Negro girl have to do with classified information that was so important as to pull one of the army's all-too-few airships off patrol. Trying to sort all this out, both took their seats. They however turned down the offer of a drink.

John started in, "Gentlemen, while it is true that we are a museum research expedition, in reality that is our cover. We are also a special government team that has been sent out here to deal with an exceptionally dangerous situation."

Major Fraser interrupted in an anything-but-friendly fashion, "Who do you work for Morton, and what is a little colored child doing here?"

Julia started to respond when John put a hand on her to restrain her. He knew how Julia tended to react to anyone making derogatory comments about Sarah. "Major, let me be frank with you. My orders come from very high up in the United States Government, which exact department you do not need to know, sir, except to say that it has the full backing and complete cooperation of the War Department. Second, you, sir, will treat my team members with respect, am I clear! This 'little colored child', as you phrased it, has risked her life to defend her friends and been an invaluable member of my team. She speaks at least four languages and can partially follow several more. Her ability to record and present information is at the very top tier of such people, and finally, and most importantly, for your safety, my wife sees her as her sister, and trust me you do not want to make the lady mad. She has already carried out several sanctions for our government. Any further comments?" At this last Sarah looked at Julia with a bit of shock.

Major Fraser looked at Morton and mentally sifted through what he had said. He looked over at Washburn who nodded as if to say he is telling you the truth. It was at this point Fraser said, "Frank, I think I will take that drink now." Fraser turned back to Morton. "Very well, Professor, tell us your tale." Meanwhile Washburn retrieved a decanter and several glasses.

Julia reached up and took her husband's hand and gave it a squeeze as if to say thank you. Sarah looked a bit upset at being part of the center of the dustup, although she was, at the same time, warmed by the way the professor stood up for her, but wondered about what the professor had said about Julia.

Morton relaxed, as he had tensed up during the responses to Fraser's questions. "Gentlemen, we think an international criminal conspiracy has been operating in the immediate area testing out what we strongly believe is a terrifying and extremely advanced weapon of war. This machine is able to tunnel through earth and rock like a fish swims through water. It leaves a tunnel for troops to follow through. As an additional problem, some of the tunnels it has left have emitted a previously unknown gas that causes mutations in various animals, including men."

This time it was Lieutenant Fox who spoke up. "What? Morton what are you talking about, mutations! This is preposterous, sir!"

Morton shook his head. "Mr. Fox, I would have said the same thing if I had not only seen it, but I almost died because of it. Your captain questioned Sarah's presence before, but let me tell you that if it had not been for her courage in helping my wife in an extremely dangerous situation, I would be dead instead of talking to you now. I was dosed, along with another member of my team, with the gas in question.

Within a short period of time, both a teammate named Carl and I were being changed into a much earlier form of man. One of the Nez Perce leaders was changed and died of it before we found out that a powerful electric shock could reverse the effects if administered immediately. His body was so changed even his family and friends did not recognize him. We have seen, been attacked by and killed creatures out of earth's prehistoric past, brutal killers, and if not carnivorous then still extremely deadly, with an array of natural weapons to challenge even the might of the United States Army."

Both officers looked at Washburn, wanting him to say this was some sort of joke. He returned their look and stated, "Ian, Bill, I have seen some of the things myself, each one worse than the one before it. A local rancher brought in a bird he had killed after it attacked and killed several of his cattle and almost made a dessert of one of his ranch hands. Yes, a bird killed a full-grown range steer, several in fact, and almost took down one of his hired men. It took all eight rounds from his Winchester to bring it down. Believe me, I thought Morton was ready for the asylum myself, but if you send him I might as well go myself because I believe him."

The two officers looked as if they had been told the United States did not exist or even God for that matter. Both took a deep sip of bourbon and looked back at Morton wondering what he was going to tell them next. Once again it was Fox who broke the silence. "Professor, you said this was a weapon of war?"

Morton relaxed a bit. He knew now that having Washburn speak up on behalf of his tale and vouch that he had seen some of the animals with his own eyes apparently gained him credibility with the two airship officers. "We are fairly sure, gentlemen. It is the only theory that fits the facts as we know them. The machine would be too expensive to operate otherwise. We have to find this machine and its crew before they escape and hopefully before more of the gas that is causing so much havoc is released. I think it would be best if Miss Liman shows you what she has found. Sarah, would you please," Morton motioned at the table.

Sarah was feeling more than a bit intimidated as she stood up, and laying her map on the table, unrolled it, and just as in the team's quarters, began to anchor it down with various objects. She looked at Julia briefly, who gave her a reassuring smile. Taking a deep breath, she started in, "This is based upon the information I received from all the various search parties of the tunnels so far discovered. I also put in the sightings and animal kills that the farmers and ranchers have supplied, and finally the same information that was supplied by the Indians. I therefore believe there is a pattern emerging." She moved her hands over the map showing the various items. "The teams of soldiers and Indians..."

She was cut off as Fraser barked out, "You have been using the Nez Perce for scouting? Are you mad?"

Surprisingly it was Colonel Washburn who replied. "Ian, I know what you are thinking but I approved it, and it has worked. First, we needed the manpower, there was just too much territory to scout; remember, we did not have the services of your ship. Second, by working together, as the priest who is part of the team suggested, it has restored some of the trust that was lost and reduced some of the tension between the whites and the Indians. The bottom line, there was not much choice. My requests for airship coverage had gone unanswered."

Fraser grunted and then, "I see your point Frank but I still do not like it." It was obvious that the Franklin's captain was still quite upset. "We cannot trust the savages."

It was Julia who responded, "You mean that the Nez Perce cannot trust the United States Government: corrupt Indian agents; being pushed off their land. As it is we are trying to build a lasting peace and it is working, Major."

The major looked at Julia as if he were ready to explode. "Madam, if it was not for your sex, I would be all too willing to give you a thrashing. Also, I do not need to be lectured by children, especially Negro children!"

Julia was becoming dangerous, so John tried to settle her down. "Julia calm yourself, we have to work together here. As for you, sir, if you want to tackle my wife you will have to go through me."

By this time, Washburn was on his feet. "Major Fraser, you will apologize to both of the ladies, both of them, immediately, am I clear!" It was obvious that the Colonel was steaming mad.

Julia seemed to calm down. John started to get very nervous as Julia was smiling her tiger smile. "Perhaps the major and I could have a chat in private, dear. That is if you do not mind Colonel; I am sure we can work this out. Perhaps if you gentlemen and Sarah would step out on the porch for a few moments."

Fraser was looking somewhat pale. "A gentleman does not strike a lady!" this last with his nose in the air.

Again that tiger smile. "Do not worry about it, Major, I am no lady."

Washburn was starting to yell now, "Ian, you will stop this now, sir, or I will have you on report! Am I clear, sir!"

Surprisingly it was Morton who spoke. "Gentlemen, Sarah, I believe we should step outside for a few moments."

Sarah was shocked, not to mention Washburn. Fox was standing there with his mouth open and no sound coming out. Morton corralled them and they went outside leaving Julia and Ian Fraser in the office.

When they were outside Washburn looked at Morton. "Sir, how could you leave your wife in there! Do you know what could happen?"

Morton said rather sickly, "All too well, Colonel."

Sarah was scared for her sister and flinched when the obvious sounds of a scuffle were heard.

John Morton sighed and went on, "Indeed I do know what could happen, Frank; I just hope Julia remembers that we need him and does not lose her temper and kill him."

Lieutenant Fox looked shocked. "Sir, I can assure you that my captain can handle himself. Colonel, we must put a stop to this!"

As suddenly as it started the noise ended with a loud thump. All the persons on the porch looked at one another. Then they heard Julia's voice, sounding distressed. "Could you all please give me some help; Major Fraser seems to have tripped and hurt himself."

As they rushed in Julia was straightening her dress and corralling a few stray curls of her raven locks while Major Fraser lay on the floor unconscious, bleeding from his nose. The map on the table was a bit messed up but not too badly. "The major seems to have tripped and hit his head on the table. Oh dear!"

Morton looked down at his wife and shook his head. Mr. Fox knelt down to check on his commanding officer. Julia asked in a concerned way, "We were just starting to discuss our differences when he caught the rug and tripped. He fell and hit his head on the table's edge. Is he all right, Mr. Fox?"

By this time Major Fraser was starting to come around, moaning. As John and Lieutenant Fox helped him to his feet, Colonel Washburn looked at him. "Ian, go use my privy over there," pointing to a door, "and clean yourself up; your nose is bleeding, sir." Fraser, groaning, mumbled something and Fox helped him over so he could get cleaned up.

Washburn looked at Julia and then turned to Morton in a bit of shock. "You live with her?"

Morton shrugged his shoulders and replied, "I think it was the comment about her sister; she is very sensitive about that."

Washburn looked at Julia and Sarah. "I believe you made your point, Mrs. Morton, and thank you for not killing him or even hurting him too badly. I have known Ian since I was a captain and when he was a new second lieutenant. He is a good man but he does carry a bit of a chip on his shoulder."

Julia looking very innocent replied, "As I said, sir, Captain Fraser simply tripped over the rug. Perhaps having a loose rug in your office is not such a good idea." She looked her innocent school girl best as she said this, while no rug was visible.

Washburn looked at her. "Well, since it was an accident, I suppose there is no reason to write anyone up. Especially since the rug in question seems to have disappeared."

"Why, I certainly do not know how that could be. It may be frowned upon but I do not believe clumsiness is covered under War Department regulations." Julia agreed most profoundly with the colonel's assessment that no one needed to be put on report.

Before long Major Fraser and Mr. Fox returned. By this time Fraser was starting to sport a black eye. Washburn looked at him. "Mrs.

Morton told me how you tripped on the rug, Ian, and hit your head on the table. I assume we need say nothing more about your bit of clumsiness, sir?"

Fraser looked at his superior officer, straightened, and then at Julia. "Indeed not, sir. I believe that I have learned my lesson about tripping over things, sir."

After a nod from John, Sarah began going over her map again.

By the time she concluded, the two officers from the Franklin had agreed to a patrol route over the area Sarah had indicated, along with a schedule to pass over the ground search parties to exchange information by way of heliograph during the day and lantern light by night if the ship could not use its landing basket. With that the meeting broke up.

As they were walking, Sarah snuck a look at Julia who was looking quite unflustered and quite the proper museum secretary. "Before you ask or even say anything, Sarah, it was just as I explained, the Major tripped and hit his head. That is the end of the story. Are we clear?"

Sarah laughed and replied, "Indeed, madam." Sarah licked her lips and asked very quietly, "Julia, when the professor said sanctions, what did he mean?"

Julia was dreading the question and even more so the answer; again the deep fear of losing Sarah. "He meant that I had to do my job, Sarah, and eliminate certain rather nasty people. The reason I have been able to train you so well is that I was so schooled. I am sorry you had to find this out, Sarah." Julia looked at her out of the corner of her eye and prayed.

Sarah seemed lost in thought, then as if making up her mind, looked at Julia. "You mean so that other little sisters would not be hurt?"

Julia breathed again. "Yes, Sarah, and not just little sisters but people of all ages and the country as a whole. It is not something I am proud of but sometimes the things we are required to do just have to be done. I am now glad I work with John on his research projects. At least virtually everything we come in contact with is long since already dead." The pair continued on their way. When they returned to their quarters, Sarah went to write out the new search plan so the teams could receive their orders.

John and Julia retired to their room. As the door closed behind him, John smiled at his wife. "I am glad you kept your temper, my love. It would have been very dicey if the Franklin lost her captain."

Julia looked somewhat less than sweet. "It was a struggle, husband. The man has an ego to match the size of his ship. If we could harness him I am sure we could inflate the Franklin what with all the hot air coming from him. No one talks about Sarah that way!" Julia looked down and she cried a little. "I had to give Sarah an answer about my former life, John."

John looked at his wife and pulled her into his arms. "Did she understand?"

Julia nodded and quietly said, "I think so, John, at least I hope and pray it is so."

John pulled her in closer. "Come here Tiger Lady."

CHAPTER 27

THE PICTURE GETS MUDDLED

As the various patrols came back in for resupply and rest, Sarah showed them the new patrol areas to be covered. After over a week of searching, both on ground and in the air, there was no sign of the men responsible.

Julia stopped in to check on Sarah. "Would you like me to make you a cup of tea, Sarah?" Julia noted how down at the mouth Sarah looked.

Sarah shrugged her shoulders and sighed, "No thank you, Julia. I do not understand; where did they go? The patrols should have spotted something by now. They cannot have just disappeared into thin air."

Julia put her arm around her and with a hug said, "They may have disappeared into solid rock, or for that matter, even bad guys take a vacation now and then. Do not worry, we will catch them. Remember, we have help from the British, Canadian and Russian governments, although in truth, I could have done without the last." Julia sighed herself at this last bit.

Sarah looked up at Julia, as her sister had not yet sat down. "Perhaps you are right, maybe some tea. Poppa and Father Peter both say tea may not fix a problem but it does make it more manageable."

As the tea was steeping, they heard the corporal of the guard yell to open the gate; a patrol was returning with wounded. Then they heard a flurry of activity on the parade ground. Rushing out, they looked at one of the patrols detailed to cover earlier ground looking for any mutated animals that might have been missed. It was not a pretty sight. Several of the troopers and Indians were badly hurt and at least two were dead.

It happened that Lieutenant Dasson was the officer of the day and ran out. "Sergeant, report!"

Jim Bodkins dismounted and saluted as best as he could although he winced in pain as he did so. "Patrol reporting, sir. Two dead; Jenkins and one of the Nez Perce, Spotted Cat. Four men injured one serious. Got banged up a bit myself, sir."

Paul looked at Bodkins. The man had, in the way of many an NCO over the centuries, transformed a raw trained-but-inexperienced second lieutenant into a first-class first lieutenant. Bodkins was the type of man that every army since the Roman Legions marched across half the world, depended on. Quietly Paul looked at him with the respect of a student for a mentor. "Jim, what happened?"

"Sir, we had been scouting, looking for more of the animals. We had seen some but nothing we could not handle, small stuff. We were bivouacked up by Lodge Pine Flat, letting the horses rest and the men heat up some food and coffee. Sir, there was a shaking like nothing I ever felt and the ground just opened up. This machine, at least I think it was a machine, exploded out of the hillside. That kid was not exaggerating, sir! My God, it was as big as the blockhouse. Horses bolted, that was what caused most of the injuries, the men got hit by the horses. The noise was like someone was trying to cut open your head from the inside. Most of us were on the ground completely shook up and crying in pain. Two of the pickets were far enough away to get a look at it and get some shots off. They just bounced off like it was armored and they were using pea shooters. No damage to whatever it was, sir."

Paul looked at Bodkins and quietly ordered, "See to your men, Sergeant, and then report to the surgeon yourself. The army cannot afford to lose you, Jim." Bodkins responded and began the task of dismissing his patrol.

Up on the porch of the team's quarters, Julia looked worried and then she glanced at Sarah who looked totally stricken. Julia grabbed her and turned her around. "Sarah, what is it?"

Sarah was mumbling, "No, that should not have happened, it was not supposed to be there. Julia I killed those men!" This last came out as a harsh cry.

Julia looked at her and holding her by the shoulders, said, "Sarah Marie Liman, you did nothing wrong, do you hear me? You are not all-knowing; you based your guess on the information you had. It was not your fault!"

Sarah looked shaken to her core. She broke free and went inside. Julia followed her and found her staring at her map with tears streaming from her eyes and running down her face.

It was later in the day when Carl, Jason and Adam, along with the detail that had accompanied them, returned to the fort after closing up several tunnels. Hearing what happened, they rushed in to talk to Julia. They found Sarah sitting, staring into space obviously feeling that whatever happened had been her fault.

Carl walked over to her. "Sarah let me see your map." Sarah just sat there as if she were alone in the room. In a much louder voice, "Sarah!"

This last seemed to have gotten through and the young girl looked up at him. "What?"

Carl spoke again, "Let me see your map, we have to figure out what changed."

Sarah shook herself and got up almost woodenly to go over to the table and unroll her map. "Here, sir, not that it is right. I was wrong and those men were hurt or died because of me." She started to cry again. Julia came over and held her.

Carl looked down at the map and noted the spot where the latest sighting was. He just stood there quietly, looking at it yet not saying a word. Suddenly, he said something in a foreign tongue and threw down his hat. Sarah looked confused and said, "What is it?"

Carl ran his hands through his hair and started muttering as if to himself and not in response to Sarah at all. "Stupid, so stupid, I should have seen it! Damn it all to hell! Not your fault Sarah, mine!" He looked at Sarah and went on, "I got lazy thinking you had nailed it down and did not look hard enough at it myself. You could not have known, but I should have."

Sarah and Julia were both staring at him. Sarah was the first one to speak. "What are you saying?"

Carl took a deep breath and spoke quietly. "Sarah it was not your fault, it was mine. Your reasoning was quite right, but you misunderstood why they were moving. Look here," pointing at the map. "These first three areas where the tunnels were found, each had a different type of subsurface condition. The area you expected them to go to has much the same type of condition as the second area. They were not moving to throw us off; they were testing the machine in different types of soils and rocks. That is why they were moving. Not your fault. You did not have the knowledge to see the pattern. I did. It is my fault. They were looking for more different materials to test the machine on."

Julia held Sarah, turned her and looked directly into her eyes. "Not your fault," she said to her.

Carl looked at the map. "However, your work was not wasted, Sarah. First, without your map and notes I would never have been able to see the pattern. Second, and possibly more important, it seems as if they want to bore at least five tunnels in the various areas in order to test their machine, which means that if this was one of their first, we still have a chance to catch up to them!"

Sarah looked at him. "You mean that my work was not wrong?"

Julia put her out at arm's length. "If Carl is right, it may be the key to unlocking this mystery."

Changing from her Big Sister persona to Agent mode she quickly said, "Sarah, go check with Sergeant Bodkins and find out all the particulars so you can update your map. I will send a messenger to meet with John's patrol so we can notify the Franklin to scout the new area. Sarah, you did well."

Sarah, looking a bit relieved but still downcast, replied, "I still got it wrong."

While all this was going on, Father Peter had come in from making rounds in the village by the fort. He heard enough to get the gist of the problem. He looked at Sarah and quietly spoke, "You are not perfect Sarah, none of us are. There is only One that is. The important thing is that when we fall down we resolve to get back up."

Sarah looked at him, and even though she was not Catholic, she still believed in him. Smiling a determined smile, "I guess I have work to do. I better go talk to the sergeant."

Julia smiled behind her. Father Peter gave his head a slight nod. "I have wounded men to visit and minister to. Would you care to join me, Miss Liman? I believe that the sergeant is still over in the post hospital." Father Peter helped Sarah on with her cape.

As the pair left, Julia went over to the table, and taking a pad began to write out a message to John whose patrol should be the one that would meet the Franklin next. In it she told him of the new developments in the pattern and Carl's beliefs. It bore instructions for the captain of the Franklin and his ship.

CHAPTER 28

THE QUARRY IS SPOTTED

ohn led his patrol in the area that they had hoped would intercept with the machine The Teamwork was using that had caused all the grief. So far they had spotted nothing but beautiful territory, nice but hardly useful in their pursuit. As they crested a slight ridge, one of the Nez Perce yelled that he heard something. They all stopped and listened. Then they heard the sound of hoofbeats in the distance. They turned to face the oncoming animal, since they were not sure if it was a rider or one of the strange creatures. Both troopers and braves drew their weapons but began to relax for they could hear a man's voice crying out to them.

Soon a rider from the fort approached, drew up and dismounted. "Major Morton," and he saluted. John, having given up any pretense at being a civilian while on this part of the mission, returned the salute. "Dispatch for you, sir. From your wife, sir."

John was a bit startled at this since he did not think that Julia was sending him out to get some extra items at the green grocer for dinner that she had forgotten, as she did at home. John took the note and read it. He was somewhat shocked to say the least. He reread the message and told the patrol to dismount. He called over a corporal and instructed him to have the men start a fire for rations and then set some wet wood on it to generate smoke to signal the Franklin.

As all this was going on, John pulled out a map and began to study it. Corporal Simons came over. "Problems, Major?" As with most army personnel, he was far more comfortable referring to John by his rank instead of his title.

John continued studying the map. "So it would seem, Corporal. This message from my wife says we have been searching the wrong area. Our quarry was spotted in a totally different area. She gave me the coordinates and the search area for the Franklin. Hopefully the Franklin will see our signal and we can be on our way before too long."

The corporal shrugged. "Guess it was not too smart relying on some darkie kid."

John turned his head quickly and looked straight at the enlisted man. "Corporal, first, that darkie as you referred to her is my wife's little sister, no matter what color she is. Let me warn you that if you want to have a long and happy life do not ever refer to her like that where my wife can hear you. Second, according to this message, Sarah's reasoning was sound but she did not know about the geological conditions. She said Carl would not have picked up on the reasoning for the change in their pattern without the aid of Sarah's records and her map. I do not expect to have this conversation again. Am I clear, Corporal!"

By now the corporal was looking quite pale. Being dressed down by a senior officer, even if he did not wear his uniform, was not a happy thing. "Yes, sir! No offense was meant, sir."

John looked at the NCO. "Apology accepted, Lew. Do not let the color of her skin or her youth fool you. Sarah is a very intelligent young lady. And believe me, I meant what I said about my wife and Sarah being like a sister to her. Now, how is the fire coming? I could use some coffee."

With pickets posted, the patrol settled in to wait for the Franklin. About two hours later one of the pickets gave a yell that the Franklin was in sight. John gave orders to break out the heliograph and began to signal her. Soon the great ship came to a halt and commenced holding position about one hundred feet overhead and sent down her landing basket. John wasted no time climbing into it. Quickly he found himself in the gondola of the airship and even more quickly was on his way to the bridge.

Captain Fraser stood on the bridge of his ship and acknowledged Morton with a frosty look. Morton, trying to avoid a repeat of their last meeting, smiled and held out his hand. Fraser looked down at it and said, "What is it, Professor Morton?" refusing to grant Morton the courtesy due his rank.

Morton looked at the man, shrugged and withdrew his hand. He pulled out the dispatch from Julia. "Do you have a map of the area, Captain?"

Fraser looked annoyed, as if he was insulted that John would even ask such a question. "Indeed, sir, we are fully equipped." Moving over to the ship's chart table he pulled out a white tube and began to unroll it. As it was unrolled the map was anchored down and when he finished Fraser looked up at Morton.

John stepped over and began to indicate the new area to be searched with a divider from the side of the table. "The dispatch from my wife indicated that there was a recent sighting here, at this ridge. Several men were hurt and at least two are dead."

Ian Fraser smiled, and not in a friendly way. "Appears your wife's sister is not so good after all, Morton."

By this time John had enough of Fraser's sorry attitude. "First of all, Captain, it is Major Morton. You will give me the courtesy of my rank. I believe I have seniority here by date of appointment. Second, I am tired of you insulting Sarah; she is a most valuable member of my team. She is brave, highly intelligent and a tireless worker. It is quite apparent that your discussion about her with my wife did not convince you of that. If I have to discuss it with you I will not be as subtle. Am I clear, sir!"

Fraser looked at Morton as if he had shot him. "What is this girl to you anyhow, Morton? Excuse me, *Major* Morton?"

John looked Fraser in the eye without any trace of warmth. "She is exactly who I said she is, Major Fraser; a young girl I rescued, and I had to kill two men to do it. A person my wife took care of, a highly trained and deadly agent in case you had not noticed, who sees Sarah as her family, her only family. And finally, a highly intelligent and extremely valuable member of my team. Now, unless you would prefer that we use the ship's landing basket and we retreat to a secluded spot to further discuss it, lose the attitude, Ian!"

As Fraser looked at Morton, one could see the wheels and gears turning around in his head as he digested all that Morton had said to him, including the implied threat of a duel. Ian Fraser regarded Morton, and thinking about some of the things the Colonel told him before the ship started this new patrol, and adding everything up, including the fact that Morton's wife had enough connections to pull his ship off its assigned patrol, he put out his hand in friendship. John let out the breath he had been holding without realizing it, smiled, and took the offered hand as if nothing had happened.

Morton told Ian how Carl had said he was to blame since he had not put the pieces together until the latest sighting. He added that Carl said he would have been unable to do it without Sarah's records. The two men worked out the new patrol route and with that Morton returned via the landing basket to his patrol. He told the men to saddle up even as the great ship moved out.

The corporal looked at Morton and noted, "The ship seems to be moving in the wrong direction, sir?"

Morton smiled and replied, "Not to worry, Corporal, the captain and I had a heartfelt discussion. She is just taking a detour to catch up to the other two patrols to let them know the change in plans. Form them up, Corporal, column of twos." Morton heard the corporal shout the order with the Nez Perce fanned out leading the way. Soon the patrol was moving out to the new area.

Since the new area was a distance away, the patrol took the rest of the day and all of the next before they found themselves in the right coordinates to hope for a sighting. They saw the Franklin and signaled her, although she was staying high so as to minimize the chance of spooking their quarry. They rode easily over the ground but nothing appeared. On the third day of scouting the Franklin signaled that she spotted a new tunnel. Morton led the patrol off at a gallop to find it.

Several hours later they reined in their horses and looked down at the tunnel. They approached, moving forward carefully in case there was any of the deadly gas. Signaling his men to dismount and form a skirmish line, they began to move in. As they approached they heard something, and all of a sudden they saw two men come clear out of the opening of the tunnel. Morton yelled to them to freeze, instead they threw down whatever it was they had been carrying, and drawing their weapons, began to fire at the patrol. Before Morton could tell his men not to fire, shots were returned. One of the men spun around and fell, the other man covering him.

Morton was getting ready to hurl one of Julia's special bombs so that they might have a chance to capture them, when there was a noise that drowned out the sound of the weapons and a giant red and metallic monster machine came part way out of the tunnel. It stopped, and for about a minute nothing happened, and then it continued its movement out of the tunnel and turned so the spot where the two had been standing was exposed. Both men were gone. John assumed they had gotten in the machine when it was stopped blocking the patrol's view of them.

As the machine turned, the patrol could see the other end of it. There were three, what looked like some kind of glass balls with bumps on them. All of a sudden there was a terrific noise like the sound of a million bees and everyone was dropping their weapons and covering their ears.

As Morton was gritting his teeth he realized that they must be using the tunneling sound-generator as a weapon. As his world was going black, he barely noted that there were a number of explosions around the machine. As suddenly as it started, the sound died off and the machine turned back to the opening and disappeared into the tunnel it had emerged from and most probably made.

Slowly the men recovered and began to regain their feet. Soon the Franklin came to a hover and the landing basket came down with Lieutenant Fox and several men to check on them.

Finding Morton, Lieutenant Fox helped John to stand up straight and the Lieutenant saluted and asked, "What happened, sir?" John looked at him, and trying to smile, gave him something between a wave and a salute. "Forgive me if I do not properly return your salute, Mr. Fox. I am more than a little shaken up. I assume the explosions were from your ship?"

Fox broke the salute, and seeing it laying there, retrieved Morton's revolver from the ground where he had dropped it and handed it to him. "Yes, sir. The Franklin is one of the newer class ships. We have several bomb racks for use, sir."

Morton, checking his gun and holstering it replied, "Please convey my compliments to Captain Fraser for his timely use of them. My God, that was terrible. I cannot describe it. The sound was like a million bees and they were all in your head." Morton shook himself. "Do you have any more of that ordinance handy, Mr. Fox?"

Fox looked at Morton. "Indeed, sir, one more rack's worth, ten bombs, sir."

John was beginning to feel a bit more like himself. Turning he yelled, "Corporal, how are the men?"

A private replied to John, "Sir, the corporal is still out of it; he is bleeding from his ears, sir!"

Still trying to shake off the last of the sound weapon, John regained command. "Wilson you just made Acting Corporal. How are the rest of the men?"

Wilson looked surprised but he too took hold of himself. "Sir, Johnson is in bad shape along with one of the Nez Perce, Black Crow."

"Mr. Fox, if Captain Fraser does not mind I would like to transfer the injured men to the ship while I try to salvage what I can here."

Fox saluted Morton. "Yes, sir, Major. I will go up with the first two men and then have the basket return for the other and my crewmen, sir."

This time Morton, slightly more recovered, returned the salute. "Carry on, Mr. Fox. Again, please give my heartfelt regards to Captain Fraser."

Lieutenant Fox began to see to the loading of the injured men while John went to check on the rest of the patrol.

The men were still shaking off the effects of the sound blast. It was lucky they had dismounted far enough back that the horse holders had retained control of their mounts. Morton had wanted to move in as quickly as possible but he already had lost a part of his command, so he took the time to check for more of the horrible gas. This tunnel at least was clear, but the machine had disappeared into the dark, plus, the air was filled with fine grit almost to the point of being a gas or fog.

The acting corporal came up and saluted John. "Sir, something you may want to look at over here, sir."

John got up and followed the man over to just inside the tunnel. There on the ground was a large stain. John got down and picked up some of it. He felt the texture and smelled it. "Good work, soldier. I think it is some kind of oil or lubricant. Our beast must have sprung a leak. That is what those two were doing outside, probably getting ready to try and fix it when we interrupted them. Hopefully we at least slowed them down some."

As the pair walked back to the tunnel mouth, John looked around at the state of the troopers and the Indians. All of them were tough men but they had been hit hard by something that they never experienced before. "Corporal, I want to set up a watch post but far enough away that we have a chance of surviving if that thing comes back. The horse holders said it was bad but they could handle it. Use that distance as a base minimum distance and set up two positions so that we can watch the tunnel from both sides. The rest can camp just on the other side of the hill here. Set it up, Corporal."

The trooper, now acting corporal, saluted and with a "Yes, sir" took off to post the guards and get the camp ready. That left John alone to ponder as to what they should do now. It was obvious that their small arms were not enough to stop that metal behemoth. Unless they could get the crew outside they would need field artillery to try and engage the beast, given the size of the thing if indeed that would do it, and how would they know where to site it so they could use it. How did you fight an enemy that could come out of the ground anywhere including right under your feet?

With these thoughts in his head, he started up the hill and decided that he might as well get some beans and hardtack with a coffee chaser. At least he could try and figure a strategy on a full stomach.

CHAPTER 29

JULIA ARRIVES

During the remainder of the day, the patrol rested and recovered from their encounter with the monstrous tunneling machine. Toward the end of the day John led a small party into the tunnel, this one at least did not leak the strange gas that caused all the mayhem. However, this foray told him nothing since it was much like all the other tunnels they had discovered and explored. Finally he settled for keeping a watch posted and having the men and mounts get some rest and sleep.

Early the next day he decided to scout the area, sending four-man teams out to do a sweep of the immediate area with several men back to keep an eye on the new tunnel. A little after midmorning, one of the pickets shouted that the Franklin was returning. Using the heliograph, John signaled her and as before, the great ship came to a hover. All too soon John could see the landing basket start its descent from the belly of the ship.

Just as it touched the ground, Julia, Isaiah and Carl climbed out. Well, to be more accurate Carl and Isaiah did and then the two men lifted Julia out, the basket's sides being somewhat too high for Julia to climb out, at least with any dignity. Julia had an annoyed-wife look on her face that caused Morton to feel very nervous. After the trio alighted, the basket rose back up into the ship. Soon it returned with several new men to make up Morton's losses.

The lady in question marched up to her husband, and not caring who was around, hugged him fiercely. Stepping back she looked at him.

"John, I saw the injured men. What happened, are you all right? I told you I need you in my life, John Morton." During this exchange both Carl and Isaiah stayed back, at least far enough to be out of the blast range in case Julia went off.

John relaxed a bit and hugged Julia back. "I am fine, Julia, shook up a bit but luckily the sound cannon has a very limited range. You can thank Major Fraser; if he had not dropped some bombs from his ship they probably would have kept coming till they killed us all. As it was, at least one of The Teamwork crewmen was wounded and the whole crew was scared off."

Julia looked a bit shocked that she had Major Fraser to thank, but recovering she replied, "Well, I guess that makes up for the minor incident in the colonel's office."

John released Julia from his arms and smiling at the two men said, "What are you all doing out here?"

Julia replied before either of them could get a word in. "Carl came to see the latest tunnel and Isaiah and I are here to see if we can figure out a way to stop this thing. Since they are operating in the area this seemed like the best chance to get a look at what was causing all the problems."

John looked thoughtful for a moment. "Julia, you know I do not like you in any danger but I have to admit that I will be needing both Isaiah's and your help on how to stop this thing. Julia, Sergeant Bodkins was not exaggerating when he said it was the size of a block house. It is huge and armored, at least enough to ignore small arms. I have no idea how I could position artillery to be ready when it appears, if indeed that is enough to stop it."

By now, Isaiah and Carl had decided it was safe enough to come up closer. Carl, seeing that things were reasonably quiet, said he was going down to check the tunnel since there had been no sign of the yellow gas that had been causing so much destruction. Both Isaiah and Julia asked John about the machine itself.

Isaiah spoke up, "John, how fast was it moving and did it seem to have any weapons other than the sound-bore cannon, I guess we should call it?"

John looked thoughtful for a moment before he replied, "I am not sure Isaiah; things were somewhat confused not to mention that the noise was unbearable. From my own recollections and what I was able to get from the rest of the patrol, best I can put together, first the machine moved on two huge metal bands that went around the wheels like an endless belt. The body was divided into three parts: First, at the front what looked like glass or crystal spheres with bumps on them, next a giant cabin of some kind, and finally three rotating pipes along with a short smoke stack. No, I do not remember seeing any Gatling guns or even gun ports. As to its speed, it was not fast, at least not much faster than a man can walk or trot, at most four or five miles per hour. Hard to tell but I would hazard a guess it was not very maneuverable based upon the way it turned around."

Julia spoke up, "Well at least that much is in our favor. It sounds much like a snapping turtle, dangerous but not fast and only dangerous on the front end. We may be able to use some kind of explosive to disrupt the bands or treads on which it moves. I wonder why it has those." She stopped for a moment then went on, "From what you say, John, trying to pierce the cabin may not be feasible unless we can bring it to a halt."

Isaiah responded to Julia's thought, "I think that the bands are there to spread out the thing's weight. It must be incredibly heavy, so they use them so it does not sink into the earth as it moves along. I wonder what it uses for a power source. I assume the tubes on the back are to pass the pulverized earth back to be thrown clear." He stopped to scratch his chin in thought and resumed, "I think you might be onto something, Julia. If we can break the band then I think it would bog down pretty quickly. Then we may have a chance to breach the hull."

Julia looked thoughtful, "It would be much easier to figure a way to disrupt it if we could get a good look at it. I do not suppose they would be cooperative enough to come up in the same place..."

John looked at her. "The question is, will they come up at all? Every time before this last one they had everything their own way. For the first several times they met no opposition or virtually no people at all.

When they did, it was just some cavalry and the Indians, which they could safely ignore. This time, we at least winged one of their men, and thanks to Ian's fast thinking dropping his ship's bombs, it showed them that we were much more prepared for them, even if it was just luck that the Franklin was here. If she had been fifteen minutes later you would probably be wearing widow's black, my love."

Julia looked shaken at this thought. "Do not even say that, John Michael Morton. I absolutely forbid you to get yourself killed, am I clear?"

John put his arm around Julia. "I will be here as long as I can reach out and touch you, my love."

Isaiah suddenly looked back at them as he had modestly been looking the other way while the two were having an intimate moment. "John, what did you just say?"

Both John and Julia looked at their friend. It was John who replied, "I said The Teamwork had it their own way. Why?"

Isaiah shook his head. "No, after that, about Julia?"

The couple looked at each other wondering where this was going. "I said something like as long as I can reach out and touch you I will be here."

Isaiah smiled. "That might be it! Remember when we first got here the colonel said something about the Nez Perce being descended from Centaur stock they rode so well?"

Julia nodded. "Indeed Isaiah, but what has that to do with our problem?"

Then Isaiah replied, "This thing is not very maneuverable or fast and as far as is known, does not have any defensive small arms, just the sound projector. If we could rig up some lances with exploding heads, and build in a small delay, the Nez Perce might be able to hit the tunneling machine from its flanks to break the bands."

Julia looked at him. "Isaiah, that is brilliant! Even a small delay should allow the Indians to get clear and the lance means they would not have to even dismount, just get close. I would guess a several-pound charge would be enough, although it is a guess not having seen the beast. They should be able to plant the charges with minimal danger to themselves." She looked at John. "Do you think they can do it, John, and furthermore, will they do it?"

John listened to the pair, trying to follow. "It sounds good. I do not think that the Nez Perce use the lance much but they are indeed splendid horsemen. Let us ask."

The three went up to where the rest of the patrol was eating and taking a break, welcoming the new replacements. John called out to Spotted Wolf as he had requested the young warrior be assigned to his patrol. Introducing Julia and Isaiah, they explained the problem to the young warrior. The young Indian looked at them. "You believe that we can kill this thing? It is hard to believe it is a machine, it is so big."

John responded, "I do not know about killing it, after all it is not alive, but if my friend and my wife are right, and they generally are in such matters, then we can cripple it and look for a way to get inside or kill the men operating it. The question is, can the Nez Perce get close enough to plant the charges with a lance? This is not supposed to be a suicide mission. They both feel, and I agree, seeing how your people ride, that they can easily outrun and outmaneuver this thing."

Spotted Wolf looked at the three of them. Drawing a line in the dirt with his foot, he moved over some twelve feet, and said, "Your lances will need to be no longer than this. If they are any longer, I do not know if we could count it as a fair kill." The lad smiled at them; it was not a nice smile.

Isaiah was somewhat taken aback and Julia smiled her tiger smile then looked at John. "Dear, Isaiah and I have work to do at the fort so we must take our leave. I need you to be careful, John. You are not a Nez Perce warrior, so do not try anything foolish. I meant what I said about you being in trouble if you get yourself killed. We should be back in a couple of days with the lances."

John looked at his wife. "You also, madam. I do not want you blowing yourself up."

Julia replied with her nose somewhat in the air. "As if, husband." Then she stood up on her toes and kissed him, not caring at that point what it did to his mantle of leadership.

John untangled himself from Julia and had one of the men signal the Franklin to send down the landing basket. He watched as she and Isaiah were lifted out of sight, Carl having decided to stay with the field team. *Now,* he thought, *where did that infernal machine go?*

Once Julia and the others were safely in the belly of the Franklin, she asked one of the crewmen if he would ask the captain if he would see her. She had avoided him on the short trip out but she thought she must see this through. Before long, the man returned to lead Julia through the great vessel to the bridge.

Ian Fraser stood there tall and imposing with his hands behind his back. They were off by themselves in the very front of the bridge; the area seeming to act almost as the captain's ready room. Julia straightened her spine and looked up at him. "Captain, I wanted to take this opportunity to thank you personally for saving my husband. He told me that it was your quick actions that saved his patrol. I know we got off on the wrong foot, but there are things I would like you to know about my relationship with Sarah."

Fraser looked down at her. "Just so *you* understand, Missus Morton, I acted to save a United States Army unit under attack along with some Nez Perce warriors who were assisting, that is all." With that, Fraser turned back to his chart table as if to say the conversation was over.

Julia sagged a bit then licked her lips and straightened up as if she was out to do something that was very hard for her, which if truth be told, it was. She quietly said, "Captain Fraser, please."

Fraser stopped what he was doing and turned back to face her, now more curious but with no sign of compassion. "What is it that you have to say, madam?"

Julia looked up at him. "Captain, do you have any siblings or any kind of family?"

Fraser looked at her wondering at this rather odd question. "Indeed, madam, I have two younger sisters. My father is dead, but my mother is still alive. Why do you ask?"

Julia started up again. "I am happy for you, truly," seeing the look of skepticism on Fraser's face. "I had no one, only having very vague memories of my mother and none of my father. My last name was found sewn into my clothes, if indeed it even was my own name. I was an orphan living on the streets. I was arrested when I was about ten or eleven for stealing an apple. I had not had anything to eat I cannot remember for how long. Instead of a workhouse or orphanage, I was sent to a special school that had a most peculiar course of study, run by the government we both serve. Among other things I did after graduation, I completed my first sanction, it is just a nice word for murder, at age sixteen. It was a minor affair and actually more of a simple training exercise to remove a small annoyance for the United States Government."

Julia stopped for a moment pulling herself together to finish her story. "When we were in the finishing school, that is what Uncle William called it, the 'Finishing School', we were taught that nothing, but nothing, came before the mission, not family or love or even decency. The mission was always first." Julia started to cry a bit at this, but sniffed it back and went on. "When John saved Sarah, we were members of a special team that had been put together. We were not married or even in love at that point, so again there was just myself. Anyway, Sarah was only ten and an orphan like I was. She had been beaten badly and a gang was about to use her when John saved her. I do not know exactly how it happened but I took care of her and we somehow bonded. She became my little sister in all but blood. I could not love her any more then I do already if we did share blood. I cannot tell you the details, classified you understand, but it was during that affair, that she taught me that there are things far more important than the mission. Until I fell in love with him and married John, she was my only family. I am not asking for your forgiveness, but your understanding. How would you have felt if someone said bad things about one of your sisters. That is all; I just wanted you to understand."

Fraser looked at her. Even as big a stuffed shirt as he was, he could see how much it had cost the woman before him to tell this story. He reached out his hand and put it on her shoulder. "I love both of my sisters very much. There was once or twice that I had to thrash a young fellow for inappropriate words or actions toward one of them. I am sorry that we got off on such a sour note. If you agree to teach me how you arranged for me to, what was it you said I did, trip on a rug? I think that will be enough. Now, madam, I have a ship to command." He turned back to the chart table again.

Julia smiled behind him. "When we have some time after the mission, Captain, it would be my pleasure."

Fraser smiled although Julia could not see it. Then she turned and left the bridge, returning to Isaiah.

CHAPTER 30

In Isaiah's Workshop

t was late in the day when Julia and Isaiah returned to the fort via the Franklin, Carl having elected to stay with John's search party. The pair joined Father Peter, Sarah, Mikhail and Detective Lestrade at dinner. The rest of the team was out patrolling with the various search teams, while Lestrade and Cznerka had been monitoring the town, just in case. The meal was quiet as each person thought about their family, friends and comrades out in the field.

Julia asked Isaiah if they could get started on the explosive lances for the Nez Perce. Isaiah looked at her. "Julia it has been a long day and I, at least, am tired. I know you want to get them ready but blowing ourselves up because we are too exhausted to do things right is not going to help anyone."

Julia looked at Isaiah for a moment, anger on her face. Father Peter reached over and put his hand over hers and nodded his head. Julia looked at him and then at Isaiah. "You are right, Isaiah, I am tired and this is no project on which to allow mistakes. Even if we survived making a mistake, we must get them right for John and the others in the field. First thing then."

Isaiah shook his head in agreement. "Right after breakfast, madam."

Sarah followed Julia to the compartment they sometimes shared and the ladies prepared for bed. Sarah looked at her sister. "Julia, what happened, why were you getting so mad at Poppa?"

Julia looked at Sarah and taking a deep breath replied, "Sarah, for the second time on this mission I have had to face the fact that I almost lost John, first to the gas and then to this diabolic machine. If he had been another fifty feet closer it might well have killed him. Oh Sarah, what will I do if I lose him? I do not know if I am as strong as Jennifer, being able to rebuild a life and raise a child by myself." Julia was shaking at this point.

Sarah perked up at this last. "Raise a child by yourself? Julia are you...?"

Julia looked at her. "I think so, Sarah, I think you are going to be an aunt."

Sarah jumped up and hugged her. "Does the professor know?"

Julia hugged her back. "Sarah, how many times must I tell you, men are delicate, sensitive creatures. Do you think for a minute that John would let me be in any kind of danger if he knew? So you cannot tell him or anyone else in case it gets back to him before we end this."

Sarah smiled and hugged Julia some more. "I understand, not a word." Looking Julia in the eye, "Sisters' Oath."

Julia smiled weakly in reply, still dealing with her husband's brush with death. "Sisters' Oath."

That solemn oath being sworn the pair finished getting ready and were soon sound asleep, at least an exhausted Julia was. Sarah was a little bit behind her excited as she was at the idea of being an aunt.

The next day found the same group around the table, with Sarah as usual helping Cook with the breakfast. Father Peter and Constable Lestrade, Father Peter being a bit old and Lestrade not being a frontiersman, stated that they were going to go back into town on the off chance that they might overhear something useful. The constable said, "What with the gang being bombed and at least one injured, I doubt that we will hear anything, but we may get lucky." With a second cup of tea for each to fortify them, the pair left.

Sarah looked at her father and Julia and asked, "Can I help?" To which both replied in unison, "NO!"

Sarah looked a bit cross at this. "Why not, Poppa? You said I was a big help in the shop back home."

Isaiah looked at his daughter and spoke firmly, "That is true, you are. However, at home we do not work on things that can go BOOM! You have your maps and records to keep up, so that should occupy your time, at least for a while, young lady."

Sarah looked at Julia for some support, but seeing the look on her sister's face realized that there was no support to be found there. "All right, but you two have to be careful too. You are my whole family."

Julia smiled at her. "We plan to be. Remember, I wanted to start last night but I had to admit your father was right to say work on it after a good night's sleep." Sarah nodded in agreement.

Isaiah spoke up, "Do you remember Sergeant Bodkins?"

Sarah replied that she did.

Isaiah continued, "I believe he may still be at the post hospital. Would you go there and ask him if we could use one or two of his best troopers for a bit?"

Both Sarah and Julia looked at him with a question on their faces. He went on, "We need a good horseman to tell us how long our lance can be and how heavy a warhead it can carry. While you are both better on a horse than I am, neither of you are as big or strong as a Nez Perce warrior."

Sarah smiled. "I will do it right away, Poppa," and she bounced up off her chair and took off.

Julia looked at Isaiah. "Good point, Isaiah. We need someone with experience on a horse to see if we can make this work," then the pair got up and headed down the train to Isaiah's workshop.

Sarah arrived at the Post Infirmary, at least that is what the sign said. She went in and politely asked the man at the desk if Sergeant

Botkins was there. He looked at her wondering what a little black girl would want with the sergeant. Still, he responded that he was in the third bed in the ward.

Sarah wasted no time and soon found him. Bodkins looked at his visitor somewhat quizzically not remembering her too well. Sarah smiled. "Hello, Sergeant. I do not know if you remember me but my name is Sarah Liman. I think you met my father, Isaiah, and my sister, Julia Morton."

Botkins looked at Sarah, now more curious than ever. "Indeed I met your father, Miss Liman, however I did not know that Missus Morton was your sister."

Sarah laughed. "We are not blood sisters but in every other way we are. The professor saved me before Poppa adopted me and Julia nursed me back to health. That was before she and the professor were married. She says it was the fact that we were both orphans that we bonded. I could not love her more."

Bodkins digested this and seemed to accept it. He had heard many a strange family story during his years in the army, what with a multitude of posts, wars and actions. "Very well, Miss Sarah. To what do I owe the pleasure of this visit?"

Sarah explained that her father and sister were trying to build a device to stop the machine but needed some advice on how long and heavy it could be so a horseman would be able to handle it. The sergeant was even more curious trying to follow what Sarah was talking about. Finally he said, "Sarah, if you would wait out front, I will get dressed and be there in a few minutes."

Sarah looked concerned. "Are you all right to leave, sir?"

Bodkins laughed. "Miss Sarah, I will be ready for the asylum if I stay here much longer. I can function as long as I take it easy."

Sarah trotted off to wait for the sergeant. When she got to the front office, she saw that the post surgeon had arrived and was checking one of the men. He was using a shaped piece of wood and with one end on the man's chest he had his ear to the other end. Sarah stood there with a mixture of curiosity and surprise on her face. The doctor looked at the trooper and told him to rest for the day and wrote a note to that effect for his sergeant. Finished, the trooper left and the doctor saw Sarah standing there. Thinking she was the daughter of a soldier since he also saw to the post's families, he asked her what her problem was.

Sarah looked at him and replied, "I am not sick, sir. I came to visit Sergeant Bodkins. If you do not mind, what were you doing just now?"

The doctor was surprised, but seemed to find it amusing that a little black girl would question him. "I was listening to the trooper's breathing and heartbeat. This device," holding up the piece of wood, "helps to transmit the sounds to my ear, so I can hear the heart better. Since you are so curious, come here and listen for a moment." With that he placed one end to his chest and Sarah come over and put her ear to the other end, quite surprised to hear the man's heartbeat.

Sarah got a look on her face like a light had gone off in there. "Thank you, sir!"

It was just at this moment when Jim Botkins came out. The doctor looked up. "Where are you going, Sergeant?"

Botkins looked at him. "Sir, I need to do something; I was never very good at just laying in bed."

The doctor, by his bars he held the rank of captain, smiled. "All right, Sergeant. I will release you on light duty, understand? If I catch you straining yourself, you will finish the rest of your recovery in the guardhouse. Am I clear?"

Bodkins drew himself upright and rendered a perfect parade ground salute. "Yes, sir!"

The doctor returned the salute and told him to stop taking up space in his infirmary. Then Sarah and Botkins left and headed for the train.

Sarah took the sergeant up to her father's shop and while he was talking to Julia and Isaiah, began to look around at the store of various components and materials Isaiah had stocked the workshop with in order to fabricate whatever was needed for the mission. She seemed to find what she was looking for and pulled it out. By this time, Isaiah noticed that his daughter was up to something and interrupted his talk with Julia and Bodkins to ask, "What are you doing there, gal, fixing something for your friend Molly?"

Sarah looked up at Isaiah and smiled. "No, Poppa, I think I may have a way to find the machine we are looking for."

At this statement, both Julia and Bodkins looked over at her in wonder. Isaiah went on, "And how do you plan to do that, young lady?"

Sarah smiled, looking confident. "By sound. I got the idea when I was waiting for the sergeant. The doctor was listening to a man's heart using a wooden device he placed against his chest. He let me try it. It was amazing how clear I could hear his heart. I thought we might be able to do the same thing in the field. If we have a string of listening posts we might be able to hear it; the louder it is, the closer. If we hear it between two of the posts we might have a good idea of the area to be searched."

The three adults glanced at each other. Julia responded, "Sarah, that is very clever, whether it works or not. We shall try it. Since we have not got to the part about loading live charges you can stay and work for now."

Sarah smiled and went back to sorting out parts and pieces for her listening devices.

Meanwhile, Julia and Isaiah explained to Sergeant Bodkins what they hoped to do to the machine when they found it. Jim looked thoughtful for a few moments. "I think it might work but I doubt that a rider, no matter how good he is, could handle much more than a pound-and-a-half warhead, otherwise it will be too hard to manage with the lance that long. I suggest we try it with some blank loads just to see how much a rider can control and if it will work."

With this advice, the pair started to work on the dummy lances. As they were doing this, Sarah began her own project since she found what she thought she would need. The three of them worked the whole day long to fabricate the various devices with a brief break for a quick lunch. By the time the test lances were ready, along with two of Sarah's listening devices, the sun was beginning to set, so the trio headed off to get some dinner and sleep. Testing would have to wait until tomorrow.

It was early the next morning after breakfast that the trio began the day's tests. Sarah and Isaiah headed out with two of the post's cavalry troopers while Julia began to formulate charges for several of the now-empty lance-head cases Isaiah had made per John's instructions.

Sarah went off some distance down the tracks and began to pound a rod into the ground as a test. One of the troopers seeing her at work came over to help. While this was happening, Isaiah and Bodkins took an empty barrel and using a rope, set it so it could be pulled along on its side to simulate the motion of the machine's wheels. While one of the troopers helped Sarah, the other went to get their horses. By then the other trooper had returned from helping Sarah who followed behind.

Bodkins and Isaiah explained to the two men what they were to try to do. "The idea is to wedge the explosive part into the dirt just in front of the moving barrel." The men looked at their NCO with a bit of nervousness on their faces. Isaiah smiled. "Do not worry, these are dummy charges, no explosives, just some smoke power in them so we can see how it works. This is to see if a rider can do it and how large a charge he can handle."

The pair looked relieved at this last bit of clarification. Obviously it was a bit safer than using live warheads. Isaiah explained that they were to come at it from the backside and wheel around to place the charge. He explained that the sound projector made any approach from the front of the machine impossible.

The men mounted and trotted off to simulate coming at the machine from a distance. Several hours later the trials proved just about what Bodkins had estimated. One pound was about the maximum charge that could be handled on a twelve foot lance. It did not seem like much, but by the time the weight of the lance and casing were added to the end of a twelve-foot pole it was quite unwieldy. Julia and Isaiah hoped that the charge would be enough to disable the monstrous machine.

While all this had been going on, Sarah, taking another of her listening devices, was moving even further down along the railroad tracks to plant it. She did all this while waiting for the engine crew to build up steam. She figured out that the train running a bit would be enough to simulate the machine boring through the earth. She was so intent on trying out her idea that she lost track of where she was in relation to the fort and had moved a fair distance away.

Sarah heard a rustling and a snort behind her and turned to see a strange creature looking at her. It was an odd-looking creature not like anything Sarah had ever seen before. She thought it looked as big as a moose, she had seen a picture of one in a book back home in Buffalo, but with horns not antlers, that were huge and pointed straight forward. It had a huge frill, not to mention the creature itself stood some ten feet or even taller at the shoulders and was colored various shades of red and brown.

Sarah, being a reasonable and resourceful young lady did the practical thing and screamed in terror!

Isaiah, the NCO and the two troopers heard her cry and the two who were mounted wheeled their horses about and headed for the sound while Isaiah and Bodkins ran as fast as they could. Julia, who had left the sliding doors of the workshop car open for ventilation and more light, it being a pleasant day out, also heard it and came down and ran toward the scream.

The mounted men were easily the first to arrive on the scene. Sarah was still standing there too afraid to move, but that did not stop her from recovering. The men rode their horses forward but the horses, catching the scent of the strange animal, were getting harder to control. Not planning on a serious amount of combat, the men were armed only with pistols, which given everything that was happening, the colonel had ordered that no one going outside the fort's walls, even if it was just down to the station, was to be unarmed. Both realized that unless they were very, very lucky, their side arms would not hurt the creature seriously but would probably just make it mad. They called out to Sarah to come over to them.

By this time Isaiah, Bodkins and Julia had arrived. Isaiah yelled for Sarah to run to him. Sarah who had been watching the creature called out, "I think I am safe, Poppa. It does not seem interested in me, it only seems to want to eat some grass or trees." The five adults watched as indeed the creature opened its mouth, which looked more like a cross between a large pinkish steam shovel and parrot's beak. The strange animal, finding a fallen tree about five inches in diameter, began to munch a bunch of leaves, then using its beak sliced off a part of the tree and swallowed it.

Julia watching this said softly so as not to spook the creature, "Sarah, come over here slowly and quietly. I think you are right, it is a plant-eater but that does not mean it is not dangerous, please note the horns and the fact that it could trample us all to death."

Sarah thought that this was indeed sound advice, in Sarah's mind almost anything Julia said was, and began to slowly and quietly move toward the rest of the group. When she got within range Isaiah grabbed her and the group moved back down the line toward the station and fort beyond.

Isaiah recovered enough to lecture Sarah about being careful. She looked down at her shoes and said, "I am sorry, Poppa, I was trying to test out my device." Gathering her courage, "You know how you are when you are working on a project, Poppa."

Isaiah looked thoughtful for a moment. "True, Sarah, but normally that is when we are at home safe in the workshop where the extent of the danger is forgetting to eat a meal, not out where there are dangerous animals and machines running about. You have to be aware of what is going on around you at all times. Are we clear?"

Sarah looked up at her father. "Yes, sir."

Isaiah smiled. "I cannot lose my family again. Now, how did your idea work out?"

Sarah shrugged her shoulders. "I do not know. The moose or whatever it is, showed up before I had a chance to test it."

The team looked back and noted that the creature had moved somewhat further away. It was at that moment that the engine let off a belch of steam from its pop valve with a very loud blast. The creature might not have been afraid of a small girl screaming, except for the annoyance factor, but the locomotive was a totally different matter, for it disappeared in a bellow of fear and a rush through the underbrush in the area.

Isaiah looked thoughtful and said, "I believe it is safe now, but I think Julia should go with you.

Julia, who had grabbed her favorite rifle when she heard Sarah scream, nodded in agreement. Sarah asked Sergeant Bodkins if he would let the train crew know to move just a bit when she had Julia fire a round from the rifle. When Julia fired again they could stop. If he and the rest of the troopers heard more than one shot they should come a-running.

With that the group broke up each to their own tasks.

As the four men returned to their makeshift evil-device stand-in barrel, they wondered what would appear next. Isaiah knew from his time working with John that if there were giant plant-eaters around in the area, it only stood to reason that there were giant meat-eaters around, plus they had seen them already. He sent one of the mounted troopers over to the locomotive to tell them of the prearranged signal from Julia. Meanwhile he had the other go further down the line to the workshop car and retrieve some heavier ordinance and ammunition. He most assuredly did not feel like being caught unprepared again.

Right after they returned to the barrel they heard a single shot, Julia's signal, and heard the train spin its wheels and move just a few feet. After that they went back to seeing if their explosive lance would be workable. The tests were going reasonably well with at least forty percent of the lance strikes being in the right position. Isaiah was hopeful. Shortly thereafter they heard another shot, but only one.

As the men were taking a break and rolling up some smokes, Julia and Sarah arrived. Isaiah looked at his daughter and noted, "I take it from the look on your face that your idea worked."

Sarah beamed with pride. "Indeed, Poppa, I could hear the train as if I were standing next to it. We should be able to get an idea where the machine is if we can plant a line of these and listen."

Isaiah looked at Julia and waited for her assessment. Julia smiled and put her hand on Sarah's shoulder. "Indeed, sir, I do believe that Sarah is right. I also listened and the sound was quite clear, perhaps not clear enough to tell that it was a train, but as John noted, it should be clear enough to tell the difference between the machine and any prehistoric gophers we might encounter."

Isaiah looked down at his daughter and said, "So what are you doing standing around, young lady? I do believe we will need more than just one or two of your devices, so get down to the shop-on-wheels and get to work."

Sarah stood up tall and saluted her father. "Yes, Sergeant!" Then she smiled and turning, trotted off down the line to the car holding Isaiah's workshop.

Isaiah smiled and laughed. "I guess that we have been spending too much time on an army post."

Julia looked at him. "I think your daughter has heard several tales about how some of your devices helped in the war. She is very proud of her father, Isaiah." Isaiah turned a bit red at his but was pleased just the same.

Later that afternoon Sarah was told in no uncertain terms that her listening devices would have to wait while she returned to help Cook and do some studying. There was still school to worry about and Isaiah and Julia were going to be preparing live warheads and fitting them to the lances.

Sarah looked at them and hugged them both. She disappeared and went to do as she was told. The preparation of the live lances took some time since neither one of the pair wanted any mistakes. Isaiah did not want Sarah to be an orphan again and neither did Julia since she was by now fairly certain she was responsible for more than just her own life.

Later they told Sarah she could return as the pair had prepared some twenty of the explosive lances. They hoped it would be enough. Sarah, with the help of Julia and Isaiah, continued to prepare more of the listening posts.

CHAPTER 31

A Terrifying Encounter

The work took another day as Isaiah insisted they try one of the lances with a half charge just to make sure that there was enough of a delay for the rider to get safely clear. It turned out that this was a wise precaution as the blast was set off prematurely when the heavier barrel rolled over it. Thus it was back to the shop to reinforce the warhead. Additionally, Sarah's listening devices, while much easier to fabricate, still took time to make enough of them and neither of the adults wanted her in the shop car while loading the live warheads on the lances.

Finally they felt all was ready for the field. Over dinner the night before they would leave, Sarah insisted on going along. "I understand the listening device and I should go and set them up and show the soldiers how to use them."

Isaiah and Julia were, to say the least, not in favor of this idea. "Sarah, being out in the field with who knows what is hardly the place I think you should be." Isaiah looked at his daughter with worry on his face.

Julia refrained from adding more but the look on her face seemed to imply that she favored Isaiah's side of the debate.

Sarah was not so easily dissuaded however. "Poppa, it will be no more dangerous than when we were scouting for signs near Los Angeles. I will keep back and be safe. Just a scouting mission, that is all."

Mikhail, who was resting after being out with a patrol for just a couple of days, that had rotated back into the fort, being bored in town trying to pick up clues, listened to all this back-and-forth. "If I might offer my services, Mister and Miss Liman," he broke in. Julia, Isaiah and Sarah looked at him as if he had appeared out of thin air. He smiled and went on, "I offer my humble services to accompany you and act as a bodyguard to Miss Sarah, if that is acceptable to you. If nothing else she can regale me with the tale of how she and Julia became sisters." Mikhail smiled and took another sip of his tea.

Julia looked at Isaiah and said, "He is very good at what he does. He also tends to keep his word."

Isaiah looked doubtful at this but Sarah still looked determined. "All right, but as soon as you hear anything, you, young lady, are to hightail it out of there. Are we clear?"

Sarah smiled innocently at her father and replied, "Yes, Poppa." Julia was very impressed. She thought that Sarah even had her beat at the little-Miss-Innocent look!

Before too much time had gone by, they heard the sentry shouting that an airship was approaching and to call out the ground crew. The quartet grabbed their various coats, capes and hats and moved down to the train to load the lances and listening devices that had been prepared into a small buckboard they had secured. Once this was done, they began heading toward the mooring mast to which the Franklin had docked by that time. They had to wait a while as the Franklin had to load some supplies before she returned to the skies that were her natural element. All this took several hours so it was late in the morning before they were able to get aboard. Isaiah noted that, in spite of the modern technology that had been added, not much really had changed since his time in the army, 'hurry up and wait'.

Shortly after they boarded, Captain Fraser gave the order and the tower's clamp was released. The handlers slowly moved along with her as her props beat a slow dead astern till she was clear of the mast. Then, like a precision drill team, the ground crew released the ropes and moved quickly out of the way as the Franklin discharged some of her water ballast and began a gentle assent toward the sun.

The crew seemed to be welcoming but Julia wondered about the captain. An enlisted man came up to them, and per the captain's request, invited them to the bridge of the great ship. As they came down the ladder onto the bridge, Sarah was speechless, gazing out the windows. This last was indeed most impressive since in the best of times Sarah tended to be a bit of a chatterbox. Mr. Fox came up to them, welcomed them and showed them forward where Captain Fraser waited for them.

Sarah looked a bit confused and asked the first officer, "I thought he was a major."

Fox looked down at her and smiled. "When we are aloft he is the captain of the vessel so that is his title. I hate to say this but it is just like in the other service, the navy." This last came out with a bit of distain.

Sarah pondered this for a bit and then seeing Fraser, looked a bit nervous remembering their last encounter. However, Captain Fraser seemed at ease with the group. He smiled at Julia and seemed genuinely pleased to see her, muttering to her that he planned to hold her to their agreement.

Sarah seemed a little confused but wisely kept silent till she could ask Julia in private. The captain then asked Sarah to show him her map and research. He did this in a polite manner, substantially different then the last time they met. Unrolling her map on the chart table while her father held down one end and the first officer held down the other, she showed the captain and first officer what she had found. She then told them how Mr. Jordan showed her where she had made her mistake.

When she finished, Fraser shook his head and said seriously, "Very meticulous work, Miss Liman. I see that both Major Morton and his wife did not exaggerate your abilities."

Sarah looked relieved at this utterance and rolled up her map. As she was doing this, the Captain spoke to Julia, "However, Missus Morton, even with the excellent work that Sarah has shown, it still leaves a lot of possible area to cover where the enemy may reappear. With teams out checking for more of the creatures in other areas we have nowhere near enough men on the ground, even with the Indians. How do you plan to cover it all?"

Julia looked at him and smiled. "Captain, Sarah is not just good at keeping records but she borrowed an idea off the post surgeon that may help us detect the machine and be ready for it."

Fraser looked somewhat startled at this, trying to sort through his thoughts about black people, that like most well-established upper-crust white families, he thought they were all right as servants and should be treated well, but otherwise not much good for anything except farming. He looked at Sarah and one could almost see the gears turning in his mind as she explained her idea to him and the listening posts she had fashioned.

He turned to Julia and Isaiah. "Well done, very ingenious. However, how do you plan to stop it once you find it? From what Mr. Fox told me it shrugged off small-arms fire. My ship cannot be everywhere along the line with its bombs."

Julia looked at him and gesturing to Isaiah, she said he should explain the explosive lances since it was his idea. Isaiah took over and told the two officers about his idea of breaking the tunneling machine's endless belts so they could stop it. He finished by saying, "If we can immobilize it, we can wait them out, if nothing else. Eventually they will run out of food, water or fuel and have to surrender."

Fraser looked satisfied but it was Fox who raised an objection. "Missus Morton, Mr. Liman, I hate to rain on your victory parade, but when you filled us in, you said one of the men was Japanese, did you not?"

Julia looked at him wondering where this was going. "Indeed, Mr. Fox, we have it from another agency that is working with us that one of the crew is from that nation. Why do you ask?"

Fox looked worried. "I spent some time in that country, attached to our embassy there. The ambassador urged us to learn as much as possible about the culture, and additionally as a military officer, the Japanese military. The Japanese officers are drawn from a warrior caste, they call themselves Samurai; they will not surrender. They consider it to be dishonorable, the greatest of dishonor, death is far preferable especially if they can take some of the enemy with them. Your plan may have a problem. One of a very deadly sort."

Julia, Isaiah and Mikhail looked at one another. It was Mikhail who broke the silence. "The Japanese sailor. We do not know much about him but what we do know is that he supposedly came from a minor noble family. He may be of this persuasion. In my country we have some knowledge of this Bushido religion."

Fraser looked at him. "Your country?"

Julia started to reply when Mikhail beat her to it. "I work for the czar. These men recognize no country, only their own power and are driven by their own lust for wealth. We may be at cross purposes on other matters, but in this we work together, da?"

Julia looked at Fraser and nodded in agreement. Fraser looked a bit stunned but shook it off; Indians, blacks and now Russians. He was heard to mutter under his breath, "This should make interesting reading in the ship's log book."

Without it showing, Julia, remembering her relations with Fraser up to this point, breathed a sigh of relief. *We may make this work after all,* she thought. However, the information supplied by Fox and confirmed by Mikhail scared her. Men who were willing to die, no, make that determined to die, for their cause where dangerous opponents indeed.

Several hours later the Franklin came to a hover over the area where Morton's patrol was camped. It was pretty much in the center of the area where they expected The Teamwork and their machine to show up. It took several trips of the landing basket, which was used since there were no landing facilities, to unload all the passengers and cargo. Julia and John hugged briefly while Mikhail, Sarah and Isaiah unloaded all the materials. After about an hour the team held a conference.

Julia and Isaiah filled John, the troopers and Indian allies in on the explosive lances. Then Sarah explained about the listening devices. John asked how they would let the other listening posts know if they heard anything. Sarah explained, "I remembered that Poppa told me how you used a rocket to signal the airship Congress when Julia was hurt on a previous expedition." She left it at that, remembering that Cee Cee and her family's origin were never to be revealed. She continued, "I brought three different colors, red, blue and white. If the listening post hears something faintly, they can fire a blue one, getting louder a white one, and if it is really loud, a red one. We should hopefully be able to get a pretty good idea of where it is from that. Also, the Franklin can see the rockets go off."

The adults all smiled at this plan. "Very well thought out, Sarah" said the professor. Nodding to the group, "All right, let us get started. Spotted Wolf, if you and the other braves would start to practice with the dummy lances Isaiah brought to get the feel of them, that would be good. We only have a limited number of the armed ones and need to make them all count. I fear if we do not get them on the first encounter they will take steps to ensure we do not have a second chance."

Spotted Wolf looked at Morton. "Do not worry, our weapons will strike true!" He looked at Isaiah, "If you will show our braves how to operate the weapon."

Isaiah and Spotted Wolf left the group to join the other Indians. There they would practice and have Isaiah show them how to arm the lance's explosive tip.

Sarah looked at the professor. "I would like to set up the listening posts, sir. I know how to install them and can show the men how to use them."

Both Morton and Julia looked somewhat less than thrilled at this idea but it was Mikhail who responded, "I would considerate it an honor if you would allow me to accompany Miss Sarah and protect her. I am still interested in her story about how she and Julia became sisters."

Sarah smiled up at the pair as if to say, "I will be safe". It was Julia who responded this time. "All right but you stay with Mikhail and do what he says. At the first sign of trouble you get out of the way. Are we clear!"

Sarah looked at Julia, her brown eyes alight with excitement. "Yes, madam. Just set up the posts and show the soldiers and Indians what to listen for and then come right back here."

The pair moved off to load Sarah's devices onto some pack horses before moving out.

John looked at Julia. Julia smiled at her husband. "It is her design, John. She needs space to grow. She will be all right. Mikhail is a top agent, even if he works for the czar."

John shook his head and returned to making plans, but not before detailing two of his small command to accompany the pair.

Since the various patrols where spread out along several miles of ridge line, it took some time for Sarah, Mikhail and the two troopers to visit all the camps. Mikhail was impressed in spite of himself, not having met many blacks since they were indeed a rare sight, one might even say a non-existent one, in Russia. He thought Sarah did a quite adequate job in explaining to the troopers and Indians what they had to do and her signaling plan. Additionally, he was fascinated with Sarah's tale of how she and Julia met, including what they had come to mean to each other. "Two orphan girls just bonding, most astounding, Miss Sarah. I can understand your fascination with Julia. She is a remarkable young woman. Likewise, I can see that you are much like her, intelligent and resourceful. You two are indeed, as you Americans say, cut from the same cloth. I can only hope my daughter grows up to be like you two."

Sarah looked over at him. "You have a daughter? What is her name? What is she like? Where does she live?"

Mikhail cut her off since having seen Sarah in action he was beginning to understand the American expression "chatterbox". "Svetlana is four years old and lives with a friend in Russia. I do not get to see her too often for her own safety. Before you ask, there are those in my country who would be happy to wipe out any trace of me and my family, including my daughter. Her mother perished from such activity some three years ago. It is hard to have a family and have to cut yourself off from them."

Sarah looked at him and tried to digest what he had just said. Thinking a bit she replied, "It must be hard for her. It must be like being an orphan. I know what that is like."

Mikhail looked back at Sarah. "She is with good friends, but yes, it is. But enough of this; we have work to do little Sarah." Saying this he spurred his horse into to a somewhat faster trot heading for the next and last unit camp before returning to the base camp as he thought of John's unit.

The sun was fading fast over the in the western sky by the time they returned to find the full team, less Lestrade and Father Peter who were still in the town, just in case, and the fact that the good father was a bit old for sleeping on the ground and the London detective was not exactly a woodsman, that set of skills not being much covered in the Metropolitan Police training.

Sarah was exhausted but she was determined to finish what she had started, so up the hill that the camp bordered on she went, Mikhail dutifully trotting along behind her. Julia seemed more relaxed now that Sarah was back where she could keep an eye on her. Isaiah had been none too happy to find out that his daughter was going over the area where the mechanical monster was believed to be ready to burst out at any moment.

Sarah, Mikhail and the two troopers had just started to pound in Sarah's listening device when they saw the first rocket, a blue one. Then there were several more blue ones from the end of the listening posts and then white ones from the posts closer on either side of them. Sarah frantically helped to finish off the one they were working on and put her ear to it. "Mikhail!," she yelled, "fire a red rocket! It sounds as if it is right under us," as she finished putting her ear back to the spike in the ground.

All further conversation was cut off by the sounds of the mammoth tunneling machine breaking forth from its subterranean world. The people in the camp scattered, knowing full well the effects of the sonic vibration on humans. Sarah's scream was lost as she fell into the void left by the machine, with Mikhail right behind her trying to grab the young girl.

Sarah hit with a thump that knocked the wind out of her and she felt herself rolling toward an enormous tube that was so hot she could feel the heat even at a distance. She was so stunned that she was unable to stop her motion and knew she was going to die in mere seconds. Just as she was truly beginning to feel pain from the intense heat, she felt herself being grabbed and slowly being pulled back to safety, or at least away from the heat.

When she looked around there was Mikhail hanging on with one hand and using the other to pull her back. Sarah managed to catch her breath and began to help, pulling herself back toward him using whatever handholds she could find. When Mikhail had an arm around her he yelled to her almost right in her ear so she could hear over all the noise, "When I first arrived in your country I went to a farming event, I think they called it a rodeo. They had an event in which the cowmen rode wild horses, perhaps you would do well in such an event little Sarah."

Sarah began to laugh and cry at the same time, her mind in a state of shock. Pulling herself together she yelled back in his ear, "I think you mean cowboys and I never want to try something like that again."

The two managed to get to their knees and look around. It was now obvious what had happened. The machine had come out almost directly under were Sarah had been setting up her last listening post. The last part of the tunnel had collapsed when the roof became too thin to support the weight. She and Mikhail had fallen right onto the back part of the machine, luckily just enough off-center to miss the rotating tubes that carried the pulverized earth behind the device. The analytical part of Sarah's mind figured out that the tubes must be hot from the friction of the earth being discharged through them.

They were suddenly aware of explosions below their somewhat precarious perch. Sarah screamed in Mikhail ear again, "The Indians must be attacking with the special lances that Poppa and Miss Julia made. We cannot stay here it is too dangerous."

Mikhail looked around and could see a giant shape in the sky closing in on their position. Mikhail returned Sarah's shout with one of his own, "The airship, she plans to bomb the machine, we have to find cover!" Mikhail glanced frantically around, then grabbing Sarah's hand began to sprint for the control cabin at the end of the gangway. "Come, we have to hope we can get inside! It is our only chance; the machine and Indians are moving too fast to dismount."

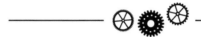

Julia was beside herself. Sarah was in danger and she could not get to her, she could not even see her. The Nez Perce reacted swiftly, like the legendary warriors they were. Led by Spotted Wolf they wheeled their ponies in close, striking the machine as they had been shown. Soon it appeared that a single charge was not enough, but as luck would have it, a second brave hit a section of the flexible steel band further down the machine's flank that had already been hit a few seconds earlier. That was enough to break the pins that held it together, a perfect strike just as the band passed under the wheel so that the blast was concentrated downward.

The Indians scattered as the machine began to spiral throwing pieces of the band everywhere, while it began to turn in a tight spiral, the sonic cannon lashing out in all directions. To make matters worse, rocks and dirt where arcing into the air from the side of the gigantic machine where the track was still in one piece. Slowly the lumbering behemoth came to a halt and just sat there. Julia, and by now Isaiah, were frantic, looking for signs of Sarah.

It was Julia who saw the open hatch on the deck of the iron monster. She grabbed Isaiah and ran for the ladder that led to the deck where she could see that there was an open door. Somehow she found the breath to pray.

John seeing his wife and one of his best friends heading toward the machine, scrambled to look for something to signal the Franklin with so that they did not bomb the machine.

Mikhail stood against the inner wall of the cabin, just inside the door he had spotted, while Sarah stuck to him like she was bolted on. She started to ask him in a quieter voice, since the noise was considerably dampened once they were inside, what they should do when he shushed her, "We need to find the control cabin. Like Julia, I have a mission to carry out; Glinka has to be captured or eliminated."

Sarah realized what he was saying; he was planning to kill a man. All of a sudden what Julia had told her she had done for the government became crystal clear. This was not exciting or glamorous but dangerous and deadly.

Mikhail bent down to her so she could hear him clearly. "Sarah I must impart some information to you; it is vitally important. If anything happens to me you must get it to Julia. Do you understand?"

Sarah, still trying to make sense of everything, nodded yes. Once he finished they were off. Sarah decided that it was safer to be with Mikhail then by herself.

With the machine ground to a halt, Julia, followed by Isaiah, fought her way to the side of the machine, the ground having been ripped up by the machine's spiraling before it came to a full stop. The pair finally found the ladder up to the after-deck of the giant tunneling mechanical and began their assent. It was made difficult by the fact that the ladder had been twisted and bent by the machine's wild gyrations when the band was broken. Additionally, everything was covered with loose dirt and mud thrown up by the same motion, but they finally made it. Julia took a quick glimpse skyward to see the Franklin beginning to move in a slow circle around them. She did not know why the airship had not loosed its bombs, but was grateful for the reprieve. Isaiah soon joined her on the walkway and the pair moved toward the hatch praying that Sarah was inside not buried or ground into the dirt that the beast had churned up.

The pair slipped in the door of the control cabin. There were several passages to take, but which one? Isaiah said quietly to her, "I will go toward the lower deck and rear, that should be where the engines are; you go forward to the control room. We have to find Sarah, there is no telling how much time we have!" One could see the look on Isaiah's face, clearly mirrored in Julia's, of their fear that Sarah was not with them anymore.

Isaiah started down a ladder just a short distance off the corridor to begin his quest. At the same time Julia slipped her derringer into her hand and started her exploration forward. Soon she could hear voices and was so intent on listening she did not see a wrench lying on a support beam in the access corridor that she tripped over. The noise sounded deafening to her ears. Then she heard a new voice quite clear.

"Whoever you are, come out and show yourself, or I will kill the child." The voice was heavily accented and sounded harsh and scared mixed in with Sarah's screams.

Julia stepped into the control room and saw the scene that was unfolding. Mikhail lay badly wounded, propped up against the cabin wall. He looked like he was seemingly dead or close to it. A man Julia did not know lay dead across what could have been some type of monstrous organ keyboard with various valves, gauges and controls added in to make an even more macabre scene. The sight that took Julia's breath away was a man holding Sarah with an evil look on his face and a short but very sharp knife at her throat. There was no way she could get a clear shot at the man the way he was holding Sarah.

The man snarled at her with the look of a cornered predator. "Throw your weapon away woman or I will cut her throat while you watch!"

Sarah looked terrified. "Julia, I am sorry."

"Quiet little black bitch, I, Glinka, will do the speaking. Now throw your weapon away."

Julia looked at him and quietly said, "All right, I am putting the gun down, only please do not hurt her, she is just a little girl." Julia set the gun on the floor plate and kicked it away from her.

"Good, now you can enjoy watching her die before I use you to get away. A pretty white woman has to be worth more than some black peasant child."

Julia looked terrified, "Please, wait. At least give us a moment."

The man laughed. "Da, go ahead, it will make an amusing story for my friends in The Teamwork. Say your piece, female."

Sarah looked hopeless, her face a mask of fear. Julia looked at her as steady as could be and said gently, "Sarah, remember, you must remember what I taught you in the baggage car about how to face such a situation, how to be brave."

Sarah looked at Julia, and swallowed.

It was just at this moment that Mikhail spoke, "Glinka, you traitorous dog."

The man whirled towards Mikhail, his knife hand dropping from Sarah's throat to an on-guard position toward the badly wounded man. Sarah did indeed remember her sister's training and snapped her hips to the left while bringing her right hand up in a vicious chop right between the man's legs. A scream of pure pain tore out of him as he doubled over, Sarah using her left hand to pull Glinka's fingers back from her shoulder in a particularly painful manner. She dashed toward Julia who, because of Sarah's rush, could not take any further action.

Glinka snarled in pain, "You will both pay for that!"

It was Mikhail who spoke barely in a whisper, "I think not." Suddenly there was a knife in Glinka's chest and a spreading red stain. Mikhail smiled as he spit at the body collapsed on the floor. "So ends the life of a traitor to the czar." Turning his gaze to the two women, "Ballistic knife, blade is spring loaded and can be fired, very handy at times. Sarah, remember to tell Julia." The girls raced to his side. Mikhail pressed something into Sarah's hand. "To identify you." His eyes looked at Julia, "Goodbye my czarina, your John is a lucky man. I take your marker to the grave. I may have to call you from beyond."

With that he was going, the handsome polished Russian was hovering over the grave.

"Julia, he saved my life," sobbed Sarah.

"Indeed, Sarah," replied Julia in a whisper as she put her arm around Sarah in a protective way. Taking a breath to steady herself, Julia looked at Sarah. "What did he mean when he said you have to tell me something?"

Sarah started to reply when she was cut off by Isaiah's somewhat dramatic arrival through the compartment entrance. Without any preamble he yelled, "We have to get out of here, now!" He stopped and looked at the scene in front of him. "Sarah!" Taking a few quick steps over and grabbing her he cried, "You are alive, oh thank you Lord. Thank God!" He shuttered and looked down. "Mikhail?"

Julia looked up at him from where she knelt by Mikhail's side. "Dying. His last act was to save Sarah."

Isaiah could see the others were dead. He pulled himself together and said, "We have to get out of here, this whole device is going to blow itself to kingdom come!"

Julia jumped up. "What are you saying? We have to try and retrieve the notes and diagrams!"

"Forget it!" yelled Isaiah. "I found the Asian crew member; he committed suicide down below, cut his guts open with a knife, and another dead, don't know which one or how. The Japanese rigged the engines to overload. I don't have enough time to undo what he did before the whole thing goes up. We have to get out of here, NOW!" With that he shoved the girls so hard it was as if he were throwing them towards the exit door. He looked down and saw the dying Russian's chest heave and steady into shallow breathing. It seemed the Russian agent's demise had been over estimated! Somehow Isaiah picked him up and staggered to the hatch. He owed him. Sarah was alive because of him.

The ladies needed no further urging and the trio, plus a badly wounded Russian made haste to the door onto the back deck and the ladder down.

In retrospect, it was amazing that none of the three mobile members broke any bones, such was their speed in descending from the gigantic machine that had caused so much grief. John, on seeing them ran toward them, but Julia's yell informed him to run away. It was the Nez Perce warriors who responded, riding their ponies in while giving forth war hoops. Spotted Wolf was first, picking Julia up in mid stride as he rode by and pulled her across his mount, followed by another warrior who did the same to Sarah. Isaiah and Mikhail were a bit bigger problem but this was solved by two pairs of the Indians riding in close and each grabbing a shoulder and riding off with Isaiah and Mikhail, each pair having one of the men in between them.

The entire rest of the force began to mount up and ride for the far side of the hill. Just as the last of the mounts and riders cleared the ridge line there was a blast which threw many of the men and horses to the ground. Screams were heard all around.

CHAPTER 32

PICKING UP THE PIECES

Some time had passed. John was beginning to re-form what was left of the unit as the various scattered details arrived. It was a miracle that no one had been killed, but several of the men had broken bones and there were enough concussions and wounds that it looked as if they had been under a major artillery barrage. Mikhail somehow amazingly was still alive, though no one could quite figure out how, so badly was he wounded. Several men had suffered shrapnel wounds from the debris that rained down upon them. Three horses had to be put down due to broken legs or other serious damage. The Franklin had taken on several of the worst of the wounded. The men from the remainder of the patrols that had been strung out on the picket line had rallied on John's command. Of the machine that had caused all the havoc, the largest part found was a two-foot by three-foot jagged piece of the hull, imbedded in the earth where the machine had stood. Taking stock, the rest of the machine was in substantially smaller chunks. Whatever power source that it used had been of immense potential.

Julia directed and then led the others to look for any paperwork or diagrams, small pieces that might give some clue as to the machine's operation. There was nothing left worth picking up. The blast had generated a ten to twelve foot hole in the ground and collapsed the cave it had emerged from so that it was corked up like a wine bottle. The Franklin had made a quick flight over the area to see if it could sight anything, but the wounded presented a more pressing problem.

Julia looked at her husband. "John, I do not think Uncle William is going to like this report. Not only were we unable to retrieve any useful information on the machine, but we could only account for four of the five Teamwork members."

John shrugged, looking over the crater at what was all that remained of the nightmare machine. "Julia, Anderson said to resolve the situation so that the Nez Perce did not jump the reservation and start a new war. That has been done. They fought for their land, again, and this time they won, with of all things, help from the army. Their courage will be the stuff of many campfire stories for generations to come. The distrust between the Indians and the army is substantially less then what it was, not gone, mind you, but reduced. Our friendly Canadian mountie is satisfied. I assume the other Crown policeman will be when he finds out all the particulars of what happened, so hopefully that tension is down a notch at least as well. Overall, wife, I think things turned out fairly well and that I was also able to retrieve several specimens for the museum, including some raptors that I found out about through our scouting, ones I believe you failed to mention, wife." With this he started to advance on Julia.

Julia looked at him and smiled a rather contented smile. "Well, since you put it that way I suppose you are right, my love. Did I forget to tell you about those beasts? Sorry, it was probably just all the confusion, you know, all the gunfire and chases, not to mention the large cat, not to mention believing that I had lost my husband to some very nasty gas because he had gone where he should not have. All very confusing, my love."

John stopped and looked at Julia. He laughed. "Well played, my love. I would hug you but I have to keep a picture of military propriety."

Julia smiled back at John and thought it wonderful that this was the man she was starting a family with. "Then it shall have to wait for later, my husband. As it is I have to talk to Sarah. Mikhail left some sort of a message for me with her and gave me a medal. Very mysterious."

The pair parted, John seeing to the final sweep of the area for any clues as to how the machine functioned and what powered the mechanical monster, then to see about organizing his remaining forces. Some would be rotated back to the fort while others would continue the sweep for any remaining creatures spawned by the strange gas or tunnels that might have been missed. John knew well that just because the machine was destroyed it did not mean all the danger was past.

In the meantime the Franklin returned with some fresh troops and to take on more of the injured, both whites and Indians. It would seem that injuries and death, at least, did not discriminate between the races.

Evening had fallen and the men set fires not only for warmth and cooking but for keeping any remaining beasts at bay. Julia was hungry but decided that she never wanted to go into the army, considering the state of army cuisine. Still, as she reminded herself, she had to eat for two. Sarah joined her, smiling. "Julia is there anything you need? I mean I can get it for you so you do not have to strain yourself."

Julia laughed at her. "Sarah, if I can manage getting out of an exploding war machine, being tossed across an Indian pony and carted off like some captured prisoner on the steed, and finally withstanding an immense explosion that rained debris all over, I think I can manage to retrieve some beans, bacon, hardtack and coffee by myself. Besides I have not had a chance to tell John yet and I want it to be a surprise."

Sarah laughed with her sister at her own silliness. "I guess indeed you can. There was just so much happening at once." Then her dark face turned somber. "Julia, I am sorry about Mikhail; he is quite a man. I hope he survives, his wounds looked very serious."

Julia looked sad also. "Yes, Sarah. He is brave and dedicated, a good man to have at your back. I did not love him. Like I told you, that is for the John Mortons of the world, but I did like him and enjoyed his company." Julia halted for a moment looking up at the sky as if hoping to see a special star for Mikhail. Finally she looked back down and pulled the medal from her pocket, turned it over in her hand and then looked at Sarah. "Sarah do you know what this is about or why Mikhail gave it to me? He said he gave you a message for me."

Looking around to see that no one could overhear them, Sarah told Julia of Mikhail's message to her about his daughter. She finished by saying, "He was terrified, Julia, that if some of his enemies in Russia heard he was dead and they found he had a child, if they could, they would hunt for Svetlana so they could kill her just to wipe out all traces of him. I do not understand, why would someone do that to a little girl?"

Julia looked away as if in thought and then back at Sarah with a sad look on her face. "Sarah, this will be hard to understand, but in some parts of the world the people carry feuds and evil on for hundreds of years. Bitterness does not die, it just keeps getting renewed and passed on to the next generation." Shaking her head she went on, "Thank God it is harder for us to understand. There are some who would do it here, but for the most part we tend to look to the future and not to the past."

Sarah looked deeply at Julia and spoke quietly, "What are we going to do about her?"

Julia looked surprised for a moment. "We, little sister, do you not mean me?"

Sarah got her mule-face on. "He saved my life too, Julia, he also has my marker even if he takes it to the grave with him."

Setting her plate and coffee cup down, she reached over and hugged Sarah. "If indeed it should come to pass, we shall have to hurry. I know the type of people Mikhail dealt with. If he dies, they will move fast as soon as they can confirm his death." Again she looked up and taking a deep breath while she marshaled her thoughts, Julia finally looked back to Sarah. "We need to return to the fort as soon as possible so I can send a message to Uncle William. He owes me and I think I need to collect on that marker. For now, we had best get some sleep; we will be busy for the next little while."

Undoing their bedrolls, the ladies did indeed get some sleep.

Dawn found the Franklin overhead. Julia explained to John and Isaiah that she and Sarah had to return to the fort so she could let Anderson as well as the colonel know what was going on. Since all of the badly wounded had already been evacuated, John agreed and the basket was let down. He explained to Julia that he wanted to do some more searching to hopefully find any remains of the machine and its power plant, although he admitted that there seemed to be little chance of it, and in addition, try to make sure no more of the strange animals were around to terrorize the area, and maybe, possibly, finding a specimen or two as well. Finally, there was still one Teamwork crewman unaccounted for.

Before long the landing basket was being retrieved and the last of the lightly wounded and the two ladies were moving out of sight.

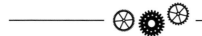

Julia and Sarah returned to the fort and the first thing Julia did was send a long coded report to Anderson along with a warning that one of Mikhail's agents might contact him. She was pleased when Anderson sent a reply that he did indeed understand the situation and he would comply with her request. Next, she and Sarah filled in Father Peter and Lestrade on what happened.

Lestrade was pleased that the machine had been destroyed but wanted to wait for Preston's report before he sent word to London. As he noted, John had told him to trust, but verify, with one of your own agents.

Julia smiled at this and decided that she was very happy she did not have to make him disappear; it would be a waste. Not the handsomest of men but a good policeman anyhow. She wondered about Lestrade's comment about wanting to return to London so he could keep an eye on some amateur who was mucking about named Holmes.

After several days of patrol, the Franklin came in for a prolonged docking period for minor repairs and routine equipment servicing, crew rotation and taking on stores. Julia and Sarah had time to show how Major Fraser could arrange for someone to trip on a rug.

By this time the worst of the wounded, including Mikhail, had been shipped out to better facilities in San Francisco, hopefully to mend. Per his word, Anderson kept Mikhail's condition secret. Word was simply sent via the Russian Consulate that he was working for an extended period with an American team to fight The Teamwork.

Several days passed by the time John returned to the fort. He had been replaced in field command by Lieutenant Dasson and was very happy to sleep in a regular bed again and eat something besides beans and hardtack biscuits.

CHAPTER 33

THE PROFESSOR IS SURPRISED

After a good night's sleep, a bath and a hearty breakfast courtesy of Sarah, John felt enough like himself to report to the post commander's quarters. He and Colonel Washburn tried to figure out exactly what to put into their joint report, at least the one that would be made public. It was a much-edited version of the preceding events. The colonel noted that Paul Dasson had been a big help and recommended him for promotion.

John prepared his special report to Anderson after he left Washburn's office. Then he went to seek his wife to go over the report with her. John might be the head of the family but he very much appreciated his wife's mind, along with the rest of her anatomy. He found Julia alone for a change in their post quarters.

As they discussed the report, John became increasingly annoyed that Julia's mind seemed to be wandering and the fact that he found out that Julia had talked to Ian without his knowledge. John looked at her and finally spoke, "Julia what did you say to Ian? I think that such a discussion breached military protocol."

Julia looked down, a very non-standard Julia look, almost as if she were guilty of something. "John, I just wanted to explain to him about my relationship to Sarah. I did not want any hard feelings to get in the way of the mission, I mean it was hard enough and confusing as it was. He seemed to find it in his heart to forgive me, at least if I promised to show him how to get someone to trip over a non-existent rug." Julia smiled weakly at John.

John absorbed this but looked worried. "Julia what is wrong, you seem distracted and hesitant. Are you feeling well?"

Julia looked at John and replied, "Nothing some rest will not clear up, husband. I am just tired, that is all".

John stood up, a very irritated look on his face and took several paces. "Julia, do not lie to me, madam. I am your husband and I know when you are adjusting the truth."

Julia smiled at him and said quite calmly, "John it is nothing that will not clear up in about six months and besides, John, you are not going to chastise the mother of your child are you?"

John stopped dead in his tracks, looked at Julia then ran to her and picking her up in his arms twirled her around. "Julia are you, are we...?"

Julia smiled. "Well if my calculations are correct, next winter we should be parents. Now put me down you silly man."

John held on to her so tight she thought he might smother her. "This, John Morton, was why I did not tell you earlier, because I just knew you were going to act like an idiot." Still she held on to him. "I hope, sir, that you will make a better father than the idiot husband I fell in love with," teasing him.

John set her down and still holding her, "Julia, have I told you how much I love you, wife?"

Julia looked up at her man and replied, "Yes, but you can do it again; I really like hearing it. Now, however, we have important matters to discuss such as what room we shall convert into a nursery." The rest of the time was spent in soft, quiet conversation interrupted with laughter and kisses.

After several more weeks of running down reports of strange animals and possible sightings of the missing Teamwork crewman, Morton decided that he had enough specimens and that the army could handle the follow-up work. The local marshal's office was notified about the unaccounted-for criminal.

An extra car was obtained for the train to fit in the various museum-bound artifacts that had been recovered, including some Nez Perce tribal items that John had received in thanks. There was nothing of value to be found of the tunneling device, much to Anderson's displeasure from the tone of his telegram back to Julia.

As the team sat around eating dinner, the discussion turned to the future. Morton started out by announcing that they would be heading out in the morning; the train's conductor already had his clearances. He told everyone that he and Julia had some redecorating to do to make room for an enlarged family. Everyone congratulated the couple, while Father Peter smiled to himself. John wondered about that but filed it away for a later time.

Lestrade, having verified John's and Julia's report to him with Preston, announced that he would be returning to London via Canada, since he felt he had imposed enough on the strained American hospitality. Preston likewise was looking forward to returning to the Yukon with King. Sarah announced that she, for one, would miss King.

It was a surprise when both Jason and Carl said they would not be leaving with the returning train. Julia looked at them and inquired what was going on.

Jason was the first to reply. "Mr. Anderson decided that having a field office in the northwest might not be a bad idea especially with a member of The Teamwork unaccounted for." Julia looked at him with a look that inquired more, her senses telling her that there was somewhat more to the story. Jason blushed a bit. "Well, I volunteered. I met this girl and thought I might like to stay on for a while longer."

Sarah, ever the nosey one, even more so than Julia who did it "only professionally", spoke out, "Who?"

Jason smiled and said, "Her name is Molly and she works at the trading post." Sarah and Julia looked at each other and smiled.

At that point John nodded to Carl and asked, "Your story, sir?"

Carl looked at him with no regrets. "Jennifer Swenson. It has been so long and it is good to be able to relax a bit. She is truly a wonderful woman, and the children need a father. With her home destroyed she is a woman strong enough to follow a mining engineer around the country."

Even Lestrade congratulated Carl. He smiled and said, "I remember that night in the saloon. A good woman indeed, sir!"

So it was the next morning that the team broke up. Preston and Lestrade with King beside them headed out of the fort on horses bound north, while Jason and Molly came down to the station to see Sarah off. While the two girls hugged each other and promised to write, Carl and Jennifer stood on the platform as Julia, John and Father Peter said goodbye. Just as they finished, the conductor shouted out, "All aboard" and the engine gave a sharp blast from its whistle to punctuate the conductor's shout.

The rest of the team had already shaken hands and boarded into their car with Tinsman seeing that everyone was set. Isaiah had already said goodbye to Carl, for the two had become fast friends, and was making sure one last time that the steam wagon was secure. Meanwhile, Peter and Lestrade had exchanged words before the two constables had headed north, as they also had formed a friendship while working together.

As the last of the passengers took their seats, they waved to those staying behind and felt the thunk of the couplers having their slack taken up and watched as the train began to roll past the station, the engine's whistle giving forth its mournful cry and its bell clanging. This time it was not as bad as at the conclusion of the Ratten business and their departure from the badlands since it was still early fall and there was no storm to outrun.

After a day's travel, John found Father Peter alone in the parlor, and sitting down by his friend, turned to him. "Peter, you did not seem very surprised when we told you that Julia was in a family way. I assume you had been forewarned?"

Peter looked over at John through the smoke from his pipe. "John, I had to promise not to tell you when she accidentally let it slip out to me." Peter continued on with a bit of a chuckle, "She told me she could not allow you to act like an idiot until the mission was completed."

John shook his head at this and thinking for a moment, laughed and replied, "I think my wife knows me too well, sir. However, something is nagging at me. When we talked on the way out it was like you had a premonition that this might happen."

Peter smiled at his friend and comrade. He spoke in his gentle way, "John, first I assumed you and Julia were simply enjoying each other's company. It was obvious to even the most blind fool how much you two love one another. Second, when you talked to me about Julia's behavior I told you I have to deal with all sorts of things in my parish. Julia might not have understood it herself, but like the specimens you invest so much interest in, she was nest building, something that God instilled in her, and you, for that matter. As I said, it is obvious how much you two care about each other."

Peter looked up as Julia entered the parlor and he spoke up, "If you two will wait here I have something for you." John and Julia looked confused but waited till Peter returned from his compartment with a stack of papers. Peter smiled and handed them to Julia and said, "Something Guiles and I discovered. You see, while the machine was being destroyed out in the field, Guiles and I had been keeping an eye open in the town as we said we would. When we saw an injured man picking up supplies who spoke with a German accent, we decided to follow him." Peter paused to empty the ashes out of his favorite pipe and prepare it again, while John wondered where this tale was going. Resuming his story, Peter continued, "It was lucky we did; he was the missing fifth crewman, the one who had been shot during the first encounter with your patrol, John. He led us back to The Teamwork's camp."

Julia looked startled. "You got the research notes!" She was looking at him, but her face grew more concerned. "They do not seem to make much sense; it is almost as if most of them are missing."

Peter nodded. "There are about half missing. Guiles Lestrade has the other half. They should prove to be as confusing to Her Majesty's government as those will be to ours."

Julia and John both looked shocked. Julia spoke, "Peter, these notes are priceless! How could you let Lestrade get away with them?"

Peter looked her in the eye and replied, "First, you are right. The machine was extremely dangerous and powerful. Both Guiles and I thought it too powerful for one country to control, especially when it is at odds with another world power. Therefore, we thought that if the two countries had to work together to salvage the research, perhaps, just like the army and the Nez Perce, it may lower tensions between them."

John replied, "That is why you waited till now to let us know, so that Lestrade would be well into Canada and safety." While Julia looked concerned, John just smiled, took out a cigar and joined Peter in a quiet smoke as the train headed back east.

It was Julia who finally spoke up, "What happened to The Teamwork member?"

Peter shrugged and replied, "We used one of your explosive devices, it worked quite well so we got the jump on him. However there was a minor problem in that it started the cabin on fire. Guiles and I raced to put it out and retrieve the papers but in the confusion the man got away. We figured that that was more important than the one man."

Julia looked annoyed. "That means more work on the device, sorry, my love," this last with a nod to John.

John took Julia in his arms. "Perhaps that should be left to someone else, wife, you have enough to do for now."

CHAPTER 34

SARAH'S EDUCATION
AND OTHER DETAILS

The journey east was a very calm affair. Julia and Sarah spent time with her studies and Sarah was teaching Julia how to knit, something that was never covered at the "finishing school". John was forward studying and preparing his new specimens while Isaiah added a few more improvements to the steam wagon. Tinsman was still working with Adam to improve his skills, while Sam, in the manner of experienced soldiers throughout history, caught up on his rest. Peter just relaxed and lent Isaiah a hand now and then.

It was some two weeks later that the train pulled into Buffalo to its usual resting place in the Buffalo Central's coach yard. The team came down, John making a bit of a fuss over Julia making sure she did not slip. Julia rolled her eyes at her husband's behavior. "John I am fine, stop being such a fuss. You see why I could not tell him, Sarah?" Sarah smiled and the two ladies nodded to each other and said in unison, "Silly creatures." This as far as they were concerned explained everything.

John left Tinsman and his two operatives to watch the train while a carriage was obtained. Soon the five were off. While John, Father Peter, Isaiah and Sarah went into the store, Julia stayed in the carriage saying that she had to meet with Sarah's teacher and fill her in on Sarah's educational activities over the last several months.

John and Peter decided that there was little enough they could do after helping with the luggage for Sarah and Isaiah since Isaiah was busy finding out what this Anderson-furnished replacement had done, as well as what might not have been done. Sarah was going through the shop's records. Jonah seemed very pleased to see his boss return since he had not had the best of relationships with his replacement, and he seemed to notice that Sarah had changed and started to develop some interesting curves. Poor Sarah was so busy with her records she did not even notice.

Seeming at loose ends, John and Peter decided to adjourn to a nearby saloon for a beer. It was over an hour and a half later that Sarah found them and asked if they would return to the shop with her because Julia had come back from her school and needed them. The two men followed without question, curious as to what had transpired.

When they reached the shop, Julia was there directing things as if she were a general in charge of an army. Jonah was busy sweeping and cleaning while Isaiah was nowhere to be seen. She looked up, "There you two are, just in time. We have a lot of work to do."

Peter and John looked at each other and wondered what was going on. John started to ask when Julia cut him off. "Miss Watson, Sarah's teacher, is coming for dinner to discuss what she learned while she has been gone and we want to make a good impression do we not?"

While both men stared at her and realized that even though it was put as a question, it was not a question but a directive. Soon John was off to retrieve his suit and one of Julia's better dresses; luckily she had not grown such that she could still fit into it. Sarah was making a list of what she needed from the butcher, green grocer and baker so Father Peter was tasked with obtaining all that, for the simple reason that he basically wore the same outfit every day, except when doing repairs around the parish or helping Isaiah or John. With all that being done and Isaiah grumbling about having to put on his Sunday best, Julia and Sarah were busy cleaning the house part of the structure behind the store.

The team was assembled and trying to look casual when the shop door opened and an attractive, modestly dressed black woman came into the store around five in the afternoon. Julia looked up and smiled along with Sarah who looked quite fashionable in her Julia-picked-out clothes. Julia looked up, smiled and said, "Miss Watson please come in."

Sarah looked nervous and smiled at the woman. "Hello, Miss Watson; I missed you."

The lady returned the greetings, and Julia went on to introduce John and Father Peter. She finally introduced Isaiah as Sarah's father. Miss Watson looked around and asked, "Where is your mother, Sarah?"

Sarah smiled at her and explained that she did not have a mother and told the story of how she had met the rest of the group and that in the end Isaiah adopted her, having lost his family. Bucking up her courage, Sarah suggested that they all adjourn to the house for dinner.

Over dinner, Miss Watson discussed what Sarah had studied on her trip. There was no mention of adventure, the dangerous aspects being carefully edited out by the five. It was obvious that Flora, for by now, except for Sarah, the group was on a first-name basis, was quite impressed with the high level of talent Sarah had for tutors.

In turn, Isaiah was quite impressed with Flora. He found her intelligent and well-schooled and, he thought, very pretty, not what he thought a schoolmarm would be like at all. In fact, he was quite intrigued with her.

After Julia was sure that Isaiah was intrigued by Flora and Flora seeming to find Isaiah of interest, being both handsome and a tinker of quite some local renown, she informed the pair that she and John would be leaving for their hotel. She explained that she was becoming somewhat more easily fatigued these days, being in a family way and all.

John looked somewhat concerned and fussed a bit, while Father Peter asked if he could share a carriage with them, as he too was feeling tired, noting that he was not as young as he once was.

As the three left, Sarah offered to see them out. This maneuver left Isaiah and Flora alone in the house. As they left, Julia winked at Sarah and whispered to her, "Now you are on your own." Sarah smiled and laughed, whispering back, "You mean Poppa is."

John who had not overheard the whispered conversation was concerned as he helped Julia into the carriage. "Sweetheart, are you all right? I mean, you have not complained before this."

Julia just rolled her eyes. "Husband, for such a learned, intelligent man you can be a complete idiot at times. I am fine but we needed to get out of their way."

Both John and Peter looked at her. "Gentlemen, I could have taken care of everything about Sarah's lessons and education at school today. That was not the point. Sarah was concerned that Isaiah needs someone more his own age to care for him and though she did not admit it, I think she wants a mother. Men!"

Peter laughed and John just said, "Oh," then smiled at his wife. "And how long have you and Sarah been cooking up this dastardly plot, madam?"

Julia gave her husband a coy smile and replied, "Why, since before we left Buffalo, sir."

The Mortons and Father Peter had long since returned to New York and their respective lives. Julia and John had been busy converting an adjoining room into a nursery when John was not busy writing up his latest finds.

They were both warmed by several letters from Sarah telling them that Isaiah was continuing to see Flora, starting with inviting her to the Baptist church where he and Sarah went on Sundays, although dating was hard since she was only allowed one day a week to see gentlemen by the terms of her employment with the school system. In late October, another letter told them that a supposedly non-Canadian, non-government official came into the shop asking after her. Both Isaiah and Sarah were a bit nervous about this, but the man explained that Her Majesty's government was quite pleased with the assistance and courtesy shown the detective and the constable, in a very non-official nothing-ever-happened-in-the-western territories sort of way. As a gesture of gratitude, he had something for Sarah from the Yukon. Surprising her, he opened the door and brought in a husky puppy, about three months old. "Miss Liman, a NWMP officer said to introduce you to Duchess. She is yours." Sarah was overwhelmed and hugged the dog. For her part Duchess appeared to be as scared as Sarah was delighted, but appeared to find Sarah comforting. Sarah finished her letter by saying that she and her dog were now inseparable, which was somewhat annoying at times since Jonah had asked her out for an ice cream and Duchess was upset that she could not go.

Of the missing Teamwork agent no sign was found. Peter admitted in a letter to Anderson that he had escaped Guiles and himself. He explained that the man had tried to destroy the cabin by fire that the Teamwork agents had been using, and they felt recovering the documents seemed the better course of action. Peter had learned from Julia about 'adjusting the truth' so that Anderson was not mad at Julia for her device starting the fire and doing the damage. Anderson was extremely put out at Peter's actions with the Scotland Yard policeman. However, as Peter had predicted, a high-level scientific working group had been set up to begin to put together the separated sections of the recovered notes much to an equal amount of displeasure on both sides of the Atlantic.

Julia was finding it difficult to get around at seven-and-a-half months and John put her under "house arrest" since he did not want any chances of her slipping on the ice or catching a cold in the New York winter.

Near the end of December their lives took a new turn when the maid announced that they had a caller, a Colonel Anderson.

The End